THE SCOTT PFEIFFER STORY PART ONE

ESCHATON

SHANE WOODS

SEVERED PRESS
HOBART TASMANIA

ESCHATON

To friends and family lost, and friends and family gained.

Thank You

PROLOGUE

This is the worst headache ever. I don't know if you've ever been knocked out, or rendered unconscious in any way, but let me tell you, it sucks. Waking up is guaranteed to be worse than the action that put your lights out in the first place. Once your brain begins to regain consciousness, pain is the first thing you register. For those first few moments, it is your entire world. Think of the migraine that ate the migraine that your wife or girlfriend always complained about. Being hungover doesn't even compare.

You guessed it. That's precisely what's going on inside my head at the moment. Musical Jolly Chimp is playing his cymbals inside of my head. Although, my brain is between them, so it's less of a cymbal crash and more of a painful *squish, squish, squish*. Each squish coinciding with the beats of my pulse. Well, there's that at least. I hurt, and I have a pulse. At least I'm not dead.

I don't dare open my eyes. Not yet. One thing at a time.

I can tell I am definitely sitting in a chair. Face down on a table or something. A cold, smooth surface under my cheek. Steel? Wood? Not sure about that, either. Probably not important. I'll get in touch with the decorator when I get a chance and see what's going on.

The sensation of a puddle around the aforementioned cheek. Drool, it has to be. Oh well, no biggie. Not the first time I've woken up in a strange place with a splitting headache and a goatee full of the results of an overactive salivary gland. I am a product of the 90's after all.

Slowly I begin to crack one eyelid open, and then the other. As my eyes adjust, I start to take in my surroundings. Bare light bulb overhead? Check. Stainless steel table under my face? Check. Okay, not a great start, but I can deal.

Next, I begin the arduous process of kicking the rest of myself into motion. Slowly lifting my head, I can hear the soft whirring of a ventilation fan. As my eyes come into focus, I can make out a very sparsely furnished room. The low level of light provides just enough illumination to show I'm alone. I can make out three bare white walls, and one with what appears to be a large mirrored window in it. How original.

Craning my head around some more shows the room to be about fifteen feet in both directions. Nothing else to it besides the chair that I'm in, and two more across the table from me. I begin thinking to myself if I just quit looking around, this whole situation could change for the better and stop becoming more and more stereotypically ominous.

Yeah. Right. Fat chance of that. I could also wish and hope for a beautiful redhead to walk in holding a platter with a cheeseburger and an ice-cold beer, speaking in one of those accents that somehow make the attractive woman even more desirable. Norwegian, British, hell, I'd even take French at this point. Very doubtful that either wish would come through at this moment. Well...maybe...focus... Yeah, not happening.

Reaching up to wipe the quickly cooling drool from my cheek and facial hair, I notice for the first time that my wrists are shackled and adjoined by a few feet of sturdy chain. Following the length of chain, I also notice that it has been routed under another length of chain around my waist, the length around my waist securing me to the chair. I was left enough room to allow for some freedom of movement of my arms, but not much else. This is looking worse and worse by the minute. I begin trying to move my feet, and, you guessed it, chained and bound, albeit much more securely in place than my arms.

I'm pretty sure I've seen this movie. It doesn't go well for me. Alright, stay calm, don't panic. You're panicking. This is not the time for panic! Apparently, Mr. Panic didn't get the memo, that bastard showed up to the party in the loudest shirt I've ever seen and didn't even bring any drinks. Instead, he injected a full load of adrenaline directly into my system. With the quickening pace of my heart, the Chimp's cymbals picked up pace as well.

SquishSquishSquishSquishSquish

I pulled every which way on my bindings. I squirmed and writhed, I exerted so much pressure I even let out a little gas. Hey, don't judge me! Put yourself in my situation and see if you keep it together!

It was no use. I was stuck fast by my bindings, and all I'd managed to do was make a little noise and change the previously sterile atmosphere of the room into something a little less than clean.

Great. Amazing. Wonderful. All of those little adjectives that people think when they are frustrated and out of luck begin to rush through my brain. Well, alright, time to check out plan B and see what the hell is going on and who's got me here.

I took a few moments to gather my breath, compose myself, all the while very prepared to stick to my usual M.O. and say the first thing to come to my mind. Nothing. My first efforts yielded nothing but a dry, dusty croak.

Clearing my throat, I decided to give it another go. This time, I managed to bellow with as much voice as I could carry. Okay, maybe it wasn't a bellow, and definitely not much in the way of even an authoritative shout, conversational volume at best, but, hey, it was something!

"I don't know what the fuck is going on here, but I definitely don't approve of bondage on the first date!"

Really, you idiot? The hero of your own story, all you've been through, and that's what you go for as the opening line of what could very well be your end?

Apparently, it was enough, because the single light over my head disappeared, to immediately be replaced by the multiple banks of fluorescent lights that, in my current state, could only have rivalled the intensity of the sun itself.

It instantly began to feel like somebody gave our little monkey friend a full-on shot of cocaine. He was going to do all the squishing, do it now, and do it forever.

Squeezing my eyes closed as tightly as I could and lowering my head, I squeaked out a meager "Not cool" as the pain in my head skyrocketed to a whole new level.

From what seemed like a million miles away I heard several sets of the heavy footfalls of boots on linoleum, followed by a loud metallic click. Doing my best to lift my head and pry my eyes open against the heavy weight of so many lumens, my eyes slowly began to adjust once again, in time to see a plain steel door swing open. Stepping through the threshold and taking up spots on each side of the doorway were two armed men, both with M4's held tightly across their chests. They were perfectly military. By that, I mean you could have copied and pasted them both out of any given recruitment poster from any given military recruiting office.

Following the two men into the room and proceeding past them, another pair presented themselves. Both with high-and-tight haircuts, although their similarities stopped there. The first wore basic dark suit pants and a plain white button-up shirt. Obviously the elder to the other man's younger, with a touch of grey interspersed through his otherwise dark hair, and a pale, though serious and heavily lined face framed by entirely utilitarian eye glasses.

The second man to enter was in his mid-twenties, a tan complexion with dark eyes, sporting a standard issue military ACU with a holstered sidearm and little more decoration than the basic unit and rank patches, along with a nameplate declaring him to be Munoz.

Okay, so we have a soldier and a suit. Wonderful.

The elder man took his seat across the table from my own. He laid a plain manila envelope on the table and motioned for the younger man to take the seat next to him.

He began to speak as he opened the folder, adjusting his glasses just a bit higher on his nose with his index finger.

"Mister...Ah, yes. Mr. Pfeiffer. My name is Agent Grayson," and, motioning to the younger man to his right," this is Sergeant Munoz."

"I'm sure the pleasure is all yours," came my reply. "I'd love to stand and shake hands, and be a proper gentleman, but you see..." and motioned to the chains still binding to my spot.

"Mr. Pfeiffer, I don't think you are grasping the gravity of your visit with us," Grayson replied," nor do you seem to understand the severity of your actions."

The man broke out his most severe expression for the occasion, and I could feel his gaze penetrating through me as he glared over the top of his glasses. Well, that's great. My first time ever being tied and bound to a chair in the same room as a suit and a soldier and I've pissed off one, maybe even both of them, though I couldn't tell as Sergeant Munoz kept his gaze clear and impassive. Why stop now? Why not go for broke?

Straightening in my seat and doing my best to fight through the pain in my head I snapped back, "Look, buddy, I don't know where you think this is going to go, holding me in this shoe box of a room as your captive audience, but we are not going anywhere until I know exactly what the hell you've done with my family and friends. Where are they?"

"Mr. Pfeiffer!" he growled, "You are hardly in a position to be difficult. You are to be facing charges of crimes against your country, including, according to our reports," as he thumbed through pages within his folder, "you and your men have murdered sixty-seven United States soldiers, as well as destroying several land vehicles, and bringing down an AH-6 Little Bird helicopter!" His voice reaching a crescendo as he spat those final words.

"Excuse me, Mr. Grayson-"

"Agent."

"-Agent Grayson, like it fucking matters, agent titles at the end of the world and such. But, excuse me, those men attacked us. No reason, no provocation. They were led by a man clearly acting outside of convention and law, but that's our fault? The fact of the matter stands that my head is absolutely fucking killing me, I've no idea where I am-"

"Mr. Pfeiffer."

"Stop interrupting me, you dick! You also still have not told me what's become of my family and friends. I'm not giving you a damned thing until this back of mine gets a little scratching! End of story!"

I was pissed. I mean, the nerve of this guy! I clasped my hands together and placed them on the table, leaning forward and attempting to meet his gaze with one equally as cold.

Considering my stance, he muttered a concessionary, "Very well then", and motioned one of the door guards over to him.

The guard, a young private, stepped forward, leaning in close so Grayson could whisper some orders to him. After a moment, the private nodded once, spun on his heels, and left the room.

Grayson leaned back in his seat, and soon Munoz and I followed suit.

"Any chance of getting my legs loosened?" I asked.

Grayson just smiled wanly, and Munoz let out a soft chuckle. Ok. I guess not.

After a few more moments, the private returned, a black poly case in one hand, and a pitcher of water in the other.

Following him into the room was a younger blonde, maybe around the same age as Munoz, wearing the pale blue scrubs of a nurse and carrying a small case of her own.

She handed a tablet in a black case to Grayson as she passed him and proceeded to stand next to me. Laying her own case on the table, she opened it, and removed a syringe, which she laid on the table.

"I'm Nurse Hannigan. We're going to get this little gremlin out of your head," she reported with a demure grin.

"Monkey," I corrected.

"I'm sorry?"

"It's a monkey in my... You know what, never mind. Let's get to it," I said, returning the smile.

She began loading the needle and swabbing my arm with a prep pad as the private set the water pitcher and some plastic cups on the middle of the table and handed the poly case off to Munoz before returning to his post near the door.

Nurse Hannigan finished cleaning the inside of my elbow, cleared the air from her syringe, and slid it into the arm with the skill of someone well versed in the subject. Within moments my head began to clear. Not entirely, but the pain and grogginess that was left became just a shadow of its former self. She produced another smile for my benefit before gathering her things and turning to leave the room. Upon passing Grayson, she nodded to him and declared, "He's all yours," before making her way through the door, closing it with a heavy clang as she departed.

Grayson nodded to me, asking, "Better?" as he started filling Styrofoam cups with water for each of us. I accepted mine, the cold water feeling like the most refreshing thing this side of...well, I don't know. Other refreshing things. Nonetheless, it was good. Damn good.

Munoz cleared his throat as he unclasped the top of the poly case.

"As Agent Grayson stated, I am Sergeant Munoz. I'm here as an observer, and for data collection. This is just a recording device."

"Ah, he does speak!" I reported to Grayson, "Does he do any other tricks?"

Munoz shot me a withering look, and began anew, "Anyway, we would ask that you start at the beginning. Leave no details out. These recordings will go higher up the ladder to determine-"

"Look, cupcake," I said, interrupting him, "Do you kiss a girl before your first dinner together? Do you like taking road trips before you fill up the tank or check the oil?"

"Excuse me, puta?" Munoz shot back.

"My head may be better," I started, "but that's only half the deal. Calm yourself. We ain't going nowhere until I know-"

Grayson's turn to interrupt somebody came, "Yes, your family. And friends. Look," and he propped the tablet on its case, bringing up a screen showing the very room we were in, all three of us seated at the table. A live feed.

"So that *is* an observation window! You clever bastard! I had no idea!" I shot out, giving him my best 'you got me' expression.

"And," Grayson said, thumbing across the screen, "your wife. Your daughter. Cute kid."

Several more panes slid by on the screen, all presumably live feeds of either cells, or rooms much like the one I was in. The only ones not kept in confinement were the children and babies, all shots showed them in either day care settings, or nurseries tended by what I assumed to be nurses.

"Now, see?" I offered, "I'm much more willing to be just a little bit more cooperative. When can I see them?"

"Soon, Mr. Pfeiffer. First things first. I believe, as you said, there are backs that need scratched?"

Sighing in resignation, I said, "Okay, okay. Name's Scott, by the way. We're not in school, and you ain't my principal, drop the last name bullshit. What do you need?"

"As Sergeant Munoz was stating, the beginning. Start just short of when you saw your first infected." And, catching my apprehension, he continued, "The charges I'd mentioned before have not been moved to convictions, and nothing has been formalized as of yet. This is more to..." he paused, then

5

continued, "to determine the validity of said charges, and determine what really happened. We have conflicting reports across the board, and also, any real-world experience you can bring to light concerning this worldwide catastrophe will of course be of great benefit."

"Alright." I conceded again, "The beginning?"

"Yes, Mr. Pf- I mean, Scott. The beginning."

I stole another sip of that God-tier water, ran my hand over the stubble on my cheeks and usually clean-shaven head, and sighed.

"Yeah. The beginning. Clench that sphincter and buckle up, man. It's been a ride."

ONE

Stepping out of the doors of the Highway 80 service plaza, I sighed. Another long trip from New York. Nah, not the city itself, I'll never take a semi into that mess. I may be a little off in the head, but I'm not crazy. Orange County, one of the places this outfit sees fit to send me, more often than somewhere that the sun actually shines.

No sun yet, but close. The rain clouds that have plagued my entire journey finally tearing themselves away from their low hanging valance in the place just over my head, revealing pin pricks of starlight for all to see. Another typical late April morning in Ohio. Rain across the entire region, only to give way to a clear sunrise, likely followed by more rain. Fine by me, I'm a whole 25 miles from my home terminal, and another little ways south to my bed.

Walking across the lot towards my truck, the morning sounds of a busy highway rest spot coming to life are all around. Other drivers grumbling their way to and fro, either running their pre-trip checks, or off to get their first coffee, and maybe a morning shower in one of the rented stalls. Some trucks here and there coughing to life in anticipation of another leg of their cross-country trek.

And there she is. My truck for the day. An absolutely hideous orange Volvo, over a million miles on the clock, hooked to a pair of brand new trailers loaded with God knows what inside. One seat in the small day cab. Never a passenger, just me. My way or the highway, amirite? Eh? Ok, I'll stop.

Nearing my rig, a large driver in a well-worn sweat suit came out of the shadows next to his tractor, leaned against the front fender, any further downward movement hampered by his ample gut, and began a deep, throaty roar of a coughing fit. Spitting oily looking gobs of expectorate all over the ground and his chrome bumper. Running his already stained sleeve across his face, leaving behind crimson and tar-colored smears.

"Damn, dude," I entreated, "you should probably get that checked out."

He grunted something unintelligible and went back to his fit. I passed him by and went about my day as well. Some people just aren't morning people.

Climbing into the driver's seat of the Giant Orange Turd, I retrieved the phone I'd ignored for most of the night. I had left my charger laying on the dining room table when I left two days previous. This meant when I started it up, I was met by a very dim screen and a battery life reading three percent. Being so close to home, and a man with his priorities in order, I ignored the 'Wife: Three Missed Calls' notification and went straight to social media. I was immediately assailed by posts speaking of everything from mass riots and unrest nationwide, to people claiming that the zombie apocalypse is upon us. Of course, the obligatory posts interspersed into the mix of the girl everyone ignores posting as much cleavage as possible, and that one smart-assed friend marking himself safe from the California earthquake, twenty-three hundred miles from his house. Well, maybe I should call the wife after all.

I pull up her number and press the little green call icon. It rings, rings some more, and goes to voicemail. Ok, we'll try this again. Once more I dial, and finally hear her voice on the other end.

"Hi, sorry, the neighbor was at the door. Where are you?"

"Almost home, had to make a piss stop, maybe thirty minutes? Which neighbor? It's five A.M!"

"Henry. Look, you need to get here. Something big is happening, we keep hearing gunshots."

"Yeah I seen some shit online about riots? Some idiots think-"

The phone starts beeping. I pull it away, and in the dimly lit screen I can see it says '218 Home Dispatch'. What the Hell? They never call. Never. Pretty sure it's against policy. Back to the wife for a moment.

"Hey, I'm going to be home as soon as I can. Hang tight, lock the doors. Dispatch is calling through. Gotta go. Love you."

"Love you too. Be careful."

Pulling the phone away, I switch to the other line.

"Heyyy Scott, it's John from dispatch."

"John? What are you doing on nights?"

"Julie was sick, got that cold that's been going around and I had to cover, but listen," John's usually cheerful voice turned very somber, "I'm not sure where you're at, but the highways are becoming totally impassible. Like, they saying it's not moving for the foreseeable future."

"Of course," I replied, sighing heavily, "I'm twenty-five fuckin miles from you and the highways are garbage. Any suggestions to get around it?"

"Nah man," John replied, "Nothing we got permits to take the double trailers down, ya know."

"Suggestions?" trying not to show my frustration, it's not his fault after all.

"I mean, you can park wherever you can and take it easy. We could pull a load rescue and get you back when it clears, or you can sit in it until it clears and safe-haven it to the terminal, I'm sure it will run you out of hours."

"Yeah, the FMCSA and their desk jockey rule making. I think I-"

And a beep. Pulling the phone away I notice it's not lighting up any more. Dead. Of course.

Allow me to interject, the people who make these phones are assholes. More computing power in one text than we could even dream of fifty years ago, you can use it for absolutely every aspect of your daily life, and they can't put a battery in the stupid thing that lasts for more than a few hours of use. Hundreds of dollars for a portable computer you can fit into your pocket, and it's useless in no time if it's not tethered to a wall or a vehicle. Thanks, guys.

Well, I might as well take it as far as I can, nap through the traffic jam, and take it the rest of the way if and when the road frees up.

I grab a cigar, cut the end off, and light it. Starting the truck and releasing the brakes, I put it in gear and begin making my way back out onto the highway. Merging into my lane, I get up to speed and crack open my last diet soda.

Not ten minutes later, I crest a hill and am met with a veritable sea of tail lights. Well shit. Here we are. A good fifteen miles left, and, according to the guy that tells me where to go, it's like this the whole way, and then some. I immediately grab my log book and begin notating the time and place of the traffic jam. If I'm sitting here forever, then I'm getting paid for every minute of it. Beginning my transfer from mileage pay to hourly rate...now.

So, I pull my brake knobs out. First trailer brakes, then tractor brakes. The brake chambers behind every set of wheels on the rig bellowing out their air in their individual exhalations. As I start to push my seat back and put my feet up on the dash, ready to take the long wait in comfort, I notice a boy of about 8 years of age smiling and waving like a lunatic from the back seat of a car. Why do they do that? The parents piss and moan about semis and make jokes about truckers, all the while the kids love us. They can be seen plastered to their windows in every state of the nation, smiling, waving, and doing the arm pump to get you to blast a shot of air from your horn. I don't get it. As a driver myself, I'll be the first to admit that a good chunk of us are pricks, and not really somebody you want your kid spending time with. Hey, kid, wanna hear about the time I tazed a lot lizard that was on my truck, leaning in my window? You could smell the menthol and poor life choices frying!

All this going through my head, and I still smiled and waved. Whatever. It's probably the kids and not the parents because the kids don't know the ways of the world yet. I'll let him keep the magic today. The boy beamed. He glowed with a smile full of chocolate bar and childlike innocence.

Pushing my seat back further I disappeared into the confines and privacy of my steel cave. I dug through my cloth insulated lunch bag and produced a container of pretzels and hummus. Yeah, I know. Big tough trucker drinking diet Pepsi and eating pretzels and hummus. What, does he drink fruit smoothies, too? Yeah. Yeah, I do. Because I'm not trying to turn into a heart attack at forty. And besides, this stuff? With the little bits of roasted red pepper mixed in? It's pretty damned tasty. I don't even know what a chickpea is, but I love them like this.

The sea of bright red brake lights began to dim as people accepted their fate and placed their vehicles in park. The usual highway crowd is gathered here. The long thin legs of a woman in a Lexus SUV can be seen from my high vantage point. An all-American pickup truck ahead of me, plastered with 'III%-er', 'Come and Take it', and other various bumper stickers. A pale blue Prius with an equal amount of stickers, all opposite to the pickup's, 'Eat Green' and 'Coexist'. A heavy man in a safety yellow vest and a ball cap proclaiming 'Dave's Hat' getting out of a beat-up Toyota Camry to see how long the traffic jam is.

Then, over the crest of the hill ahead, a figure barely shown in the now early dawn light, running. Running very awkwardly, his arms flailing almost uselessly at his sides, head back towards the sky, but running nonetheless. Then the shadows of more people. Three, then five, then a dozen, all coming over the hill. Some trying to get into the vehicles, but a few seemed to zero in on the first of several people who had left their cars to stretch or inspect traffic. They hit the first guy hard. I mean real hard. Watch any footage of the Cleveland Browns playing in the last thirty years. See the quarterback? See him get nailed, again?

That hard. The guy's head must have hit the ground before the rest of him even knew it was falling.

At this point, everybody started running. Not just our new friends, but their new friends as well. I couldn't see what happened to the first guy, but it seemed to have a pretty negative effect on those that did. Within moments, however, both of them were up and running like nothing ever happened. Running together. Joining the growing throng of sprinters. A few passed my position, but before I could even follow them in my mirrors, my attention was drawn to a pair attacking a silver car about fifty yards ahead of me. One, and then the other, arched their heads back and erupted all over the side and front of the vehicle with a viscous dark crimson vomit.

What the hell is going on here???

I watched, awestruck, leaning forward over my steering wheel as the people running away fell to more tackles, obscured by the other vehicles trapped on the highway. Another duo lunged for the pickup truck with all the stickers. The one nearest the driver's door expels his own blast of the oily vomit as he slams his fists against the window. True to his nature, Mr. Gun Sticker opens fire. A half dozen shots, muffled by my own vehicle, paired with the outwardly exploding glass from his window. The man attacking the truck took every round center mass, slumped against the Prius next to them, and then...What? How the fuck? He got back up. The fucking guy got back up!!! Who does that? Before I could shuffle any more of my uncomprehending thoughts, the guy, who should by all accounts have just died, *lunged* through the now missing window. The remaining shards of glass tinkling to the ground in an oil slicked crystalline waterfall. More shots rang out, blasting through the man's missing window, the roof of his truck, and were cut short as the inside of the truck splattered with the bright crimson of arterial spray.

The woman in the Prius flung open her door, screaming, and took off at full speed. She didn't even reach the car behind her when she too was tackled to the ground. The woman that nailed her brought her face down in an arc and sunk her teeth deeply into her chest. She brought her head back to the brightening sky, swallowing a ragged chunk of flesh and torn clothing. The woman in the Lexus took her turn to run, and the... cannibal?...on top of the first woman pursued.

As I watched, the woman who was just bitten twitched, one final arcing rainbow of blood leaving her gaping chest wound, she twitched again, and let out a shriek so ear splitting I could almost feel it reverberating within the confines of my truck. She then took on a wholly unnatural posture, laying on the ground, wrists down, palms up, fingers bent and twisted into claws. She shrieked again as her back arched, shoulder blades now firmly to the pavement, and her head began shaking side to side in a manner so quick that her facial features nearly blurred. Within a second, rivulets of blood began to flow like thick tears from her eyes, and she was up. Angling to her feet, her head rose, and she locked eyes with me.

In an instant, the entire realization that this is not just another day, and I should do something washed over me like an ocean of ice water. Or maybe that was the cold sweat I'd become drenched in while watching this horrific scene unfold. Either way, my trance of disbelief broke, and I was in motion. No, not superhero motion. Not Arnold Schwarzenegger circa 1985 motion, not even good old Arnold today, aging and weak but still badass. But, more like exactly what I was. A terrified man, who may or may not have let a small trickle of urine go. I'm not telling, and you weren't there, so it's my secret.

I locked the doors. I locked the doors and slid off of my seat and into the cavity where a passenger seat would normally go. The entire tractor rocked as something, or someone, hit my driver's door full bore. Then again.

Listening to the impacts on my truck, still drenched in icy sweat, I fumbled with the zipper of my travel suitcase. Flipping the top and scattering my two days' worth of clothes on the floor of the truck, my fingers found the Velcro strip that concealed my secret. I reached into the recess and withdrew my Smith and Wesson 6906. A handy, easy to conceal little 9mm handgun. Company policy says no, but, by permit, I was legal to carry in all of the states East of the big river that I traveled to. Except New York. Shush. We all do things we aren't supposed to from time to time. Checking the magazine, and withdrawing the two spare mags, and box of fifty rounds, I withdrew from the task at hand enough to take notice of the distinct lack of impacts on my truck. Did she leave? Die? Or did she decide to take heed of her bumper sticker and start coexisting?

I'm not looking. No way. Not sticking my head back up and becoming a target again. Looking up at my driver's window, I remember the mirror switch. Reaching out and fumbling with the controls, I could see much of the same thing as before. People running. People falling. People biting and killing, and others rising and joining the fray. I suddenly wished I could be anywhere but here. Lord, take me away. Or at least make this into one big bad hallucination, maybe an extreme acid flashback from years past. Anything.

Another impact, seeming to come from further forward of my truck brought me back to reality, and I looked up to the side mirror to see one of the runners stumble into view, go down to a knee, then take off in pursuit of someone. Ok, so it's still real.

"Oh God," I moan, "shit shit shit shit."

I did the only thing I could. I curled up, low to the floor of my truck, gripping my gun, and tried my best not to be noticed.

At some point, among the shrieks, screams, occasional shots, and thuds against the truck, I fell asleep. Maybe. Maybe I fell asleep, passed out, went into shock, another state of consciousness, or even left to another plane of existence. I don't know. I do know that by the time I was plummeted back into the midst of this hellish nightmare, the sun had surpassed its noon-time apex, and moved well into afternoon.

I grab up my phone and try turning it on to call the wife again. I have enough battery again to make a few mildly informational blurts, and that is it.

"Take girls, hide, grab guns, coming home soon as I can. Love you."

And before she gets a chance to get one word in, the phone goes dead again.

Well, wonderful. Here I am. No phone, stuck on a highway surrounded by something I don't understand. I slumped back against the back of the cab interior. For the first time in my life, I'd give anything for a sleeper cab with a bunk to rest in, and the usual supply of food and drinks that a long-haul guy would have. Hell, some of them even have refrigerators and generators. I'd have beer in mine. Man, a beer would be good right now.

I look up to my mirrors again. Bodies lay in the highway, slow roasting in the strengthening Springtime sun. Some have these...these things...crouched over them, gorging themselves on their flesh.

I can see some people in their cars still. Not quite sure if they are dead or alive, either way, they remain quite still. Some cars are crumpled up into each other, obvious attempts to escape the horrors that have been witnessed on this typically fast-flowing three lane stretch of asphalt. Blood drips down the sides of some of them, others with interiors sprayed like a living Jackson Pollock work done in viscera and blood.

Gathering my nerves enough to take a quick peek out of my front window. The shoulder has a couple of cars visible, and more bodies as well, making it tough, but not totally blocked. Taking stock of what I've got, I have a 9mm with three twelve-round magazines, a box of fifty additional rounds, half of a flat soft drink, and a small pack of salted almonds. I've also got an eighty-thousand-pound tractor trailer setup. And I'm in the right lane. When your vehicle is governed to a whopping sixty-three miles per hour, the right lane is your home.

Deciding that my only option is to bully my way down the shoulder and try to get as close to home as I can, I reach up and click the key into the 'Start' position. Instantly I can hear the multitude of soft clicks as all the relays begin doing their thing, and the glow plugs begin cycling.

Sliding into the driver's seat, I crank the key forward and hear the big diesel cough to life. Every head in sight turns my way. Frantically I push both air valves in, only to have them pop right back out. The mechanical beeping of my 'Low Air' indicator mocking me in its monosyllabic voice.

"Fuck!" I shout as I smash the pedal to the floor to speed up the compressor and get my pressure up to where it should be.

Then the shrieks begin. I look up from the gauges to see at least two dozen abominations sprinting full-bore right at me. Some weaving between the vehicles, others clambering their way over the tops. Several of them impact the front and sides of the tractor, several more slam headlong into the front half of my lead trailer.

But several of them run straight past me. They're heading for the semi stopped just off the back of my second trailer, his truck going through the same struggle as mine as black and grey smoke belches forth from his twin exhaust stacks, the driver in the same panicked situation as myself.

My truck rocked as the running monsters collided with it over and over again. One managed to climb its way up the two steps leading to my seat. Hanging on the mirror with one hand, he let out an ear-piercing howl of a scream and started beating on my widow with his free hand. Then I notice the hat. It was Dave. He was still wearing Dave's hat. Poor Dave.

Finally, my air pressure gauge read that it was in the safe zone, and I jammed both valves into place on the dashboard. Slamming my foot down on the clutch, I rowed the truck into gear and took off at the whopping speed of molasses. It's a semi, not a Ferrari.

The truck began to climb in speed, and a glance in my mirror showed the one behind me doing the same thing as we both angled onto the shoulder and began our arduous journey out of Hell.

Another bang on my window brought me back to the more pressing issue. Some of the creatures were now getting dragged under the massive vehicle, popping like balloons full of spaghetti and gristle as the tires churned them into the pavement. The one on my window let out another loud shriek, which was cut short halfway through and replaced with a loud, low gurgle as he let loose a black and crimson tinted torrent all over the glass. He began to shake his head, almost as if the action stunned him, and I rolled the window down a few inches to angle my firearm downward in his direction. Letting loose four shots, the small caliber still loud enough to make my ears ring at this range and close quarters, I struck him in the chest and neck with three of them. The exit wounds taking chunks of poor Dave with them, taking his balance and he dropped to the pavement, immediately recovering, stumbling, and getting taken back down as the lead edge of my second trailer clipped him on the side of his face.

Making it to the relative safety of the shoulder and both trucks picking up speed, it became apparent how many people were still alive in their vehicles. It seemed as though every fifth car or pickup truck had some movement inside. Some with faces and mouths pleading for help, some pounding on their windows in a vain effort to get help, only to draw the attention of some straggling runners. Two people flung open the doors of a blue minivan and ran to catch the trucks, only to be brought down before making it a dozen yards, and left as dessert for the runners, dying face down screaming their pleas to the roadway.

The Orange Turd lurched and tried to change direction as it met with the front half of a silver BMW, halfway onto the shoulder, bringing me back to the windshield for focus. I wrenched the wheel and got it straightened back around, both trailers swaying threateningly because I dared to disrupt their direction of travel so quickly.

Looking again in the mirrors, a wave of relief washing over me as the attackers began to break away, one at a time, giving up their pursuit for some more captive prey. The second truck still right on my tail, and only the occasional shudder from my own as I clipped more vehicles not completely in their lane. Here and there other, smaller vehicles would try to muscle their way through the traffic in our wake, only to be stopped by debris and bodies, blocked in by others, or, in one case, to slide slowly and with no sign of grace down the slick grass towards the tree line. Before much longer, the first exit showed itself, and the pursuing trucker took it, tailed by two other vehicles. I wished them luck as I drove on following my own plans of making it home.

Another twenty minutes and the signs for Route 8 started showing themselves. No longer caring about the career I've sacrificed so much for, I took the exit, and continued towards my house. Route 8 was worse than I-80. Where vehicles had mostly come to a peaceful stop on 80, casually awaiting their fates, Route 8 was a wreck. Literally, a wreck. Vehicles still smoldering, twice the number of dead visible, and signs of last stands everywhere. Akron was a dangerous enough city, but most of these fuckers couldn't shoot. Bodies lay in the evening sun, surrounded by empty casings and discarded small arms. I'd have given anything to scavenge what I could, but *they* were there, too. At least a hundred visible, and surely many more hidden as they feasted.

I continued on, never slowing more than a little bit for obstructions on the shoulder. A few miles later, the truck began to reek of the sickly-sweet smell of hot coolant after colliding with a small pickup truck. Steam rising up from under the cracked and partially desecrated fiberglass hood, and the fan kicking on to work overtime at keeping the pig cooled down.

I figured now would be a good time to find easier venues of travel. Following the exit for Cuyahoga Falls, I maneuvered my mini road-train onto the main street, and immediately dropped down onto Second Street, heading southbound, the sounds of tree branches and low hanging power lines snapping as I turned down side street after side street, none of which were designed for such a tall rig to be traversing.

The side streets were mostly free of traffic and people. Runners here and there, as well as the odd one or two vehicle accidents, all of which were quickly picked over by the monstrosities, the only signs people having been there before were the puddles of blood and remains looking like something that had been through an industrial blender. How had the neighborhoods I've spent the last ten years frequenting transformed into something straight out of a horror flick so quickly? No signs of 'normal' people out and about, tending to their daily lives. No cute girls out for an evening jog in small shorts and tank tops. No retirees taking in the mild temperatures, walking yippy nippy purse dogs. No kids playing basketball while dads trimmed hedges or mowed lawns. None of it. Just accidents, fires, and destruction gone widespread in the matter of, what, a day? Two? It just didn't make sense.

Maneuvering through the odd wreck or signs of struggle, and keeping a wary eye out for the monsters, I zigged and zagged through the side streets without stopping or slowing. Every turn making my trailers sway and rock, creaking in protest.

Finally, down to one of the larger roads, Falls Avenue, there was some traffic backed up. An apparent crash sealing the fate of the people stuck in the intersection waiting for help and road clearing crews that would never arrive. Looking around, taking stock of my options, and pounding the steering wheel, I decided I had to drop into low gear and muscle the truck through, hoping against hope that it didn't take its final breath there, and leave me stranded and naked so close to my home. Being physically impossible to reverse a set of double trailers, forward was my only option anyway. Not a whole lot of choice there.

Deciding the left side was the least crowded, I angled the truck towards the curb, then, up and over with my driver's side. Tree branches scraping and snapping along the roof of my trailers on one side, the creak and screech of steel on steel on the other. Then, a loud bang, similar to a shotgun going off. In fact, that was my first thought, was that I'd been shot at. Nope. A trailer tire had given up the ghost, exhaling its 100+ PSI of air pressure in one resounding burst.

And then the shriek. Followed by several more. As I angled my lumbering beast through the most sparsely populated part of the intersection, pushing a couple of cars and a small pickup truck as I went, several running forms began charging in from all directions, like sharks sensing the blood in the water. Freak after freak began running headlong into the sides of the tractor and both trailers, oblivious to what they were really after, but knowing there was a pile of meat sitting somewhere close by. Several others began making their way over the cars surrounding the intersection, some unfortunate enough to be dragged under by the truck and the cars it was knocking about like a bulldozer does rocks in a quarry. A couple even ended up sandwiched between the cars as they were moved, the sickening crunch and pop of limbs and bodies audible even over the ensuing racket of their chase, and my escape attempts.

Bursting forth from the entanglement, splitting the last two vehicles to each side like a giant mechanical Moses, I throttled down, making another dreadfully slow progressive climb through the numbers on the speedometer. Now over twenty-five miles per hour, the exploded tire began adding in its own two cents, throwing long black alligator shreds of rubber all over the street as the runners pursued, only to be gradually outpaced by my remaining twenty-one tires. Another two much less packed intersections, and I began to allow my speed to scrub off as I started formulating a plan. One turn and seven blocks from my home, and hopefully, safety and family. I grab the phone, turn it on, and it shuts right back off before the 'Shittiest cell phone provider on the face of the planet' title screen completes. Okay, so that's not really their name, but they both start with an 'S', so we'll take it. At any rate, the option of calling once more to home and cooperating on a plan is no longer present.

Well, I had few good options. As much as I wanted to, I couldn't rightfully pull up next to my house in a bright orange semi, making all the noise in the world, and let the brakes whoosh and walk right through the door. 'Honey! I'm home! Some really weird shit going on out there but man I'm hungry, is that pizza?' Yeah, probably not an option at this point. But...

Large noisy vehicle. Neighborhood full of angry hungry fuckers that are attracted to every mouse fart and insect flight? I've got it!

I worked the truck to a street about two blocks south of my house. Turning onto the road, I cut the turn tight intentionally. Half smiling, half grimacing as my second trailer ran itself along the side of a telephone pole. The bending and twisting metal meeting the unyielding wood and letting out a sound reminiscent of the world's longest nails being raked across the world's nastiest black board.

Pulling free of the pole, the noise persisted. No, never mind, those were shrieks. Fucking worked like a charm! I pull my damaged, smoking, straining rig about halfway down the block, well within earshot of my house, and pull the knob for the trailer brakes. More cringe-worthy noise flooded the neighborhood as the pneumatic brake chambers let out their last long hiss of air. Then, ignoring the usual need to lower my landing gear (those little support legs for the trailer, for you non-truckers), I flipped the switch to uncouple the lead trailer from the tractor, slammed the truck into third gear, and flew out from under the trailer. The trailer, and its twenty-five thousand pounds of cargo weight, dropped clear of the back of the tractor and slammed to the ground, turning its own landing gear to bits of tin foil, and making an earth-shattering BANG in the evening quiet. As the tractor advanced away from the cacophony, the last I heard of the mess was my air and electric lines breaking free, impacting the back of the cab, and shrieks and calls from all over the neighborhood.

Smiling at my grand distraction, I followed the straight street a few short blocks back out to the main road through the neighborhood. The tractor, much lighter and very much nimbler with its 34-ton weight loss, shot up the stretch of North Howard to its next turn a couple blocks north of my own street. Once making the turn, I killed the engine and let the truck coast the next few blocks until it lost momentum. Leaving it parked in gear, instead of making more noise by applying the tractor brake, I began to gather what was important. I moved fast, though I was sure my distraction left nobody but my tire noise on the road to whisper my location to the world. Clipping my gun holster to my belt, spare mags, my last two cigars, and stuffing my bills of lading into my cloth lunch bag, I checked my surroundings and left the truck, making my way quickly to a house on the street that I knew had been vacant for years.

Once on the porch of the house, I retrieved my trusty folding knife from its pocket clip, worked the front window until I could get the lock to pop, and entered, drawing my pistol on the way in. Closing the window behind me, I began to slice the pie around every corner, clearing the first floor of the empty structure, and then made my way up to the second floor, doing much the same. Confident that I was alone, I'd relaxed for the first time since this whole ordeal began.

I moved to the front windows to look out and view my truck. Through the dust covered pane of glass, I could make out a good half dozen of the creatures all around the truck. Watching as one walked a few feet away from where I'd just exited, she threw her head back, and I could hear the sharp intake of breath as she inhaled sharply through what was left of her nose, and then darted back to the open driver's door of the truck. Was she...scenting me? Trying to find a trail? Another loud snorting sniff, and then a series of short, sharp coughs, and all present made their way to be near where she was. I couldn't be sure, but if I was being tracked, I'd have to guess the pungent interior of the truck, saturated with the ass and sweat of every trucker in the company might have just saved my bacon. Hey, I'm not saying truckers are dirty, but a vehicle with over 1.5 million miles of us in and out of it will have a certain... aroma about it.

Moving back toward the rear bedrooms of the house, I could see no movement on this side. I decided that waiting until it started to get dark was my best option, and that's just what I did. Although, right as I pressed my back to the wall, ready for my posterior to make friends with the dusty wood floor, I heard a series of shrieks from my friends out front. Gripping the S&W tightly in one hand, my small blade in the other, I crept quietly and quickly back to the front window, only to be met with relief that they were in fact running away from my hiding spot. That relief quickly dissipated as they disappeared around the side of a house across the street, and some obviously human screams echoed throughout the rows of houses.

Deciding rest was not going to come, and dark was within an hour away, I waited. Watching out the windows like an old spinster worried about what's become of the world, I saw the most reassuring thing I'd seen all day. Nothing. No crazed fucks running around, no people running from them, nothing at all. It was more tranquil, somehow, than a late Sunday evening.

Gradually, darkness began to blanket the Earth, and, gradually, I began to get up the nerve to make my move. Once the street lights came on, I moved down to the first floor and eased my way out of the rear entrance of the house, slipping as quickly and quietly through the tall grass of the forgotten back yard, into the yard of the house behind it, and up to the side. Sweeping my gaze up and down the street, and across the visages of the houses lining the sidewalks, I saw nothing. The only apparent sign that something was not right with the world was two bodies lain in the street, directly behind a half-rusted Oldsmobile with giant chrome wheels. You know, the kind that some people think are cool, so they slap them on a car worth a fraction of the price of the wheels, and wonder why the rest of the world cringes? Yeah, those. One body lay completely still, the other weakly moving its head, though the twin trails of blood trickling from its eyes told me right off that it wasn't someone I should talk to.

I snatched a small rock off the ground and threw it down the street, and, waiting several seconds to make sure nobody would come to investigate, I darted across to the other side, making sure to stay to the shadows between the pools of light from the street lamps. Once across and sliding almost noiselessly down the side of the next house, my own dwelling came immediately into view. The same basic two-floor home with an attic and small garage that you can find in any inner-city housing row across the country. Nothing special, but it was mine, and being on a double lot, we had one of a very few actual back yards worth mowing in the neighborhood. That's special. Well, unless you don't like having a yard to mow, then I don't know what to tell you.

As far as mowing was concerned, the lot abutting to the back of my yard hadn't seen a mower in many months. Funny, how that works, the city will come by if yours has gone for a couple of weeks and post a notice to mow or be fined for your lack of attentiveness, yet once they knock a house down, it sees their blades maybe twice a summer. Less often than that, usually.

I took advantage of this and sprang from my hiding spot, crossing one small empty lot, and dropping into the waist high grass in the one behind mine. Moving low and slow, I carefully made my way to the back of the lot, painfully aware the sounds of each blade of grass as it parted to make way for my large frame. Sneaking comes easily to some people. The heavier and taller you are, those talents become much easier to obtain. At six-one, I wasn't overly tall, and not overly heavy, fairly well-built two hundred and twenty pounds, but just enough to let me know I was no stealth ninja that could drop out of a rafter in the ceiling and assassinate someone.

Making my not entirely stealthy way through the tall grass, I reached the back of the lot. There it was. My house, hopefully with my wife and daughters still safe and sound, and maybe even a neighbor inside helping keep them safe.

Looking at the house from my vantage point, I could see the attached garage, a first and a second-floor back window, and the attic window. How am I to signal them now, or let them know I'm here without catching a bullet? My wife could shoot, and I wasn't going to tempt fate by rushing right up to the house, so I retrieved my lighter from my pocket. Striking the flint with the wheel, I signal three short, three long, three short-SOS. Waiting a few moments, I try it again. Nothing. Maybe nobody's looking, I think, as I scan the ground around me and come up with a few stones. Flinging the first two at the lower windows, nothing happens, so I throw a couple more at the side of the house and the attic window. There it is. I saw movement in the attic, so I tried the lighter again. And again. Finally, three single flashes of sparks in the attic window.

Relief found me instantly, feeling like a previously unnoticed weight had slid off my shoulders. Scanning my surroundings, and determining the coast to be clear, I low-ran across my back yard, behind my pickup truck in the driveway, and stood below the attic. The window opened, swinging inward on its hinges, and the beautiful mess of dirty-blonde hair that is my wife poked itself outside.

"Oh, thank God, you're here!" she called in an excited whisper.

"Yeah," I replied, also whispering loudly," traffic and shit. Are you bugged in up there?"

"Me, the girls, and Henry," she replied.

"That's awesome!" I replied, nearly breaking the quiet in my excitement. "Is the downstairs open?"

"No, Henry- "she began, but I cut her off.

"Later. I need a way in. Tell Henry to grab my extension ladder. I'm coming in through the bedroom here."

"Okay hold on, it might be a minute," came the reply.

Without another word, she disappeared from the window, and I moved back behind my truck to keep out of sight. Several minutes passed, and I could hear footsteps, and the sound of my aluminum ladder jostling in the garage next to me.

A few moments later, the bedroom window, then the outer storm window slid open, and my old rickety ladder made its way out, then down, followed by Henry's smiling chocolate brown face.

"And a good evening to you, my brother!" he called quietly, in his perpetually cheerful, but bass-drum deep voice, "you gotta have God himself on your side to be out in all this!"

"Good to see you, I'm coming up, man," I replied, and started making my way up the ladder, cringing with every creak and pop of the aluminum as I worked my way up. Henry's face vanished as I ascended.

I clambered through the window, and into my bedroom over the nightstand. Checking the closet, and not surprised to see not one gun or scrap of ammunition in sight, I left the room and went straight up the narrow stairway to the attic, only to nearly run headlong into the three smiling forms of my wife and girls.

"Oh my God, I'm so happy you're all alright!" I exclaimed, hugging both girls and then my wife.

Moving further up into the attic together, I looked around and noticed somebody was missing.

"Where's Henry?" I asked.

"He went back downstairs to re-block the door between the garage and the kitchen," explained my wife. "He had to remove everything to get your ladder."

"Nice. Is the whole downstairs blocked up?"

"Yeah," she said, hesitating, "but you kind of don't have walls in your garage anymore. He used all the plywood to cover the windows and doors."

"That's fine, it went to a good use."

Then a loud and shrill "DA-DA!" nearly echoed throughout the small attic as Gwen made her way back to me and latched onto my leg. Melissa immediately made her way over to her much younger sister, trying to shush her, but I scooped the toddler up, tussling her sloppy blonde hair and planting a kiss right on her cheek.

"She's cool, dude," I told Melissa, "just excited. Has she been good? Quiet?"

"Mostly good, but not very quiet," replied Melissa, her dark hair and eyes very weary already, giving her age beyond her twelve years.

"What about you?" I asked.

"Scared," she said in her usual quiet voice, "we were so worried about you, and those things!"

"Yeah, well I'm here now, and we're all safe, right?" I tried to reassure.

"Right" she said meekly and went back to her sleeping mat in the middle of the attic.

Gwen started fussing, so I put her down and she took off like a jet to her pile of foam rubber building blocks, scattering them in every direction and giggling.

"You haven't been outside, right? They haven't seen you guys?" I asked, turning to my wife.

"No," she replied, motioning to the girls. "Melissa has been helping her best with keeping Gwen occupied while Henry and I kept an eye on the outside. Those things."

Picking up where she trailed off, I offered, "Yeah, they're fucked up. I don't know what's going on, but I'm happy I was able to make it back."

"We heard a bunch of noise a few hours ago, like a semi-truck," as she buried her face in my shoulder.

"Yeah, I had a plan, and for once, it worked!" I said, squeezing her tight.

Just then, Henry made his way up the steps. "Hey hey neighbor," he said jovially, "brother it's so good to have you back here," taking one of my hands and embracing me with his free arm.

"Yeah no shit, it's good to be here," I told him, "thanks so much brother, I could damn near kiss you on your bald ass head!"

Henry was a good neighbor. A damned good one. He'd help the wife with things if she needed it and keep an eye on things when we'd go on vacations. Always respectful, helpful, and as happy to see you as a Golden Retriever. Not overly imposing, a few inches shorter than me, but he was built like a freaking pit bull and Lord help you if you ever got on Mr. Henry's bad side.

Motioning to my youngest, he opined, "The little one sure been a handful. She's good for a bit, but good Lord that girl has some lungs when she wants your attention. Me and Miss Jennifer," motioning to my wife, "been keeping an eye on the outside. We got the water shut off to the house, all the sinks and tub filled, and been boilin' it to make sure it's safe."

"Yeah she doesn't really seem to understand why we're up here," said Jennifer.

"Probably for the better, anyway. Y'all been holding up ok though?" I asked "Got any food? I'm starving."

"Yeah," Jennifer said, offering me a can of beef ravioli.

I took the can and started to sit, but then heard a commotion out front. All of us moved to the front attic window and watched the scene unfolding.

The neighbors across the street and one over decided to make a run for it, probably hoping to use the cover of darkness the same as I had. The commotion we heard was their own great escape, botched before they made it one step outside their front door. Two of the five people made it outside and were making their way down the front steps toward street level. The third one fell, right across the door jam, making a resounding thud on the porch which was followed almost immediately by a chorus of shrieks and howls as several runners made their way from the surrounding yards and driveways.

"Ah shit," I muttered, looking back to see Melissa watching from behind us.

"Go over with your sister, you don't need to watch this," Jennifer shot at her, and Melissa slunk away.

A scream drew our attention back to the drama, a thin sheet of glass now our own television screen to the horrors. The other two neighbors, Christ, they haven't even been there long enough for me to know their names, dragged the third back inside as two runners shot up the front steps towards them. The other two made it safely to their car, slamming the doors just as three more impacted the doors just a fraction of a second later. With little hesitation, they started the car and left the others to fend for themselves.

The two runners made it up the steps, one crashing clean through the not-quite-closed front door, the other bursting inside hot on its heels. Screaming echoed out of the house, reverberating off of the houses. One runner began backing out of the house, dragging what looked like the teenage daughter with it, the handle of what appeared to be a butcher's knife sticking out of its chest. It dragged the girl across the porch, leaving a thickening trail of blood as he bounced her head down the steps, her screams long silenced, turning into gurgled moans, thanks to the large chunk of missing flesh from her neck and down her shoulder. As the runner dragged her body across the devil strip, the three that had attacked the car joined him. Nipping at her legs and removing long strips of blood and sinew-decorated meat.

In the midst of all of this, the one that remained in the house showed itself at the front door, issued several loud, barking coughs, and three of the four attacking the now lifeless body rushed inside the house, and within moments, crimson lines and splatters painted the white of the open front door as a dark, but visible, pool spread its way to the door jam.

The guy dragging the body away was now out of sight, a trail of blood marking their journey to the area of Henry's driveway. The others in the house were now quiet, presumably feasting on the two left inside, and the sounds of the engine making its escape faded away. Moments later, we heard the screech of tires, a crash, a single gunshot, and then silence.

"I guess, guess they didn't make it, either," Henry said, looking a bit sick.

"No," I replied, "they went south."

"What's south?" Jennifer asked.

"That's where I dropped my trailers," I explained, as realization spread across their faces.

Leaning against the wall near the window, and sliding down until I was sitting, I began to realize for the first time that I was soaked with a cold sweat. I'd just seen my neighbors slaughtered right in front of my eyes. Jennifer looked about the same as I felt, pale faced and breathing kind of hard. Henry had disappeared back down to the second floor. He came back up with, of all things, a twelve-pack of Miller High Life.

"I need me one of these babies," he said, offering me one of my own.

I took the proffered can, and, cracking it open, remarked, "I didn't want to admit it, but I guess this is how you know the world has gone to shit." And took a swig.

"What you mean?" Henry asked, eyeballing me.

"Because you finally convinced me to drink this piss water," I said, and was met with a soft chuckle.

"Brother," he said, "drink about six more of these, and you won't care how they taste. Trust me."

Taking another long draw from the can, I looked around the attic. It was pretty average for an unfinished storage area. Wood plank floor, peaked ceiling with no actual walls aside from the slope of the roof interior, and a window on each end. At least it was secure. That was something. We had a whole house full of supplies to sustain us for a while, guns, ammo, and a high vantage point. Henry had stripped the interior of the walls in my garage, and used the plywood, along with a whole box of wood screws, to cover the windows and doors on the first floor.

Finishing my beer, and feeling we were fairly safe in our little hideout, I decided going to bed was the next proper step to take. I had been up for over twenty-four hours at this point, and, though not unusual or difficult for a truck driver, the events of the day made it quite a bit tougher to pull off. Locating a pile of musty blankets in the corner, I instructed Jennifer to lock the door at the bottom of the attic steps, and we all lay down for bed, except Henry.

"You ain't tired, man?" I asked.

"Somebody gotta stay awake to keep an eye on things, brother. Get some rest, I'll wake you when I feel too tired." And, holding the remainder of his twelve- pack up, "Somebody's got to keep these guys company, anyway."

"Alright, man. Good night," I replied, and lay my head down, pulling Jennifer in close.

"Sleep well, my brother," he wished and turned back to the window.

TWO

I awoke some time later to see light streaming through the windows. It had definitely been more than a few hours. Both girls were awake and playing quietly in a corner, Melissa drawing, and baby Gwen back at it with her blocks and an assortment of stuffed animals scattered around her haphazardly.

"You're up," Jennifer observed, handing me a steaming cup of black coffee.

"Nobody woke me up to keep watch?" I asked, eyeballing her.

"Your day was longer than ours, and you weren't moving, anyway," she laughed, leaning in to give me a kiss.

Henry made his presence known, appearing on the steps, "Whoa now, there's children present here!" and laughed.

"Jealous" I admonished with a smile.

"Nah brother, that one's all yours. Too crazy for me." He grinned, "I had to nudge you with my foot a dozen times. With your snoring..." He trailed off, shaking his head and grinning.

"Yeah," Jennifer chimed in, "We thought you were going to lead them right to us."

We all had a laugh, and then Henry turned serious. "Jennifer and I checked what we have, for supplies."

"Yeah?" I asked, sipping my coffee.

"About one and a half months, if we're easy on it." Jennifer said, "We figured we'd leave it up to you, whether you want to stay or leave."

"Right," I said, then added, "No fuckin way are we leaving. Not yet. Not with the girls, and with how fast those things are. We have a month and a half of supplies, we stay for one month, and take what we have on the road then."

"Where would we go though?" Jennifer asked.

"Don't know yet, woman, I just woke up. Let's take it easy for now," I explained.

"Man needs some time," Henry opined.

"Yeah, this is a lot to take in, man," I offered, then, "We should gather what we have and bring it all up here, this is the safest spot we have. Keep perishable food where it is for now and bring everything else up here. Did you count the MRE's in the closet downstairs?" I asked Jennifer.

"Shit, no," she said." That gives us... what?"

"Another two weeks," I explained. "Get everything. Guns and ammo are all up here, but get both med kits, both bug-out bags, tarps, hand tools, batteries, the kids' stuff, couple changes of clothes, get everything. Is my phone charged?"

"Yeah, I plugged it in when I got up," Jennifer explained.

"Cool, I'm going to call my mom, see if they're alright and what's going on there," I said, and got up to retrieve my phone. Grabbing the device, and seeing it had fifty-percent battery, I brought up my mom in my contacts.

Selecting her number and putting the phone to my ear, I heard silence for a few seconds, then a beep, and the phone went back to the contacts menu. Pulling it away and looking at the screen, I saw 'No service' displayed at the bottom of the screen.

"No phones. No service," I said and turned to see that the other two had already left to gather our supplies up. "You girls doing good?" I asked my daughters.

"Yeah," Melissa said, "I'm kind of scared."

"I know," I said, giving her a hug with one arm, "we got this though, kid. We'll be alright."

"Okay," she said meekly, then went back to her sister, who was now busy filling in an entire coloring book page with blue marker.

A few minutes later, Jennifer and Henry came up the narrow attic stairs, each with one of the bug-out packs on their backs, and arms full of various supplies. Placing them in one corner, Jennifer turned to me.

"Any luck?" she asked.

"Nah, no service," I explained.

"Yeah, I checked mine downstairs, it said the same thing."

"Mom's too stubborn, Dad's too smart. I'm sure they're alright," I said.

I left Jennifer to sort and stack supplies and left down the stairs with Henry to grab the rest of our stuff. The rest of that day, and the next couple of days after that passed by without too much drama. The occasional freak, or small group of them, could be seen running between houses and down the streets, chasing anything that moved. I got quite a good laugh watching them at the bushes across the street, next to a neighbor's house. The perpetual flock of little brown sparrows that lived there seemed to be taunting them. They would land, chirping and squeaking loudly, one of the runners would sprint head-long into the bushes, bounce off, and all the tiny birds would fly up to the roof tops, only to return a few moments later to taunt their predator again.

We began keeping watch in shifts at night, each person on-duty for three hours, effectively giving us all six hours of sleep a night. We knew we were in danger, but, from our elevated position, we were more like observers, as opposed to prey.

Four days into our new lives as the silent watchers of our new world, we heard a commotion on the street adjoining our own. A Hispanic man, named Jose, and his family had tried making a run to their SUV that was parked on the street. As soon as the side door to their home opened, the shrieks of those running freaks could be heard. We watched in horror as Jose drew a pistol and fired, hitting one of the monstrosities in the chest, and another in the head. The one that he hit in the chest stumbled and fell, but almost immediately found her feet, and lunged for Jose's wife, taking the small woman to the ground like a tiger leaping on its prey, and tearing long strings of flesh and cloth free from her shoulder blades that glistened in the sun.

Jose spun when the implications of this new development sunk home, and he started firing blindly. They had now attracted a small flock of about a dozen runners. Jose's rounds had practically no effect as he squeezed the trigger again and again. He stopped shooting when the group got closer, and turned the gun on his young son, pulling the trigger on the young boy of about 6, then turning the gun on himself. As the spray of skull fragments and brain matter left the top of his head, looking much like the world's most disgusting party popper, I turned and vomited into our restroom bucket.

No sooner had I lifted my head and began wiping my mouth, Jennifer followed suit, filling the entire attic with the sounds and smells of sickness and second-hand beef ravioli. Henry just walked away, muttering and wiping sweat from his forehead, finding a seat next to the kids, and offering them comfort.

I returned to the window for just a moment, long enough to see the freaks dragging Jose and his wife off to locations unknown. The remainder of their Devil's dinner party stayed behind, and began pulling on the boy's body, twisting his small limbs about, pulling and tearing until each had their own meal. I left the window as the sounds of popping bones and tearing cartilage reached me, followed by sounds similar to ripping a wet wash rag as I traversed the wood plank floor.

"Brother, you made a wise choice to stay, I think," Henry remarked somberly.

"I'm going to get a beer. I have Guinness," I replied and made my way down the stairway to my fridge on the first floor.

THREE

Thankfully, the next two days once again passed without much drama, though the neighborhood was beginning to already look worse for wear. Dried blood and gore now splattered across the house of two of my closer neighbor's properties. Long-dried streaks stuck and baked to the pavement from the first encounter, where the woman was dragged across the street to Henry's driveway. Similar marks and puddles littered Jose's driveway. A few abandoned vehicles here and there, the bright blue collar of somebody's dog in the nearby intersection, surrounded by more witness markings of horrible scenes.

The one thing that kept drawing my attention was the runner that Jose managed to shoot in the head. It lay still and hadn't moved or been touched since it took its last moment of life face down in the grass of the small house's front lawn. I remarked about it to Jennifer, who promptly wrote it down in her notebook she had begun keeping, the front of the lime green pack of bound paper promptly labelled 'How to Survive Monsters'.

On the third day of silence, at dawn, I heard the sounds of distant gunfire. Full automatic, the far away thump of what could only be a .50 caliber machine gun. The sound of small explosions, softened by distance, reverberated through the empty streets.

"Hey, guys!" I announced, waking up Jennifer and Henry.

Waking wide eyed, and exchanging glances all around, Jennifer was the first to speak.

"What is that?" she asked, already fully awake.

"Is that…?" Henry asked, trailing off.

"Gotta be the fuckin military, man. Gotta be!" I exclaimed.

Our excitement was short lived, soon to be replaced with apprehension and confusion as the power to the house shut off and was soon replaced by a far-off klaxon emanating from the downtown area of Akron.

"Hey, Scott, what is that?" Henry asked, motioning out the back window towards the sky.

I moved into a position next to him as the unmistakable shape of several military aircraft flew in a formation just over the treetops. Their silhouettes letting anyone even remotely interested in military aircraft know that it was a swarm of A-10 attack aircraft. They flew low and fast, barely missing the tallest treetops as the sound of their twin jet engines shook the house on their pass.

Running to the front of the house, the backs of their aircraft wavering in the heat of their exhaust, I watched, and waited. We all did. All curious as to the intentions of a formation of one of the modern military's most impressive airborne killers. They flew out of sight, though the sounds of their powerful engines remained.

The streets almost immediately filled with pack after pack of running freaks, all turning their attention skyward, then downtown, all wondering what was making this much noise in their part of the city, and if they could eat said intruder.

As the aircraft made their second pass, then a third and a fourth, more and more runners moved through the neighborhoods. There were so many of them, more than any of us had ever imagined there could be, making me all the more thankful that we hadn't decided to fight our way out of town. Despite years of seeing armchair apocalypse experts offer advice on the internet, bugging in, as opposed to bugging out, had been an apparently smart move.

The groups of running cannibals began sprinting toward the direction of all the commotion. Eventually, the sounds of gunfire and explosions lessened, then lessened even more, and their near-continuous drum beat was replaced by only sporadic fire.

Finally, on what I recalled to be their eighth pass overhead, and towards downtown, the aircraft began to split away from each other, zeroing in on targets as they started to open fire. The massive *BRRRRRTTTT* of their nose guns, sounding for all to hear like God himself playing with a giant cosmic zipper, filled the air. Massive 30mm rounds from the GAU-8 Avenger cannons laying waste to targets within the downtown area of the city, followed by loud thunderous *BOOMS* of explosions from ordinance being dropped from their pods on the Warthogs' wings.

In very little time at all, the clear blue sky was pockmarked with rising columns of black smoke. Downtown must have become no-man's land in just a matter of moments. The aircraft made another pass, then a third, each pass shaking the entire world with the Hellfire sounds of explosions and plumes of thick, roiling, oily smoke. Then it hit me, what they were doing became very apparent, and I sat down and started laughing.

"What's funny?" Henry asked.

Through my bursts of laughter, I replied, "We're fucked. They just said so! We're done, gotta be, you don't fire-bomb a city you intend to save. Christ, they swooped in, scorched the earth, and dipped out!"

That realization began to sink in with the others, and in short order, everybody looked like they needed a drink and a vacation. I wonder if there are these monsters in the Caribbean? Christ, I hope not. St. Thomas doesn't deserve that. Maybe Barbados and Cuba, but please, not the Virgin Islands.

We sat around, talking idly and just passing the time for the rest of the day, each of us with one eye on each other, and one to the outside world, but this time equally as interested in the sky as we were with what was on the ground. They didn't return for the rest of that day, as we sat long until evening acting like the world hadn't fallen apart around us in the past week.

The power never came back on after the military had their way with the city. My city. This wasn't a huge concern, as we barely used any light, and none at night time due to the concerns of being spotted and swarmed. I never had air conditioning in the attic, as it was nowhere near being a finished room, but...

Something was nagging me as we sat watching out of the windows while the girls played. I just couldn't put a name to it. Then it started to come to me. Like a swirling mist of a thought materializing, right up until you realize there's a Mack truck hidden behind that fog, and it nails you while you're not paying attention.

I shot up from my seat on a roll of rugs by the front window.

"Shit!" I nearly shouted.

"What? What's going on?" I heard from my wife, as Henry ran to my window and began scanning the outside world, returning his gaze to me with a questioning expression.

"The fridge!" I explained, "The fucking fridge, man. Our food. No power. Shit shit shit!" And I ran down the stairs as if the food were on fire, as opposed to on its way to a quicker-than-planned expiration. Henry and Jennifer followed me down, and, right as I reached the fridge, an idea dawned on me.

"Ok, woman, go grab the camp stove from the basement, Henry, get our butcher knives and a bunch of pots and pans and shit, man, we got some cooking and prepping to do!" I directed, and then, on another thought, called down the basement steps to my wife, "Hey grab them Ziploc bags, too, all of them! We got this!"

"Uhmm, Okay," she replied, then asked, "Do you want the cooler, too?"

"Yeah! Good thinking!" She brought the cooler halfway up, I grabbed it from her and shot a quick "Thanks" as I went back to the kitchen with it and began packing it full of foods from the freezer. Opening the cabinet and grabbing a large handful of grocery bags, I began emptying the refrigerator into those, and making the typical efforts of a man carrying bags of groceries. I *will* get these all in one trip.

Okay, scratch that, maybe the second trip.

Nope, but the third one is in the bag, no pun intended. Alright, pun intended a little bit.

Making my final trip up to the attic, two full flights of steps, and sweating like Richard Simmons in the 80's, I placed my final load of cargo in the pile and looked around to the faces of everybody, even the baby, looking at me like I'd lost my mind.

"Alright, get that stove fired up," I instructed Jennifer. "Tonight, we eat chicken and fish. I'm going to let the pork and beef thaw, slice it thin, salt the hell out of it, and roast it until it's jerky. While we wait for the meats to thaw, I'm going to start salting and slow roasting the vegetables. Going to make all this corn crunchy like Corn Nuts, it should keep for a while longer like that, and we can grind some of it into corn meal."

"Is he for real?" Henry asked Jennifer.

"Do you know how much he's got locked in that head of his?" she replied, laughing. "If he says it, I'm going to listen."

"If you say so," he replied, with a slight shrug.

"Melissa," I said to my oldest girl, "Dude, run down to the kitchen, fill a grocery bag with spices, and grab the big container of pepper, we'll need it."

"Okay," she replied, with mild enthusiasm, probably simply happy to lend a hand, and disappeared down the steps, returning a few moments later with a bag filled with spice containers, and an econo-sized tin of black pepper in the other hand.

"Why do we need all that pepper?" Henry asked.

"Because," I replied, "salt preserves, pepper repels bugs and vermin."

Henry returned to separating the food, now with a thoughtful look on his face as he placed packs of meat here and there to thaw.

We spent the rest of that evening cooking and preparing food, hanging what we'd roasted and dried on cloths and in small sacks made from coffee filters and rubber bands. We cooked a whole bag of salmon fillets, and a couple of packs of seasoned chicken breasts and ate until our bellies were about to burst. Both girls having eaten so much they were fast asleep on their sleeping mats way earlier than they usually would. My wife was reclined back on our pile of blankets, busily writing notes about everything that had happened into her binder. Henry and I were at our respective window seats, a weapon loaded and lain within reach of each of us.

"Shoot brother," Henry breathed out, loosening his belt, "y'all even eat well at the end of days."

Chuckling, I replied, "You can do a lot to Germans, dude, but you can't starve us."

"I believe that's right, my friend!" he said, letting out a long sigh. "Hey, let me ask you something."

"Shoot."

"I boarded up the first floor. We can block them steps up real nice, why don't you sleep in your beds?"

"Easy," I offered, "This is the highest, and most defensible spot in the house. Barring a house fire, this is the smartest place, best view of the neighborhood, and tough to get into, especially with them narrow stairs coming up to here. Plus, it keeps us all accounted for, and in one larger room, instead of spread out in three bedrooms over a whole floor."

"Makes sense to me," he replied, "my brother got it all figured out." As he finished with a smile.

"Yes sir, I'm trying to at least. I'm kind of a rookie at this whole apocalypse thing," then suggested, "You get some rest, man, I'll take the first watch."

"Not about to argue with you there," as Henry laid down by his window. "I'll see you in a while."

"Sleep well, man," I told him, as he drifted off to sleep in moments, the postprandial somnolence food coma taking him over in apparent waves.

FOUR

The next week, or as best I could tell it was a week, passed by with little to no nuance. It reminded me of my early adulthood, spending time behind bars. Was it two weeks, or had it been three already? Or only one? The only things missing were the sounds of arguing over the microwave and phones, set to a steady background of loud voices, the slap of cards on the table, and the clink of dominoes. I'd rather this than jail, though. Here, I was with family and a good friend, though the guards were a lot scarier here, and I probably had as much chance here as there for a good solid escape.

At any rate, as best I could figure, it had been another week. Sometime around what I'd assumed to be midnight, I heard something out of place. Straining my ears to listen more closely, I was met with silence for several moments. Just as I was about to relax, I heard it again. It was outside, from right around the back window. Then a third noise there, and I realized I was listening to the sounds of something on, or around, my ladder. We never brought it back in through the window after I'd entered, intending to leave it in case we needed to make a quick escape. I'd seen runners close to it a couple of times, but none of them even acknowledged its existence. Had one of them figured out what it was?

Another noise from below, this one the sounds of weight being applied to the first rung, and I was quickly brought back to the present time. I reached out and shook both Jennifer and Henry awake, motioning to my ears, and then the window.

"Get your guns ready," I whispered, almost inaudibly, nearly mouthing the words, then, "Jennifer, you watch from up here, Henry, come with me, provide cover from the back of the room, something's coming up the fucking ladder."

They both nodded, Jennifer taking her place, her Sig Sauer .45, a beautiful Nightmare 1911 model, at the low ready, close enough to the window to watch, but far enough back to be as close to invisible as possible. Henry grabbed his .357 Taurus revolver and followed me down the steps. We reached the closed bedroom door, my twelve-gauge Remington ready, resting on the crook of my arm to keep it aimed into the room as I reached for the door knob, the stock collapsed all the way in to make it as far from unwieldy as I could.

I slowly turned the knob, and shoved the door quickly, bringing the shotgun to my shoulder and scanning the obviously empty room. The only movement being the curtains blowing slowly with the breeze from the open window.

Then, another creak and pop of the ladder as another slow, careful step was taken. I brought the shotgun in as I crouched in a low cover position at the end of my dresser, Henry hugging the open doorway with his massive wheel-gun aimed for the open window.

I could all but physically feel Henry tense up behind me. I turned to him, mouthing *return fire only*, and he replied with a nearly imperceptible nod, his affirmative response telling me that maybe we wouldn't shred somebody we knew, or somebody innocent, if it wasn't a runner. Maybe.

A couple more creaks of the ladder, and I began to make out a form in the moonlit darkness. The top of a head, and a shock of wild, unkempt red hair backlit by silver from our lunar nightlight. Then, the figure rose some more, I could make out a face. Pale skin on a freckled forehead, then the eyes peeked carefully over the edge. It was definitely a man, the eyes showed none of what we came to know as signs of the infected. No blackening of the iris, no bloody tears streaming down the cheeks.

He turned his gaze back to the back yard, then back into the room, apparently missing my still figure, and Henry's dark complexion, in the unlit darkness of the room. He made another move upward, and, once a full face was visible, I clicked on the 800 lumen Streamlight mounted to my weapon, and issued one clear, but low, order.

"Don't...fucking...move..." as I rose, the light turning his pupils to mere pinpricks, illuminating ice blue irises, he nearly fell off the ladder in surprise and realization, but regained his balance.

"Henry, watch my ass," I instructed.

"I got you, neighbor," he replied.

The face in the window took on a look of pure shock upon finding out there was more than one of us present, and we were obviously armed.

"I...H...I...friendly..." was all the man in the window could stammer out, a low, scratchy voice emanating from his open mouth, as he raised his hand in a placating gesture.

"Who are you?" I shot at him, irritated. "Belay that, we're going to draw attention. Are you armed?"

"Y...y...yes," the man replied.

"Pass it butt first through the window, then stand tall enough to show me your waist line," I instructed, then added a very deliberate, "*Slowly,* fucker, I don't know you."

He nodded, then, with his free hand, very slowly reached into his belt and began moving his weapon toward the window. It crested the bottom of the window sill with all the speed of a July sunrise, and I braced my shotgun under my right shoulder, and snatched the small revolver with my left hand, and tossed it on the floor behind me without breaking eye contact with the man. He then rose a bit higher on the ladder, bringing his waist line in view of the window, twisting one side to the next.

"Get in, feet apart, hands on your head," I instructed him, as he nodded and climbed in the window.

He stood nearly a full head shorter than myself but was fairly-well built. He stood up straight, palms on top of his head, feet apart, just as instructed.

"Henry, search him," I ordered, training the barrel of the Remington on the man's chest, his eyes going just a bit wider.

"Now hold up," Henry objected, "why I gotta feel up all over this guy, I don't know him, don't know where he's been, either!"

"Because," I shot back, impatiently, "we have to make sure he ain't armed, and while your gun will ventilate him, a slug from this will vaporize his ass if he wants to be stupid tonight."

Henry grudgingly moved forward, leaning in and patting the man down. Pulling one shoulder, he got the man to turn around, and repeated the process, pulling a long fixed-blade hunting knife from the man's thigh, and another, though much smaller blade, from a sheath on his ankle, and he tossed both blades into the hallway.

"You alone?" I asked the guy as I clicked the light off on my gun.

"No," he replied. "My wife and our friend are waiting out there. They…. they're armed, too."

"Alright, go get them, we'll watch the area around the house from up here. Bring their weapons, and anything else you have," I instructed, "then you all can come up."

"How do I know you won't just take our things and lock us out?" he questioned.

"Dude," I said wearily, "we have more firearms and ammo here than we could possibly carry, even if everybody carried a double load. Let me see that pistol, Henry."

"Oh, here you go," and he produced the small silver revolver.

"This a fuckin' .32," I chuckled. "You couldn't give it to me, man."

"Alright," he said, looking mildly offended, "I'll go get them."

He disappeared back out of the window and down the ladder, and I whispered details of what was going on up to my wife, and told her to keep watch for anything suspicious, but not to fire unless somebody draws. She replied in the affirmative, and by the time I got back into the room, the red-haired guy was making his way up the ladder with two large backpacks.

"This it?" I asked him.

"Yeah man it's all there," he replied, "And they're both out there disarmed, waiting."

"No knives or other bullshit?" I said with a small grin.

"Yeah, no," he said, chuckling, "Sorry about that."

"I can't blame you, I'd have kept a piece or two also, we don't know each other," Henry opined.

"Alright, Henry's going to check you out again," I told him. "Once you're good, go wait at the back of this room. We'll get through this quick as we can."

The man nodded as he assumed his earlier position, and let Henry pat him down, spun, and did it again, then he moved to the furthest corner of the room. I moved to the window, clicked my tongue a couple of times, and motioned with my arm. Two figures rose from the grass where I'd originally approached the house from and began to make their way across my small back yard to the ladder.

The first to reach the window was a woman, presumably the guy's wife, her small wiry frame and dark hair appearing at the window and stopping, looking right into the barrel of my shotgun, then over to the red-haired man; he nodded, and she slowly made her way into the room. I held her the same as I held him, at gunpoint, and Henry made the pat-down, but with no words of argument this time. While he was searching the small woman, the other person appeared at the window. A face about the same age as the others, around late twenties, and short cropped dark hair. I held my hand out to halt him.

"Hold up, boss," I said calmly. "You each are getting searched and kept unarmed until we know who you are, as well your intentions."

He eyed me suspiciously, and was about to say something, but the first man shook his head and held up a hand, and he remained quiet. Henry finished patting down the girl and motioned for her to go stand with the guy near the corner.

The final piece of their trio got the signal from me and began making his way into the room. Actually, he almost squeezed through the window, as opposed to climbing through. This guy was freaking *huge*. Standing a head taller than myself, in stark contrast to the first guy's small size, this one was tall, and looked solid, aside from a healthy beer belly. Short dark hair, and tattoos starting at his jawline and fingertips, disappearing into his striped polo shirt. His dark eyes narrowed, and his eyebrows shot up as if to say '*Well, I'm here, now what?*'.

Henry approached, hesitated, and the first man offered a light-hearted, "He don't bite." Henry began going through the motions as I wondered if a shotgun slug would even do the job. The man turned, showing his back, and Henry patted him down once again.

"They all clean, brother," Henry shared.

"Okay," I replied, still eyeballing the ink-covered, bipedal behemoth that was blocking the entire window.

"Chris," the man said, low in pitch and volume. "Chris Simons," he said, as he shook my hand.

We all made our introductions, Chris Simons, Rich Lester, and Rich's wife, Carolyn. 'Doctor. Doctor? Doctor. Doctor. Doctor? Doctor.'

I asked my first question, "What the fuck made you come up my ladder?"

"It was there," Rich replied, his voice seemingly perpetually rough, "the house looked empty, first floor was boarded up solid, there was a ladder, so we figured it was a good high ground."

"Right," I said shortly, instantly regretting leaving our quick escape in place.

"Well, let's get back to rest," Henry offered.

"Yeah," I agreed, "I've got another two hours on my shift for watch. Rich, we'll roll out some more bedrolls for you guys, you sleep through the night, get washed up in the morning. We've got a bird bath setup to keep clean, and y'all look and smell like shit."

Laughing, Rich agreed, "I imagine we do, we've been through a lot."

"Well, we're using the upstairs for our stronghold, follow me, but keep quiet. Kids are sleeping," I explained, motioning for them to follow me up the stairs, myself leading, and Henry taking up the rear.

Upon entering the attic, Jennifer giving the new guests a wary look, I grabbed an armload of blankets, a few cans of food, and some bottles of water.

Grabbing his can from me, as well as a water and plastic fork, Rich said, "Thank you. So, have you guys been here since the beginning?"

"They have. I was at work, drove my semi here through this shit," I replied. "Probably my worst day of work ever. Well, maybe second, there was that one time I had to spend the night in Scranton, Pennsylvania..." I trailed off, shrugging.

"That was your truck?" Carolyn asked, her first time saying much of anything, and every word coated with a heavy French accent.

"Yes, it was," Henry pitched in, "Crazy man drove it all the way here."

"Jesus," Chris said, looking at me in a new light already.

"We travelled, too," Rich explained, "From Canada. Easiest border crossing I ever had."

"You're from fucking Canada?" I exclaimed, "Why come down here? Why risk all that for Akron, Ohio, of all places?"

"My folks are from here, I grew up around here," he said, then, motioning to Carolyn, "She's from Canada, I moved up there a couple years ago when we got married, but when all this happened, I had to see if my family was alright."

"My parents worked for the local hospital," Carolyn picked up where Rich left off. "We tried to get to them, but it was so overrun. There were thousands of *them*! No way anybody around survived, so we left. We came across border to find his family."

"And?" I urged them on.

"No good, man," Rich said solemnly, "My stepdad was nowhere to be found. My mom and sister, well, we found them. And we ran from them."

Henry bowed his head, lips moving, obviously in prayer.

"That's shitty, man," I offered, "real shitty. I'm sorry."

"We have had time to come to terms," Carolyn said, "but we are strong. We are still here."

"We ran into Chris," Rich continued, "his big ass was scrounging the liquor store east of here."

"No family, Chris?" I asked.

"Nah," he replied, "They all got got. My mom never made it home, I couldn't find my dad, so I went to go get something to drink."

"We holed up in the back of a restaurant," Rich explained further, "then those planes came in, we knew downtown would be off limits, so we started moving at night when we could sneak and sleeping where we could find shelter during the day."

"None of them things caused you much trouble?" I asked.

"Nope." A bit of pride in Rich's voice, "A few run-ins, but nothing big. Some of them are slower now, too."

"Slower?" I asked.

"Yes," Carolyn said. "We watched one for nearly a week from where we hid. He stayed near same house, he was a runner, now he's not. I don't know," she finished, splaying her hands in uncertainty.

I motioned to my wife, and she retrieved her notebook and started writing.

"What's she doing?" Carolyn asked.

"Anything noteworthy or possibly useful for survival," I said, motioning to her notebook, "gets written in there. Sun Tzu, man, know your enemy better than you know yourself. We're learning."

"Smart," Chris opined.

"So, your journey to survive, what? Led you to the next safe looking place to chill, and that ended up being here?" I asked them and was met with nods to the affirmative all around.

"We should consider sticking together, you know," Rich offered.

"We'll consider it, but I want to know you three a bit better," I replied. "I've got kids, man. Gotta consider them, as well as the rest of our safety. You'll draw on our supplies, and a bigger group is even easier to spot."

"That safety in numbers, though," Henry added from his window seat.

"He's right," Chris added.

"Fuck it," I relented. "Maybe, but we'll talk about it once I've rested. And y'all still stink, so get some rest, clean up in the morning, we'll talk then."

"Sounds good to me," Rich said with a smile. "I'll see you in the morning."

"Yeah, goodnight, dude. Get some rest," I commanded.

FIVE

The rest of the night went quickly. We opted to hold vigil as always, not including our guests, partially to allow them time to rest, but also partially because we simply did not know them. The next morning, we all sat around, and had our talk over coffee. Jennifer and I at our seats, by the windows on opposite ends of the attic, and Henry keeping a watchful eye on the girls.

"Okay, look," I opened up, "I need to know some things before I make any choices."

"Shoot," Rich said.

"Yeah, that's the first one. Can y'all shoot? Ain't got to be professionals, but can you hold a gun steady, pull the trigger, and hit something?"

Affirmative nods all around.

"Good," I continued. "Obviously, you have survival instincts, you two made it from Canada, he's survived this city. No kid touchers, sex freaks, or hard drug addicts here?"

Negative head shakes instantly from Rich and Carolyn, but a hesitation from Chris.

"Chris?" I urged.

"Nah man, I been clean for six months," he said.

"Right. Whatever, I'd imagine whoever you got whatever from is gone anyway," I said, with just a touch of malice hidden in my words. "Alright. We haven't touched your bags and shit since we put them in the bedroom last night. Go grab them and let's see how you're set up."

Rich and Chris left to gather their things while Carolyn sat enjoying her cup of coffee. They returned just a moment later with two large backpacks and a long canvass duffel bag. Opening the bags in turn, they set their weapons aside and started going through what they had. Some food, some water, maybe a few days' worth of each for the three of them, as well as some very basic medical supplies and water purification tablets.

Bringing their guns forward, Rich had the .32 caliber pistol he'd handed me the night before, and a Ruger 10/22 rifle with an oil filter screwed onto the end of it.

I eyeballed the contraption, and smiled, "I like that."

Grinning ear to ear he offered, "I saw these silencer setups on YouTube a couple of years ago and made my own in my dad's garage when I still lived down here. It was still in his gun cabinet, but it was one of very few left there."

"Suppressor, not silencer," I corrected.

"Suppressor, whatever, but it works good," he said, still grinning.

I pulled a couple more weapons out of the duffel bag, a Taurus 9mm, and a lever action Marlin chambered in .30-30. Not great, but not bad. Even a good pellet rifle, or a machete, would be better than nothing. Almost as if on cue with my thoughts, the last thing in their bag was a pair of machetes, still with the price tags on them.

"Not great, not bad. A couple of boxes of ammo for each, at least you're not dry," I said appraisingly. "Chris what do you have?"

He grinned, and pulled out a Ka-Bar fighting knife, and then said, "I also got my Glock .40, it's my problem solver." As he produced a black handgun and handed it to me with all the enthusiasm of a child showing a new drawing to his parents.

I took the proffered handgun and groaned inwardly. Dropping the magazine, I shucked the rounds out of it onto the floor.

"The fuck you doing?" Chris asked, angrily.

"Well, it's a .40," I explained, "but it's not a fuckin Glock, man. This is a Hi-Point. That's Chinese for 'fancy hammer'. It's garbage."

"Man, I gave my cousin three hundred bucks for that thing," he shot back at me, anger rising in his voice. "He said it's a Glock!"

I opened the footlocker next to me and handed him one of my pistols.

"This is a Beretta 92FS. It's a 9mm, better than a Glock *or* a Hi-Point," I told him, watching him look the new gun over, and the smile begin to spread across his face. I then added, "Keep it."

"Damn, for real?" he questioned, then, "Thanks, man!"

His grin faltered a bit though when I opened the window next to me, and unceremoniously flung the Hi-Point out the window, over my porch roof, and we both watched it as it clattered to the street, struck the curb, and finally ceased its motion in the middle of the road.

The weapon landing was almost immediately followed by the shriek of one of the runners as it burst out from the still-open front door where the family across the street tried to make their escape. She shot down the stairs in front of the house, skipping three at a time, out into the street, and finally skidded to a halt right next to the discarded firearm, studying it. Her head tilted back, she sniffed the air, and ran off in the opposite direction.

"See?" I said, as if that reaction were planned, "Not even the infected fuckers want it."

This was met by soft laughter from everybody. The laughter stopped at a new sound, the sound of several gargled gasps and low growls. In a few more beats, more infected made their way to the commotion, but, just as Rich had said, they were slower. Moving not much faster than a speed walk as they moved to inspect the weapon, and then moved on to wherever the runner had gone.

Closing the window, I turned back to the group and said, "I guess Rich wasn't bullshitting us. Some of them seem to have slowed down." Then I added, "Considering that, and the new load on our resources, it may be approaching a good time to move on to somewhere with easier scavenging, more resources, and more room."

A few nods, then the question from Carolyn, "Where are we to go? You mean to stay?"

"Yeah,", I replied, "and I think I know where."

"You talkin about the place?" Henry asked.

"Yeah, that's as good an idea as any," Jennifer added.

"Probably it," I said, then explained to Rich, Chris, and Carolyn, "We've had many, many talks about different scenarios. A few friends, Henry, and me. Usually late-night drunk fun talk, but we kept focusing on this pair of apartment buildings north of here, maybe about five miles. Lots of rooms in both buildings to scavenge, security doors, and the stairs can be blocked to limit anything getting higher than the first floor. Good, high vantage point, too, and it's residential around it with a view of the highway. If these fuckers are slowing down, I'm ready to move."

Rich shrugged, and replied, "Sounds good to me! The nomad lifestyle sucks lately."

The others echoed their agreement, and we began to formulate a plan.

"Henry has his Escalade. I've got my crew cab down there. Let's start gathering up everything we can, I've got to get some things from deeper in the house. Wrap everything up like giant hobo bundles in those sheets, a little of everything in each pack in case one or two gets left."

"Yes, Sir!" Jennifer said sarcastically, amid the others' agreements. While they gathered up things in the attic, I trekked down the stairs to the basement. There, I grabbed a couple bundles of 550 paracord, and a bundle of heavier nylon rope. Hoisting the bundles in one arm, I grabbed our recurve hunting bows and a narrow, long box full of various arrows in the other.

One more trip down into the house, I looked, and came up empty on further survival supplies. The wife and neighbor had done very well clearing us out previously, so I grabbed a handful of tools from the basement and made my final trip back up to the attic.

"Alright," I told the gathered group, "I've got everything we have left. We'll use this rope to lower all our things out the window, and into the bed of my truck. But, we'll do that tomorrow. We have to plan how to get there, how to get out of here safely, and where to call safe until we clear the building. Can't exactly have a toddler and a kid sweeping a building for us."

"Whatever you think, you're the boss man now!" Henry said with a grin.

"This should help," Rich said, as he produced a map of the entire country from his pack. "Now we just plan a route and a way to distract those freaks."

"Yeah, you're right, dude, whoever goes with Henry has more ground to cover than we do. 'Only right next door' may as well be a mile now," I observed. "So we'll need to distract them hungry fuckers long enough to get in the vehicles and get moving faster than them. Any ideas?"

"I've got one!" Jennifer exclaimed. "I'll be right back!"

As she disappeared down the stairs, we began planning our route. Deciding that the bridge over the river, and one of only a couple of routes across the highway were going to be our only choke points, we quickly determined paths through the neighborhoods based on what I'd seen on my way in, and the path that my semi had cleared was going to be the clearest, easiest way to our destination.

"Cluster of houses here about a block from the buildings," Rich pointed out, "we can leave the kids and someone to guard them there, while the rest of us check the buildings."

"Yeah, agreed," I said as Jennifer came back upstairs.

"We forgot about these!" she said, obviously proud of herself, and displaying two large brown paper bags full of various fireworks.

"Nah," I replied, "Pack them, they might come in handy, but I don't know if they'll last long enough to give the distraction we need. We need a longer-term device. An alarm clock or something."

"My stereo is loud," the usually quiet Melissa chimed in.

Sitting back for a moment and thinking, I looked at her and said, "Good idea kid, go grab it, and some of my CD's."

She took off down to her bedroom, returning shortly with her stereo, a five-disc changer with two big mounted speakers, and a handful of large D-cell batteries. I pulled an arrow out of a box, and began tying a rope around it, just below the hunting broad head.

"I've seen this in a movie or something," I said to the confused faces around me. "Should be able to get it further from the house without breaking it. Get the truck loaded up."

They began relaying large packs of supplies to Chris at the window, who lowered them each into the empty bed of the pickup truck. While they worked, I further fastened the rope to the arrow with Gorilla Glue and set the contraption aside to set up. I loaded the batteries into the back of the stereo, removing the wall plug, and selecting my choice of CD to insert.

"It's almost dark now," I told the group. "We'll eat, and bed down tonight, and we move first thing in the morning."

"Our food," Jennifer said sheepishly, motioning to my pickup truck, "is all down there."

"Well then we'll just go to sleep. Can't eat if you're sleeping, anyway," I replied with a reassuring smile.

SIX

Thankfully, the next morning came quickly, and uneventfully. Jennifer gathered up the kids and had them ready while Henry and I opened up the path to the garage door and shot two full cans of oil on every moving bit of it to make it as silent as possible. Everybody else policed the weapons and a few lighter packs that got left behind, and we gathered back in the attic.

The plan was simple, but we all understood so much could go wrong in almost no time at all. It was agreed that Jennifer, Melissa, and Gwen would ride with me. My diesel Ford outweighed Henry's SUV and had a nice deer catcher on the front that had proven itself time and time again with no more than a small dent on it. Henry, Rich, Chris, and Carolyn would go together.

Basically, we'd lay out the distraction, and book it. Get in the vehicles and get moving as fast as possible.

I guessed how much rope I'd need to reach my target and handed the end of it to Rich. Nocking the arrow, I opened the front attic window, drew the sixty-pound string to full draw, and let it loose. The arrow shot, well, straight as an arrow, if you can imagine, through the sky, through the window of Bill's house across the street, and struck home with a loud, solid *THUD*. Grinning, Rich wrapped the rope around a nearby roof support.

Hoisting my daughter's stereo in one arm, I quietly instructed them to be ready to book it as soon as we were sure it worked, as there was no way to signal either way.

Everyone gathered on or around the steps, Jennifer holding little Gwen in one arm, with the other around Melissa's hand. Everyone else crowded close, looking like they were all but weighed down with apprehension, all except for Chris, who actually looked bored. Bored! I couldn't believe the guy!

Nonetheless, I untied our end of the rope, looped it through the carrying handle on the stereo, set the thing to play, then paused it as I cranked the volume to the max. Re-lashing the rope to provide an anchor point, I pressed play, and let the device free from its window frame-perch. Immediately, loud crashing drums and a heavy metal guitar began screaming out of the speakers as it slid down the length of rope, and crashed right through the partially busted window, right into Bill's living room.

"What the Hell was that?" Henry asked, eyeballing me.

"Cannibal Corpse!" I replied, trying not to laugh at my cleverness. He shook his head, letting out a chuckle, as did everyone else.

Almost as soon as the stereo stopped its forward progress, the shrieks and growls began. Both runners, and the slower variety, began coming out of the woodwork to greet whatever was creating such a cacophony in their neighborhood. Though in much smaller numbers than at the beginning, probably thanks to the military's earlier actions, there was still plenty enough to give pause and cause a bit of concern.

Upon realization of my success, I turned, and spoke firmly, but not loudly enough for the monsters to hear us, "Remote start's going on my truck, it'll fire up as soon as the glow plugs cycle, we need to move, *NOW PEOPLE*!!!"

Everybody rushed the stairs, me in the back of the group now, and through the house. Opening the garage door only enough to duck under, one group went to Henry's, and mine stepped to my truck. A short moment after mine fired up, and we got the doors closed, we heard a horn blasting. I immediately began to dread the worst had happened, and we were being signaled for help.

It was not so.

No sooner had the horn began, Henry's wine-red SUV burst between the gap between his house and his garage, and the whole vehicle listed and began sliding sideways as he applied full throttle through my back yard, closing rapidly.

I threw my truck into drive, shouting, "Fuck! Hang on tight!" as we smoked the rear tires the short length of my driveway, drifting the eight-thousand pound crew cab sideways onto the street, as Henry's Escalade slid dead sideways, across the sidewalk, and out onto the street in the same direction as me, both of his rear tires billowing smoke in answer to mine as four infected runners rounded the front corner of my house.

"They fucking made it!" I shouted, high-fiving my wife before gripping the wheel once again to take the next hard right, again sliding the truck, combining white tire smoke with heavy black clouds of roiling smoke from my exhaust, the entire scene sounding like the world's angriest jetliner at full take-off. Melissa buckled herself into her seat with Gwen squeezed right up against her, looking bewildered, excited, and scared shitless all at the same time as both trucks formed one long wine-red and chrome blur, rocketing down the street.

One more right onto North Howard a few blocks later and easing our pace now that our escape was won, we made our way back to Cuyahoga, hoping and praying that the way my semi had cleared was still open.

A few blocks down Cuyahoga revealed that we weren't the only ones to attempt escape. The intersection I'd scraped through previously had been reclogged, a pair of pickup trucks wedged soundly in what was once free and clear. Bodies, or, more accurately, puddles of half-dried gristle and gore wearing scraps of clothing, littered the intersection, as well as the bodies of several infected, and a liberal smattering of discarded weapons and spent casings.

Looking around from my vantage point, the only way around, without backtracking, was the driveway next to me. I reversed a few feet, cut my wheel left, and rumbled up the concrete strip toward the flimsy privacy fence, crossing my fingers that somebody hadn't built a barbecue pit on the other side.

My luck held out as thin wood beams shattered and splintered like toothpicks, and I wrenched the wheel, the truck sliding on the slick grass, catching, and whipping to the other side as we made another Wile E. Coyote hole through the next fence, and back out onto the road in time to take a pair of running infected head-on, splattering their bodies across the front of the truck. I watched them tumble as Henry's SUV burst in much the same way through the gap, onto the street, and leaving roadkill-esque tire tracks over the bodies as he kept pursuit.

After travelling a couple of blocks further, I steered toward the right of the road, and slowed to a stop. Rolling down the window, and motioning for Henry to pull alongside, I waited. He slowed to a stop next to me, rolling his window down, looking expectantly.

"Let's take it slow," I advised. "We were kind of bottle-necked back there, and I would like to keep an eye open for other survivors if we can."

"Sounds good to me, my brother," he replied. "You lead, I follow."

As we progressed at a much slower rate, the rapid degradation of the neighborhood became startlingly apparent. Cuyahoga Falls was typically a largely peaceful place. Warm clear evenings saw senior citizens walking little yippy dogs, children playing in yards, people going for jogs or bike rides around the lazy streets.

There was none of that now. The streets were still largely quiet, save for the steady rumble and long low whistle of my turbo-diesel pickup stalking its way through the dead avenues. The shining new vehicles usually parked on the sides of the street were less in number, instead having been replaced with wrecked vehicles, a few of which were nothing more than burnt-out husks of Fords and Kias. Apparently, no matter who made them, they burnt the same.

The same thing went for the houses. Some shutters hanging loose, doors swung wide open here and there, windows smashed open, some with garage doors in various states of revealing their interiors. Once clean, freshly power washed siding and sidewalks were crisscrossed with smears of blood. Smoke rising lazily from a pair near one corner that had burnt to the foundations, the siding on the next nearest house melted and running toward the ground in thick, now dried, drips.

The thing that got to each of us the most were the distinct lack of bodies. Oh, the carnage was there, but there were almost zero whole bodies. A handful of dead infected lay intact, sure, but nothing else. A memory of a scene outside of my own home could be had in front of one house, a large splattered puddle of blood, as if it had been placed right dead center of the driveway. In the puddle lay a still bright blue collar, surrounded by clumps of golden-yellow fur. A few bones, very little gristle left on them, and having been chewed stark white in spots.

I tried to turn my head and focus on something, anything else besides Fido, but scenes like this and worse were a dime-a-dozen here. A car interior filled with arterial spatter, nothing but torn jeans left in the driver's seat. Nearby that, a Little Tikes Cozy Coupe in much the same condition, not so much in stark contrast as it was blatant mimicry, both vehicles exhibiting long trails of blood which led into the front door of the nearest home. Were they homes any more, or just houses? Surely, they were homes to somebody still, as every bit of our progress made still was not enough to shake the feeling of being watched.

We neared the point where we needed to turn onto the main road, out of the neighborhood and back in between rows of businesses advertising sales that were no longer relevant. It's kind of ironic, you get that vehicle, find a financier with the lowest APR, go to work to pay for that and many similar items, make sure every payment is in on time, tracked, accounted for, and how much does it matter now? None. Already it was apparent to me that survival was the only thing that mattered.

As we approached the overpass that traversed the width of the highway, our smooth cruise hit another snag. Somebody had moved a number of vehicles across the narrow roadway, creating a funnel that almost imperceptibly narrowed to the point of being impassible. Obviously meant to entrap, but while they were focused on robbing people that were just passing through, they seemed to have met their own well-deserved fate. A handful of bullet casings littered the scene, alongside the obligatory compliment of gore and blood.

I parked the truck, instructing Jennifer and the others to watch over us and provide 360-degree cover while I hooked up a tow rope and Chris rounded up any weapons that looked to be in fair shape, as well as any ammunition.

Retrieving the heavy tow rope from behind the crew cab's back seat, I looped one end through one of the tow hooks in my front bumper, and the other end around the rear wheel of a Honda CRV to the side of the road block. Motioning to Henry to move his Cadillac to the side as I got back in my driver's seat.

Dropping the transmission into reverse, the truck backed up until the tow rope was held nice and taught, then stopped. Pressing on the throttle just a bit, the big pickup grunted, the bumper of the CRV scraped against the vehicle it sat against, and the tires began to squeal as the vehicle was dragged sideways out of its resting spot with minimal effort.

I throttled down a bit harder and completed moving the vehicle out of our path before getting out and retrieving my tow rope, looking up to catch a nod from Henry that was half approval, half vehicular admiration. Dropping the rope lazily onto the floorboards in case it was needed again, I climbed back into the seat and proceeded forward.

We started up the incline, passing the old Riverfront Mall, and at the crest of the hill, the highway was clearly visible. Stretching on in both directions, absolutely jam-packed with vehicles that would never move again in both directions, as well as plenty of infected. The problem, on their end, was that they could see us, but could not figure out how to get to us. Some of them were definitely of the quicker variety, but the large majority were either the laziest freaks we'd encountered yet, or the slow type. It didn't matter to me. This overpass? This is the VIP section. They can have the dance floor.

Dropping down the decline of the raised roadway, we continued through the last leg of our journey. Back into residential areas, it was the same scenes that had played out earlier. The one nuance was a home with 'HELP' scrawled across the garage door in bright red spray paint that dribbled down the door, much like the blood across the living room windows. Some comedian had come along, hopefully after the fact, and scrawled a big 'NO' underneath the plea in their own black paint. I quickly decided the front door hanging open, leaning on a single hinge, had intended to tell me that it's too late to find anything alive inside of that structure.

Our final destination visible through the trees and some houses on the left, we continued on another block east, and one north. Here, we stopped about halfway down the block, in front of a single-story ranch home with a two-car garage. The home looked intact and unmolested, save for the garage door a fraction of the way open, exposing nothing but ample empty space for our vehicles. Henry pulled alongside my vehicle, rolling his window down to communicate.

"This the spot?" he asked.

"Yep," I replied evenly. "Rich and Chris, you two sweep that house. Attic and basement, too, if it has one. We'll circle the apartments and come back, should give you plenty of time. Once you're done, open the garage door up and we'll pull in. Be quick but be thorough and safe."

The passenger door opened, and Chris' large frame stepped out, followed by the back door disgorging Rich, before both doors were pushed quietly closed. They nodded, and embarked for the next hideout, while Henry and I pulled away from the scene.

We rounded the corner to pass around behind the north building. The apartment complex was fairly large. A pair of 9-story brick buildings, both positioned longitudinally parallel to one another, and separated by a split driveway that straddled a large swimming pool and led back to an above-ground parking lot, and an underground parking garage.

Both buildings sat a couple of blocks into the neighborhood from the main road, but had a clear view of the highway, and sat only a block's worth of tenant parking off of the Cuyahoga River. They offered space, sturdy construction, nearby water, and the surrounding neighborhoods would offer plenty of scavenging. Perfect, right?

We passed slowly behind the north building, trying to be as quiet as we could with the vehicle we had. Rounding the next corner, we started heading south.

Both buildings seemed empty. No movement to be had from any of the windows or balconies, the parking lot was empty of life, roof tops empty. Looked good so far, God willing, the insides would be devoid of issues as well. The good news was, both buildings had no apparent damage. No fires, broken windows, nothing. Sitting just far enough outside of the main area of town, and a bit into the neighborhood, it seemed as though most of the chaos had forgotten the large structures.

We rounded the next corner, heading back toward our hideout again, and were relieved to find a row of trees and houses blocked much of the buildings from view of the main thoroughfare. I was beginning to feel pretty damned good about this, but that still didn't say much. Looking back at my line of ex-girlfriends was proof on its own that an initial good feeling, when I'm involved, means absolutely dick.

Upon returning to the point where we'd dropped the guys off, we found the garage door of the house we'd chosen wide open, and could just barely make out Chris and Rich, one to each side of the opening, standing guard and waiting for our return.

Pulling both vehicles inside, the guys worked in tandem to lower the heavy rolling door back into place. I stepped out of my truck into the middle of every garage in every city in the country. It was very basic, a few shelves and tool racks holding the usual display of shovels, rakes, some hand wrenches, and a couple of racks that seemed to have once held canned goods, though they were bare now. Nothing but the rings of cans left behind in a thin layer of dust.

Rich was the first to speak up.

"Looks clear. No food in here though, only one gun in an upstairs closet. I think the people that lived here cleared it out looking for somewhere to go."

"What gives you that impression?" I asked him.

"All the doors going outside were locked. Nothing's been broken, but all the food has been taken, except for a bunch left to rot in the refrigerator."

"Sounds about right to me," Henry added.

"So now what do we do?" Jennifer asked.

"Well," I began, "kids look tired and hungry. So am I. Let's camp out here for the night, we'll go to the towers in the morning and start sweeping them. They looked good from the outside."

"Seemed like as good a spot as any," Henry opined.

"Good," Rich stated. "Well let's eat and sleep then."

"Yeah," I agreed, then, to Jennifer, "hey, grab heavier foods, canned goods and stuff. We'll save the jerky and stuff for travelling light."

"You just want all the jerky to yourself," she teased.

"Ha-ha, funny, woman," I shot back. "Rich, you said y'all found a gun?"

"Here," Chris said in his typically wordy manner, "Shotgun."

He handed it to me from where he had it leaning against the wall. It was a very basic twelve-gauge, single shot with a break barrel. Not much good here, as our opponents were either very fast, or travelled in groups, or both, and the gun would simply be too slow to do much with. Much like Rich's .32 revolver, it was better than nothing, but we already had better.

"Shells?" I asked, eyeing Chris.

"Yeah, some slugs," he stated and handed me a small stack of 5 round boxes of 1 oz Remington slugs.

I tossed the gun aside and received the rounds from Chris' outstretched hand. I explained, "A single shot is junk, especially for clearing buildings and stuff. We ain't hunting deer here, I'll keep my pump. We have a Mossberg pump gun, too, so that..." I trailed off, shrugging.

Jennifer began handing out cans of food, and we realized our first mistake in our supply packing. No can opener. Shit. Nobody said anything, and Rich got up, grinning, and disappeared through the door into the house. A moment later he returned, still grinning, and handed out forks and spoons. He produced a can opener, opened his green beans, and passed the can opener to Jennifer so she could open the girls' food first.

"Didn't think of that," I said sheepishly.

"I know," Rich said, ribbing me, "but I don't think the people that lived here thought of that, either. This is their can opener."

We all laughed about the irony. Once all of our cans were opened, we began to eat. Jennifer was taking turns eating her own and feeding bites to little Gwen so she didn't cut her hand on the can. The toddler didn't seem too pleased with the cold food, but she accepted it anyway. Probably same as the rest of us, too hungry to be picky.

While we ate, I began laying out the plan for the next morning.

"So, we're going to leave for the apartments around dawn. Rich and Chris, you'll go with me. We can't take the kids to sweep a building, so that leaves my wife, Carolyn, and Henry to stay here and hold down the fort until we get back."

"I don't like you guys going off alone," Carolyn immediately objected.

"He's right though," Henry interrupted. "Gotta watch the babies, we need to make a safe place to live."

"Exactly," I continued, "Rich, Chris, either of you familiar with stack and clear?"

"I mean," Rich said, "I know the theory, but I've never done it."

"So, we have the same experience level," I smiled. "Chris?"

"Nah." The man of many words said, "I mean, I know a little, but…"

"That's fine. You're rear guard," I directed. "All you gotta do is watch our backs and make sure nothing sneaks up. Easy job, but if I get bit in the ass, you're the first fucker I attack when I turn."

Soft laughter all around, then I continued, "We'll take two days each worth of food and water. Pack light. Small foods, minimal water, guns, ammo, and a light if your gun ain't got one. Rich, you'll get the Mossberg, Chris, you have the Beretta, and you can use the Sig 220 as backup. Sorry, we're kind of limited on bigger weapons. The wife has her AR-15, but I doubt she's giving it up."

"Nope!" Jennifer said, smiling.

"This girl…" Henry trailed off, shaking a finger at her and laughing.

"Yeah, she's a trip," I said, chuckling as my darling wife stuck her tongue out at me.

"So, what's the rest of the plan?" Chris asked.

"We pick a building, and make sure there's nothing that can hurt us in it. Then we find a way to secure it and start turning it into a home," I explained. "Once it's safe, we clear it of supplies, then do the next building. Eventually we should have this neighborhood cleared, and hopefully pick up some help along the way."

"Simple." Rich added, "I like simple."

"Well, let's get some sleep," I instructed, throwing my empty food can in the trash can. "Tonight's last watch shift, wake us all up an hour before dawn. We'll pack and head out with the sun. Count on one day or less, but we'll prepare for two. I don't know how much can happen one block from here, but I don't wanna take chances."

We all found a place to rest for the night, most of us in the vehicles, Chris sprawled out in a lawn chair he pulled off the wall, and we tucked in for the night as Henry took his first turn on watch.

SEVEN

We awoke as planned, about an hour before the sun crested the horizon. Rich, Chris, and I grabbed a backpack, emptied out the contents, and replaced them with our own. We took three bottles of water each, and enough food to allow us to scrape by for 48 hours. Loading our pockets and weapons with ammo, and, nearly overlooking such an item, I threw a small med-kit in my bag. It was a simple camping affair from Wal-Mart, bolstered with a fire starter kit, a small Purell bottle full of rubbing alcohol, and a basic suture kit and pack of razor blades. I'd assembled a half dozen such kits over the years, though I never expected them to come in handy.

I instructed the wife to keep little Gwen occupied, thinking it better she didn't realize that I was leaving, to prevent the fit that toddlers are prone to throwing every time a parent walks out of the room.

Melissa stopped me, wrapping her arms around me in a hug, and said in her soft voice, "Be careful, Dad."

This nearly stopped my heart. I've known the girl as her stepfather for around eight years now. Only on Father's Day has she ever called me *Dad*, and even then, only in cards, never spoken. I returned her hug and gave her my word in my most self-assured voice.

"No worries, kid. You know I'll be alright. Love ya," I said, then moved on to hugging and kissing Jennifer, and repeating the process for little Gwen, who hasn't quite gotten the concept of a kiss. She instead opened her mouth and left a big smear of toddler drool on my cheek, then let out a giggle.

Returning Gwen to her mother to distract, I turned to Henry. I shook his hand as Rich bid goodbye to Carolyn, and Chris looked typically bored. I told Henry to watch over the rest of them, he assured me he would. Chris damn near rolled his eyes.

"Hey, Jolly-fuckin'-Green," I said to the large man, "If you're feeling unloved, Henry can wish you goodbye, just don't expect an 'I love you' from him."

The big man actually smiled like that was the funniest thing he'd heard all week.

"Hug," I instructed, jokingly. Chris made a move toward Henry, following the punchline of the joke, and just before the much smaller black man was swallowed up by the tattooed goliath, Henry pushed him back with a jovial shout.

"Hey, watch out now!" he exclaimed. "We ain't that friendly!" Then, chuckling, he shook Chris' hand and wished him to be safe and come back in one piece.

We left the garage through the interior door after all of our farewells and made our way out the sliding back door of the small ranch, pushing it firmly closed as Henry followed and locked it from the inside in our wake.

We moved across the open back yard and hopped the short chain link fence onto the next and moved through that one as well. Passing several children's toys and a cheap wooden playground in the next yard, we came up to the privacy fence of the next property.

I boosted Rich's small frame up and over, then clambered over after him. After a moment, the gate at the end of the fence opened, and Chris waltzed through. As he eyed us, both standing there looking bewildered at our own overzealous actions, his expression was a mix of judgement and bemusement.

"You get one of those a day," I shot at him quietly.

His face lit up in silent laughter, and we continued, no gate this time, so we all scrambled over the next section of fence and dropped onto the sidewalk that signified the end of the block. The apartments loomed ahead of us, two brick sentries keeping watch in the early dawn light. I could still see no movement in any of the visible windows, though that may have been impossible anyway due to the way the sun hit the glass and reflected into a blinding glare.

We kept low and fast, and moved across the street, squeezing between a small gap in a hedgerow that bordered this section of the property. We all immediately froze. Not five yards ahead of us stood a figure. Its pale skin, veins visible and arms twitching, it did not make any larger movements. It stood there just staring in the direction of the north building.

Chris began to raise his pistol, but Rich put his hand over the slide, causing him to lower it back down. We looked at Rich to see what he was stopping him for, and he put a finger over his lips telling us to remain quiet. Then he unsnapped the loop around the hunting knife he carried, and approached the creature, moving low and slow. Once he got close, the freak's head twitched, and we all froze, thinking he had heard Rich regardless of how much stealth he exercised.

The thing's head twitched a few more times, and it remained there, once again still as a statue, aside from the occasional muscle spasm. Rich covered the remaining few feet between he and it, and, drawing his arm back, swung the blade tip-first in a long arc. The blade found its way right into the side of the creature's skull, and it began to drop instantly. Rich wrapped his arms around its mid-section in a bear hug, and followed it quickly to the ground, dropping it soundlessly in the grass. Then he retrieved his blade from the thing's skull and motioned us forward.

We regained formation, myself in the lead, followed by Rich, and Chris covering our rear. Approaching the side of the building, I checked around the corner to the front once, then disappeared around the corner, the other two in tow, Rich's hand on the middle of my back as he followed to let me know he was right behind me.

I reached the front door of the South Building. It was a pair of doors actually, set into metal frames with large panes of glass in similar frames on each side. A second matching set of doors was set about ten feet behind this one, allowing access to the building. The first set swung open easily, and we made our way inside. The second set proved to be locked, and I could see why when Chris tapped my shoulder and pointed to the card reader on the interior wall, with an intercom system set into the wall next to it, a list of apartments and corresponding buttons next to the speaker.

I moved to the pane of glass next to the door, turned my Remington so it was butt-first, and was about to break the glass when we heard a short burst of gunfire, followed by two single shots. All shots were muffled, whether from distance, or location, we couldn't tell. All three of us froze and listened, trying to split one ear between the outdoors, and the other to the interior of the building we were trying to enter.

A few moments later, we heard another short burst of automatic weapons fire. Rich motioned to the north building. I glanced at Chris, who shrugged, and Rich did the same. Not wanting to be left out of the club, I shrugged as well, and we made our way back outside into the sunlight.

We once again moved low and fast, away from the front of the south building, and up against the iron fence surrounding the pool between the driveways. Looking through the bars of the fence, the area looked still and clear, and we broke cover, again moving low, and took up spots on each side of the front entrance to the north building. It was a disaster scene.

Somebody had driven a Honda Civic straight through both sets of front doors. The charcoal paint of the car was splattered and dripping with blood, the dark, nearly black blood of the freaks. More blood, as well as the bodies of at least ten infected littered the scene for a good ten yards all around the entryway's exterior. Scattered liberally as if they were confetti, were the empty casings from several calibers of firearms.

Taking a couple of quick peeks inside, we decided the immediate scene was clear. Making our way to the back of the car, peering through the smoke of the wreckage, the hallway in both directions looked just as lonesome. Good.

I bent down and inspected many of the rounds at our feet. 9mm, probably a pistol. Several much larger rifle rounds lay around, composed of two more varieties. .308 was scattered sporadically, as well as what appeared to be one empty ten-round magazine. I shrugged to the other two as I set it quietly back down on the blood-soaked carpet. The final, and most prevalent, was casings from a 7.62X39. Considering the amount present, I took a guess, and whispered "AK-47" to my friends. Almost as if on cue, another choppy burst of full-auto fire echoed down from the floors above us.

"Ok," I said in barely a whisper, "Weapons hot, clear each room and hallway. Don't fire unless they threaten us directly. Chris, cover our backs. Rich, you take lefts, I'll keep right."

The other two nodded, and we made our way quietly over the wrecked Honda and into the first hallway. We swept a long combination in both directions of two- and three-bedroom apartments. All were basic units, with nothing left alive in them. The bodies of a half dozen infected were scattered throughout the floor, dark plumes of blood spatter, brain tissue, and skull fragments littered walls and furniture behind where each corpse lay. The carpet was doing its level best to soak up ever-expanding pools of freak blood, and the whole place smelled of copper and iron, and the cordite scent of burnt gunpowder hung in the air.

It was much the same through the entire floor, until we reached the last apartment. It was decorated with muted colors, and furniture that, while tasteful, looked like it had been purchased forty years prior. The walls were decorated with the basics of a lone senior's dwelling. A few cross-stitch images, with pictures of children and adults alike thrown in. A pile of yarn at the end of an aging green sofa, knitting needles left lying on the coffee table beside a pair of reading glasses and a small army of prescription medications. The whole scene appeared as it should, until we got to the bathroom. The crumpled body of an elderly lady lay there, and at first glance, we passed her off as another dead infected, until Rich quietly pointed out the distinct lack of blood seeping from her eyes. He pried one eyelid open and reported that the pupils were fine, not dilated, no broken blood vessels. This lady was not infected, but she was killed all the same, hiding in her bathroom. Christ, she lived a long, full life, only to be gunned down in the midst of the end of the world.

Shaking the scene from my mind, and doing my best to regain my stomach, I motioned for my friends to follow me up the stairwell to the next floor.

We moved the same as we had thus far and swept each room of each apartment in turn; Chris hanging back within view of the front door while Rich and I pushed onward into every dwelling. Another burst of fire, this time a heavy semi-auto *BOOM* interspersed with the quieter pop of a handgun, sounding much closer.

"Next floor up," I said to the others. "Let's go meet whoever's keeping the neighbors awake. Y'all ready?"

Rich nodded slowly, Chris uttered a firm "Good", and we made our way into the next stairwell. This time, instead of pushing straight through the door, we checked, ensured the hallway was clear, and sat quietly with the door open, listening.

We heard a small chorus of voices.

"Dude leave it. We'll come back."

"Fuckin thirsty."

"He's right, building first, beer later, dipshit."

"What the fuck ever. Fine. It's gone."

I couldn't make out much more, as they seemed to be an apartment or two down. I had the brilliant idea to make our presence known. Shrugging off my backpack, I opened the top flap and retrieved a bottle of water. Setting the bag next to me, and readying my shotgun, I sent the bottle flying down the hallway. It hit the floor, careened off of a wall, and rolled to a stop about a third of the way down.

Immediately a voice spoke up from the second apartment on the right.

"What the fuck? I thought we cleared this floor?"

"Go check it out!" instructed a second, slower voice.

I called out, "We're friendly, don't shoot!"

"Yeah, fuck you, dude!" called back the first voice, then said something I couldn't decipher to his friends. He was met with a chorus of "STOP" and "No, wait".

The asshole didn't listen, as his head peeked out of a doorway to look down the hall in the direction the bottle had landed. His head then swiveled in my direction. It was pretty dark in the hallway, and I couldn't make out much aside from a full head of dark hair, and the shoulder straps of a white tank top.

"I said we're friendly, don't fire!" I challenged.

"Yeah well I'm fuckin' *NOT!*" the man shot back and strolled out of the doorway. I called it previously, there was an AK-47 being used, and this guy held it at the low ready as he walked.

I wasted no time at all. I brought my 870 to bear, clicked on the light, and squeezed the trigger. Nothing happened. Then, the world slowed down.

Almost as if watching from a third person, I checked my gun. The slide was locked, indicating it was ready to go. As I stared at my gun for just a moment of panicked confusion, I realized the safety...the damned safety...was still engaged. I'd cleared two whole floors already with my damned safety on! What an asshole!

While I tried figuring out the gun I've shot a hundred times, the man recoiled in surprise from my light. He took a step back and began bringing his own gun to bear. Firing as he started to raise it, rounds chewing up the carpet in front of me, he ceased his backward step and stood firm. I clicked the safety off of my own weapon as I shouldered it, though through the pulse pounding in my ears and the cacophony unleased by his Kalashnikov, I could never tell you if the small safety device actually *clicked.*

Squeezing my now very much alive trigger, I sent a load of double-ought buckshot down the hallway, peppering the guy in the thighs just as I could feel-literally, *feel*- a couple of his rounds pass under my right armpit. He started flailing backward, yelling, and I worked the pump of my gun to send another load of lead his direction. The second blast took him right in the chest, throwing him back with the force of a linebacker.

My ears now pretty much useless from the sounds of two large guns being fired together in such tight quarters, and relying totally on sight, I could make out yelling, but not voices or what was being said. No sooner had the first guy hit the ground, a plume of blood leaving his lips as his breath burst out of him, then two more appeared. They came out of the room at a run, nearly side-by-side, and opened fire on my doorway at the end of the corridor. I ducked my head back inside as rounds filled the space I'd just occupied, impacting the door frame and shredding the metal of the door itself. I motioned for the other two to open fire as I covered my ears, trying to regain a bit of that sense of sound.

Rich and Chris ducked back in, and no rounds followed them. I could hear yelling from down the hall, but still could not entirely make out what was being said.

I looked pleadingly at Rich, who cupped his hands to his mouth and yelled to me, despite our four-foot space between us.

"He said cease fire!" Rich shouted. "He wants us to drop our weapons! I told him we won't!"

As the ringing in my ears began to subside, I thanked Rich for the relay of information. Rubbing my ears made it feel like my sense of sound was coming back, but I wasn't sure. Maybe it was a mind trick, but Rich's next words were much clearer despite them being directed down the hallway, instead of shouted directly to me.

"You drop your weapons!" he called. "Your guy started it!"

Then, a very familiar voice shouted back, "Yeah, he was an asshole, but, fuck, man!"

I listened to the exchange, and as my hearing started nearing normal, it dawned on me.

"Rich, shut up for a second," I told him, and was met with an angry glare. "Nah man, I know who that is," I explained.

Rich sat back against the wall, relenting.

"Hey, you fuck!" I shouted from around the shattered door frame, "We've got hookers wrapped in cornbread!!!"

The next short moment was filled with nothing but confused looks from my friends, and some murmurs from the other party. Finally, an eruption of laughter that I knew so well echoed down the hall.

"Scott?" the man said, "Dude you fuckin' shot Seamus! You killed him!"

"Who the fuck is Seamus?" I asked, and then to my team, "Guys, lower your weapons. He's a friend. A damn good friend."

Rich and Chris eyed each other for a moment, then lowered their guns. I stepped out from the doorway, side-stepped the body, and began walking down the hallway. My life-long friend then stepped out from the second apartment, with a grin stretching ear to ear.

"Tony-fucking-Harris!" I exclaimed, embracing him in a bear-hug. "Holy shit dude, you're here! You're alive!"

"Man, I'm glad to see you!" he shouted, returning the hug. "Who are these guys?"

"Oh, right, that's Rich, and the ogre is Chris. They found us at my house. Decent guys," I explained to him. "Jennifer and the girls are held up in a hideout down the street with Henry."

"Nice, man! Everybody healthy?" he asked.

"Oh, yeah, dude," I answered. "Doing fine. We were going to make this place home like you and I always talked about."

"Yeah, same here," he replied, then called behind him, "Hey Dave, it's Scott! And Willy, you too!"

"Dude!" I said, happily, "Dave's here?"

On cue, Dave walked out of the apartment, letting out a near perfect Tommy Chong impression, "Nah man, Dave's not here," and embraced me in a hug that matched Tony's.

These were all very manly hugs, by the way. We're not pussies or anything. Don't judge.

Tony, Dave, and I have been friends for years. No, we never grew up together, in fact, I didn't meet Tony until we were both adults slaving away at the same dead-end job. I met Dave about six months later. They were a stark contrast to each other. Tony, a bit shorter than myself, stocky, ex-Army infantry, and a beer guy to the core. Dave was taller than either of us, but rail-thin, long dreadlocks, and I'm pretty sure the guy keeps a bag in his pocket that stays magically filled with pot. Some kind of ancient genie trick, I guess. However you chop it, these two were buddies. Near permanent fixtures in my house every time I came home from driving across my half of the country. Many drunken, friendly nights would be an understatement.

Just as mine and Dave's manly hug broke apart, a third figure appeared. The man was average height, with thick glasses, and thick, short, curly black hair that looked like it hadn't seen shampoo in months. He was introduced as Willy Grey, and left the area making retching sounds after taking one look at Seamus' body lying in the center of the hallway. I looked at Tony, he shrugged, and mouthed the words 'useless pussy'.

"So, who was Seamus?" I asked, motioning to the dead guy, "And was he someone important? You're not acting like it, so I'm guessing…not?"

"The dude was such an asshole. Name was Seamus Mahoning." Dave said levelly.

"Yeah, he pulled the trigger on that old lady downstairs," Tony explained. "Not the first time he's fucked up, either. He's a loose cannon. Or, he was. We were going to sweep the building, and then find some way to get rid of him."

"Nice," I said. "Guy sounds like a real winner."

Dave went over and picked up Seamus' AK-47, and, inspecting it, slung it over his shoulder.

"It's mine now," he said, grinning, then spat, "Fucker."

"That's great that your family is okay, man," Tony commented, bringing the subject back around, "And Henry, too? How's the old timer holding up?"

"Man, you know Mr. Algood," I said laughing. "Dude's as level headed as ever, with the same old touch of mean. He's alright. Been a hell of a help."

"Sweet," Tony replied. "Well, let's take a moment here man, catch our breath. You down to clear the rest of this place with us?"

I nodded in the affirmative.

"That's what I like to hear," he said, taking a long swig from his water bottle.

At some point during our breather, Willy came back, wiping his mouth. He moved far to the other side of the hallway from Seamus' body, and slumped against the wall with his bottle of water. I'd grabbed the one I threw previously and took a long draw from it.

"Nice fuckin' technique, by the way," Tony said, congratulatorily.

"Well, yeah, I wasn't going to just walk right up to the door, man," I replied. "Especially now that I know the room was full of assholes."

"Wait, what?" Tony asked.

Dave laughed and said, "He called you an asshole, dumb shit!"

We all had a laugh, except Willy, who still looked pale, and kept taking glances at the body.

"What's wrong, dude?" I asked him, trying to draw his attention for a moment.

He just motioned to Seamus, and I think I could actually see him start sweating heavier, right before my eyes.

"Yeah?" I replied, "It's the end of the world, you ain't seen a body yet? They kept you blindfolded?"

"He has," Dave replied, "Little Willy just ain't cut out for this shit."

"I told you to stop calling me that!" Willy nearly wailed.

"Christ," I muttered. "Alright, let's get kitted back up. We have six more floors to push, I'd like to call this dump home by nightfall."

"Right?" Dave agreed, "You heard the dumb trucker, let's go guys!"

"And you guys are supposed to be friends?" Rich asked, appearing with Chris from the first apartment.

"With friends like these, right?" I said amiably and reloaded my shotgun. The others all checked their weapons, and we quickly formed up in a new pattern, clearing the rest of the floor with ease.

EIGHT

We moved cautiously up the stairs to the next floor. Stacking up on the door like a budget SWAT team of rookies, but damn we felt right together. Unlike the other ones, this door seemed locked. As it would happen, the door handle would turn, but the door would only budge a fraction of an inch. Looking through the window revealed a wooden plank across the door, about midway up. We moved to each side of the door, and I pointed to Chris, then to the door. He grinned.

One heavy impact from what seemed like a size thirty-seven Air Jordan, and the wood morphed into toothpicks as the door flew open, impacted the wall, and bounced back into the closed position. This time, turning the handle, it swung easily open, and revealed an infected, running full bore down the length of the hallway. Its throat was lain open, long strands of gristle dangling and bouncing with every step it took. He seemed unable to scream, or shriek, or whatever it is they do, because of the damage. I had no further time to contemplate it, however, as Tony's M1A SOCOM pushed a round out of its barrel on the tip of a fireball and sent it straight into the running freak's sinus cavity, blowing its skull out. It stumbled, hit the carpet, and slid another ten feet before stopping. No sooner had its motion ceased then two others came out of an apartment to the left. A pair of blasts from mine and Rich's pump guns cured their infections, and we moved on.

We swept the open rooms first, since we had an ample rear guard now, we felt a bit more comfortable leaving closed doors shut and dealing with them after the rest of the floor was cleared to limit contact. Moving quickly through the floor, we reached the end, and back-tracked to the first of three locked apartments. Replacing the buckshot in my shotgun with a couple of lead slugs, I placed the muzzle right against the spot where the deadbolt connected into the door frame and waited.

"Friendly! Anybody home?" Tony shouted, pounding hard three times on the door.

We waited for a five-count, heard no replies, and I squeezed the trigger. My ears now plugged with scraps of cloth, the report was still devastating but not on the damaging level it had been previously. The locking mechanism of the door buckled a bit but did not give. I worked the slide, ejecting one shell and slamming another home, and repeated the process. The deadbolt gave way in a shower of steel fragments, so I placed the muzzle lower, and blew out the section of frame that the door catch was mounted to. The door swung open slowly, and we flooded the apartment, everybody taking a section of pie, leaving Chris and Willy to provide guard on the door we came through.

This process was repeated on the next two locked doors; one more empty apartment; one contained a man with a .38 revolver in one hand, face down on the floor in a puddle of dried blood. Looks like he decided to take the easy road.

We moved up to the next floor and were met with a varied version of the last floor. A couple of infected, no living, but no dead this time. Deciding to take a breather again, we stopped just long enough to intake some water. I tore open one of the packs of jerky and handed out a piece to everybody present. Nothing was said between us, all communication nonverbal. We held no illusions that the reports of heavy caliber weapons, shouts of announcement at doors, and the consequent cries of "CLEAR" announced the presence of an armed group moving through the building, but, when we weren't moving and looking, it made sense to not announce our positions. The last thing any of us wanted was to be found, jerky in mouth, water in one hand, and a gun cradled uselessly in an armpit.

We cut our quick break, and, despite the moaning protest from Willy, and sighs from a couple of others, we moved on. Floor five, up to floor six. We stacked up on the door at the beginning of the next floor, and, trying the handle, found this one to be stuck firmly in place. Several boards this time could be seen holding it in its spot.

"Man, somebody got this fucker barricaded real tight," I observed, mildly out of breath. "You think they're still around?"

"I don't know man," Tony replied, and, looking through the narrow window, "Not seeing anybody in the hallway."

"Knock, knock!" Dave shouted, pounding on the door. "Anybody home?"

Rich moved forward, and, butt-stroking the glass from the window with his Mossberg, tried in his own gruff, scratchy voice, "We're friendlies, anybody in here?"

We waited several moments and had no response.

"Ok, well, Chris," I said, motioning to the door.

The big man gave a half roll of his eyes, stepped back, and hit the door with a mighty kick. Nothing happened. He nailed it several more times. Nothing happened still. Letting out a frustrated half-yell, half-growl, he booted it three more times before stopping, hands on his knees, and breathing heavily.

"Fuck, man. No good." He breathed.

"Alright. New tactic. Smarter brute force," I offered, grinning. "Check it out, we got boards here, here, here, and here," I said, drawing my knife and scratching an 'X' into the paint of the door to mark the ends of each board.

"So, we can also assume there are boards here, here, and here," I finished, scratching more markings. "Rich, together." And we began loading slugs into our respective twelve gauges.

Within moments, we were loaded up. Pressing the muzzles of our guns on each side, we began blasting holes through the door, and through the wood holding up the other side. Even with our ears filled with rags, the noise was immense. Each concussive blast of the shotguns felt as much as heard, shrapnel peppering our arms and faces, and the small area began to quickly fill up with smoke. Reloading for the final few boards, damn near slipping on the quickly growing floor covering of spent green plastic casings, we began blasting again. Once we were satisfied and laughing as Dave and Tony high-fived each other, we called Chris forward again. His next kick nearly cost him his balance as the door didn't just open, but fell forward, landing flat in the hallway. Man, we felt like some badasses right then and there. I wish it could have been filmed and put on the internet.

Rich and I slung our long guns over our shoulder, now empty, and followed Tony and Dave through the doorway with our pistols drawn. Nothing came to meet us. Nobody moved in the long, darkened corridor. We swept quickly through the floor, finding that, oddly, every door was unlocked. We reached one about midway down that was locked tight, and, deciding to stick to our M.O. we'd come back, we moved on.

Nothing.

No infected, no dead. No food, no drinks, nothing. Every apartment on this floor was swept clear of everything that could be used. Approaching the end of the hallway, we noted that this stairwell door was also blocked up with nearly a dozen lengths of board, all fastened with screws to the surrounds of the doorway.

I motioned to it, then back to the single locked door. Tony nodded in understanding. Somebody is still here, or at least, they were. We moved back to the locked door. We took a moment to reload the shotguns, mine set with three slugs, and two buckshot. Same as before, we prepped to clear the apartment.

"We're friendlies!" Tony shouted. "Looking to make contact with survivors! Five seconds to answer or we assume this space is empty and remove the door!"

He followed with his usual three pounds on the door, and then the wait. This time, the empty space of apprehension felt more…. loaded… than it had in the past. My muzzle pressed against the deadbolt, hand squeezing the pistol grip, stock buried deep into my shoulder, I waited. The five-count passed, seeming like minutes instead of seconds.

"Wreck that fucker," Tony called, patting my shoulder.

Just as I began applying pressure to the trigger, we were met with a female voice from the other side of the door.

"Wait!" she said. "Just…just hold on a second."

Tony let out a firm, "Hold fire!" The statement unnecessary for myself, likely meant to appease whoever was talking through the door.

"How do we know you're good?" the voice asked.

"Well," I started, "we're holding fire, aren't we?"

A snicker from Dave and Rich, then the voice again, "Well, okay, that's a start, but I mean…" she trailed off.

"I know, I know," Dave said. "The world's gone to shit, and now you got guys with guns at your door."

"Look," I added, "we're trying to find a safe place to call home. We'd decided on this place for SHTF years ago. I have a wife and kids waiting on me to get back and move them here. We're all friends here. No harm meant."

A pause, then, "Okay just hold on. One second," she replied and said something inaudible behind the door.

The sounds of screeching, and several heavy objects being moved could be heard. This was followed by another pause, then the metallic clicks of locks being disengaged. The door opened only a little bit, held still by a chain lock, and part of a pale, round face, and single green eye could be seen.

"You're sure you guys are okay?" she asked.

"Ma'am," I started.

"I know, I'm sorry," she replied, cutting me off, "we just haven't met anybody else."

"Lots of room in this building. We just need a safe place to hold up," Tony implored.

"Yeah," she replied. "Yeah, okay. You're right. I'm sorry, hold on."

She closed the door, and we could hear the chain lock sliding loose, more indecipherable talking, hers and a male's voice, and the door opened slowly. The girl we were talking to was fairly small in stature. Ok, let's not sugar coat it. She was fucking *short*. Maybe five-foot-tall in the right shoes. The aforementioned pale, round face and green eyes framed by dark red hair, and, Jesus, no way could those be real. Pulling my eyes back up from her chest in time to catch her outstretched hand and grasp it in a firm shake.

"I'm Shannon," she declared, "Shannon Lytle, and the first one to make a joke about my last name, and my height, is getting punched right in the ballbag."

This was met with laughter, then, Tony, "We'll let Willy make the remarks. I'm pretty sure he doesn't have a ballbag, anyway."

More uproarious laughter from our team, and soon, more people let themselves be shown in the dark of the room. There were seven of them all told, and they looked pretty rough. The odor of B.O. was prevalent in the room, trash bags piled up in one corner of the kitchen that was visible from the door. We moved inside, the small group separating as we walked through. Dave made a beeline to the couch, and sat down heavily, grunting, cursing, and pulling an action figure out from under him.

"Kids here?" Rich asked, noticing the toy.

"My husband was with them, they never…" and Shannon trailed off, tears beginning to spill down her cheeks.

"Ah shit man," I consoled. "I'm sorry."

"Yeah, great condolences," said a wiry man with glasses, who looked like he could be Willy's shorter, younger brother. "I hope you're better with rescue than you are with saying the right thing."

Great, I thought, one of these. "What's your name, son?" I asked him.

"It's Parker," he puffed his chest up, trying to impose all 140 pounds of himself. "Parker Elwood, *not* son."

Dave snickered, and responded, "Who the fuck names their kid Parker?"

"Hey hey hey chill the fuck out," Tony scolded. "Hearts and minds, dick."

"Yeah," I added. "He can't help his name. Not his fault his parents are hipsters."

Laughter all around, mixed with Shannon scolding Parker.

"I'm sorry," Shannon apologized. "We've been stuck up here pretty much since the beginning. We're all just a little tense."

"Since the beginning?" I asked. "You mean, you guys haven't left?"

"We only had one gun," said a slightly built guy, tattoos stuck haphazardly to his dark skin. "James, by the way. Name's James. We stayed here, we still have plenty of food, some water, and we made this floor safe enough. Those things are on the other floors, though."

"We tried to get to the other floors," said a chubby blonde. "James killed one, but I don't know. There's just so many of them."

"Well," I said, "we've got it cleared up to here. We are going to sweep the other floors and leave a few of us behind to keep guard while I go get the rest of my people. We'll make this building safe. Promise."

"We think a guy on the third floor had guns," Shannon supplied. "He worked construction, and had a pickup truck covered with gun stickers."

"Alright," I replied, "Rich, Chris, go with her and check that apartment. Willy, stay here, be their new gun while we finish up here. Tony and Dave, with me, let's go upstairs. Get this whole fuckin' place locked down so these people can get cleaned up, fed, and have some breathing room. Let's move, guys."

And with that, we all split up and went our own ways. As Rich, Chris, and Shannon went back the way we came, Tony, Dave and I moved to the end of the hallway and began unfastening the boards on the door. Once the wood was removed, we proceeded to move up to the next floor.

We moved room to room in much the same manner as before. Three infected on floor seven, no survivors. The slow, arduous process continued, much the same for the final two floors. Four infected, two runners and two slow, on floor eight, and only one slow female on the top, floor nine.

Moving through floor nine, we reached the stairwell at the end. This door was padlocked and chained, presumably leading to the attic. Instead of my shotgun, Tony lined up his .308 on the lock, and blew it into shrapnel with one squeeze of the trigger. Pushing the door open, we moved up the steps, bound for the roof.

Blowing the second locked door, we stepped out into a beautiful, bright, sunny day. The roof was now in full early afternoon light, no more than a few lazy, fluffy clouds speckled the sky, backed in brilliant blue. The sky was amazing. This had to be the first time I'd had a chance to view it properly since the military blew downtown Akron into a third world country.

The landscape was a different story. Our immediate surroundings seemed to be frozen in time, barely a thing touched. The only scene to give away the fact that this was no longer our world was had by looking straight off the edge, where the carnage from Tony and his crew could still be seen.

"Nice fuckin' work, I forgot to pat your back on that one," I said to my friends.

"Dude that was nuts," Dave added. "We stopped, they came from everywhere."

"Yeah man," Tony continued, "we parked the car and they came, so we got back in, circled the lot, and I just floored it right at the building."

"If it fits, it ships," I commented, and we shared a laugh.

Dave brought out a cigarette pack and a lighter. When he opened the pack, what was inside was most definitely not a Newport. He held the near perfectly rolled twist of plant and paper up to the sun, then turned to Tony and I and grinned.

"This guy," I lamented. "Even in the end of days," and I shook my head.

I began to take in our true surroundings. I could see the house where my family and neighbor, as well as Rich's wife, had taken up temporary residence. In the distance, as well as a few spots throughout the neighborhood, black plumes of smoke rose up like some form of disgusting trees. The highway stretched on its own longitude, packed to the brim with cars. A few figures could be seen walking among the wreckage, too upright and too nonchalant to be regular people. Beneath that, the Cuyahoga River flowed lazily, not giving the slightest hint of a care that most of the people dumping garbage and pollutants into it were no more. It had its own business to attend to.

I felt a tap on my shoulder and turned to see Tony coughing and holding his hand out to me.

"Nah," I said, "I'm good man. Wanna keep clear still, I've got to get my family in here by nightfall."

"Fair enough," Tony said, and began a coughing fit, exhaling puffs of the acrid smoke with each bark.

"Dave?" I asked. "Give me a smoke. A cigarette."

Dave fished the pack out of his pocket, opened it, and handed me a smoke.

NINE

After finishing our respective smoke sessions, we vacated the roof top. Moving back down, flight after flight, until we reached the floor that Shannon and company had held up on.

The scene was much more relaxed as we reached the apartment. The others had returned from their trek to the third floor. The blinds had been opened to reveal the apartment, much cleaner than I'd expected it to be, all things considered. It was a typical two-bedroom affair. Both bedrooms with a nearby bathroom in a hallway, a living area, and a small kitchen.

"Any guns?" Tony asked.

"Two. Nothing special, though," Rich replied.

"I was sure he'd have more," Shannon commented. "His truck was covered in stickers, he wore camo all the time, I'd have thought he would have a lot of guns in there."

"He probably did on the internet," Dave added, laughing.

What was found was a basic Taurus 9mm, and a .30-06 hunting rifle. Still better than nothing. It effectively tripled the number of guns they already had to defend themselves with. Now three of the seven residing in that apartment were armed.

"The rest of the building is cleared," I stated. "All the way to the roof."

"Well, what now?" Shannon asked.

"Now," I began, "we bring my family in. Wife and two little girls. I'll leave some of us here to help keep this place secure, then we'll block the first floor off from the second, catch some rest, and start planning."

"So, you guys are going to be here for a while?" Shannon queried.

"Yeah," I answered, "Yeah, we will be. We have a plan for this place dating back from before things even went bad. Back when beer was still cold."

"Don't worry," Tony added, "It'll be a good place to hold up when we're done."

"Great," Parker's whiny voice challenged. "You guys really think you can just come in and take over? What if we don't want you to? We were doing just fine!"

"Shut the fuck up, Parker," James and the blonde said almost in unison.

"Yeah, seriously," Shannon added, offering us a smile. "We were pretty much trapped on this floor. This place is already doing better with them here."

"Any other agreements or objections?" I asked the group.

I was met with nods from the other handful of survivors, all of whom had remained pretty much silent through everything.

"I think we are all in agreement here," said a heavy-set middle-aged man with dark hair and eyes. "I'm Rob. I was just a computer tech before, but I'll be glad to help where I can."

"Glad to have you, Rob," I said, shaking his hand, then, "Once we get situated, we will definitely have a spot for everyone to pitch in."

Parker harrumphed.

"Let's go get your family, man," Tony pitched in.

"Yeah," I agreed. "Dave, Chris, Willy, stay here with these people. Rich and Tony, with me. We'll try to be back by nightfall. I'll have my truck, Henry will have his Caddy. Everybody with a gun follow us down to the first floor and guard the entrances."

This was met with agreements, and those with guns grabbed them, and we made our way back down the hallway and to the stairwell to head back down to Floor One. Once at the front doors, we wished everyone the best and promised a speedy return.

Tony, Rich and I climbed over Tony's disabled Honda, glass and empty brass crunching underfoot, and moved to where the exterior door had been.

Moving low, fast, and spread about arm's length apart, we moved across the blacktop and back across the street.

We took the same route to get back to the house as I had come early in the morning with Rich and Chris. This time, however, we all went through the gate, Rich and I sharing a look and small chuckle at the morning's shenanigans.

We rounded the corner of the final house on our approach, the late afternoon sun lowering itself into early evening. Nothing looked out of place, but I still wanted to be damned cautious. I had no idea if all remained well, and no idea how jumpy my wife and Henry would be. Both were typically fairly level-headed, but I can only assume being left on your own in a strange place while fast, intelligent cannibals roamed the streets would put just about anybody on edge.

I motioned for Tony and Rich to stack up to one side of the sliding glass door, watching as they carefully stayed to the near side to prevent being seen. I then moved behind them, then slowly up next to Tony, touching each of their outer shoulders to let them know I was moving by. I bolted to the other side of the door, my back pressed firmly against the siding of the house, crouched, and shotgun held low over my knee.

I reached just to the edge of the door, gave three knocks, then three more. We really should have thought of a signal to make this easier. I guess we will keep that in mind for future reference, too late to make one now.

Within moments, I heard a very familiar deep bellowing voice from within the structure.

"Who's out there?" Henry shouted through the closed door.

Not wanting to yell back and make our presence known to anyone, or anything outside, I placed my shotgun in clear view on the patio in front of the door, rolled up my left sleeve to show my tattoos, and waved my arm in front of the glass.

"That you, Scott?" Henry challenged.

Giving a thumbs up, then retracting my hand and retrieving my shotgun, I tried sliding the door open. Nothing. Locked.

"Hold on a minute, brother Scott," Henry instructed, and soon I heard the click of the lock opening.

I remained out of view but slid the door back by about a foot.

"It's me, Henry, I have Rich and Tony with me. Everything good?" I asked.

"Tony?" he replied, slightly shocked and confused. "Where's the big guy?"

"Safe, back at the apartments waiting with others," I answered, then moved into view, Henry and I lowering our weapons at the sight of each other.

I pushed the door the rest of the way open, scanned the inside of the house, and motioned for the other two to follow me in.

Once inside, and the door shut behind us, Tony grinned ear to ear at the sight of Henry and they embraced in a quick man-hug and exchanged pleasantries.

"You said you found others?" Henry asked.

"Yeah," I offered. "Tony, our friend Dave, some bitchy dude they found, and about seven others that made the sixth floor their sorta-home. How's Jennifer and the girls? Carolyn?"

"Oh, they doing just fine," Henry said with a smile. "Melissa and Gwen are napping, I think Jennifer laid down with them. Carolyn was in the garage, too, but I don't think she can sleep, girl's a wreck."

"Good, cool. And Rich is here now," I said, then Rich and I moved to the garage to get them woken up and start getting ready to move. Conversation between the two guys followed me down the hallway, into the kitchen, and into the garage. Tony and Henry had shared many drinks with me, one a good friend, and the other a friend and neighbor, and they had some catching up to do.

Rich went straight to the corner where Carolyn sat and began comforting her. She spoke in half French, half English, and frantically, but it seemed as though just seeing him okay and alive had begun having a calming effect. I left them to their business and continued.

I made my way past the vehicles and saw nobody. Looking around I discovered all three of my ladies had made themselves a comfy spot under my massive pickup. Probably felt safer under there, and likely, it was. I woke the three of them softly and was met with a neck-crushing hug from Jennifer when she slid from under the truck.

Gwen awoke, made her way out, and toddled right into my arms, laughing the whole way.

Melissa was last out, and she gave me a hug, then immediately inquired if she could get something to eat. I retrieved a pack of crackers for her and then began laying out a plan with Jennifer.

"Tony's here?" she asked, still sleepy sounding.

"Hey guys!" I called in, and soon all three appeared, Tony wrapping each of my family in a hug. Gwen was a bit reluctant, at the tail end of her shy stage, so I instructed, "You get your tiny butt over there, that's your Uncle Tony!"

She slowly complied, and he swept her up in a big soft hug. She smiled, and he returned a "Hi sweetness" and gave her another squeeze before placing her back on the garage floor.

"You been okay? Been behaving?" he asked Melissa.

She replied with her usual quietness, "Yeah. I'm glad you're okay."

"Me too," he said, returning a second hug from her, and we started going over the plan again.

"There's more people in the apartments. We met Tony and Dave there- "

"Dave, too?" Jennifer interrupted excitedly, and absolutely beamed at the unlikely luck that we had friends now.

"Dave too," I smiled, "there's also seven other survivors present, and some guy Dave and Tony met along their way. north building is secure, so, once we get the vehicles packed up, we will leave. Tony is, uh, kind of blocking the entrance with his car."

"It fuckin' worked though!" Tony exclaimed with a wicked grin.

"Yeah well since you did it," I explained, "you help clean it up, dude. I'll nose up to the entrance, we'll have my tow-rope attached to the front of my truck already, so just grab it and find somewhere solid to loop it onto your car. I'll yank it out of there, and we can move in supplies and people. Henry's SUV sits lower, so once it's open and we have everyone and every*thing* inside, we'll park it there for now to close up the entrance."

Everyone agreed to the plan, and we began putting away all of our things at once.

"What about all their things?" Henry asked.

"Whose things?" I asked back.

"This house," he replied, motioning, "I know they didn't take everything, I've been snooping."

"Yup, let's each pick a room, search it, clear it, and bring it all back to your ride. My bed's full on the truck."

TEN

Within an hour, the house had been emptied of anything useful from basement to attic, and all its remaining contents was packed into both vehicles, strapped to tailgates, and shoved wherever it would fit. We concluded that we were ready to head out and loaded into both vehicles. Then, I got back out, and opened the garage door. Okay, maybe we're all a bit out of it, it's been a long day.

Backing cautiously out of the garage, my rig first, then Henry's, we moved into the driveway. I got out, instructing them all to watch our surroundings. I grabbed an armload of cans of spray paint from the garage, tossed all but one into my truck, and returned to shut the door. Once the white door of the two-car garage was closed, I moved to the front door of the house and set quickly to work.

I sprayed a big orange 'X'. Known as the FEMA X, or Katrina X, due to its widespread use in the aftermath of the hurricane. I then marked the upper quadrant with a '5-18', denoting the date it was searched and cleared. The right quadrant received a '0', denoting no dangers or supplies were present. The lower quadrant of the X got another '0', meaning nobody dead was left inside, and finally, I marked the left quadrant with an 'S.P.', the initials of the last person to search it. I moved back to the large garage door and sprayed a large 'CLEAN' across it before getting back into my vehicle. I explained the markings to my wife, who was eyeing me very curiously as I closed the door.

I stopped momentarily to chuckle as I heard Tony's hushed voice from somewhere behind me.

"Hey, Scott!" he called, "Draw a penis!"

Taking another beat to recover from my chuckling, I departed the scene.

Motioning to Henry, we departed for the apartment complex, and hopefully onto better sustainability and survivability than the cramped, hot attic of my own home.

We approached the north building and proceeded exactly as planned. Henry waited back a bit, Tony jumped out of the SUV and quickly attached the tow rope to, of all places, the bumper. Okay, yeah, the guy is great with guns, great with surviving and tactics, but toss him a Chilton's mechanics manual and watch his eyes go blank. I went along with it, put the truck in reverse, and promptly ripped the plastic rear bumper off of the smaller vehicle. He stared at me, bewildered. I just motioned to the car, and this time, he hooked it to the steel bumper support instead.

I put my truck in reverse, it grunted, the turbo letting out its long low whistle, and the car began to pull free with a cacophony of screeching metal and rubber, taking bits of the wall away with it, and dragging a large section of door frame with it. In short order, the Honda was wrenched free, and I dragged it far enough away to allow us plenty of clearance and room for Henry's Escalade when we were done. I detached the tow rope as the others began moving supplies to more people waiting inside to carry them up into the complex.

All told, it took a small number of trips to get everything moved inside, and I directed everyone to move the things up to the ninth floor. I wanted a high vantage, and as much building as possible between my family and anything that would make it into the ground floor. Most complained quietly at the prospect of climbing nine floors of stairs loaded with supplies, but acquiesced when I gave my reasoning, and the assurance that I'd be suffering along with them. The only one to seek relief was Carolyn, whom was left behind upstairs to care for Gwen as we worked.

We made one final trip to the truck, four of us loading our arms with supplies. Seeing that this was the final trip, Rich and Tony departed their guard and began loading up with bags and packs to take upstairs.

Henry carried his load in, and just as he cleared the threshold, an ear-splitting shriek filled the evening. It was met quickly by three more, and then another, and shortly after, a loud coughing rasp. Shit they were close. We froze stupidly, not one of us more than ten yards from the door, save for me, having just left the truck to lock it up and heft a case of canned goods and a backpack full of ammunition.

"Gotta move!" I ordered, and just then, six running freaks came seemingly out of nowhere. They ran with the speed of Olympic sprinters, trailing the side of the building, one running its cracked and bloody fingers down the side of the building.

"FUCK!!!" I shouted, nearly a scream, then, *"RUN! FUCKING RUN!!! FUCK!"*

Jennifer moved first. Almost as if made from stone, she took one step, then another, moving as fast as she could with an armload of survival goodies.

Melissa froze.

Goddammit the kid *froze.*

Of all her years of doing her best not to listen to us, this was *not* the time for an encore. The infected zeroed in almost instinctually on this hesitation. They shrieked again, they let out those disgusting phlegmy barks again, and eyes full of burst blood vessels narrowed and marked Melissa, who still stood there in terror.

My entire world seized up, then began moving again in agonizing slow motion. I could hear myself shouting. I could feel my throat burn from the force of the yell. It didn't even feel like I was there.

"MELISSA!!!" I could hear myself screaming, "RUN DAMN YOU, *RUN!!!"*

Finally, as if someone slapped her, she listened. She dropped her load of supplies and ran. Left. The fucking kid ran *left*, the door to relative safely was *forward*, not left!

Shouting my new favorite expletive of the day, I bellowed, "FUCK!" one last time.

My world still moving at a crawl, the nasty freaks now just a few yards from the girl, *my* girl. She moved as fast as I'd ever seen her move, and they closed. I dropped my own supplies with a crash and withdrew my 9mm.

Losing all the discipline I'd thought I had learned at the range, I fired before even bringing the gun all the way on target. The first shot missing by a country mile, hitting the pavement and ricocheting into the building. Bringing my second hand onto the weapon, I squeezed the trigger again. Fuck they were fast. The next three shots did nothing but send chips of the brick walls flying. A fourth and fifth striking the lead creature in the shoulder and back, then finally one caught its head. It tumbled, tripping up the next two in line, and Tony's .308 began to erupt like Mt. Krakatoa, sending the skull and brains of another into orbit in a hull red and white spray.

Two down, four left. I felt like I actually had time to formulate this thought at the rate everything still moved.

I could see Jennifer being held back from running out the front of the building. Her fighting and jerking, pulling against his arms, a silent scream flying up her throat and dying on her lips. I could see Henry shouting, veins popping out under his dark skin as he fought to keep my wife from running straight into danger.

I turned my full attention back, seeing Tony taking a knee to elevate the angle of his shots and keep Melissa in the clear.

Then time began to move again. Not slowly falling back into focus, but more as if I had been pulled by the undertow of a mighty sea swell, only to have another wave bury me in a breathless fury of movement.

Melissa ran, *they* ran, we fired. Pieces of shoulder and brick flew from one creature, and one wall. It did nothing to ease the chase. Another's chest exploded outward from a rifle round in the chest, and the forward motion of its stumble actually seemed to accelerate its gait. I squeezed again, three times, more brick erupted from the building and my third shot only grazed a skull as my gun locked open.

In the bare moment it took to reload my weapon, and for Tony to pump his dry, we lost. The lead freak reached Melissa's back, latched on, and she fell in a heavy heap. They slid together on the pavement as the other three reached her, and the first took a chunk square out of the center of her back before their motion even ceased.

My throat hoarse, my mouth open, the realization that we had not won this one hitting me, I continued dumping round after round into the backs, shoulders, and heads of the disgusting forms gathered around her. I struck two in the heads, and they fell over her in heaps as the others gorged themselves, blood arcing its way into the air in misty spurts.

One monster lifted its head and looked our way, the remaining section of its jaw moving hungrily and packed full of meat and scraps of pink t-shirt. Tony wasted no time in vaporizing the horrifying visage with another heavy round of fire, turning his attention to the last one.

Melissa began convulsing, her head jerking, and though we couldn't tell if it was from pain or infection, we knew at once that there was no coming back for her. All those years of raising her as my own, ever since I'd met my wife. The good and the bad, all gone in one furious instant. I stopped several paces away, and Tony approached from behind, placing his hand on my shoulder. I looked down at the locked slide and empty chamber of my weapon, loaded another magazine, thumbed the slide release, and he stopped me.

"Nah," he said firmly. "She's my niece, and you're my family. Go inside."

I eyed him stupidly, my mouth hanging open, and he repeated his order to get in the building. I complied.

I walked numbly several steps away, head down, and heard the start of a much smaller-than-usual shriek of the infected, and a single shot silencing it.

I fell to my knees, right there among the blood, brick fragments, glass, and other debris. I dropped and cried. My eyes burning now as much as my throat. I looked up and found my wife to be in much the same position, the same condition, and Henry doing his best to comfort her from one side, Dave to the other.

Tony came and helped me back to my feet and led me to the front door, his expression solemn. Not one word was spoken as I helped my wife to her feet, wrapped my arms around her, and supported her as she collapsed into heavy sobs against my chest.

The light of the day soon mostly vanished as Henry's SUV moved across the entrance. The others milled around as we wept quietly together. A twin pillar of sadness in the middle of a crowd.

ELEVEN

I awoke, but I didn't open my eyes yet. I had no idea where I was, and the pain raging through my head was excruciating. I felt something land on my leg. At least, I think it landed. Hit? Impacted? Then the sensation of whatever…it… was, crawling its way up my torso.

This is it, I thought, *this is how it ends. One of those freaks has me and…fuck it. Take me.*

I felt something warm, wet, and slimy drag its way across my face. Was it…*licking* me? What kind of fresh hell is this?

The weight of the form on top of me became heavier on my chest.

SLAP!

"Da-DA! We GO! DA-DA!"

It was Gwen. Jesus Christ and all that is holy, it was Gwen. Where are we?

I opened my eyes a bit, sunlight streaming in through the cracks of the blinds. My toddler perched on my chest like a bird of prey inspecting its kill, and the mess of dark blonde hair that could only be my wife, lying next to me.

Inspecting the little one, I found the wet, sticky sensation. Yup, I'd been clobbered with a small hand loaded with drool. Two-year molars suck, both for child and parent.

Then, one by one, and carried by the medium of a heavy hangover, the memories of the night before came flying in, like cyclists crossing the finish line. The clearing of the building. Retrieving my family and friends. Moving our things into our new home. Then, Melissa. Oh, God, Melissa, I'm so sorry.

I let out a long groan as I began mentally encouraging myself to move, my stomach lurching at the mere thought of such action. I remember losing it. We left the entryway, and a handful of us made it to the roof. My friends in mourning with us, while offering support. Trying to joke to lighten the evening. Somebody showed up with a handle of Jack, that's 1.75 liters of Jack Daniels for those who missed their party phase, and Jennifer and I hogged the majority of it. I'm fairly certain we also helped smoke a couple of those funny looking cigarettes that Tony and Dave always had.

The night was a blur, probably not the proper way to mourn, and no way to tell if it eased the pain yet, but it was what we had.

Little Gwen lost faith in Daddy returning to this plane of existence and moved onto Mommy instead. She repeated the same process, and, upon getting her bearings, my wife wrapped the small child in a hug and began to sob while she whispered love to the toddler.

I started getting up, out of whoever's bed I occupied, and nearly as soon as my feet hit the floor, I grabbed the nearby waste bin and began retching into it. With not much in my stomach, it was not what you would call a fun thing to do.

Jennifer, finally sitting up, wiping her eyes, moved in next to me. Without a word, she slid her Gwen-free arm around me and buried her face into my shoulder.

"I'm so sorry," I started, burying my face in my hands. "I should have- "

"No," she stated firmly, cutting me off. "We're not doing the blame thing. It was the monsters. The freaks, mutants, whatever. You did your best. Everybody did."

"I can't accept that," I retorted, voice flattened. "I should have seen it co- "

"Goddammit!" She snapped, "Stop it, Scott. You did literally all you could. I've got to get Gwen changed. You want to blame something? Blame the monsters. Remember her every time you kill one of them."

I had no answer and gave just as much. I was still numb inside. Jennifer got up and left the room with Gwen. Once she opened the door, the sounds of chatter and the smell of some kind of food flooded the small bedroom. The smell brought another dry heave, and, a few minutes later, I dragged myself along the wall and into the kitchen, where Tony, Dave, Shannon, and Carolyn sat, a lively conversation going and several M.R.E.'s laid out on the table. All the meals were Menu 20, breakfast. Well, the best way to beat a hangover is to hydrate, and pack that gut full of heavy food. If military Meals Ready to Eat didn't fit the latter, nothing but prison nutraloaf would.

"Holy fuck, it's alive!" Tony exclaimed.

"Doesn't smell that way," Dave commented, and was met by soft laughter.

I ignored the comments, sat at the table, and began preparing my MRE. Moments after adding water, it began to heat up, and soon, I was shoveling spoonfuls into my mouth. I hadn't even realized until I'd slammed a whole meal, and two bottles of water, that the whole table had fallen silent.

Tony was the first to speak up.

"Look, man, I'm sorry."

"Don't talk about it. There's a time to mourn and apologize, right now, we need to get things in motion."

Shannon got up from her spot at the table, cleared the debris from everyone's meal, and went into the second bedroom to talk to Jennifer. Rich came in and asked to borrow Carolyn, and she left as well.

Leaning back in the chair, I grabbed one of my cigars and retrieved the ever-present cutter and lighter from my pocket. I snipped the end off with the cutter, held the end to be lit over the flame for a moment, then lit it and inhaled.

"How did I get down here?" I asked, through a blast of smoke.

"You're a heavy fucker," Dave replied vaguely, lighting a cigarette.

"Yeah man," Tony added. "You just kind of stood up, and then you fell over, puked on the roof, and started snoring."

"That explains that," I grunted. "Who's bed was that?"

"Don't know," they replied, nearly in unison.

I gave another grunt and took another pull from the cigar. A cheap Dominican, one of my daily smokers, but it beats cigarettes. I hate those things, and only smoke it when what I consider to be a real smoke isn't available.

"Well," I started, "we need to get a plan moving. This is home now, but it's not safe. Let's get everyone together, say, in the hallway outside of Shannon's place?"

"Works for me," Tony said.

"We'll start getting people gathered together down there," Dave added.

"I'll be down in thirty," I stated.

With that, my two friends departed, and Shannon and Jennifer returned to the room. Jennifer began preparing a meal for her and Gwen. Shannon, having heard the conversation, left to begin getting people gathered up as well.

"You alright?" I asked Jennifer. She simply shook her head, a single tear falling down her cheek.

"Yeah, me either," I offered. "We can't dwell, I think. If we don't get moving and make this place survivable, it'll have gone for nothing. She'll… have gone for nothing. I'm going to lay this place out real sweet, we all will. It'll be in her memory, then."

Jennifer just nodded and began feeding Gwen. We continued to sit there and made the smallest of small talk while they ate. After, she cleaned up the mess, and followed me down to Floor Six.

TWELVE

Down on the sixth floor, everybody present was gathered loosely in the hallway. The apartment doors all opened, and several candles burned, providing enough light to make it suitable for a group meeting, but not much more. I had noticed several present would not meet my eyes. I didn't let it bother me. They could feel guilty, unsure, insecure, I couldn't really care less.

"We need to make this place to live a home," I opened up. "We need security, and sustainability. My group can't do it on our own, so I'm asking everyone to pitch in."

"Excuse me," Parker piped up, "but I don't think we even asked for your presence, much less voted you as leader!"

"I never said I was the leader, Parker," I retorted, "but so far, we've opened up your one solitary floor into a whole building. We've multiplied the available supplies nine-fold in doing so and brought the security of several people with more guns than we can possibly carry, all who know how to use them. We. Not *me*. Does anybody else want to step up and take the reign?"

Nobody stepped forward. Most of the people gathered shook their heads in the negative.

"Tell me, Parker," I continued, "What would be your plan? How would you bolster the food supplies for... almost twenty people? Water is a finite supply, as well. How would you go about getting it stored in advance, so we don't run out? How would you back up the security of the building? Whose talents would be best used *where*, Parker?"

Parker simply shrank back, the fight in him leaving.

"Where do we start?" To my surprise, it was Shannon who asked the first question.

"Shelter. The first item to covet when surviving. We have it, but how to make it sustainable, and safe? Ideas?"

A murmur began to spread throughout everyone, most seeming to be surprised to be included, their opinions polled. Then ideas started coming out, most of them leaning towards building a wall of some sort. Other options came spilling forth. Somebody, I think it was Rich, going by the unique voice, suggested a moat. A fucking moat. Really? Cut the power off and we move back to kings and castles?

"Actually," Tony piped up, stealing the moment, "a moat of sorts isn't a bad idea, but we shouldn't waste water on it. What about a deep dry moat?"

"Could build it outside the wall at a later point. Line it with punji sticks," James suggested.

"We'd need to locate and bring in some kind of equipment," I admonished. "That will have to come later, we have bigger matters, but it will stay in the top half of the list. I like it. First, the wall. Materials."

More murmurs shot through the group, except for Chris, who remained largely silent. Finally, he spoke up.

"Take fences from houses. Privacy, chain link, all that shit."

"He's got an idea there. We could layer them and build them up real nice like," Henry agreed.

"Sounds like a plan so far. We'll set up a team, maybe ten of us in the morning. Leave some here to hold down the fort, I'll go with the outbound. I won't ask anyone to do anything I wouldn't take part in." Then, I added, "Calories and hydration are a concern for work teams though. We'll spend three days, get as much fence as we can torn down and put back up. Then, we run through the South Building, bolster our supplies, and get back to work on fencing."

"How big are we building this thing?" Rob, the computer guy asked.

"Big as we can, I'd imagine," James opined.

"Big enough to circle both buildings, and probably at least to the streets on all sides," I suggested, "preferably the opposite side of the street or further. It would be smart to leave as much open ground as possible between the wall and the buildings, just in case."

"We could stretch it to the river over there," the blonde we'd met the day before added.

"That's a good idea," I said supportively. "I'm sorry, I don't think we ever got your name."

"It's okay," she said with a beaming smile, "you guys were rushed. I'm Briana, just call me Bri."

"Well, that's a damn good idea, Bri," I said.

"Yeah nice," Tony agreed. "Keeps us in clean water, but we don't know if those fuckers can swim. Might be wise to chain-link that section and put in a heavy gate."

"Man's got a point," James remarked.

"Yeah, for sure," I agreed, "no loopholes."

"So, what do we do for the rest of today?" Dave asked.

"We start checking this place out in detail," I replied. "I'd like to see the top floor used for command and administration. We could reserve it for meetings and shit and build it up real nice. Maybe the eighth floor for supply storage. The rest for living, with Floor One sealed up, and Floor Two left empty for now. Keep it clean for security purposes."

As everyone began to disperse, Tony clapped his hand over my shoulder, and cheerily said to me, "Well, you don't want it, but it looks like you're leading this now!"

"Don't," I warned him. "Don't do that, fuck head."

Tony walked away smiling, trailed by a laughing Dave. Those two. God what am I going to do with such a crew? The best we can, I guess. I think we've got this one.

FOURTEEN

We spent the rest of that day moving everything around the entire building. Beds and couches were removed from the top two floors and dispersed into several mostly empty rooms throughout the structure. All food, cleaning products, drinks, and much more were brought up to the eighth floor, with anything having gone to spoil moved outside, with plans to take it to the river and send it downstream. I highly doubt anyone else would be along the way to mind if a wooden pallet stacked with rotten vegetables and spoiled milk floats on past. I hoped.

The ninth floor was set up with most of the rooms containing various types of desks from throughout the building, and one apartment had actually been made into a meeting room by ripping out the walls for the two bedrooms, thus creating a much larger space in which several tables were pushed together to make a pseudo-conference table. Other whole apartments had been stripped, walls roughly removed, to be patched in later to make more large spaces to open it up and allow for several people to work in each space at once.

The eighth floor was undergoing a truly special process. Plans were laid, and some underway, to open up much of the floor via different doorways knocked straight through the walls, creating a place with many rooms for storage of everything we had, all able to be accessed directly. More talk was being had about making a sort of 'office' near the stairwell entrance and bolting the door at the other end of the hallway shut to keep the place secured.

All in all, it seemed as though the group was actually having fun laying it out. I have to admit, it's kind of cool. Imagine, how would you lay out a pair of buildings to survive the end of the world and keep you and yours safe, effective, and efficient? Most importantly, to me, everyone was already working together. A few didn't seem to want to pull their weight, but I never even had to mention it, as the other members of the group got them going good and strong.

We all rounded out the evening by having a meal together. It was Shannon's suggestion, and all of our agreeance, that everyone ate as a group. Breaking bread together and all that. Dinner was a blast for most, though it consisted of a mix of MRE contents, as well as some canned food that had been heated to lukewarm by the MRE heaters. It wasn't great fare, but it was edible, and better than nothing.

Given some downtime, a point in the day in which there was little to focus on and occupy our minds, myself, Jennifer, and even Tony fell into somber moods. The loss of Melissa still weighing heavily on the three of us. Jennifer's daughter, my step-daughter, and every bit as good as a niece to Tony. This would surely be a wound that only time would heal.

We could see the occasional freak running, or walking, through the area. A couple of times the entire group collectively held our breaths as one would approach the front entrance, only to reappear within minutes heading in another direction, obviously not finding anything of interest, or at least not a way to get to it. Henry's SUV was still firmly set longways against the front of the building, various debris shoved underneath it to effectively seal off the front of the building.

After dinner, it was suggested that more alcohol be brought out. This is where a stand had to be made. Not only did my stomach turn at the mere thought of drinking again, but there were other reasons.

"We should save the alcohol," I started, rising to a stand, and was immediately met by several groans. "Look, I know, the world's gone to shit and it would be immensely easier to drink it all under the table. Alcohol has a shit load of other uses, the one at the front of my mind, mild anesthesia, as well as sanitation. We can drink the beer, but please, save some for me. I love beer."

This was met with laughter, then, Rob, "What about the cheap gas station stuff?"

"Drink it. Wine, low proof liquor, beer, drink it. Move anything eighty proof or higher up to supply and keep it there," I instructed. "We need to save what we can, starting right now. That goes for everything. We may have to consider rationing."

"But we've got plenty of food, lots to drink, and all those houses…" Rob stated.

"And the other building," Chris pitched in.

"And what happens when that runs out?" I asked. "Or when we find more survivors, our numbers increase, or we simply burn through it all living like kings? We scavenge the countryside until, what, we find someone to go to war with, risk our own asses to grab some more short-term foodstuffs?" Come on, people! Think about it!"

The previously upbeat dinner mood dampened a bit, but after a few minutes, general agreement prevailed, and the group fell in with the plan to conserve.

Jennifer got up to head off to bed, bidding Shannon and the others good night. Since working together, the two were already becoming friends, maybe at Shannon's push, or maybe naturally, but it was good for my wife to have someone female to talk to and pal around with. Honestly, that may just be the thing to keep her from sailing over the edge.

As Jennifer grabbed Gwen to head off to our new quarters, I got up as well. Turning to the group, I commented, "Whatever you do drink, do it in moderation. My work ethic is a fucking beast, and we'll start our early morning push for wall materials first thing, hangovers or not. Get some rest, people! Good night!"

I left, moving out of the doorway and down the hall, a smile creeping over my face at the sound of a few groans, and a few others bidding each other good night. Tony caught up to me just before I reached my family's apartment.

"Hey man," he started, "you doing alright there, buddy?"

"Nah, not at all," I replied, "but we'll get there. Lot of fuckin' work to do here, good time to bury my head in some. You good?"

"Yeah," he breathed, "I'll be alright. I just…I don't know. Fuck it. Have a good night man."

"Yeah you too," I replied, then headed into our three-bedroom affair to curl up and go to sleep. I climbed into bed next to Jennifer, Gwen already fast asleep in the next room. I kissed Jennifer, and just held her tight. It seemed like a decade passed, but soon, her soft breaths signaled her to be asleep in my arms, and soon, I followed her into dreamland.

FIFTEEN

The following morning, I awoke a bit before dawn. Shaking the wife awake, I set off to find some form of caffeine, only to find several of our friends, both new and old, gathered around a dining table in an empty apartment down the hall. I walked into the apartment, scratching myself with one hand while rubbing the sleep from my eyes with the other. Somebody had rescued a case of energy drinks from one of the apartments. It wasn't coffee, but the coffee wasn't exactly flowing freely yet with no power, and nobody wanted to burn a fire. A fire indoors presented the obvious dangers; outdoors, it would have drawn too much attention.

Just as the sun began to poke itself above the horizon, we set off to work. Five of us pulling security detail, five working on carefully, quietly, removing fencing from nearby houses. Everybody armed to the teeth. We moved a lifted pickup truck over to where we worked so a pair of sentries could provide watch from the higher vantage point.

The day was clear, the sun rising lazily into the sky as it slowly climbed. It was warm, but still not late enough in the year to be torture, as Ohio summers can occasionally be. In my thirty years living here, I've seen summers over a hundred degrees, and winters more than ten below.

The fencing began to slowly stack up very nicely. The neat piles lining the sides of the street consisting of everything from solid wood planking, to cheap plastic jobs, to chain link and wrought iron. The plan was to bring it back together and put it up with the weaker stuff sandwiched between stronger material. Privacy and security all in one sloppy package.

Near mid-day, just before we changed shifts, moving sentries to work and workers to provide overwatch, we encountered an issue.

"Hey," Rich hissed, "stop working, stop moving. I've got one down the street here!"

"Can you hit it?" Chris asked, motioning to the lever-action .45-70 rifle I'd loaned Rich.

"Maybe," Rich replied with a hushed tone. "Wait. Nah there's more. I've got three. Now six. Ah fuck. Ah fuck man, we gotta go. Ah fuck."

Seeing the sweat beading across his brow as he chanted the vulgarity, I climbed onto one of the oversized tires of the pickup truck and looked with a pair of binoculars.

"Not good man," I replied, cursing. "Shit there's at least two dozen now."

"They're coming this way," Henry realized as he came alongside me.

"Yeah," I said. "This way, inside. Find the fuckin' attic, we gotta *move* y'all."

I motioned to the nearest house, and all ten of us began to move. Dave ran back over by the truck and grabbed two gallon jugs each of ammonia and bleach. We approached the back door, an easy journey since the home's eight-foot privacy fence was now lain in a neat pile by the road.

Tony breached the door with the crow bar he'd been working with; it opened a bit, the wood splintering, but held fast by a pair of deadbolts. A few strong kicks, and the door gave way, exposing a tidy dining area. We quickly fanned out until a shout from Rob confirmed that the house had an attic, and he had found it. We began moving through the house to his location, flowing into the area like water seeking a low spot.

We could hear the infected approaching already. Scrapes of feet on the street surface, a few coughing barks, some sniffling, grunts and groans. They were a chorus of disgust, and Dave returned to our point of entry and began emptying both jugs of bleach on the back porch as the sounds drew closer.

The first monstrosity appeared, right near our guard post/truck. It arched its neck and inhaled sharply, gathering the scent of ten people sweating in the sun. Christ, it must have smelled like a buffet to them. The freak let out the trademark series of coughs and barks, and more began to appear as Dave added a puddle of ammonia to the bleach from both bottles. He then threw all the jugs onto the wooden decking and booked it back to the rest of us.

Closing and latching the door behind everybody, we moved upstairs. Most stayed out of sight, toward the middle of the attic area. Tony and I stayed near the window to the back of the house and watched. The freaks were swarming the house, from right where we'd entered.

"This is problematic, dude," Tony declared.

"Nah man, check it out. They're confused," I replied.

Sure enough, they got right to the empty bottles, right in the midst of four gallons of chemicals intertwining into a mix, creating a haze of chloramine vapor. There, they'd stop, having lost the scent they were trailing, and start giving out the call of sharp inhalations. In little time at all, they would start clawing their throats, and collapsing into piles on the deck, allowing room for a handful more to spill in and meet the same fate. In just a matter of minutes, there were no more freaks left to tail us.

"Let's move. We gotta finish them off while they're down," Tony ordered, but I held everyone back for just a few minutes.

"No, wait a few minutes," I stated, motioning out the window. "Wait for the vapor to clear, unless you want to nap with them."

So, we waited. Each minute, every second, feeling like a life time as we watched in apprehension. Nobody sure if they'd get back up, stay down, or what else could happen as we waited for the airspace to free up. Finally, after what I'd calculated to be at least a decade of time, we moved.

Out of the attic we went, and back into the sunshine. The air still smelled faintly of chemicals, but it didn't seem to have much effect. We set to work on the craniums of the freaks lain about the deck, slumped over chairs, one leaned up against a Char-Broil grill as if she was just relaxing. Working with shovels, spud bars, screwdrivers, and other hand tools, we shut down every skull that still had shape to it.

Moving back to the truck, we waited. Passing around a water jug, we watched and listened. Nothing made noise, nothing moved. After several minutes, we set back to work.

By the end of the day, we had nearly an entire block's worth of fencing stripped and laid by the road. We had started on the next block alongside the complex, got through two properties' worth of material, and decided to call it quits. Tony, Rich and I left to go retrieve my pickup truck as the others dragged a landscaping trailer from the driveway we found it in, and got it lined up to hook up to my truck.

Once the trailer was connected, we started working to load the trailer with fencing, and unload it near the apartment complex, laying it in a long line as we went to mark the new fence.

As the sun neared the end of its descent to the horizon, we were calling it a day, and returned back to the apartments for a meal and rehydration.

We explained the events that left us trapped and surrounded in the house across the street, and detailed what saved our bacon, all while Jennifer wrote every note she could down in her notebook, save for the things we'd already learned and recorded.

Once dinner was complete, we all retired to our respective dwellings for some much-needed rest. I spent some time cuddling and talking to little Gwen and took a bird bath with a jug of river water.

As I lay in bed next to my wife, I took note of her short breaths and occasional sniffle. A cry that could be sensed from my perspective more than it could be heard. I looped my arm around her, pulled her in tight, and there we lay until we both eventually found sleep.

SIXTEEN

It took three more days to procure enough material to build a wall we were comfortable with, complete with one single rolling gate. The gate had been found at a nearby auto garage, which had also provided us with a whole lot of sturdy, tall chain-link to reinforce our rapidly growing collection. A second trip to that location provided us with a literal truckload of tools at Henry's insistence.

Henry found a pair of post hole diggers in two different garages we were working near, and on the third day, he took a team consisting of himself, and three other people and started setting to work. They dug holes at intervals all around the compound, making places to set the fencing into. In addition, he found many bags of concrete in the maintenance area of the complex's parking garage, and laid those out at intervals as well.

As they labored away at the start of our security system, I gathered up Tony, Dave, and Rich. We armed up, long guns and pistols, with enough ammunition to sustain a ten-minute firefight, and moved to the South Building.

Upon reaching the main front doors, we found the outer pair to be unlocked. We moved in, two of us at all times watching both inside and out of the building. Rich and I found the inner set of doors to be locked tight, not even enough clearance to rattle when the handles were pulled. On the wall between the entrances, there sat a basic card reader, and a large box for an intercom with a series of buttons, each button corresponding to an apartment number.

"Press a button," I said, shrugging.

Rich pressed a button and waited. Nothing. He pressed another, then another, and still nothing.

"I don't get it. It looks like it has power. The card reader's lights are on," I observed.

"Battery backup?" Tony wondered aloud.

"I got their backup," Dave declared, bringing his rifle butt-first to stroke the glass from the door. Rich stopped him with an outstretched arm.

"Wait a minute," he instructed. "I was ready for this, we have the same setup in our building."

To our three confused faces, he smiled. The cocky little shit smiled! I kind of liked this guy. He then produced a 9-volt battery, a knife, and a length of wire. Within about thirty seconds, he had the card reader broken open, wired up, and, upon touching the leads to the small battery, we all heard a click from the inner set of doors. Dave gave them a pull, and they swung right open.

I couldn't even think of what to say. I mean, looking at the guy, perpetually unkempt red hair, crooked half-toothed smile, short stature, you wouldn't expect him to be as outright damned handy as he was. I just shrugged. And returned his smile. It was all I could do.

We moved into the building, fanning out into a close facsimile of combat intervals, Dave watching the rear, and began to move. It was much like clearing the north building had been. The first floor was devoid of all life, and empty of anything made of flesh at all.

Moving up the stairs, we encountered only two freaks, and the remnants of a single body that they'd been sharing. The pile of gore nothing more than a pile of jelly and discarded bones, though its odor was still very prevalent, permeating the entire floor with a putrid stench of rot and decay. The freaks sharing the meal didn't even see or hear us, and they were quickly dispatched with a pair of shots let loose by Tony and Rich, adding their own package of nastiness to the scene.

We moved on and found much the same as before on each floor. One floor would be empty, another occupied, and the most we had found in the entire complex was on the top floor. Upon opening the door to Floor Nine, we were immediately greeted by a female who had clearly seen better days.

At first, she just kind of stared, almost as if perplexed. We stared back, for just a moment. Did she see us? Smell us? What was she doing?

Then the freak made her intentions clear. All at once, it was as if the realization of what was happening hit her. She dropped her jaw as if on a hinge, and let out an ear-splitting shriek, that, at this range, seemed to fill the entire world and permeate every part of my being.

At the very tail-end of her oration, we heard a loud gurgling, as if she'd just eaten an entire batch of atomic wings and found out too late that they didn't agree with her. Following the grotesque series of noises, you could almost see her throat expand as a blob of the vomit I'd seen many times before began making its way up from her digestive tract.

Rich was the first to move, raising the hand with his small .32 revolver, and sending one of the small-caliber rounds straight through the thing's forehead. She fell over flat backwards, almost as if she were in a cartoon, and as her back struck the floor of the hallway an eruption of dark crimson left her parted lips. The sick soup rose a solid five feet into the air, and then came crashing back down like the world's most disgusting geyser.

The scene departed our line of sight and revealed three more monstrosities running to our location from the other end of the hallway. At that moment, we were all spurred into action, and at once, we unleashed a mad minute of directed fire into the forms. Rounds ripped through clothing and flesh alike, painting the walls, floors, and ceiling. Rounds missing their target torn into walls, exploding plaster, and hole-punched the door at the other end of the hallway.

At the end of our firing session, we reloaded, stinging fingers from negligently touching warm gun parts, and coughing from the smoke screen we had built up. Not one freak moved. Nothing moved. Silence once again took over the floor. After a few minutes, we started moving, but we had barely touched the door of the first apartment when Henry's bellowing voice called from behind us.

"Friendlies!" he called. "We heard shooting, everyone alright?"

I started to reply but was cut short by a muffled shout from the other end of the hallway.

"Hold position!" I shouted down, motioning for my friends to be prepared. "Don't move, we are coming to you!"

We moved rapidly down the hallway, a centipede of legs with porcupine quills of gun barrels sweeping through every open doorway and covering every corner and recess. In short order we reached the door to the last apartment.

The door was the same basic steel entry door with a peephole that you see in apartments and hotels worldwide. What was different was the collage of dents, dings, scratches, and scrapes marring the entire surface of the door.

Approaching it, I called out, "Hello? Friendlies here. Who's there?"

The clicking of locks and scraping of furniture followed, and soon the door swung open exposing a family of four. The husband, a short, well-built man, made the first introduction.

"God we're glad to see you! I'm Frank," he declared, shaking hands. "This is my wife, Clara, and our kids, Robbie and Tanya." He informed us this, motioning to a short, very thin brunette with deep set eyes, and a pair of very scared looking children, both near the age of ten.

"Y'all been here since the start?" I asked, and he nodded, so I continued, "Any guns? Drug issues? Anything we need to know about you? How about health conditions?"

He shook his head in the negative to each of these, except the last one, "I've got a bad back, but I don't let it slow me down. My wife... she's prediabetic, but it's controllable with diet. We were trapped in here by those things."

"Get them some food and water," I said to Dave and Tony, who set to preparing the only MRE's they brought, one from each man, and handed out a couple of bottles of water.

"Are you the military?" Clara asked.

"No ma'am," I replied. "Well, Tony here was, but he discharged well before it all went bad."

"Ma'am." Tony nodded.

"Are they coming?" Frank inquired.

"Don't think so," I explained. "They blew up downtown and we haven't seen a sign of them since. We've got a group of survivors in the north building, and we are constructing a containment wall to make these buildings safe. You're welcome to join us if you wish. We just expect you to help out when and where needed. No bullshit, no theft, full rationing. Basic respect and honor system."

"Oh God, thank you so much!" Clara exclaimed.

"Not a problem," I replied. "Go with Henry and his group here. They'll escort you to the north building and introduce you to the others." Then, turning to Henry, "Get them set with the others, Jennifer and Shannon will settle them in and help them. Get me a group of five to come start transferring everything usable to our building."

"Will do, my friend," he replied kindly enough, and then departed as we began to empty everything we could find in each apartment into a couple of large rolling laundry carts and transporting them to the end of the hallway.

In little time, we had a full crew working on clearing out the building, and a line moving between the two, carrying food, toiletries, medicines and everything else we could find a use for. By the end of the day, we had the building emptied, and much of our haul had been moved to the supply floor of the north building, awaiting to be catalogued by Jennifer and Shannon, and stored for rationing.

Then the shrieks started. That awful coughing bark, and a chorus of shrieks and groans. At first, we couldn't locate them. Then, in short time, figures began moving with the speed of a crackhead being chased by the police, all in our directions. Heads falling back to shriek, then snapping back to focus full attention on our group.

"Drop supplies, *FALL BACK! MAIN ENTRANCE!!!*" Tony bellowed, as he began cracking off shots with his SOCOM.

The entire group of gatherers began to fall back to the main entrance of the south building, where we started loosing shot after shot into the figures enclosing from all sides.

"Them fuckers have flanked us!" I exclaimed over the din of gunfire. "They tried surprising us!"

"I think you're right!" Dave shouted back, and, as if all signaled at once, our people from the other building made their way onto the balconies across the third floor and opened fire.

Skulls, necks, and torsos exploded in mists of tainted flesh and bodily fluids. The attacking horde began closing in as we thinned them out, and soon we fell back into the first-floor hallway and pushed back into the gloomy darkness as several creatures spilled from the front entrance and into the hallway. Switching to my shotgun, along with Rich and Dave, we started unloading round after round of full-on buckshot into the forms as they fought to gather their footing.

Several more crashed through the entrance, striking the wall, some slipping in the growing puddle of blood and brackish vomit expelled from their comrades. They too fought to climb through or over the growing pile of bodies as we pushed further back into the hallway. Several collapsed momentarily as rifle rounds from the outside ripped through their legs, shattering bone and leaving them to drag their way to their prey.

During one of several reloads, I heard shouting and more gunfire behind us as glass shattered down the hallway. Turning to look, I could swear I felt my balls shrivel up and try to hide. A second mass of infected fucks had found the side door at the end of the hall, and broken through, as the members to the back of our group unleashed a volley of gunfire. The rounds screamed down the length of the space and ripped through flesh, making our attackers look like the front line of Revolutionary War fighters, falling one after the other, only to expose more moving in behind them.

The sustained fire began leaving the hallway choked with smoke and bodies. We had to move a good ten feet further in at one point as people were starting to slip on spent casings in nearly every caliber imaginable. Sweat poured down my face, stinging my eyes. Tony's rifle rounds flew past my vision, a couple of hot brass cylinders pelting the side of my head as he fired his gun dry, dropping it to hang on its sling as he drew his Beretta and continued firing.

I also pulled my pistol; the shotgun and AR-15 both had run dry. The trusty Smith and Wesson jerking in my hand with every expulsion of full metal jacketed bullets that it produced. Running one magazine empty and slamming home another, the mass of death behind us had stopped growing, and the whole group refocused fire on those coming in ahead of us.

Two magazines worth of time, by my count, and the group ahead had ceased to grow as well.

We nearly all collapsed back to the ground, all gasping for fresher air at our new lower altitude. So much brass littered the carpet that it'd started to melt the fibers in some spots. You could have practically made a statue out of what was left from the fight.

"Fucking…fucking…ambush. Bastards…" I said between heavy breaths, as the adrenaline began leaving my system, causing my hands to shake.

"I think they are smarter than we gave them credit for," Tony lamented.

Before I could utter a response, we heard footfalls outside. Running steps.

"Ah shit," I said, pulling the magazine from my pistol, seeing six rounds left, and sliding it back in place. I raised my gun-arm to the entrance like a world-weary gunslinger and waited. Tony and Henry followed suit. A moment later, a familiar face appeared. It was James.

"Hold fire," I coughed out, and we all lowered our guns.

"Guys!" James yelled over his shoulder, "They're all alright! You're good, right guys? They're okay!"

Bri, Shannon, and Frank all followed him in. They helped us to our feet and carried the last load of supplies as we all made our way to the north building. The simple twenty-five yard journey seemingly miles long in our fatigued conditions. Even Chris' big ass allowed his load to be carried as we went home to recoup and wind down.

Once in my own apartment, I surrendered myself to my wife's care and admonishments while Gwen climbed all over my outstretched legs mumbling in the odd way that young toddlers do.

"It's not safe out there," Jennifer scolded.

"No, and it never will be unless we make it that way," I countered.

"We've got people, and you still have a family," Jennifer replied.

"Most of one," I shot back angrily, immediately regretting it as I observed her facial expression. I softened my tone, "I'm sorry. Really, I should be easier. I'm just fucked with stress right now. Look, even this building isn't safe until we make it that way, then we have to keep on living." I sighed heavily, "I have a feeling this is just the beginning."

"I know," she relented. "I just worry about you, Scott. And me, and I worry for Gwen. Everything's just gone to shit, and I- "

"Yeah, but look," I picked up where she trailed off, "if the humans that have tried to end me couldn't, a bunch of mindless fucks won't, either. Besides, I worked nearly eighty hours a week to keep our house afloat, and now I'll work to make sure you are all good here. I can't sit back and just direct everyone else without joining in anyway, it wouldn't be right at all."

"Yeah," she replied softly. "Just…just be careful. Always come back to me. Promise?"

"You ain't been able to get rid of me yet, and you never will," I replied with a grin.

With that, we settled in for bed, and were fast asleep.

SEVENTEEN

We woke up, again just before first light as per usual, and set about our morning routine. This meant brush teeth, eat a light breakfast, find caffeine, and set out to working on whatever was next.

This day, we split into two parties of five each. One was on wall duties, the other used my truck and the landscaping trailer to start cleaning up the bodies from the evening before. I joined the wall-building team, and we began making good progress. By noontime, we had half of the compound surrounded with a three-layer wall, sandwiched together and then secured with bolts, chain, wire, and whatever else we could use. One section even had a gallon jug of wood glue poured between two sections to stick them together nice and strong. It was nothing pretty, but the sections that were up were strong. Very strong.

About the time we settled down for a break, Henry came back with the truck. They had finished cleaning the first floor, and he'd left three people. One cleaning spent casings, in case we ever found reloading equipment, and the other two bleaching and cleaning the gore out of the low pile carpeting.

"One hundred, and sixty-seven," Henry said as he and the others disgorged from the truck.

"Huh?" I asked.

"That's how many of them there were between the building and the parking lot."

"Jesus Christ," I muttered.

"They almost got us," he noted. "They worked together, I think. Real smart like."

"Yeah I noticed," I stated. "You and your crew got some wind left to you? Another day of this and we'll have the fence together. Gate should be reinforced before we start losing light today, too."

"Yeah we got you brother man," he said smiling. "You know, you really starting to pull this place together in a hurry. I'm sit my ass right here for a second, then we can get started."

"Man," I started, "not just me, we. We are pulling this together. All of us."

I saw grins and agreeing faces on all nine of the people sitting with us as they took drinks of water and ate a light lunch.

"You know what it is?" Henry replied. "We won't worry about that mule going blind, just sit right back and hold the line my friend!" He slapped my shoulder, and we all got up and set back to work on the wall. Man, he loves that line. In the eight years we've lived next to each other, I've heard it more times than I can count, and it still brings a smile to my face.

We toiled and worked the rest of the day on our first line of defense. The work was long, but not difficult, and we rotated one group from guarding to building, and the other to guarding, so everybody was able to relax and enjoy some relative downtime.

The rest of the day passed with a fair amount of monotony. By the time the sun swung lower in its journey, we had much of the complex surrounded. Maybe another day of work, and one more testing and fixing obvious issues, and we could have some safety and security.

We retired to the north building and gathered outside for a breather. All ten of us were tired, sweat-stained, and dirty. Despite our physical conditions, everyone was in high spirits and joked with one another, chatting aimlessly, while Tony and Dave went back and forth like an old married couple. It felt good. Nah, scratch that. It felt great.

Upon returning to the building we discovered that we weren't the only ones busting our asses all day. The other twelve people had been busy indoors. The first floor was entirely bare. Nothing but walls and carpet. No doors, no furniture.

The second floor had also been mostly cleared out, appearing just as empty as the first. The main difference was that the doors were left intact, and there appeared to be a single bed left in the front room of every apartment we passed.

The third floor was a completely different story. It seemed like everything that required power was on this floor. Apartments were filled with computers, televisions, lamps, even an aquarium. It seemed like this was now chosen as a storage floor.

Moving up to the fourth floor it had the looks of a living floor. The first few apartments we passed had been laid out nicely. A bit of extra furniture here and there, and the rooms had been cleaned and cleared of anything vital. Now, they had taken on the look of some well cared for living quarters. Near the end of the hallway, coming from one of the last apartments, we heard voices conversing easily, a few laughs here and there. I approached the doorway and found Jennifer and Shannon.

"Y'all look tired as shit," I grumbled as I walked through the doorway, easing my weight into the first chair I found.

"Gee, thanks," Shannon grinned.

"We've been busting our asses in here!" Jennifer added enthusiastically, then, "everyone has. Even the new people, Clara and…Frank. Sorry."

"Yeah no shit you have," I admired. "Good work! I like the direction you're going, living spaces up higher."

"There's dinner cooking on the roof," Jennifer grinned.

"It should be almost done, we should go!" Shannon added.

"Nice. Alright guys," I called to our wall party. "Rooftop in ten minutes. Let's get some warm food."

Everybody departed to go get somewhat cleaned up before we ate. Just the prospect of having hot food again made my mouth water. After maybe two whole months, I think and even a can of warmed green beans sounded like it was fit for a king, I couldn't wait to see what they had in store for us.

Having done my best to freshen up with baby wipes, I met the rest of the group on the rooftop. It was a very well thought out idea to dine up here. The sun still hung in the sky, and at the mid-way point in the year, it was warm, but not uncomfortable, as it would be in another month or so. The sky was blue and clear, save for a few lazy cotton balls of cloud watching over the Earth. A very light breeze capped off the cheery mood that mother nature had worn for the day.

I was very surprised to see a patio grill had been dragged to the rooftop as well, and the smell of dinner finishing up inside of it made my stomach twist and gnaw at the rest of me in anticipation. As it happens, it was James and Parker paired up preparing what was seeming to be a feast for our small community.

The meal finished cooking right as I was directed to a seat at the head of the table. As it turns out, in a world prior to the end of everything we knew, grilled spam, canned ham, and canned vegetables most certainly would not have been a king's feast. Today was not that kind of day, and this meal suited us just fine.

The group was sat at a couple of long folding tables set end-to-end, and a variety of folding chairs were gathered around. It looked for all the world to be a setup for royalty on a budget. Food was plated by a few and passed on to the rest. I was given my plate first, and I passed it along to Rob. I would receive mine last, just in case one plate was scraps and bits, so everyone else could have their fill.

Once everybody was seated with a plate of food and can of whatever beverage was on hand, they dug in.

Conversation was nearly muted entirely as everyone shoved fork after fork of food into their mouths, as if we hadn't eaten in days. Frank, Clara, and their children ate greedily, nodding their thanks to anyone who even looked their way. It kind of made me feel a bit guilty. Guilty that we hadn't thought to clear that building sooner. Being in a room facing away from the entrances, they had no idea anybody was even around, save for the occasional gunshot.

The one exception to the light mood was Jennifer. She sat nearby, conversing mutely with Shannon, and despite her new buddy's best efforts, her mood appeared somber at best. She simply wasn't great at bottling her emotions, the inverse of myself. She never could accomplish this feat, but that's not to say she wasn't putting her best effort forth.

Conversation picked up as the meal went on, and in short order, it turned into planning.

"What do you think we should do first?" Bri asked me.

"Power," was my quick reply. "We get some lights and basic utilities going first and foremost, as soon as the wall is complete."

"You can do that?" Parker questioned.

"Absolutely," I replied, more to the group as a whole. "Several homes and businesses, as well as construction and highway signage, all have solar panels. We take them. I doubt anyone will miss them right now. There's also a house I can see from here that has a few small wind collectors on top of it. We take them all."

"How we going to store the power?" asked Henry.

"Will that be enough?" came another question, then a few others that got mixed together and lost in the small commotion.

I held my hands up as a signal to chill out, and everyone did.

"We find out who's good at what," I started, "and then, we begin rerouting the main power lines to a storage bank. We can run series and parallel setups of as many deep cycle batteries as we can find. It's not difficult. We then grab power inverters from wherever we can find them and run it through those to the building supply. Just ration the power out until we can build it into a robust enough system."

"I can set that up and help others along the way," James offered. "We can make that the next big work party."

"Once the wall is done, and we can find all we need," I explained, and James nodded as he took in his last bite of food.

"But that's an awful lot to do," Clara began. "I mean, I'm sure somebody will come and give us aid, right? Why don't we just wait?"

"Lady, where have you been?" Rob shot at her.

"Nah," I replied, motioning to Rob to chill out. "Maybe they will, but I doubt it, and I'm not going to put people's lives in the hands of hope. Makes no sense to act like tomorrow will be better, when it's smarter survival to plan for next year being worse."

Nods and solemn faces all around the table.

"We gonna have food?" Chris questioned.

"We're going to work on it, dude," Anthony added, since my mouth was full of peas and carrots.

"Farm lands start maybe five or six miles from here," I added, swallowing my final bite of food. "I'd like to see sometime if there's any animals around, pigs and goats and things like that. I've got a long-term bag loaded with seeds, it's too late to plant now, but we could start in the spring."

"Too late?" Shannon asked.

"Won't have enough time to grow much before the first frost. We're already well into summer," James added. "We'll get by from scavenging for now, maybe hunting, too?" he looked to me, and I nodded, pantomiming drawing back a bowstring and releasing it.

Turning away from a now satisfied Gwen, the toddler's face a thoroughly disgusting mess of food, Jennifer gave her opinion, "We'll need water. I mean, the river is right there, but is it safe to drink?"

"Once the wall is built, I can build a still for purifying the water," Rich suggested, and I liked that idea.

"Large scale operation?" I asked him, and he nodded in the positive.

"Oh yeah," Rich grinned. "We can rebuild swimming pools and tanks on the rooftops to store it and collect rainwater. I can start putting it together whenever you're ready."

"We're going to need vehicles, too," Jennifer added. "We have a lot of shit to start collecting."

"Henry's a mechanic," I offered. "If he's down for it, we could start checking the underground parking, maybe set him up a motor pool."

"That'd suit me just fine my brother," Henry said, smiling ear to ear.

"We need a way to keep track of everything we see out there," I said, motioning to the landscape. "That way we can build a map of what's where, and start planning scavenging routes. Make things real efficient, ya know?"

"I can start setting up the command floor with maps and I can help keep track of things!" Jennifer said assuredly.

"If you're restoring power," Rob, adding his input, "I can run a separate power bank and we could run security monitors and cameras. Maybe even a desktop you can load digital camera images taken from scouting runs onto and build a database."

"You can do that shit?" Dave asked with no small amount of skepticism.

"Uhhh yeah," Rob smiled. "I'm a computer tech. Well, I was, but it's not like I would forget simple things like that. I did it for 17 years before it all went bad here."

"Dude!" Anthony began, "I like it man. Let's do it!"

"We found a bunch of all of that in the buildings," Jennifer added. "TV's, cameras, computers and laptops, the apartment buildings already have security cameras. We could find more and just add to it."

The talk continued on for a few hours, long into and through the evening. Everyone adding their own input, and Jennifer dutifully adding it all into her notebook. It was agreed that the first three things we would do, after the wall was finished, would be to start up a small power grid, start scouting, and locate some construction equipment to begin Rich's dry moat.

All of this was great, but it meant something more to me. I had no clue if anybody else noticed it, but the planning and banter had brought everybody together. It made us a community, right there at that roof top dinner table. It also gave us purpose, and a way to forget just a little bit of what was really out there behind our nearly finished wall.

One after another, people began to break off from the impromptu meeting and head down to their quarters for bed. Before much longer, the rest of us followed. After wishing each other a good night, we retired for bed.

"Night bye!" little Gwen chirped as I tucked her in. She reached out for her stuffed animal, a dinosaur of mine I'd somehow kept over the years and passed down to her. Being one of the few things of hers we departed home with, it stayed in her new bedroom so as not to get lost.

"I love you, baby," I said and kissed her on the forehead as I covered her up and left the room.

Jennifer was already in our room, and under the covers. I stripped down to my boxer shorts and slid under the sheets next to her; she laid her head on my chest, and we were asleep without even a chance to wish each other a good night.

EIGHTEEN

I heard the commotion and started groaning and mumbling for whomever it was to go the fuck away. They weren't listening. It was Tony. He never listened.

"Dude wake the fuck up!" he yelled as he pounded on the bedroom door.

"What the hell, man!" I yelled back, then another voice joined Tony's.

"Hey man, it's Dave, we have people at the gate!" Dave shouted through the closed door.

"Dave?" I replied, my sleep-addled mind still not grasping the latter of his statement. "Dave's not here!"

"Baby!" Jennifer scolded. "Wake your ass up and go see what's happening!"

Okay. I can ignore my friends, but, when the wife says move, I have to comply.

I rolled out from under the sheets and began sliding on a pair of pants, and, after a moment of thought, grabbed the Sig Sauer P226 off of my night stand and slid it into my front pocket.

The knocking and voices on my door continued, and I finally opened the door and pushed my way between them.

"What time is it?" I muttered, still not fully awake.

"It's morning now, fuck face," Dave replied, then stopped when he saw the lack of amusement in my face.

I left the apartment to find Rich and Carolyn in the hallway.

"You," I said, pointing to Carolyn, "please go help Jennifer with Gwen, and get some coffee going. Hopefully we won't be long. Rich, come with us. You got a gun?"

"I got my upgrade I found in the gun room, hope that's alright," Rich replied and flashed the .454 Casul Ruger I brought from home.

"Take good care of her, or I'll take good care of you," I growled, making a mental note that guns should be checked out through inventory from here on.

Rich fell in with the rest of us, and we made our way down to the front gate. Standing there was a group of what I counted to be eight people, a few with long guns, and a fairly even mix of men, women, and children. A fairly heavyset brunette with a face full of freckles was the first one to speak up.

"Well, are you guys going to let us in?" she demanded, and a man in a cowboy hat standing behind her put his hand on her shoulder.

"I'm sorry, what was your name?" I asked.

"Katie," she said, folding her arms over her chest, "but I don't know why that's important. You're already treating us like criminals. We aren't bad, just let us in! It's not safe out here!"

"Yeah," I replied sarcastically. "That's why we built a fence. Drop the attitude. We're just trying to stay safe, too."

"Look, mister," cowboy hat started, "I'm sorry for my wife. She hasn't been in the best of temperaments lately with all that's gone on. She's just upset. I'm Wayne, by the way. Wayne Howard, sir."

"Well, Wayne," I started. "We have a protocol here for new arrivals. Problem is, we're so newly established that we don't know what they are yet, so bear with me. I've got friends and family here, as well as other kids, so we're going to take this nice and easy."

Just blank stares, and a few slight nods. Great. I've been awake exactly four minutes, and I'm in the spotlight.

"Any felons? Criminals of any type?" I started. "Drug or alcohol dependencies? Medical conditions? Pregnancy? Bites?"

Katie scoffed, and the rest of them shook their heads. Negative.

"Dave, go get a few more men down here, and have Shannon and Bri meet us on the second floor," I instructed, and Dave turned to leave. I called after him, "Let's be quick, too, so we can get these people inside of the wire."

While we waited, I tried making some small talk to get a feel for the group.

"You in the lead of this party, Wayne?" I asked.

"Yes sir, it seems so, at least," he replied.

"How'd you find us?" I asked in return.

"We saw the wall you built, and your man on the rooftop." He motioned to Henry. I immediately regretted having someone up there. Henry was clear as day against the morning sky. Patrols would be kept to the ninth floor balconies from now on. And maybe some guard towers would be a good idea.

"Well, I'm going to start out giving y'all the benefit of the doubt for a start," I opined.

"I appreciate that, sir. Awfully understanding, you are." The last two words, in his southern drawl coming out as 'yar'.

"I figure you aren't here with ill intent. You've seen the wall. Showing up at dawn tells me you've at least known about us for a night, minimum," I observed. "Which, in turn, means you probably saw that our wall isn't finished. But you still came to the front gate and waited."

Just as I'd finished speaking, Dave came down with Rob, James, and Chris. I drew Tony and Rich in close to me, whispered a location, and they left the area to check. With the rest of the guard detail fanned out around me, I motioned for Dave to open the gate and let the group inside. He closed the gate behind them, latching it and driving a steel bar through the catch and into the ground.

Wayne opened his mouth to say something, and I motioned for him to wait a moment. I pulled a pack of cigarettes out of Dave's shirt pocket, lit one for myself, and waited as I took a long drag from it.

Within a minute tops, three shapes emerged from the front entrance of the empty South Building. Rich and Tony took up the rear and pushed forward a lanky man dressed in jeans and a denim jacket. When they reached us, Tony unslung a new rifle from his shoulder, a Ruger bolt action with a long eye relief scope attached to it. I grabbed the guy by the shoulder and helped him on his way to stand with the group of arrivals.

"One of yours?" I asked Wayne. He just smiled.

"Third floor, the room with the sliding door open. Just like you said," Rich offered.

"That's Fred," Wayne said. "He was just watching our backs."

"Sure," I replied. "Okay. Disarm, we'll lead you in to be screened and searched before we lay down the ground rules here. Follow Dave."

"You're not putting a hand on me," Katie said indignantly.

"You ain't my type, anyway, sweetheart. Shannon or Bri will check the women and children out," I shot back at her, then added, "I'm essentially letting you into my home for as long as you choose, you should be more civil."

She scoffed again. This was fast becoming a trademark of hers, and I was already getting tired of it.

Their group disarmed and handed over their weapons and bags. We led them up to the second floor and they waited in the hallway as one person at a time went into an apartment with someone who matched their gender to be checked for more weapons and bites, or anything else that would be harmful to our group.

As the others began checking them out, I disappeared, heading back upstairs to my apartment, and a cup of coffee.

Shuffling through my door, I found Jennifer and the baby awake, already starting breakfast. Carolyn was at the counter apparently putting together something for her to eat as well.

I sat heavily at the kitchen table, a cold brewed cup of coffee already sitting in what I'd nonverbally claimed as my spot. Carolyn was good. I've got no idea how she made coffee without heat, but it did the trick.

"Well?" Jennifer asked.

"Eleven new people," I replied, rubbing my eyes. "Well, ten and a bitch with an attitude. Shannon and Bri have them down on Floor Two checking them out for any bites or medical issues."

"Are you going to let them stay?" Jennifer asked, apparently trying to force more details from me.

"I don't really see why not, so long as nobody's dangerous in any way," I lamented. "There's safety in numbers, there's also more hands to help build this place up real sweet. Plus, there's kids. Four of them."

"Where were they staying?" Carolyn asked, joining the interrogation.

"Fuck if I know. They're dirty, but they seem to have been eating," I observed.

We continued making small talk until Shannon and Rich showed up to announce that everybody seemed alright. I instructed them to gather all the residents, new and old, and to bring everybody up to the roof.

I picked Gwen out of her seat, wiping off a bit of food from her cheek as she babbled to me, and motioned for Carolyn and Jennifer to follow. We made it to the rooftop ahead of everybody else and grabbed some seats. Since the tables and chairs were still set up from our dinner, there should be seating for just about everybody.

Within moments, people began trickling through the doorway and into the morning sunlight illuminating the open space. Some still looked as if they were asleep, others, like Dave and Tony, were wide awake. After about ten minutes, the final person made their way up, and we began a bit of morning planning and discussion.

"Morning!" I said, trying to sound cheery. It fell on deaf ears and was met with mostly little more than grunts. "Yeah, fuck mornings. I suggest you all learn from Carolyn here. She makes coffee. It's cold, but it works. Alright. You've obviously noticed there's some new faces that have joined us this morning. Welcome them, but that brings us to the first thing on my mind for this morning."

Everybody made their own introductions. I missed two of the names, but the other younger couple, aside from Wayne and Katie, had two boys of their own. I'd caught Max and Aiden for the kids, and Zack and Ashley for the couple. Both were about mid-twenties. Zack was tall and lean, with an honest attempt at a beard going on his chin and cheeks and a mop of scraggly brown hair. Ashley was short, pretty overall but with hair dye that hadn't lasted the end of the world too well without maintenance.

Once everyone had made their introductions, the attention turned back to our impromptu meeting.

"This group was kind enough to come to our front gate," I explained, "but they had a sniper of sorts inside already. So, Henry…"

"I need some people," Henry said, catching my intentions. "We'll have the wall finished up before lunch, I suppose."

"We need to start looking for supplies," Tony interrupted.

"Yeah, we need to divide our parties up smartly," I suggested. "An outside crew, an inside crew, and a scavenging crew. We have about thirty people, but seven are kids, Carolyn to watch them, so, seven-ish per party, give or take?"

"Sounds right," Rich offered.

"Well," I started, "let's start with scavengers. Y'all know these things are fast and dangerous. I need at least eight people who are motherfuckers with a weapon. Tony, Dave, Rich, Chris, James. Who else?"

"I'll volunteer myself," Wayne said, stepping forward. "Fred's a pretty nice shot, too."

"And Clara," Frank added and was met with a barely concealed scowl from Clara.

"That's eight," I observed. "Nine including me. Head down to the Command Floor, we'll get a plan going after I'm done up here. Grab your favorite guns and some ammo."

"You heard him!" Tony said, grinning. "Let's get ready for some fun!"

"I'll carry your ammo so you don't get winded, sugar," Dave said, patting Tony on the back.

"Why thank you, sweetness!" Tony said back, then, "but you're too skinny for the extra weight. I'll be fine."

As they left, laughing and joking, Wayne looked my way with an expression of pure uncertainty.

"Don't worry," I chuckled, "they're straight, they've just known each other for too long."

Wayne nodded, and followed the rest of the group through the door and down the steps.

Turning to everybody else, I began again.

"Henry needs people for two jobs today."

"Two?" Henry questioned.

"Two," I confirmed. "Priority is getting the wall finished. Afterwards, go look at the parking lot and underground parking. You're our mechanic, you can have the area as your motor pool. Think survival. Scavenging, defense, fighting, and working. We have a basket of keys down in supply, find out what you need and what runs."

"Oh, brother I'm sure I'll find a use for all of it!" Henry said, his eyes gleaming with excitement "Or at least a purpose, I suppose."

"Good shit, man," I replied, happy that he was happy. "Take notes. Anything you need, make a note. It's all free now, so long as it can be found. Give your list to Jennifer or Shannon, and we'll add it to scavenge orders."

"Will do, my friend!" Henry said, enthusiasm in his voice.

"He needs five or six people to help him with labor down there," I instructed, motioning over the edge of the roof. "Half armed, work in two hour shifts and switch."

A handful of the people gathered around volunteered, so some of them were volun-told to fill out Henry's requirements.

"Zack, was it?" I asked. "What did you do for a living?"

"Yeah, it's Zack," he replied. "I was a cook, then a manager of the restaurant."

"You're with Henry. So is Frank, and Bri. Henry that should give you seven, correct?"

"Yes sir, that should do it," Henry said. "Let's go then people, we have a wall to finish!"

As Henry's group began filing off of the roof, some grumbling, I turned to the rest of the group.

"I...I can watch the kids," Parker suggested.

"No," I replied. This guy really thinks he'll avoid any lifting or work and watch the kids?

"Carolyn has been watching them," Shannon suggested. "She's really good with them!"

Carolyn smiled and said, "It's not a problem! I don't mind."

"Cool. It's settled," I agreed. "The rest of you will help Jennifer. We need a command floor put together, and let's get the supply floor started if you have time."

"We can also lay out a plan for the second floor," Shannon supplied.

"What? Why?" I asked, a bit confused.

"For intaking new people," she replied. "At least as a good place to take them to check them out and interview them! That Ashley girl said she was a medical assistant, she could be some help."

"I like it," I said thoughtfully. "Maybe do a medical and a quarantine or containment floor once we get the south building secured. Good shit! An extra ration of rum for the pocket-sized lady!"

Yeah, I dipped the fuck out before she could do anything damaging to my manhood in exchange for the short joke. I might be tough, but, at the end of the day, having a set of balls is usually what saves me. Though those are figurative, I don't want to find out what happens to them if some small lady removes the physical set.

Having made my escape from Shannon, I went down to our currently barren Command Center. Putting aside my curiosity for what Jennifer and Shannon would come up with, we began laying out plans for the day.

"Well, I'm thinking power. Power, and any weapons or food we find along the way," I began, then, "We won't totally clean anything out today, so we won't mark them as such, but keep track of places with the most useful shit along the way. Right now, it's all good. From guns to clothing. Toiletries, all that, but not for now. Let's get the lights turned on."

"We can start with the house with those wind collectors you pointed out," Dave suggested.

"We'll need batteries and shit, too," Tony added.

"Batteries and equipment are heavy," Rich observed. "We can put all that by the front door and come back before dark with the truck."

"Sounds like a plan," Tony said.

"Yeah, works for me," I supplied. "I'd love to have more people. One for basic scavenging, one to come by the next morning with a vehicle and load up once we're done, and maybe a couple smaller long-range scout teams."

"Lots of things to consider. We ready to go?" Clara asked, just a hint of impatience in her tone.

"Yeah, move out. We'll head west to the house first, then make a plan from there," I ordered. "Let's go!"

NINETEEN

Closing the gate behind us, we set out. It still felt so damn alien. No cars moving, no people aside from us, oh, and, we just left the safety of a giant hodge podge wall surrounding a two-building apartment complex. Yeah, world's gone tits up. Boy, has it ever. But it was nice in its own way. Sure, we had death staring us in the eye everywhere we looked, but there was none of the other stuff. No work, taxes, riots or protests, no politics. Christ, I've spent so much of my life battling out politics with people online that I'd never even met, now it was all gone, and I kind of felt good about it.

Of course, it held a heavy price. So many people gone. I couldn't help but wonder about my parents. They lived in the country, the second dirt road off of the secondary road, they might be okay, but Melissa was gone. I felt a pang of grief when I struck this thought and decided to discard my internal dialogue and focus on the matter at hand.

The neighborhood looked even more alien on these nearby streets. There were the now commonplace sights of a world gone kaput, but it was made even odder to behold by the lack of any fencing or barriers. Bare lines of dirt, or the inverse, overgrown lines between properties where the fencing we appropriated had divided neighbor from neighbor. No need for privacy now, I guess. No need to worry about your dog biting a neighbor kid, or that same kid gaining access to your swimming pool. Hell, nobody even needed to mow anymore.

We moved quietly, split into two groups, one on each side of the street on the sidewalks. It reminded me of stories I'd read about wars past, soldiers moving on each side of the road, eyes shifting, looking for Krauts or Charlie or whomever we were throwing lead at that decade. I was on point in my line-up, Tony heading his formation.

We reached the end of the second block, and the end of our fencing thievery. The scene here was much more foreboding, due to the presence of so many more hiding places for pretty much anything hostile.

I stopped moving at our edge of the intersection, and motioned Dave up to me. As he approached, I whispered for him to find something heavy and breakable in a nearby trash can, and then motioned for everybody to fan out around the street and hunker down. I took a crouching position myself, waiting, and watching.

Dave returned a moment later with three empty beer bottles and took a knee next to me. On a silent three-count, we both let a couple of the bottles fly as far down the street as we could. The containers flew through the air, both striking the pavement and shattering within a dozen feet of each other. We heard nothing at first.

A few beats later, a fast fucker came running out from between two houses. No shriek, no barking, she just took off. She stood right in the center of where the bottles shattered, making motions like she was sniffing the air, but all that came out was a sickening gurgling sound. I threw the third bottle, this one landing much closer to us, and her head snapped in our direction. The freak bolted in our direction, hit the landing site of the bottle, and just stopped, looking around and gurgling as she tried to sniff again.

Nobody moved, and nobody fired. Could she not see us? She was obviously having problems scenting us, but could she not see us, either? She could detect the bottles, why not us?

I motioned for Dave to go back in line, across the street, over by Rich. As soon as he moved, the bitch zeroed in on him and shot off like a starting gun had been fired. I said as quietly as I could for all to still hear that everybody holds their fire. I didn't want to make a bunch of noise this early in our day.

She continued after Dave, now zeroed in on him like a missile. As she hit the intersection, we could make out more detail. The freak was average height, but rail-thin. Dressed in a black uniform with the logo of a nearby gas station on it, the Get-Go. She had a round face, and a thin pair of glasses that slid down her nose more with every step. And bare feet. Bare feet? Yeah, bare feet. Don't ask me, I'm just living it, I didn't write this!

Her feet slapped the pavement with every step as she drew closer, and just as she was about to fly by Tony and get to Dave, Tony stepped up. He drew out a police-style black collapsible baton, and, in one solid motion, swung it overhand directly at the thing's face. She ran, he swung, and the baton impacted the freak right square in the lower forehead. Shit, he nailed her. All conventional forward momentum ceased as her feet left the pavement, arcing up into the air as her head rushed to make friends with the street surface.

She hit, damn did she hit. A second sickening crunch echoed through the neighborhood as the back of her skull connected with the ground, followed by several more as Dave moved forward and butt-stroked her cranium a half-dozen times.

"Why didn't that one make noise?" James asked, his voice rising with every word. "Why didn't we hear it? Why didn't it scream? FUCK!!!"

We quieted James down, and all that could be heard now was Dave's panting. Rich and James stepped forward to inspect the fresh corpse.

"That explains it. Good Lord," James said softly.

"No throat," Rich observed. "No throat, no scream, no grunt, no sniff. This one's defective."

He garnered a few chuckles with this, so I added, "Yeah, must have been a smoker."

With the mood lightened, we proceeded on to our destination. Dave fished another pair of bottles out of the garbage and passed them to me and grabbed two more for himself.

We passed by several more houses, and Dave held the group up, so he could throw a bottle. Nothing came out to meet us. In fact, the street was abnormally quiet. We followed this process for the next two blocks, until we reached the house we were looking for.

The house was very average for the neighborhood. Set near the middle of its block, the only thing about it that stuck out and made it noticeable was three garbage can-sized bladed cylinders on the rooftop, and row after row of solar panels lining the rooftop. I couldn't make these out from the apartment, being blocks away from the dwelling, but man, this was good. This made the trip even more worth it, but it also meant we had much more work ahead of us.

The house itself was a basic small ranch. Pale blue in color, set back just a bit from the sidewalk with a small patch of front yard, and neatly trimmed hedges rising over a wrap-around flower bed with not a single weed in sight. A door in the middle, and a driveway up one side of the fenced-in property leading back to a single car garage. It looked…well…it looked exactly like a hundred other houses within walking distance.

"Damn," James stated, stepping up next to me. "This guy got a whole lot of power collection for one house."

"What do you mean?" I asked, looking between him and the house.

"A house this size?" he started. "Shit, he should only need a quarter of this."

"What do you think he needs the extra power for?" I asked, then ordered, "Tony, Dave, Rich, check around the building. Make sure we're alone."

The three nodded and left as James continued, "I don't know, man. Maybe a nice garage setup, but he just got the one-car."

"I guess we're about to find out," I said, as Rich came around the corner, shaking his head in the negative.

"Nothing man. We're good," Rich stated.

"Okay, cool," I replied, then another order, this time to everyone, "Clara, with me. We'll knock. James, Wayne, you two provide rear cover. The rest of you, be ready to breach it on my signal if I don't get an answer. Two teams. Us, and Tony and Dave. We go right. Fan out and clear. Keep low on your corners."

I received affirmative nods all around, and Clara and I approached the front door. I slung my shotgun forward and ready, but still on its sling over my shoulder, muzzle down.

Now at the door, Clara gave me a thumbs-up, and I knocked a few times, softly, with my knuckles. We waited several beats, and there was no answer. I pounded harder the second time, still no answer. Clara reached out and rang the doorbell. I was perplexed at the ringing noise until the reason we were here flashed in my mind; renewable energy. Of course. This house was actually not off the grid, because they had their own grid.

"Hello?" I called out. "We would like to know if you're willing to sign up to receive a lower rate on your gas bill! Hello? We have some great deals!"

Clara rolled her eyes. Okay, humor not appreciated here.

I signaled the group, took a step back, and put all of my two hundred and twenty pounds behind a solid kick just beside the doorknob. As soon as the doorframe splintered, I dropped low and moved aside. Tony was first through the door, followed by Dave. I squeezed in behind the latter, and Clara followed, tailed by the rest of the group.

The second group went left through a dining room of sorts. We were immediately in a living room. Or, a family room, if you're an oddball like my wife.

A gruesome sight greeted us. In the still glowing lamplight from an end table near the couch, we could see a corpse sprawled out. He was leaned back, as if he were relaxing with his arms out, staring at the ceiling. A dead dog, looking to have once been a pit bull, had its massive head in his lap.

There was blood everywhere, and the stench of the room was enough to be nearly visible. Flies buzzed around, three of us retched, and Clara immediately grabbed a trash can and vomited into it, adding her own aroma to the mix.

It looked as though the owner killed his dog, then, judging by the .38 revolver still clutched in his hand, took his own life. The blood spatter on the wall behind him was almost impressive in its height, reaching up to the ceiling, and still holding a few small fragments of where it started within the medium.

There was obviously nothing alive left in this room, save for the swarm of flies, and we continued onward. We poured into a hallway behind the living room, Tony kicking open a door to a microscopic master bathroom, while Clara and I breached a sparsely furnished bedroom. Nothing.

We regrouped and checked the closet at the end of the hallway. Nothing but towels and toiletries, so we opened the final door. It opened into a master bedroom, and the stench of death greeted us again.

We steeled ourselves against the horrific odor and entered the room. Tied wrists and ankles to the bed in the middle of the room was a woman about the same age as the man we already located. Her eyes oozed the bloody streams of the infected, but she did not move. There was a single darkened black hole right in the center of her forehead, and the bed coverings and mattress paid the price for the aftermath. Her white night gown was also stained with the ugly brownish hue of blood gone bad.

"Clear!" I yelled back into the house. Almost as if on cue, Rich and James came around the corner to the hallway.

"Dude, you gotta see this," Rich exclaimed, still panting from clearing their end of the house.

"Alright. Let's go. Clara, go block off the front door. No surprises," I instructed, then the rest of us followed Rich.

We made our way through a few rooms adjoining the main living area, and to a doorway with a set of stairs going down to a basement. Immediately a new, somewhat- okay, not somewhat, a very familiar scent had replaced the stench of the rest of the house. Looking down the stairs, the basement was flooded with more light than had ever seemed possible.

Moving down the steps, we met the others in a totally open basement area. The place *reeked* of marijuana. The lights were going full-bore, illuminating several rows of man-sized plants. Topping the plants, and growing throughout their sections, were buds of nearly every color imaginable. Below the plants were long handmade boxes filled with water, instead of dirt. Upon closer inspection, everything in the basement was run on mechanical timers. Each vat of water was set up with its own pumping and filtration systems, and there were even fish swimming around in the boxes. Air filtration was running to the outside with huge carbon filters set inline, each canister seemed to be made from two five-gallon buckets joined together. The walls appeared to all be double insulated, and then covered with some reflective material that seemed to be foil, but upon closer inspection it was some other material I'd never seen before.

I was astounded. This was hands-down the most impressive grow room for weed I'd ever seen in my life. The couple of dead people relaxing upstairs were absolute masterminds!

"I...well...wow" James said, stepping up next to me. "I guess now we know why they were running so much power off of the grid. Shit."

"Holy sweet fucking mother of Jesus," Tony said, stepping up next to me.

"Dude. Fuck. Dude. Wow man. Dude," came Dave's reply, apparently having run out of better words to describe the moment.

"Jesus, you guys are like a couple of kids in a candy store," Clara observed, rolling her eyes.

"Hell, even I'm impressed," I added.

"And these. Wow!" James exclaimed, motioning to a series of strange looking boxes on the wall, "Do you know what those are?"

"Expensive?" I asked, trying to use humor to take the place of ignorance.

"Yeah, they are," James explained. "Those just came out. Tesla Powerwall boxes. They can store a couple days or so of power in each one. Like a long-term capacitor for your home. They use- "

"Can we use them then?" I asked, cutting James off.

"Yeah. Sure!" James said, excited. "We can use this whole system. This is perfect!"

"Okay well we are still time crunched," I began. "James, you and Rich are coming with me. We need to get back to Henry so he can set up a work party to your specs, James, and begin converting our building. Or at least the command and storage floor."

"Okay, I know just what we need," James grinned.

"Tony, Dave," I began, feeling like I was about to tell them they'd won a prize, "six hours. Full harvest. Let's get all this dismantled and saved by then, and I'll bring the truck around. Then we can remove the power system tomorrow."

Their eyes lit up, and they high fived like high-schoolers.

"You mean," Dave began, "we can keep them?"

"Yeah dude," I answered, "what the fuck? Like y'all asking about a puppy. Yes, we keep it all. We strip this house bare and bury the owners. Show them respect for helping us so much after death. The rest of you, start clearing the first floor. Keep watch and block the door behind us when we leave."

With not a word, everybody started moving and tending to their duties. I stopped and turned back before leaving.

"Save the fish and water for last," I instructed. "Farmers use fish in water crops for parasite control and supplemental fertilizer. Dismantle the bucket filters and save what you can."

I was met with an enthusiastic nod and grin from Dave, and I walked out the front door with James and Rich trailing.

We stepped out into the light of the outdoors, and nearly as soon as we made our way down the single step near the front door, Clara closed the house up behind us. Almost as if it were planned, the sun slowly started to disappear behind a light, fluffy cloud.

Instead of following straight back down the street we'd come from, I led Rich and James across the street, where we disappeared between a house and its detached garage.

"Where we going?" James inquired.

"Couple blocks over, then back home," I explained. "No point covering the same ground twice, when we have so much to scout still."

Both guys nonverbally agreed, and we made our way through a gap in the fence along the back of the property, and into the next yard.

We made it to the second street over, and, coming to a stop near the corner of another small ranch house, we saw our second freak for the day. It was a lone male, wearing the outfit of a mailman, but I don't think he could even tell what address he was at anymore. The guy looked ragged. His uniform soiled and filthy, torn in several spots, his trademark hat was missing, and he still wore one of two earbuds to a pair of headphones that were no longer plugged into anything.

Rich was the first to move. He slowly pulled his long hunting knife and started to step forward. I caught him just before he broke cover, motioning to a couple of houses down the street in response to his inquisitive expression. We only had a moment to wait before three freaks appeared in a driveway, walking casually down the slight slope of the pavement towards the street as if they belonged there. A moment later, two more crept out of the open front door of a house, stepped onto the lawn, turned, and disappeared along the side of the house, only to return a moment later, the female in the lead sniffing the air in several directions. She meandered a moment, went back to sniffing, and darted back into the house with the other following. She appeared just a second later, standing pressed against the door frame, and began issuing a few of those barking coughs before going back inside.

"What the fuck are they doing?" James asked, his voice low and very shaky.

"I...I don't know man," I replied, my eyes never leaving the scene.

"They look like they're hunting," James opined.

No sooner had he said that, then Rich tapped my shoulder, pointing to the house with the female freak on the first floor.

"Yeah," I replied, "I've been watching her."

"No," Rich said back and pointed again.

I followed the path of his finger, and realized he was pointing up, not across. In the very same house with the freaks inside was a woman. She appeared to be middle aged, and as soon as she knew we saw her, she began motioning frantically. Mouthing what I could only interpret as 'Help me!' again and again as she waved her arms. Then it all happened so damn quickly. So quickly.

Her movements caught a lamp on a stand next to her. The lamp fell, her face fell, I stared, James gasped, and Rich cursed quietly, all at the exact same time.

In the near silence of the street scene, the lamp was like thunder crashing as it hit the floor and broke. Even through the closed window and from across the street, it sounded unreasonably loud. The infected hunting party never missed a beat. In the time it would take you to snap your fingers, their numbers doubled, mostly fresher runners, some slow guys and gals. The fast ones hit the front doorframe, wedged each other for a moment, and began flooding the house like water breaking through a breached submarine.

The woman's shrieks and screams mixed in with those of the infected as her motions became more frantic. She started fighting with the window, which was apparently locked, as she stole glances over her shoulders.

I pushed James and Rich back a step and motioned to the pavement in front of me.

"Bleach the ground. Do it now!" I ordered in a loud whisper.

"But, we gotta help, man! We gotta!" James began to wail.

"We can't fucking help them all, dude, there's over a dozen of them, three of us. We can't do a fucking thing! Move!" I ordered as the last trickles of bleach left Rich's jug. I motioned for them to fall back to the fence between the yards as I fumbled with my backpack to retrieve my jug of ammonia.

Twisting off my cap, I watched the scene unfold in front of me. The woman's actions were beyond panicked, miles past frantic as she beat the window keeping her from safety. I wanted so badly to just put a bullet in her, at least save her the pain of their attack, but we had to keep the attention off of us.

I started to pour the chemicals into Rich's puddle on the ground as a resounding crash of splintering wood resounded from the house. No sooner had the sound ended, it was followed by one solo freak screech, and a moment later, the window exploded outward. The woman exited the house like a mangled Superman with a monstrosity belonging to the devil himself wrapped tightly around her. Her scream was short lived, stopping as she impacted the ground, only to pick up again as the infected fuck helping her fly found its feet and began dragging her toward the back yard of the house by her hair, moving way too fast, considering he had the weight of an adult human dragging him down.

In the time it took to empty my jug on the driveway, she'd hit the ground and disappeared with her captor, no trace, save for a thin blood trail and a heavy sound signature as she screamed in pure terror. A trail of freaks followed the scene, around the house and out of sight.

It was about this time I decided the bleach and ammonia would do their own thing without my supervision, and I spun to run back to the others.

We had just crested the fence as a trio when the sound of several bones twisting and snapping at once echoed through the neighborhood like a series of small caliber gunshots, and the screams silenced immediately.

We ran. Ho-Lee-SHIT we ran.

We left the area so fast, we were several blocks away, and at the road nearest the apartment buildings in what seemed to be just a blink.

James reached the gate first, and upon seeing and hearing us, Henry made his way over from his work party and released the locks to allow us entry. All three panting and gasping for breath, I slid back against the interior of our now amazingly beautiful protective fencing and let my feet out from under me. The other two did the same, Henry buzzing around us like an upset mother, rapid firing questions.

I finally got a grip on my breathing enough to grab a couple of gulps of water from my water bottle and relayed the story to him. Rich and James interjected their own bits here and there, and in no time, Henry was all caught up to speed as he peered thoughtfully through the chain link roller gate.

"And this was where?" he asked, wonder in his voice.

"Maybe a half dozen blocks that way," Rich said, "they're smarter than we gave them credit, too. Most of them were hiding, waiting."

"Yeah," I interjected, noticing Jennifer as she came out from the front doors of the north building. "We need a better plan for scouting. We also still have to pick up the other six people and all that they are scavenging from the house."

"So, the others are safe?" Henry asked.

"As far as I know," I replied. "Lot of shit at that house. Going to take the truck, the trailer, and maybe two trips."

"Oh no," Henry started, "you know me, brother, we'll get it good and get it right."

"Yeah, true, but right this moment," I said, motioning to my approaching wife, "I've got another issue to worry about."

All at once, everybody turned to see Jennifer making her way across the parking lot. She didn't look happy, her face was more a mixture of worry and a touch of anger. With each step, her thick thighs and wide hips moved in a way that always reminded me of why I fell for her in the first place. By the time that thought had strolled across my mind, she had reached my position.

"What the hell happened?" she challenged. "And where is everybody else? Are they okay?"

"They're fine," I replied. "They're back at the house, stripping it. We needed to call for the truck, so we scouted a few blocks over and back to here."

I then related the events of the day thus far to her, and she listened intently, and though I could see the anger and worry beginning to fade, it hadn't dissipated entirely.

"You guys still shouldn't have split up," she scolded. "It's clearly not safe. You could have gotten killed!"

"Yeah, I know," I replied somberly, "but there was no better option. We need to get power restored here, and there was simply way too much equipment there to leave and come back for. We needed the majority of the party to stay put behind closed doors and on the rooftop to strip as much as we could as quickly as possible."

"I still don't like it," she replied.

"Yeah, well, it's the end of the world," I said with a soft chuckle, "there's going to be a whole lot of things you don't like. I don't like it, either, but I've got to do what I've got to do. Anyway, Henry, this is where you come in. What's the progress on the wall?"

"Wall's done my friend." He grinned, "We just been messing around in the garage, got that most the way done, too."

"Cool. I'll check that out in a minute," I replied, then explained, "Take some time to button it up, though. Then you're going to lead a crew with the truck and trailer, plus two lighter vehicles to get the people and equipment from that house. Make sure you have room to bring the other six back with you inside the cars."

"Alright, I got you." Henry nodded.

"Be damned careful though," I warned. "Those fuckers are a lot closer to the site than I feel comfortable with. Be quick, but be quiet, and stay safe. A guard to each person type of safe. You feel me?"

"Yes sir I do," he replied.

"Alright, let's go check out this garage of yours," I replied, and we began walking that way, Rich and James following.

We walked past the pool along the driveway dividing the two large apartment buildings. I noticed that the fencing from that had been removed, too, and made a mental note to enquire about it. I didn't want to seem imposing, but I also wanted to have a log and track of every scrap of everything. Nothing could go to waste now, and each trip into the shell of the world that used to be reinforced that.

Henry led the way, talking excitedly about everything that had been done, and things he wanted to set up, but I barely heard it. I was lost in my own world, thinking about what we needed, what we could do, and, possibly most importantly, what the hell were we doing anyway? Could we continue living like this? Would it get better? Worse? Everybody seemed happy, but how much of that was true, and how much of it was just veneer? Does it matter, anyway? As long as we still survive, anyway. Afterall, that's what humans were best at. That's one of the military's most cherished mantras. Adapt, Overcome. We got this. We'll have this. We'll beat it all. At least I don't have to work for anyone else any more.

Nah, scratch that. These people are now my employers, each and every one of them. I work for them. We work for us. I've just got to make sure we all keep tracking that point. Make sure we all stay in this together, and help each person grow into their new shoes.

Henry led us down the gradient of concrete that disappeared into the relative darkness. Somebody had set up a couple of mirrors to reflect some light, and the low beams of a number of cars blazed in an effort to do their best to slap back the darkness.

The garage was long and low, and allowed for three rows of parking, left, right, and center. Henry had the center row completely cleared out.

"We keepin' those, they'll be useful," he said, motioning to the right side, where a row of small and large pickup trucks sat among a small herd of hybrids and minivans, with a couple of full-time electric cars mixed in.

"Those are for scavenging what we can and using the rest to push up against the walls and give them strength," he continued, as he motioned to the left side, where a row of basic vehicles sat. Everything from an older Ford Taurus to a newer PT Cruiser sat there. Honda Civics, an older Gran Marquis, and various nondescript Toyotas and Kia's sat along this side. Even, heartbreakingly to me, a newer two-door BMW. Damn those were handsome cars, too bad it was now labelled as 'useless'.

Near the back of the garage, nearly hidden in a corner by the shadows of the garage, was a long low shape hidden by a vinyl car tarp. Now what does he have here?

"Henry?" I asked, motioning to the form.

He grinned ear to ear, like a damned child.

"Oh that?" he asked, still grinning. "That's my new baby. Somebody done left me a real sweet girl. All original, convertible, and just my shade of red."

"What is it, man?" I asked, growing only slightly impatient.

"1967 Cadillac Coupe Deville. Convertible." He beamed.

I don't know to this day if I groaned vocally, or inwardly, but it was there. Henry is a damn good man, damn reliable, damn smart, but he had his own… character. We'll call it character.

"But, as I was saying before," he began, continuing the conversation that I hadn't heard, "we need tools down here. All kinds. Maintenance done left me a good start, but you can never have enough. Fluids of all kinds, too. Oils, tranny and brake fluid, any fuel you can find. Matter of fact, my dear friend, if anyone here comes across some work trucks…"

"Like those pickups you have right there?" I inquired.

"Oh, no," he corrected. "Work truck work trucks. Roadside repair, construction rigs, even railroad maintenance. They got generators, welders, tool sets, auxiliary fuel tanks, the works. They'd be perfect for our cause."

"Alright, yeah," I agreed, his enthusiasm seeping into my own soul. "Yeah man we can look around for those. We'll see about getting you some real lighting down here, too. See if we can't find you your own solar and wind setup. That house can't be the only one running something like that in this city."

Once again, like he was describing his 'new' Caddy, he beamed. This was one happy man.

"Thank you! Thank you so much," he exclaimed, clapping me on the back, then, "We'll get things wrapped up here and get ready to head to that house. Same one we been looking at?"

"One and the same, dude," I told him. "Remember, be safe. I'm going up to see how the ladies have been doing on the indoors side of things."

Now it was Jennifer's turn to exude pure pride at what they'd accomplished.

"I think we did good." She smiled.

"Let's go look." I returned the grin, and, putting my hand in hers, walked up the ramp and back out into the sunlight, blinking as my eyes came into focus from the now brilliant sunlight.

We crossed the driveway, and up onto the sidewalk. In through the still ruined front entrance, we made our way to the stairwell at the end of the long hallway. Jennifer, same as Henry, was talking about all they had accomplished, and, just the same as with him, I found my way back into my own thoughts. Thankfully, I was thinking smaller than the whole picture.

We needed things for Henry, a good motor pool and happy mechanic could make or break our survival, especially when it comes to scavenging once the cold weather gets here. This is Ohio, after all. We can hover around one hundred degrees in the summer and drop down to well below negative zero in the winter. It can get downright nasty, and I for one am not in the least interested in going on runs on foot throughout the entire season.

Jesus. Halfway up the stairs and I was already breathing heavy. Nine floors. Looks like it may be a good thing that cigars and cigarettes aren't going to be manufactured any more.

We reached the top of the final flight of stairs, and through the doorway to the ninth floor.

Immediately the smell of dust and plaster assailed my sinuses, forcing out a sneeze.

"Yeah, sorry," Jennifer said apologetically. "We're still cleaning up from the work we did today."

"Oh, that's cool," I replied, "let's go check it out!"

She led me down the hallway toward the central apartments, then, through the doorway.

I was astounded at the amount of work they had already completed. I mean, it was as rough as a hangover, but, for the small amount of time they were on the job, they still did a lot. The wall between two apartments had been knocked out, making one large area with the space of the two living rooms that were now attached. Blackout curtains had been hung, then tucked up high to leave daylight to work by. A full wall had been layered with plywood and plastered with various flat screen TV's from the other apartments, as well as a couple of nice-looking desktop computers. Office desks had been arrayed in front of the monitors to make work stations, with a couple of filing cabinets separating them.

Another couple of tables had been arranged in the middle of the room, and on them lay an assortment of digital cameras, sign out sheets, and a bin with a number of various SD cards and batteries inside.

Just then, Rob approached. He ran a hand through his dark hair and eyed the equipment.

"You know, we found the entire complex to have security cameras," he began.

"Yeah?" I replied, what was he getting at? Did they catch something?

"I can use the hard drive they feed to and wire up more," he explained, "then we can wire them through these TV sets and set this up as a security room when we get the power ran. Well, I can, at least, with some help."

"Oh, shit that's right," I said, as it dawned on me, "computer guy. Man, we're going to love you up here."

Rob smiled wanly and nodded his head, "Anything I can do to help, sir."

"Don't call me sir, dude," I said as pleasantly as I could. "I've kind of been shunted into this role, I'm just floating along and trying to do the best I can."

"I think you're doing great," Rob said, smiling again. Is he kissing my ass or just socially ungainly?

"Thanks, Rob," I said, smiling again, then, to the small group gathered around, "I'm going to drop down a floor and see what's going on with our supply floor. Y'all are doing great here, keep it up."

I left before I could receive any more awkward praise. Don't get me wrong, I appreciate it, but I still don't want the damned role of leader, or mayor, or governor or whatever they think I am. I'll accept it, I guess, but it just doesn't seem right to me. I guess, it kind of makes me uncomfortable.

Forgetting all that, I walked down one flight of stairs to the eighth floor. As I crossed the threshold from the stairs to the hallway, I was met with a much different sight, though the same sinus killing scents filled the air. Right near the entrance to the stairwell, both apartment doors at that end of the hallway had been blocked off and shut by plywood sheeting that was screwed into the door frames. Maybe a half-dozen feet down from that, a steel office desk spanned most of the width of the hall. On it was a neatly sorted stack of papers, and a bin labeled 'In' and 'Out' with little hearts and smiley faces drawn by the words.

I made my way past the narrow walkway left by the desk and moved further down the hallway, and my movements were quickly halted by footsteps and a voice.

"Rob did you-Oh!" Bri exclaimed as she realized who had invaded her area. "Hi Scott! Come to see the progress?"

"Yeah I figured I'd make my rounds now that I'm back for now," I replied.

"Did they have any issues getting the equipment?" she asked.

I shrugged, "Don't know. We came back early and left a good chunk of the crew there to finish up. Henry should be going to get them with the truck soon. Let's see what you've got here while I wait."

Bri showed me around the floor, pointing things out in part like a tour guide, part like an overly excited home and garden show host exhibiting all the things they'd done while the home owner was 'away'. Both sides of the hallway showed bathrooms ripped bare. There were also rough doorways cut between apartments, allowing free access amongst the goods, which were already being slowly slotted away in an order that, I'm sure, only Bri could find the rhyme and reason for.

The door at the far end of the hallway had been blocked, covered with plywood, and reinforced, leaving only one way into and out of the floor. Christ, they were setting it up like a bank!

Before Bri had any further time to explain, Jennifer found us.

"You two about done?" she asked. "Shannon's down on Floor Two with the rest of the work crew now."

"Christ, do I want to know?" I said with a laugh.

"Actually," Jennifer began, "she's got some pretty good ideas going on. Come on!"

"You guys have fun!" Bri called after us as I was led to the stairs again.

The damned stairs. Okay, we were going down this time, but I'm deciding on quitting smoking. It's happening, especially in a world with no elevators.

We made it to Floor Two, and it was a beehive of activity. Shannon had managed to sequester pretty much anybody that wasn't already working upstairs or out with Henry in the garage. People were moving in all directions, some carrying things, others on their way to move more things around, some cutting through walls and a couple making marks in chalk lines on the carpet.

"What the hell?" I asked, amazed at all the movement.

As if on cue, Shannon appeared, grabbing me and Jennifer by the arms and leading us to a quiet corner.

"Okay, first," she began, "sorry I didn't run all this by you first, but you've got to hear it, then yell at me if you think you want to. But, I think you'll be okay with this. Maybe. I don't know, but-"

"Shannon!" I cut her off, this girl was like a squirrel, moving a million miles a second. "Just chill, breathe, and give me the details. One thing at a time."

"Okay, okay," she replied, taking in a breath, then, "we are making the second floor an intake for new members. A waiting room in the first apartment on the right, and an exam room in the first one on the left. Since there's going to be three of us in medicine-"

"Three?" I cut her off again.

"Well, yeah, I've got some background, Ashley, and, well..." and she motioned to Jennifer, who added her own information.

"I'm, well, they found some medical journals and textbooks," she began, "and I'm going to learn on the fly. I can at least assist them, and they're learning more advanced medicine than they already know, like emergency care and stuff."

"Oh, uhhhh okay then," I said uncertainly, unsure of how to respond. "Okay Shannon, let's hear the rest."

She beamed. I had the feeling she exhibited both pride, and relief that she wasn't getting chewed out in that smile. Am I really that bad? Maybe she's just being cautious, just in case I am, I thought.

"Okay, where was I?" Shannon asked to nobody in particular. "Oh! Right, okay! Waiting room and exam. And the rest of the space we are breaking into smaller rooms, making the walls double thick, strong doors, and using them for quarantine."

I eyed her questioningly.

"You know," she recovered, "in case anyone is sick with something bad, like the flu, or we think they might turn."

"Makes sense," I replied. "Maybe give the first floor the same treatment when you guys are done, but with stronger walls and doors. We could turn them into security rooms in case we have any major issues with anyone."

"Like a jail?" Jennifer asked.

"Who's going to jail?" Henry asked, his concerned expression showing as he approached.

"Nobody hopefully," I replied with a laugh. "What's up, boss, you making good progress out there?"

"Oh, brother we done for the day," he advised. "I was coming to tell you that we are going out with the truck to get the electrical things. I found a flare gun in one of the vehicles, we'll signal if we need help."

"Sounds good man," I said. "Be careful, be quick. Remember, half on security, half on work. When you come back, we'll have another town meeting. I've got some ideas regarding those things out there we should all discuss."

A town meeting. Town. Now that's an interesting thought.

"Okay, take care brother," Henry said as he turned to leave.

"Yeah, you too man," I replied, then turned back to the ladies. "Yeah, like a jail, kind of. Maybe even a place to restrain some infected, in case y'all feel adventurous enough to do some testing sometime."

Jennifer looked appalled, like I was insane for even mentioning it. Shannon, on the other hand, replied with mild enthusiasm and curiosity.

"That might actually be very helpful! Good thinking! Anyway, we've got more plans here," she continued as Jennifer began mulling over things in her head. "I want to turn the whole third floor into a miniature hospital. We could do one room as a basic exam room, another with beds for major work, like surgery or severe injuries. The rest can be long term recovery rooms, and one apartment barred off and locked up tight for storage of anything medical."

"Sounds good to me, really," I encouraged her. "Anything you need, write it down, give it to Bri. She's officially in charge of all of our supply handling, she can pass the message on to where it needs to go and make sure anyone who goes to scavenge will keep their eyes open."

"Okay!" she replied, that damn smile shining brightly. "Thanks, Scott!"

"Yup," I replied in kind. "Now, we're going to go to the south building to check on Carolyn and the kids, and get Gwen to come home for some food."

"Awe she's such a cutie," Shannon replied, "see you later!"

Jennifer and I departed, went down to the first floor and out into the bright sun and early summer warmth. It had turned into a very pleasant day, weather wise. In all the hustle of everything going on inside, I had nearly pushed the earlier events out of my mind.

We approached the south building in silence, Jennifer still mulling things over regarding work in the north building, myself thinking over the mess of infected so close to home. We entered the main doors and went straight to the second floor. Nobody used the first floor, not after we got trapped by those things in a hallway full of places for them to flank us. We had become as apes, everyone feeling safer the further from ground level they could get. I don't blame them. I kind of did, too, and for that reason I was happy our apartment was the only one on the top floor by the security center.

We made our way into the second floor hallway, where Carolyn had every child in the compound under age 10 running and laughing as they sprinted the length of the space.

Little Gwen ran part way down and stopped to turn as if to remember what she was doing, and spotted her mother and I. So, she instead made a beeline right for us. Jennifer held her arms out, Gwen let out a loud "DA!" and latched onto my legs. Seeing the jealousy in Jennifer's eyes, I picked Gwen up and handed her to my wife.

"You are taking her?" Carolyn asked, smiling at Gwen.

"Yeah, I'm due for a break, Jennifer's got her covered for the rest of the day. She's been no trouble?"

"No! No no she's great for me!" Carolyn replied. "I just wish we had more for them to do. I have them run around, I'd try hide and seek but the little ones just don't understand."

"Get a list, bring it up to supply, we'll put in the request through Bri," I said, then realizing, "Actually, Bri is going to have a ton to do, and lots to track. Maybe, if you're not watching kids and have nothing to cover, see if she needs a hand with things? I'm sure she'd appreciate it."

"Yeah, okay!" Carolyn agreed. "I would like to help, and get to know more people."

"Well, there you go!" I smiled encouragingly. "Alright Carolyn, you're doing great, and, thank you. We're off again!"

"Okay!" she said cheerily. "See you!"

We left, and made our way towards our building again, when Jennifer stopped with Gwen.

"It's a nice day out," she smiled, setting the little girl down. "I'm going to let her run off some more energy out here. You going up for lunch?"

"Yeah," I confirmed. "Yeah I think I'll scavenge something up."

"Okay," she said, giving me a kiss. "Love you. We'll be up later."

"Love you too," I said, returning the kiss, and turned to walk away.

TWENTY

Back upstairs, once again breathing heavy from more stairs than I was accustomed to, I disappeared into our apartment, closing the door behind me once I was sure it had nobody inside. Time for some peace and quiet.

I grabbed a cigar from my small humidor. I wasn't about to leave the house without my full supply of cheap Dominicans. Shoving the cigar, a cutter, and my torch lighter in my pocket, I moved to the back bedroom. After rummaging in one of the boxes we had stashed under the bed, I found what I was looking for. The prize of all prizes. My personal treat to…well, to myself.

Menu Number Ten MRE. Chili Mac. Hey, unless you've tried it, you have no idea what kind of wonderful things one of these compact light brown vacuum bags can give you, especially if you're hungry and finer dining isn't an option. A hot, usually tasty meal so long as you have ten minutes and a bottle of water. Just don't eat too many of these for too many days in a row if you like your digestive system.

Don't ask.

Just trust me.

I shoved the food bag under my arm and refilled my cup with the last of the cold brewed coffee and grabbed two bottles of water from the kitchen cabinet.

Moving through the sliding door of the apartment and onto the balcony, and, thankful there was no wind at the moment, I found a deck chair and cringed as it creaked when my weight rested on it.

Now for the surprise. Okay, look, what is on the front of the MRE is guaranteed. What else in there is not, aside from a bag with a heavy green plastic spoon, salt, pepper, toilet paper, and a chemical heater for your main course and coffee.

I pulled out the main course and grabbed the chemical heater. Adding water to the line on the heater, I slid it and the food pouch into the cardboard sleeve and leaned them at an angle against the bottom of the balcony railing. The instructions, very specific, state to lean it "against a rock or something". So, this is my 'or something', I guess.

Digging through the bag, I realized I'd grabbed the king's feast of all Meal-Ready-Eat packages. A bag of Skittles dated only eight years ago. A pack of plain dry crackers. And the real treats; a vacuum bag with a small slab of marble cake, a pack of Jalapeno cheese spread, and a resealable bag of French Vanilla Cappuccino powder. Nice! Today was a good day.

After organizing my haul in front of me, I checked and found the main course to be warm, and ready to eat, so I added some water to the coffee mix and replaced the main course with that to let it heat up. Hot coffee coming soon. Only guy in town with any, I was sure.

I poured the contents of a pack labeled 'hot pepper seasoning' into the bag of chili mac, mixed it around, and let my mind wander as I took the first bite.

I began thinking about Melissa, growing numb as I did. She was only my stepdaughter, but I loved her as my own. The wound from losing her so brutally was way too fresh. I'd stayed as busy as I could to avoid thinking about her, though I could never be sure if Jennifer found the same success in her endeavors to do the same. My wife seemed so different after Melissa passed, but she never talked about it.

Thankfully, thoughts of Melissa turned towards happy memories this time, as opposed to the sadness that had been causing me to fall asleep nearly every night with a single tear streaking away to make friends with my pillow.

I thought back to Christmas time. My parents lived in Kansas City, but they'd make the journey out here to Ohio every Christmas. That was one holiday us Pfeiffer's ritualistically spent together at all costs.

We never had much until I got into my recently lost career of hauling freight around my portion of the United States. Then the money started coming in, and we always laughed inwardly as my mother and father would scold us for going overboard. We'd tell them every time, looking at the pile of gifts that would, some years, all but hide our six-foot-tall plastic tree, that we'd always felt bad. We never had much and struggled to give even a little while we received and received. Now, it was our turn.

The older I'd get, the less I'd care about getting as opposed to giving. I was overjoyed to see the smiles on my family members' faces as they opened perfect gift after perfect gift. I was a Thanksgiving giver, meaning, I'd give until the whole family was too stuffed with goodness to move. I lived for it.

It was also the only time of the year we ever actually decorated the house. Inside and out, decorations and lights everywhere. Each thing meticulously positioned to compliment the next, but never overdone. Unfortunately, we never had a fireplace to finish the effect. So, instead, we'd put Fireplace on Demand on our 65-inch TV and accept that it was as good as it gets.

Damn I missed my big screen now.

As I continued thinking about the wife, kids, and my parents smiling happily, laughing at gag gifts, and just all around carrying on in joyous fashion, I pushed the last bite of my meal, the marble cake, into my mouth. I leaned back, snipped the shoulder of my cigar, and just as I touched the flame of the lighter to it, I heard a gunshot off in the distance.

I finished lighting the stick of tobacco and heard a few more rifle pops. No sooner had I turned my head to try to track their location, I heard another softer pop and watched as the glowing red visage of a flare rose up into the air in a lazy arc. Then the general area of our scavenging party erupted into bursts and pops of gunfire as I heard the sound of the truck's engine racing. I stood up and could just make out the shapes, blocks away, of a few vehicles rushing our way, picking up speed as they approached.

"Trouble!" I shouted down to the small groups in the courtyard. "Fuck! Get the kids inside, get guns, and for fuck's sake, open the gate!"

People began rushing around in every direction as a couple made their way to the gate and began sliding it open on its rollers.

I threw my cigar down and bolted through the open door, grabbing my pump shotgun off the kitchen table as I ran by, then down the hallway to take the stairs two and three at a time on my way down to the ground floor. Rounding the corner of the doorway and down the hall as fast as my feet could carry me, I took one final left, and exited the building just as a pale blue Toyota Prius came barreling nearly sideways through the open gate, breaking right to allow its passengers to disgorge from the vehicle as Dave provided the others cover, sitting on the sill of his car window and firing bursts from the AK-47 over the roof.

Next came the truck and trailer, Chris and Carla hanging precariously onto the loading ramp as they fired behind them, their pursuers finally coming into view as I ran toward the scene.

It was definitely the horde from earlier that day, the worn and tattered mailman leading the way, twisting and plowing the street with his face as a burst from Dave's rifle shredded his chest and neck, a couple of the rounds punching through to slam into the runner behind him. Fuck they were thick, there was easily 40 runners coming into view as the truck blew through the open space between gate and wall, the trailer weaving and swaying precariously, nearly dumping its passengers to the ground.

The third and final vehicle made its approach, another Prius, this one maroon in color. At the last second, it weaved into a Scandinavian flick and slide dead sideways, hitting the gate and wall and creating a blockage for the runners as the driver's door was flung open and Tony came scrambling out, loosing shots over his shoulder as the passenger window exploded inward when a freak dove headlong into the glass. That infected fell on impact, but the gap allowed another to dive through, and it fought for purchase frantically as Tony stumbled out an escape from the vehicle.

I approached just as the runner burst from the driver's side of the vehicle. It stopped long enough to arch its back, palms out, face to the sky, and let out a horrendous shriek of rage and hunger.

"DUCK!" I screamed at Tony.

He hit the ground without a thought, and, as the freak dropped to all fours behind him, I dumped a full load of three-inch double-ought buckshot, peppering the monstrosity across the face and shoulders. The force of the impact jerked it back as pellets ripped through and into the hybrid that birthed it, spraying blood and tissue like confetti from a T-shirt cannon. I worked the pump and launched another load of death through the car's interior as another freak fell, blocking their way through the vehicle.

Everybody else present opened fire as monsters began impacting the gate and wall at a dead run, each hit shaking the structures violently.

"CLOSE THE GATE! CLOSE THE FUCKING GATE!!!" I bellowed over the charge of withering gunfire as more hell spawn was shredded by lead and copper from the assortment of weapons present.

Several people grabbed the gate and rammed it home, Dave joining and driving the locking bars into place right before he fed the Russian rifle another magazine and let out a long burst into the last 15 infected around, the others joining him, and myself as well, as my shotgun dug in with every blast, surely leaving lasting bruises in the meat of my shoulder.

Within moments the last few enemies fell in showers of gore as each one that dropped brought more guns to sight in on whoever was left. Then I began to take charge of the aftermath.

"Is everyone here? Anyone hurt?" I asked around to a concert of wide-eyed people. What I heard next made my heart sink nearly to my knees.

"Wayne?" Clara shouted. "Has anybody seen Wayne?"

"Shit," I muttered, then I also shouted, "Wayne! You here? You good?"

To my relief, I felt a presence approaching behind me, and heard Wayne's voice asking me why I was yelling, he's right here. Okay, cool, one crisis averted. Next thing's next, don't let anyone focus on the drama lest they lose themselves over what just happened.

"Alright people, everyone accounted for?" I asked, and was met by weary nods all around. "Good. James!"

"Yeah boss," James responded, stepping forward.

"You're my finish foreman," I instructed. "Everything off the truck and to the roof that you need. Any other supplies, take them to Bri. Everything in its place. I need that car off the gate, take it to the garage for Henry to deal with, leave the dead infected outside the gate, we'll clean them up once the outside is secure tomorrow. Got me?"

James nodded vigorously, then, to the group gathered around, "Alright people, you heard him, let's go!"

"I need all of the good bullet casings gathered in buckets," Wayne began explaining to them, "we'll take them and the reloading equipment to Rich's room."

I heard Rich question Wayne, "Reloading equipment?"

"Yessir," Wayne replied. "Place was a good haul. Just you wait."

"Alright," I began. "Henry, Tony, Dave, ninth floor. Now, guys."

"What about the plants?" Dave and Tony asked, nearly in unison.

"Fuck them for now guys," I admonished, "they'll go to Bri to ration out, just like everyone else will be rationed things."

They reluctantly resigned themselves to this, and made their way inside with Henry. I then motioned Jennifer over.

"They're going to have to open the gate back up to get that car," I explained. "Get the kids inside with Carolyn where it's safe, keep them calm and help her out.

"Okay," Jennifer said, giving me a kiss and departing.

"Shannon! Ashley!" I yelled over to the pair, who both approached.

"Check everybody out," I ordered. "Treat every cut as an infection ready to happen. If nobody needs to be patched up, then help the cleanup crew."

They both nodded and accepted their directive and got to work as I spun and moved inside the building to follow my crew leaders upstairs.

Joining my three buddies in the command room, I gave them a moment to marvel at the progress, then interrupted their banter.

"Okay," I began. "What the fuck happened out there?"

"Uhhh we were attacked?" Tony said.

"Yeah no shit," I retorted. "But why? How?"

"One of them things found us," Dave began, "from the south. I snuck him with a knife, but others saw and called more to them."

"Yeah," I concurred, "that seems to be how they work. Apparently, these things are smarter than Hollywood ever let us believe."

"We got almost everything, though," Tony reassured me.

"What's almost?" I asked.

"Like," he started, "everything we came for, plus a whole lot more. We pretty much only left clothes and bed linens, we were about to load those up when we got hit."

Almost as if on cue, James passed our doorway leading a convoy of people carrying solar panels in pairs. I crossed the room and shut the door, nodding to the passing work crew as they made their way to the roof access.

"Anything good, besides electricity?" I asked.

"We got these," Tony said, unzipping his rucksack and producing one two-way radio after another, to a count of six, then adding, "I checked them out. Range of ten miles, channel lock, they had fresh battery packs and spare packs on a row of chargers."

"Those will come in handy, because I've got a plan for the morning," I advised. "We're going to make our streets a bit safer before any crews go out, and we're going to do it every morning."

"We also found some shit that you'll really like. Like, a lot, dude," Dave said, a grin spreading across his face.

"Yeah?" I replied. "Shoot."

"Ex-fuckin-zactly, man!" Tony exclaimed. "Reloading gear, powder, ammo casings, primer, they had a nice ass setup and a fuck ton of guns in a big cabinet in one of the back rooms."

"No shit?" I said, barely able to contain my excitement.

"Yeah man, these people had some strange shit," Dave picked up where Tony left off, "gas masks, guns and gear, military equipment, whole bunch of stuff. Even some weird posters about Rhodesia on the wall, and a badass computer setup. They were loaded, man. We left the furry costume we found though."

"Yeah, good thinking," I chuckled, "don't know where that thing's been."

So, the in-town pot farmers turned out to be probably the best place to hit in the neighborhood. Good, maybe we could take it easy for now with the scouting parties. I doubted it, but it was a nice, placating thought to hold onto for now, considering the closest friends I had left on this planet were just chased by death itself.

"Alright guys, good shit," I congratulated. "Henry, make sure the work crews are in order and everyone is pulling their weight, even Katie's big ass. Dave and Tony, go around and inform everyone that we are having a meeting after dinner tonight. Everyone shows up, we've got stuff to do. And it's time we assign some solid positions for people to hold down, for anyone that doesn't have one, or is unclear of who does what around here."

They all nodded, confirmed, and left the room. I began walking around the new command center, admiring the work that the crew, my crew, had done. I didn't want the role of leadership, but having a good percentage of the crew here as reliable and hard-working as they were, I was feeling better about it every time I looked around at our progress. We had a good thing going here. Every single day that passed, in one way or another, this was becoming a better place to call home.

I passed through the balcony door and leaned over to watch, people moved about all over, even a couple of the older kids. Everybody was working together, except for two. I watched as Katie and Parker stood sideline, leaned in toward one another and talking in what appeared to be hushed tones. That is, until Henry appeared, marching straight toward them from the front of the building. I couldn't quite make out what he was saying from my vantage, but I could distinguish the tone, and just imagine what he was barking at the pair. They immediately went to the bed of the truck and began carrying armloads of stuff into the building. Henry paused, looked around a bit, looked right up at me, and issued a thumbs-up and a big grin before grabbing his own armload of things and disappearing toward his garage with the items.

I heard James pass by with another crew in the hallway and decided to follow them up and see what they were up to.

Making a left out of my office, and passing my own apartment on the way, I climbed the single flight of stairs and stepped out into the clear, unfiltered sunshine bouncing off of the off-white apartment roof. James and his crew were moving along quite well. One side of the flat roof was already lined with solar panels, all arrayed with their mounts and coils of wire set up at regular intervals, laid out like a living instruction manual and ready to be worked on. As I watched them set down the last of their loads and listened as James directed each item to where it belonged, they stopped.

"Okay people," James barked. "Five-minute rest, then we should only have one more load to the rooftop."

He looked my way from the other end of the roof and smiled, then waved, but didn't have time to approach or start conversation before Bri found me.

"There you are!" she said, smiling. "Hey, uhm, the people whose house it was, I don't know, some of the guys are calling them the Rhodesians, but, anyway-"

"What's up, Bri?" I asked, hoping to break her up enough so she could regain her thought process.

"Right," she continued, "they had a bunch of food in their freezers, some of it was freezer burnt, but there was still a lot of ground beef and a whole bunch of chicken tenders. The problem is, we have no way to keep it, and James doesn't know when we will have enough power to run my chest freezers. What do we do?"

"Well," I replied, "I hate to let good food go to waste, so, let's not do that. Have the ladies get the grills ready, and we'll cook it all up. We'll feast tonight. Everyone's working hard as hell today anyway, I'm sure they can use the calories and protein."

"Okay!" she said cheerfully. "I'll see what they suggest! Thanks!"

She left in a rush before I could get another word out. I chuckled to myself, and turned to head back downstairs, intent on retrieving the cigar that I never got to smoke.

I was met with disappointment in that area, as all that was left of my Cheap Bastard cigar was a black mark and some ash where I'd dropped it. Apparently, it rolled off the balcony at some point. Great. Not like I really needed the thing anyway, but it made a nice way to relax.

I instead plopped down in my deck chair, took a swig of the coffee I'd had left behind, and promptly fell asleep with the mug still in my hand. I know, it sounds counter-intuitive. Drink coffee, fall asleep, but it's not uncommon for me. The coffee is a luxury, but the caffeine does little. My wife has picked on me many times in the past for falling asleep sitting up with an empty energy drink can still grasped in my hand.

TWENTY-ONE

I was awoken some time later by a nudge to my arm, and Jennifer's voice.

"Hey," she chided. "Everyone else is hard at work, and I find our fearless leader passed out in a deck chair on the balcony. Come on hero, dinner's ready, everyone is heading up to eat outside again."

I groaned, then grunted a response as I stretched and she scooped Gwen up to head upstairs. I heard Shannon and Ashley say something and the three of them laughed, presumably at my expense.

Making my way onto the balcony, I was greeted by a cacophony of scents. I could smell chicken, beef, what smelled like beef stroganoff, and an undertone of B.O. from a herd of hard-working people who didn't have access to clean showers. We'll have to find a way to remedy that. Personally, I'd been sneaking and using baby wipes, but for a guy who was accustomed to daily showers, even that didn't feel like it was enough. And it was a bitch shaving with little more than a large bowl of water and a bar of soap, especially for those of us who chose to remove a whole head of stubble every three days.

I sat at my spot at the head of the table and began eating. Hamburger Helper and a pile of chicken tenders and fries for each person. The fries had a kind of smoky taste, and I would bet that they'd been done on the grill, too. Probably on a baking sheet, but it was actually quite nice. They were likely healthier than when done in the fryer, and the addition of grill smoke added a level of flavor that kind of made me wish I'd thought about doing them this way pre-infection.

Conversation was kept light, though I was so deep in thought I didn't take part in it. For the most part, families and friends stuck with each other, but banter was spread around the tables as a whole. I did notice Dave and Bri sitting unusually close, talking quieter and amongst only themselves. I wondered what was going on there.

Jennifer, Shannon, and Ashley sat together, nearer to me, with Gwen among them and they all seemed to be getting along very well. It was interesting, to say the least, if you could just sit back and observe as I was doing, you could see groups and cliques forming up. Mostly for the better, but I didn't like the way that my two least favorite people, Katie and Parker, had glued themselves together and always seemed to be conspiring about things while they avoided doing any real work. That's fine, I'll be remedying that, as well. I've got the perfect idea for those two.

As the meal began to grind slower and slower, people obviously getting their fill, I figured this would be the best time to start directing their attention towards our next steps, and what needed to be done for the community as far as safety and prosperity. I drained the last of the Guinness from my bottle, stood up, and clanged my fork against it like a wedding guest about to give a speech or prepare a toast.

"Y'all, this food won't keep. Eat up, let's not waste it," I began, and was met by clapping and laughter, and several jokes and jabs at one another. I continued once the dust had settled, "Now that we have essentially all experienced the danger out there first hand, we need to make a plan."

"Let's hear it, my brother," Henry encouraged. Great, instead of pitching in, my friends had spotlighted me. Okay, here goes nothing.

"Departments," I started, and was met with blank stares. "Look, we have some people who have already claimed places in our little community here, others will be given things to do. We all pitch in, we all have an important role in surviving in comfort. I don't want to see us living like animals within a year from now."

"I like what I'm doing though," Bri began, to which I put up a hand to calm her.

"Tony," I started again. "Tony is for all intents and purposes, my second in command here. He's also going to essentially be in charge of making sure each of you know what you're doing when you pick up a weapon. He was an infantryman in the Army, I've known him for many years, I'd trust my life, and any here at the table to his hands."

Tony sat back, hands clasped behind his head, both his tattooed arms and casual grin on full display for the group.

"Does anyone have any objections to this?" I asked in earnest, then rolled my eyes as Katie's hand shot up. Of course, she did. I motioned for her, and she stood.

"Why do you get to just nominate your best friend?" she challenged. "Don't any of us have a say in this?"

"First off," I started in on her, "I never said best friend. Don't twist things. Second, this is why I literally just asked if there were any issues with it. Anyone here who disagrees with the choice, let's see some hands."

My gaze never left hers, but I could see the only other hand that went up was Parker's, right next to her.

"Then it's decided," I continued. "Tony is it. Anyone develops a problem with this, or his way of doing things, bring it to me directly. No consequence. I'm trying to lead, not be a damned tyrant."

This actually seemed to put a lot of people at ease. Cool. This was more what I wanted, cooperation.

"Anyway," I spoke up again, "Tony leads security and any weapons ventures we run, and he will have a hand in tactics and planning when we make bigger moves from now on. This brings me to my next order for the night," I took a pause, waiting, as Parker and Katie murmured to each other. "Parker, Billy. Both of you. You're with Tony. You will be his support, and he will mentor the both of you on how to handle yourselves. Get up, go stand by him. Now."

It had the effect I desired, that was for sure. Tony stopped chewing and just stared at me like he was waiting for the punchline. Katie's jaw dropped. Both Parker and Billy, surprisingly, kept their mouths shut in resignation, jaws tight, and moved to stand behind Tony's seat. Tony, upon realizing that I was serious, and possibly figuring my plan, went back to being at ease and continued chewing his last bites of chicken.

"Very good," I remarked, satisfied. "Briana, Carolyn. You two are next."

Both ladies eyed me wearily, looking at each other, Bri swallowing hard on a bite of food, then they looked back at me.

"Relax," I told them both. "You two are happy where you are, yeah? And you're both good at it. Carolyn, if you'll have it, you'll assist Briana whenever you're not loaded down at the daycare. And we will be building that floor into a daycare for you to run how you see fit. Briana, the supply floor is yours."

The pair looked both relived and grateful. They both spoke thanks, and I kept on moving. I had great momentum going, and the more people who were pleased, the easier it would be to keep them all happy. That told me the directions I would need to give next would have to be another guaranteed easy selection.

"Henry," I called out, as Henry shoved his last bit of chicken in his mouth and wiped away a bit of barbecue sauce. "You are pretty much set for our motor pool, and I want you to focus there. You'll be given help if need be, and I'm sure you've got a mile-long list of things to give to Bri. If you don't, then get the list going soon so we can start scouting things out to help you. You're also going to be pulled from construction projects."

Henry looked confused, and almost a bit offended, so I explained.

"I just want to lighten your load, man. We need survival vehicles. We need cages welded and weak points on our scavenging rigs hardened. We'll put some work trucks for you on the top of the list. You're going to need the generators and equipment they can provide you."

"Alright alright my friend," Henry beamed, "thank you very much."

"Not a problem," I replied, then moved on. "James, that leaves you. You have knowledge in planning, construction, plumbing, and renewable energy. You're our crew leader for that now full time. Same as with Henry, you're going to need some serious shit. Make a list, give it to Supply."

James seemed to be very pleased with this and agreed that he'd get his list of needs sent up as soon as he could.

"Alright now, Rob," I started again, going down my list. "Once we get power back, you're our computer guy. Get it all set up and running smoothly. There's no internet, so you should be pretty well free of viruses and porn spam."

Everyone laughed, Rob himself letting out a barking laugh from the heart that seemed to help relax the group even further.

"But, there's limited need for such trade, so, when you have no computer or electronics work to do, you'll be a go-between. Find a crew that needs help and do it. Good?" I asked.

"Yes, oh definitely," Rob agreed. "Will do, boss."

"Ashley, Shannon and my wife have already claimed medical." I explained further, "they are either all experienced, or learning quickly. Let's see here. Ah, yes, Dave! If you can grow pot you can grow vegetables. Fourth floor. That's where those hydroponics will be set up once we have the extra power in place to run them, and, if we secure enough land to start farming, you run that, too. If you don't know for sure, get a book."

Dave just kind of stared at me, his pale eyes focused on my face.

"Hey, every job is important. Until we're ready for you to do your thing, you can get it all set up and ready, then be another go-between guy like Rob."

He put his back against his chair, exhaled a plume of cigarette smoke, and mumbled something that I couldn't hear, and I don't know if I cared to.

"We need a weapons guy. Tony is already going to have his hands full, we have reloading equipment now, we need to find whomever is left with the talent to at least learn maintenance and be able to put some tricks together." I continued on before I lost steam, "We'll get whatever we can find to help you learn. Anarchist Cookbook, military manuals, whatever. Anyone?"

Rich raised his hand instantly. He looked like he was back in the third grade and had just been asked a question he'd been waiting on.

"Rich? You?" I asked, not even trying to hide my curiosity.

"Uhhh yeah, for sure," he grinned, his gravelly voice showing excitement. "Just think of me as the mad scientist of ordinance. We could be here all night if you wanted to know what I know, just trust me."

I raised my hands in resignation and placation, "Nope, I'll take you at your word. What do you need right off the rip?"

"I'll make a list," He assured. "I'd also like to drain the swimming pool, I'll be working with some things that I'm sure you don't want in the living quarters. I can wall it up and roof it in with James' help and make a bunker out of it to work in."

"Okay," I conceded. "We'll use the river for our water anyway, with no more pollution going into it, we can test it and determine how to make it safe."

Rich, clearly not finished, displayed the attitude of a loyal dog, ready to please. I admired that in him, actually. His eagerness rubbed off on the others.

"I've already got plans drawn up for a still," he advised.

"We need clean water, not liquor, so you mean a water still, right?" I asked.

"Absolutely!" he grinned.

"Alright then." I smiled back to him, then, "I mentioned securing for agriculture. I want another wall further out, two or three blocks, I figure we can even raze homes that we've cleared in the immediate area and use the materials to build it with. It'll also add some more security."

"Heavy equipment will speed that process up," James advised. "We can, uh, liberate some from any construction sites we come by."

"Maybe even a dry moat around the walls," Rich began, and was met by sporadic laughter, leaving a scorned expression on his face.

"No, now you guys shut up, let's hear him out," I admonished, and Rich began again, renewed at my giving him support.

"If we already have equipment, and we're building a wall, we dig a dry moat," He suggested. "Eight feet across, and just as deep should stop runners from even reaching the walls, use the dirt we dig up to put behind the walls for support, we could even line it with spikes. The dirt backing the walls would also be a bullet stop if there's any hostile humans out there, and give us a way to make patrol paths behind the wall itself."

"I kind of like that, actually," I concurred. "Get with James about that, and about your pool bunker thing."

Rich agreed, smiled, and visibly relaxed.

"My final order of business for this evening," I set off again, gathering the attention of the group, "we almost lost some people today. Good people. I propose drawing these things to us."

This was not well received. Gasps, complaints, and about three people telling Parker to shut the fuck up.

"You all done?" I asked when it had quieted down. "Look, we've got walls, we have trucks to elevate people on to shoot over those walls. We make some noise, draw them in, mow them down at the wall like we did earlier. Boom, streets are clearer, scavenging close by is safer, it's less of a risk then to open and close the gate."

I don't think they had originally considered this. Now that they were beginning to, the group seemed to be more malleable to the idea. Good.

"Henry, after we adjourn, get a few people, get some trucks, position them around the walls, mostly to the southeast corner," I ordered. "James, get a crew to double check the walls before dark is here tonight. We start at the break of dawn. Medical team, be up early, be on standby. Carolyn will hide with the kids in the south building. Tomorrow, a quarter hour before dawn, every single person not on medical or childcare get a truck, take a position, and have a gun. Henry, Tony, Dave and I will set this powder keg off, and command via the two-ways they brought back today. All anyone else has to do is shoot to kill. We go until we run out of moving freaks. We're adjourned. Guys, outside. Tony, command center. Ladies, take stock of your supplies with Bri and let's get ready."

With that, everyone reluctantly departed, led by their new crew leaders. Tony and I made our way down to command and began a plan. We would shoot from the south rooftop. Whatever we saw that wasn't human. Tony and I both agreed we would use the Mosin Nagant. It was far from accurate, but could reach out to about three-hundred yards without much issue. The draw to using that rifle was a fast, heavy round, and it was loud. Very loud. It would easily gather as much attention as possible.

Tony left to go set up a shooting position on the south rooftop for the morning, and I stayed in the command center and began fiddling with the radios to make sure they all worked, had a charge, and were keyed to work with each other.

Satisfied that they were, I went next door to my apartment and pulled out my rifle, pistol, and shotgun, bringing them all to the kitchen table to use the remainder of the daylight to break each of them down, clean, lube, and inspect.

Before long, I was just finishing up my work, sliding the bolt into the rifle and giving the trigger a squeeze to release it and slide it the rest of the way home.

About this time, Jennifer walked in, Gwen following along at her heels, though barely. Both girls looked absolutely exhausted. I gave Gwen a hug, and a kiss, and watched as Jennifer led her in to brush her teeth using the basin of water, then took her off to bed.

I laid out an assortment of ammunition for each gun, then followed Jennifer in. Grabbing the battery powered alarm clock, setting the time, and sliding under the covers. Jennifer had already fallen asleep, so I draped an arm over her and followed suit.

TWENTY-TWO

The following morning found myself, Tony, and Dave on the rooftop of the south building. Just as the sun's rays began to peak over the horizon and shed brilliant light on our surroundings. Dropping the stub of my cigar to the rooftop and squashing it with my foot, I brought the radio up to my mouth. Man, I felt like a badass. I was the rifleman, we had a plan, I was in charge of it, and we were actually doing things. Check it out, we even had walkie talkies!

"Henry, wait for my mark. Shoot any movement on my shot. Over." I instructed through the radio. See how fucking cool that was?

"Okay, my friend," came Henry's voice through the box in my hand. Then, I waited. Nothing. He was supposed to say 'over'. Oh well.

I went to the other end of the roof and laid on the picnic table that Tony had pre-positioned the evening before. It put the main road about 200 yards away from us. Just a bit down the street, I could see the slow movement of someone, or something, walking right down the middle of the street.

I called the target to Tony, who kneeled against the low roof wall just a few feet to my left, with binoculars in hand, and Dave leant against the wall just to his left.

"Yeah, I see them," he confirmed, and brought his binos to his eyes to put glass on the target.

As Tony did this, I brought my rifle into position. Stock buried firmly in my shoulder, sling wrapped around my arm and pulled tight to steady the heavy chunk of iron and wood. I scanned through a blurred mess of foliage until the street and what turned out to be a pair of infected came into view. I twisted the focus adjustment on the rifle scope and stopped. Well, that's odd.

"What the fuck is this?" I asked Tony, who was already beginning to chuckle.

"Dude," he declared. "What a fucking way to go. I almost feel like we should leave them and find another target."

"Nah, bro," I challenged. "She was a cutie at one point. I'd be contented to die like that."

"Naked and handcuffed to your girl." Tony sighed, laughing and shaking his head, "and, oh shit dude. Is that what I think it is?"

I refocused on the unfortunate pair and suppressed a roar of laughter.

"I think it is!" I said between spasms of laughter, "I'll be damned if it isn't. No fucking way, man!"

Dave, impatient without a set of mechanical eyes of his own, grabbed Tony's glass and put it on target.

"Well, that is awkward," Dave said, grinning and exhaling a puff of smoke as he spoke. "Wait a second, what the hell?"

Tony and I were no help, already useless with laughter.

"How does this bitch have a tail? She's naked!" Dave said, astounded.

"Dude, think!" Tony said, wiping tears of laughter from his eyes.

"Just take a moment if you need to, Dave," I added, clearing away my own laughter.

"Huh?" Dave questioned, then, "Oh. Oh HELL no. That's nasty, man. What a little freak!"

In that instant, mine and Tony's laugher picked back up, and Dave joined in. Okay, we have to regain the situation here. And, I guess, we were no longer as cool as I thought we'd looked, useless with laughter on the rooftop in the morning sun like a group of high school boys.

Okay, clear yourself up, Scott. We have a job to do here. Jesus.

"Okay, Tony, back on target, spot me," I ordered once our laughter faded to chuckles.

"I got you, man," he advised. "Looks like 275, no wind. Easy shot."

"Got it," I replied, tightening my grip once again, ready for the bite of the steel butt plate on the rifle to force its way into my shoulder as I fired.

I lined up the female's head in the sighting reticule. The stock felt cool, comfortable and firm against my cheek. I waited for a break in the monster's pace, where the target would give me just a moment of still to take advantage of.

WHAM!

The rifle bucked, shouted its report to the heavens, and sent 7.62mm of supersonic metal downrange.

Hit.

The freak's head snapped forward as the bullet hit dead center in the back of her skull, and exited the face, taking a shower of blood, bone and tissue with it. It painted the pavement with what little thought process it possessed in a large arc. The monstrosity hit the ground face first, stumbling her captive partner as she dropped. And, yeah, the tail fell out. I could have gone a lifetime without seeing that one and been much happier.

Regaining its balance, her partner zeroed right in on us. He bent his head back to the sky and let out a shriek that chilled my blood and bones together. Then, more shrieks came from much closer to us as the male sex fiend turned fully toward us.

He began an arduous charge, dragging his still cuffed partner with him as he went, the rough pavement peeling and pulling at bits of her exposed flesh.

I cycled the bolt, ejecting the spent round, and replacing it with a fresh one as gunfire began to open up below us like a thunderstorm.

I sent the next round low in my hurry, taking rib meat and lung on a journey it was never meant to go on. The second shot dropped him, but he began getting back up almost immediately after.

The third round fired poked a very neat hole just below his deformed right eye, blowing a salad bowl sized hole from the back of his skull.

Before he even finished falling, the three of us were making our way across the roof to where the rest of the action was. I saw movement outside the walls, took a knee, focused my optics on it, and what I saw made me freeze.

It was a boy of about eight years old. He ran at a good clip despite a chunk of the thigh and his pants on his left leg being removed. I had no choice. Infected is infected.

No. God, no. I don't want to do this. I'm a father, for fuck's sake.

WHAM!

He never even saw the round that ended his sickness. I didn't even stick around to confirm the aftermath, either. As Dave and Tony opened fire from their vantage, I leaned over my arm and vomited right there on the roof. Too much. Too goddamn much.

Grabbing the radio, I keyed it, realizing Henry was ground level directing people from our spots and reports.

"Henry!" I shouted into the mic. "Southeast corner, about fifty are coming in one group!"

"Ok buddy we got it, over!" he replied.

"Hey Henry," I added, "No matter what they see, remind them, these things are no longer human. NOT HUMAN! Over."

"Uh, solid copy, boss," Henry said, a touch of confusion in his voice. "Will relay that. Over."

The fusillade of gunfire continued. The infected barked and grunted to each other, even as they fell. In no time, the first line began throwing themselves into the fence, struggling for purchase and leaving the people on the pickup trucks firing almost straight down at targets.

They kept impacting the same section of fence, one after another, as their comrades fell to fire from nearly every common caliber of weapon conceivable. At first, I thought they were trying to break through. Adult after adult, thankfully, but they kept going for the same small point, the bodies piling up right on our boundary.

Then it hit me. They weren't trying to break through, these smart fuckers were piling up to make a hill to get over!

Then, the sight I wanted to see the least approached from around the corner of the house, just as the pile by the fence grew tall enough for them to reach. About a half dozen young infected, appearing to be aged anywhere from five to about twelve. They moved fast. Damn fast and could have easily outpaced the adult counterparts in a foot race.

A few of our people had the gumption to keep shooting, regardless of what these things looked like. All but one of the young ones fell as our people abandoned the trucks to handle a few adults that made it over the fence.

My rifle ran dry. I pulled the shotgun up. Then so much happened at once it was hard to track. The sole young girl infected that was left hit the pile of corpses. She climbed, found the top of the fence, and pulled herself over.

Dave and Tony both had to pull a reload at the same time, Tony swapping a magazine, Dave grabbing an empty mag and fumbling as he forced rounds into it.

Most of the people inside the wire were preoccupied with the infected that got inside. I still don't think anyone except for Henry and I saw her, and he froze.

Her feet hit the ground, and all Henry knew was the young form of a child running at him full bore. Head full of dark hair bouncing with every step, shoe, foot, shoe, foot, and he froze solid, his face twisting into an expression of fear that I don't even think carries a description.

I fired once. The light shotgun nearly jumping out of my hands at that angle when it loosed its heavy load. I didn't miss, but the spread of shot did. The second round went off seemingly without my permission. The little girl did some kind of weird juke or jive, and her feet collapsed under her, followed by the rest as she hit the pavement and slid several feet before finding a cessation to her motion.

We would later find out that it was one single lucky pellet from a three-inch magnum shell that saved Henry's life. One, tiny little .32 caliber shotgun pellet that entered the top of her head and drove the message home; You're not welcome in our castle.

I glanced at Dave, who looked steadily down at the mess below us. Tony, however, turned his head away and…was that a tear I saw? I wasn't going to push it, but he looked how I felt at that moment. Despair would have been a vacation. Kids. Child infected. Of all the fucking things in this world, sweet little Suzy wasn't the little girl down the street any longer. And my people, none of them looked too cheerful after these events. I chose not to let them dwell too much.

"Clean up here, meet me by the pool with the rest of the people when you're done," I instructed Dave and Tony, then added, "Just the shells, save them for reloading if we can."

I moved down the stairs to join the rest of our community. Stopping at the bottom, before coming into view, I took as deep a breath as I could, let it out, and strode through the south building doors and into the courtyard like I had a purpose the whole time.

Come on, Scott, you're in control.

"Everybody by the pool. NOW!" I barked, smiling internally as people snapped into motion like they were kicked. Good, nobody has lost it yet, it seems.

I thought too soon, Henry began moving, approached my direction, and kept on going.

"You good, boss?" I asked him.

"I'm going to my garage," he muttered, though his gaze seemed to look way beyond all of that.

"I'll be down in a bit, man. Try to relax," I called after him, unsure if the words even found their target. He looked bad and as ghost pale as I'd ever seen a black man before. Not good.

Turning to the gathering crowd, none of them appeared well, but they were all accounted for, Dave and Tony taking up the rear of the lineup as they exited the building.

"Alright, people." I spoke, as loud and clear as I could through the fog my head was swimming through.

"I'm not going to force anyone. There's going to be some infected lying out there that nobody should ever have to see, but we have to get this mess cleaned up." I continued in explanation, "I need Parker, Billy, Rob, Clara, Frank, and Fred to head up to command, I'll meet you there. I need six more of you on volunteer duty to clean these infected up and put them over the highway overpass."

The group that was told to do so departed, heading for the north building. Katie tried following Parker. Nope, not today. She's going to learn when the bullshit stops.

"Katie, thank you very much!" I called cheerfully, satisfied at the look of surprise on her face. She tried to start protesting, and I intervened.

"Katie, thank you very much. I admire your dedication and being the first to volunteer for cleanup!" I commended. Boy was I full of shit, but I was floating on this pleasure. "I need at least five more of you."

Rich's hand went up, then Bri, Jennifer, Shannon, Ashley, and, at Ashley's not so subtle urging, Zach. Excellent.

"Rich, take the truck with the trailer. You run cleanup today. Thanks man," I said directly.

"Everybody else, go with James," I ordered. "James, I need people working in the buildings. Follow Shannon's suggestion chart that she put upstairs, and, if you have time, start draining the pool. When Rich is done, get together with him, he has a plan to keep us in a steady water supply."

"You got it, man," James replied, then, "You heard him, people, let's get rockin'."

Calling Tony and Dave to follow me, we moved to the north building.

"You guys good?" I prodded.

Dave nodded, and spat on the concrete as we walked. Tony stayed quiet.

"Tony, you need to talk, you know where to find me. Otherwise, I think it's best we all keep our minds busy."

Tony simply nodded, mumbled something to the effect of him being alright, and they followed me up the million flights of stairs to the ninth floor.

TWENTY-THREE

Striding into the command room with the same level of purpose I'd displayed outdoors, I sat at the sole desk facing back into the room, the large sliding doors behind me offering a view of a good chunk of our compound and the lands beyond.

"Billy, Parker," I began. "You two need a lot of work. I don't see you guys surviving long without some help. You go with Dave and Tony. South of here. Just pure scouting, no house clearing, but find these things if you can."

I slid a list of supplies we needed the most across the table. Tony picked it up, reading it over as his lips moved. Dave, Billy, and Parker all shared the same look of surprise.

I slid a digital camera, fresh memory card, and two sets of batteries across the table, and then did the same in Clara's direction.

My instruction to Tony continued, "Take a pad and pen down to supply, two days of supplies for each of you, mark what you took, and leave it on Bri's desk. Take a hybrid from the lot out there, leave Henry be, just make sure it's got fuel. Be safe."

We said our goodbye's, and they departed, Tony already moving into his role of the E4 barking at Privates when giving the weaker two their directions.

"Clara, you're getting the same speech, so I'll save it," I continued once the others had left. "Except, your team is going west."

"And why are we going west? We don't know what's over there yet," she advised.

"I know a little," I replied. "There was road construction going on just past Second Street after the highway, about a block north of the main drag not too long ago. Scout it. We need any heavy equipment we can. Also, look for these…"

I slid another ready-made list to her.

"Got plans for rebuilding some roads or something?" she asked sarcastically.

"Nah, but this morning, the way they made it over our fence," I began, "Rich's dry moat sounds pretty fuckin' sweet to me. And we need more of a gap, so we need another wall further out, and houses need to come down. This means we need equipment."

"Okay." She agreed with a shrug, "You heard him, let's go."

I watched her leave, then almost as soon as the last person left, I reached into the bottom drawer of my desk and drew a small glass, and a bottle of Johnnie Walker Double Black.

I poured four fingers of the potent scotch into the glass, took a long swallow so it looked like only two fingers, then paused. I grabbed another glass, poured three, and replaced the bottle in the drawer, closed it, and departed.

***

I followed the slope of the parking lot as it disappeared into the underground garage. Somebody had removed a number of mirrors from the apartments and angled them inward so they'd reflect the sun into the cavernous space. It wasn't well lit, but the mirrors provided enough reflected light to see by.

Henry sat on a bright orange milk crate over near one of the toolboxes, a couple of crumpled beer cans near his feet already.

"Here." I guided, handing a glass of the beautiful dark scotch to him. "It's not your Canadian Club, but it should do the trick."

"Thank you, my brother," he said, though without his usual cheer and fervor. Poor guy.

"So. Let's have it," I started, taking in a sip of my own glass, and feeling the spiced burn as it trickled down my throat.

"Why-I mean, I never thought..." he trailed off, a hint of a shudder in his usually strong voice. "The kids. Nobody was spared, but I don't know. I just never considered, I mean, we've never seen, and then- "

He stopped as he shot the rest of his glass straight down his throat.

"I know," I replied. "I shot the first one and puked."

"I'm Uncle Henry," he said, nearly regretfully, as his eyes met mine and turned away.

Henry was essentially the uncle or the grandpa to every kid in the neighborhood, whether he actually was or not, he was in spirit. This was a blow to the man. He'd have fixed a bike, given a water to, or mediated any kid in this city, good or bad.

"We're in for some shit, dude." I began again, "None of it's going to be pretty. You don't have to put yourself in there if you don't feel you honestly can. You're important enough that we can keep you too busy to put another trigger under your finger. I've got you, man."

"Thanks, my friend," Henry said without cheer or relief, "but I think I'm going to take it one day at a time. I'll be alright, brother. I'm just going to try to not worry about the mule going blind."

He produced a large bottle full of an even darker liquor from the bottom of his tool box.

"And I've always got my Canadian Club. You keep that fancy stuff," he said, in his best attempt to be humorous. I downed the last of my glass without even a grimace. I figured I'd save the faces for what he was about to pour for the two of us. I hated good old CC.

He poured a glass for each of us. I took my first sip tentatively, this cheaper whiskey always did funny things to my stomach, but this man loved it, and I wasn't about to complain about something so petty given the circumstances.

***

I'm not sure how much time we spent in that garage together, switching from liquor to beer and back again, but I know we both ended up with quite a good buzz, and the sun had passed its apogee in the sky. The day was sticky and humid, but the garage stayed cool.

My mission was accomplished though, I got Henry laughing. I took that as my cue to depart, before we became useless in our intoxication, or before the conversation turned somber again.

I hugged him as friends, as brothers, and left to go outside.

I nearly ran headlong into my wife as I turned the corner by the pool.

Was it my eyes? Could she smell me? Was she watching or listening?

"You're fucking kidding me!" she started in immediately. "You're drunk. Why are you drunk?"

"Henry needed some help," I retorted, hoping the vagueness of the phrase would save me. It didn't.

"Yeah, that's not the first time I've heard that one. Why? And with what?" she shot back, and, shit, she was right. Henry and I were neighbors before the change. I've been in hot water more than once after disappearing for hours and coming back home drunk. The excuse? Every single time, Henry needed help with something. Oops.

Luckily, she stormed away before I had to find a shield and spear.

I quickly found Rich and James, they were both directing others and doing their own part in slowly draining the giant outdoor swimming pool. The water was already disgusting, filled with leaves, dirt, bugs, trash, and turning a sick shade of green.

"James, I know you can drive construction equipment," I advised. "Can you, Rich?"

"I can drive some," he replied. "My dad had some farm tractors when we were young."

"Good," I said, smiling, "because you're getting your dry moat. This morning made it sound like one of our best defensive moves. James, make up a rudimentary plan I can present to everyone after dinner tonight. I want to push this second wall and dry moat two or three blocks out from here, full coverage."

James and Rich both looked intrigued, perplexed, and amused all at the same time. But neither of them answered, so I filled it in for them.

"Couldn't have said it better myself, boys. Good work. Extra rations of rum tonight." And I began to wobble away.

No sooner had I gotten a half-dozen yards from them, I began hearing the low rumble of a diesel engine off to the west. What the hell?

The sound approached, crossing the overpass and continuing in our direction. As it passed our wall along the main road, and turned to near our front gate, it dawned on my drunken mind that there was something unfamiliar approaching us and I should do something.

"Everyone with a gun, let's go!" I ordered, drawing my pistol and moving toward the front gate. Just then, the nose of a white Dodge Ram with a work flatbed on it rounded the corner, pulled toward the gate, and Clara stepped out of it, rushing over to meet me at the front gate.

"We have one badly injured!" she shouted. "Open the fucking gate, Scott!"

I did so, and watched as the truck rolled in, right to the front of the north building.

I slammed the gate back shut and began jogging to where the truck came to a rest. The scene was already chaos as Clara was doing her best to direct people despite her obvious tense mood. The reason became apparent as Frank was being pulled from the backseat of the crew cab Dodge.

His head seemed to be wrapped in a t-shirt, as well as another on his leg, and he was clearly in distress, and a fair amount of pain. As I arrived at the site of all the confusion, I started trying to project my voice to gain some level of control over the situation.

"Shannon, Ashley, Jennifer!" I shouted, and all three were present at once, "Get him up to medical. Everybody else, clear out, give them some room, you all have work to do."

"You're not gonna fucking believe this..." Clara began, then exclaimed again, "FUCK!"

"Not here. Upstairs," I directed, "they have Frank, he'll be okay. Command floor, I'll be up shortly."

"Okay," she replied. "Okay, yeah. Should I bring Tony and Dave? This is big."

"Yeah, get them," I instructed, before turning to the people moving about. "BRI! Where's Bri?"

"Over here! Coming!" she shouted back, and then came jogging over to me.

"Up to medical, they're going to need supplies, I think," I ordered, and she went with just a nod of the head.

I began making my way up those damn stairs, thinking about all the issues we were facing today, and in the future. Wondering what revelation Clara had come to bear with all the drama she brought back today. Frank was injured, but despite his apparent pain, he didn't look to be fatally so. Henry was a wreck, and I vowed to leave him to himself for a little while. Everybody else seemed to be mostly keeping their heads about them, and for that, I was thankful. There's enough fires for me to extinguish around here anyway.

I walked through the command room door and came to a heavy rest in the chair at the head of the meeting table. Clara, Tony, and Dave were already there, every one of them looked somber.

"Okay, good news first." I nodded to Clara, "You found a work truck for Henry, that's good."

"Found your damn construction equipment, too," Clara shot back. "Almost cost me my Frank. What the hell-"

"No, one thing at a time," I cautioned, then lied, "I stopped by on the way up here, he's fine, just out of the game for a while. Relax. Tell me about the equipment."

"Okay." She began, catching herself, "Half mile west of here, right down the main stretch. There's an excavator, a backhoe, a couple of dump trucks, and the work truck we took."

"Okay, good, we'll send out a retrieval party. You did good." Then, noticing the exchange of looks between the three of them, Dave and Tony clearly having been caught up to speed, "Alright, yeah, the bad news now. What happened to Frank? He looks like he was in a car crash."

Clara didn't respond verbally. She instead flipped on the digital camera she held, and once it came to life, slid it across the table to me. I caught it as it slid, and picked it up.

"What the fuck is this?" I asked, unable to hide my confusion.

"A big one," Clara replied flatly.

"A big one?" I asked again, then, seeing its size next to the other infected in the frame, "Oh. Oh shit."

I zoomed in on the beast in the screen. If I were to judge, based on the other freaks near it, this thing was easily eight to ten feet tall. It was bipedal, but that's where the similarity to the others ended. Pale, grayish skin stretched over what caught me as a Lou Ferrigno build. The skin was stretched so taught that it was torn in places, exposing a disgusting off-pink colored flesh that looked wet to the touch, and every inch of skin was spiderwebbed with thick veins. Its head a small bulb on top of a tree, as it seemed to be the only part of the beast that hadn't enlarged.

"Frank, in all his wisdom," Clara continued, "didn't make sure the flash was off when he started taking pictures. They saw, it saw, and they came. We got most of the little ones, the normal sized, I mean, but we couldn't stop the big one."

"You run out of ammo or something?" I inquired.

"No, oh no we still have plenty left," she explained. "It just did fuck all to it. Even the couple of headshots I managed barely fazed it."

"Jesus," I said, lamenting. "Okay. Get our best gunners up here, I need six people. Get them up to speed. I also want maps of the area this is at, if we have any. Tony, get our heaviest guns together. We'll just have to make a plan."

"Scott," Clara started, "it hit Frank once, threw him like a toy."

"Yeah, it hasn't tried to hit me yet. Won't know what hit it back," I replied, as I got up and started to leave.

"Where you going dude?" Tony spoke after me.

"I'm taking a nap. Don't bother Henry, either. Wake me for dinner," I instructed as I left.

***

I awoke from my heavy alcohol induced sleep to the sounds of Tony's voice calling my name. Clearly they had come back from their short range scouting.

"Scott! Hey, SCOTT!" Wake up dude!" he said excitedly. "Dude! There's a fire on the roof, come on!"

"Fire? Ah no, okay, I'm getting up," I replied groggily.

There was no answer, except for the sound of his footsteps moving away. I piled out of bed, rushed to the door, ran back to grab a bucket of water from the kitchen, and left the apartment. Last thing we needed was our home going up in flames, Christ, why can't it ever be something simple?

Bursting through the door to the rooftop, I stopped cold in my tracks. There was a fire, a pretty good sized one, but it was contained to a burning pit that had been constructed.

So, there I stood. Our entire community also standing, my crazed appearance ceasing their movement as they went about setting up another rooftop dinner. And there's me. My long goatee an absolute mess, shirtless, barefoot, nothing but my...don't judge...Harry Potter pajama pants, and a bucket of water. Tony and Dave were shaking with unsuppressed laughter. Taking the scene in, and realizing the joke was very clearly on me, and everybody else was in on it, I stepped toward them.

"You fuckers," I challenged, then dumped the entire bucket over both of them, which was met by a crowd's worth of laughter. Okay, I was on the spot, but I think we all needed this, just a little bit.

Easing myself into my seat, Jennifer met me with a steaming plate of fried spam and vegetables, and a very warm beer. Everyone began finding their seats, and we all ate. The sounds of laughter and conversation were a welcome scene, and, despite what we had been going through, everybody seemed to be in relatively high spirits. Even Henry was doing his best to keep a smile, if nothing else for the benefit of the people around him.

I eyeballed Tony and Dave talking kind of quietly to each other, across from me. I threw a carrot, bouncing right off of Dave's forehead, and landing it in Tony's lap. They both looked over, grinning.

"What's baldy think?" Dave said, smiling even broader.

"I'm not bald, I'm shaved, you hippie fuck," I called back, jovially, then, "Think about what?"

"Bri, man, Dave here has himself a crush!" Tony jeered.

"Crushes are for kids, but I'm just saying, I'd smash," Dave said through a fork full of food that he held like it would help him drive home his point, "she got that booty like POW, man!"

They both dissolved into laughter, as I rolled my eyes and joined in.

"Go for it, dude," I challenged, "she ain't got anybody."

"I'm about to," Dave replied, then got up.

"Watch this shit," I suggested to anybody listening.

Dave made his way over by Bri, took the empty chair next to her, and leaned right up against her saying something we couldn't quite hear. She promptly pushed him away, but she did so laughing.

"I'll be damned." I called to Tony, "I think our boy's in there."

We turned our attention away from Dave and his exploits and finished up our meals with some light conversation. Once the dinner was over I rang my beer bottle with my fork. Fun's over, time for the serious side of things. I brought everybody up to speed regarding our new large find. Some looked scared, some almost sick, and others looked downright curious.

"Tony, go get those guns. Dave, go help him, please," I instructed, they both replied in the affirmative and left the rooftop. "Jennifer, why don't you go get my Mosin, and the shotgun, and grab that black box of shotgun shells."

"Okay," she replied as she got up to leave, "do you want the bandolier, too?"

"Yeah, definitely," I replied, then turned to Clara. "Did you get those maps?"

"Yes I did, right here," she said as she pushed plates out of the way and laid the maps on the table. She then began detailing the best she could where everything was situated.

I lit a cigar and studied the info, and then sat back in my seat. A few minutes later everybody out on errands had come back to the rooftop and the table, and the others gathered around. The plates cleared, Tony and Dave began laying out weapons on the table. Large rifles, a few shotguns, and some revolvers.

"This is the heaviest shit we have?" I asked, dismayed. "I mean, they're all great manstoppers, but this isn't a man."

"Maybe we should start scouting south, too." Tony suggested.

"He's right," Jennifer interjected, "we could see if the military left anything we can use behind."

"Yeah maybe," I said thoughtfully. "But, I've got a plan for tomorrow. We need that equipment, and I want this big bastard erased. He doesn't need to keep living and presenting a threat to us."

"Let's hear it," Dave challenged, and everybody else seemed to move in closer.

"Scott, Tony, Dave, Rich, James, and myself will go," Clara offered.

"Sounds good," I agreed. "We'll take a single light pickup, that leaves enough of us to drive what's there. Rich and James can jerk each other off over who takes which equipment, Clara and I will take a dump truck each if we can, they may be useful later."

"Those dumps are automatic, we were already going to take one, but we were a little preoccupied," Clara explained.

"Are we just- excuse me," Katie broke in from the back of the group, "are we just going to ignore the fact that you guys murdered kids this morning?"

I was about to speak when Jennifer stepped up.

"I'll take this one," she said, and grabbed Katie by the wrist and led the large, whining woman off to the stairwell.

Rich mouthed 'Oh shit' and several of us tried to cover laughter at the thought of the bitching out Katie was about to receive by my wife.

"Anyway, there's a business here," I pointed to a spot on the map, and the team leaned in, "I want to set up on the rooftop. I know it, it's a brick building with limited entry points and roof access. It should be about a hundred yards from the site."

"Sounds like a solid plan," Tony concurred. "When did you want to do this?"

"Seeing as how the building is east of the site, I say we leave at 0400," I offered. "Come in quiet, get set up, and wait until the sun breaks the horizon to use it like old WWI fighter pilots. We start shooting then. Hopefully the light on our backs, and in their eyes, will cover our position. I don't know if it will buy us any time, but any advantage we can gather I'm willing to try."

"That's fuckin' genius," Rich chimed in, "then we clean out any other infected, and walk away with the machines?"

"Pretty much," I agreed. "So, no drinking, no bullshit, you all get to bed once you've set up your kit. Two days supplies, med pack for each person, I've got a couple of trauma kits I'll take. I will be up at 0330, so no dicking around. Meet at the motor pool at a quarter till."

Everybody agreed and began packing up weapons and talking strategy. I began loading my shotgun for the next day. It was then Tony looked over, probably noticing the glint in the end of the shells as I loaded the magazine tube and began adding more to the shell holder on the side of the collapsing stock. He, naturally, picked one up and inspected it.

"No shit?" he asked, a touch of wonder to his voice. "I didn't know you had these!"

"Yup," I replied. "Remington copper SABOT slugs. Should give a bit of extra punch if he gets close enough to need them."

"That's what's up, man, nice!" he said as he replaced the round on the table.

I bade everybody goodnight as I gathered my stuff up from the table and departed to make my way to bed. Tomorrow was likely to be an interesting day.

TWENTY-FOUR

As promised, my alarm brought its dream killing tone right on time, and I was up and on my feet. I'm one of those rare people who have no issues being able to be up with the bell. My wife, on the other hand...

Well, I kissed her on the forehead as she remained asleep, then turned to begin getting dressed and putting my things in order. Within a few minutes, I was on my way out the door, a Styrofoam cup of cold coffee from yesterday in my hand. I arrived at the motor pool a few short minutes later, and lit a smoke as I waited for my team to arrive. My scavenged Timex told me they had three minutes.

Surely enough, they arrived together, and four minutes late. Whatever, close enough, I guess.

We made basic pleasantries, and light, hushed conversation as we loaded things into the small Ford Ranger, and then we piled in, me driving, Tony sitting alongside, and the others piled into the bed, all sitting low.

Henry met us at the gate, and as he rolled it aside, he stopped us to lean inside and give me a friendly hug along with a word of thanks and well-wishing. I returned it in kind, and we were off, the gate rolling shut behind us.

We took an immediate right and headed the half block south from the complex before cutting another right to take the main road westbound to the site.

Keeping the small four-cylinder engine of the truck running low, and the lights off, to keep our profile low, we rolled past what used to be a familiar landscape. Now painted with the markings of death, and the stench of all the rotting infected we'd been dumping off the overpass onto the freeway. It was an alien place to venture into.

We rolled the main strip anyway, and no conversation was made. Every person not responsible for driving was watching in all directions to make sure we remained alone as we picked up speed in the moonlit darkness.

Within minutes we were close enough to our destination that I killed the engine and took the truck out of gear to let it roll a little closer. It stopped nearly a full block from where we wanted, so we got out and pushed it over to our destination. The light truck was nothing to us, and we made quick work of it, then proceeded to unload and clear the target building. Once we were satisfied that the building was empty, we made our way through the door to access the rooftop.

From there, I quietly instructed the others. James and Clara were to provide a rear guard, in case any runners made it past and into the building. I absolutely did not want to be boxed onto a rooftop. Myself, Rich, Tony, and Dave would wait until the sun was up and bright behind us to start taking shots. Rich and Dave would target the smaller guys, Tony and I would have a go at the big guy. This should work. I hope.

We settled in, with a bit over an hour and a half until true sunrise, and we each opened a bottle of water and an MRE to begin some breakfast. In little time, the light smell of heating food pervaded our area. That was fine, the freaks didn't seem too keen on 'people food', just people.

Occasional peeks over the parapet showed our target zone. A number of smaller infected milled around the chosen equipment. Not much more to look at than a herd of alien cattle bumping around here and there. The machines were relatively close together, parked and waiting for a day that would never come. That's fine, you and I both know these crews weren't the most expeditious in the best of times.

As I poked my head up and watched a third time, the breaking sun slowly bringing the landscape into sharper contrast, I saw him. The big fucker was everything he appeared to be and more. He took a few steps into view, appearing from alongside a Mack dump truck, looked around slowly, and settled into a kneeling position. It was almost as if he were conserving what energy it took to get his large frame in motion. In a way, it kind of reminded me of our very own Chris Simmons in the morning.

With no small amount of effort, I pulled my attention away from the scene, mentally counting and marking positions as I did, and returned to my meal.

One-hundred and twenty-five yards. About. Well, I think, at least.

Two-dozen or so little guys, one big fucker.

Okay, yeah, sure, we've got this. Stick to the plan. The plan, man.

Nobody uttered more than a couple of soft words. The only thing to break up our open-air dining was the occasional noise from one of the distant infected, and what I could only assume was the odor of the big thing. Clara confirmed this, and it turned my stomach. The damn thing stunk of rotten fish. It was disgusting, and it made eating the years-old food in the MRE's that much more of a challenge.

In what seemed like way too short of an amount of time, the sun fully crested the horizon. It couldn't have worked better if it were placed there. We broke the line perfectly between it and the grouping of sick fucks gathered around our nice shining construction equipment.

We began setting up, everybody picking a target and waiting with all the patience of a dog with a snack on its nose. You could feel the air. The breeze had stopped completely, leaving us wrapped in a blanket of early morning humidity. The sun grew slowly in intensity, and I was ready to give the signal.

"All good?" I asked in a rough whisper and waited until I heard five replies to the positive.

"Okay, on three. Pick a target. Tony, you and I both go for the big fucker's head," I instructed, then began the countdown.

"Three…"

"Two…"

"One."

The contrast between that last syllable and the eruption of gunfire that followed was concussive, to put it lightly. Rifles in the .30 caliber range all started barking hard orders to die as smaller infected started to drop one by one.

The shots fired by Tony and myself found their marks nearly simultaneously, striking the large monstrosity square in the side of the head. It dropped. Perfect.

"WE GOT HIM!!!" I shouted, and followed with a new order, "Strike the little fuckers, everybody slow and steady!"

Shouts of acquiescence followed and the gunfire spread out to the smaller creatures, already running our way as they took shots that dropped and stumbled them.

The big guy, laying on the ground, brought an arm to his face. I watched on in shock and fascination as it began to try to force its way to a standing position.

There's...no...fucking...way. We killed this thing! A pair of rifle rounds hit their marks, and it was dazed. Dazed, really?

"BIG BITCH LIVES!" I called out again, "Refocus on him!"

As I said this, and as the hail of rifle bullets moved to this next target, he released a bellow that sounded startlingly similar to the T-Rex from Jurassic Park, then, the thing went immediately into a full sprint in our direction as bullets peppered him and...did nothing. Was it armored? What am I missing here?

In the time it took me to switch from rifle to shotgun, our rear guard began to fire into the stairwell at smaller infected, er, normal sized ones, that had already found their way in and up to where we held tight.

As I checked the load in my shotgun, this living, breathing freight train covered the ground in a way that was graceful, yet drunken at the same time. At one point stumbling on a large piece of chewed up asphalt and going sidelong into the driver's door of a nearby Camry, crumpling the impact zone like tin foil.

Rounds peppered the beast and the ground around it, doing no more apparent damage than a spring powered pellet rifle would to the average man. The plus-sized freak finished his enraged journey and plummeted headlong into our little slice of safety.

It hit the flat side of the brick building hard enough to shake the rooftop under our feet, and began pounding its closed fists into the wall, breaking loose chunks of brick as it went. If it wasn't going to fit inside, it was clearly aiming to bring us down to his level. Each strike of its enormous fists rumbling the brick and mortar structure like a 3 AM drunk upstairs neighbor.

Three of us began dropping shots down onto its head and torso and while chunks of skin flew, not much more happened. Even Tony's .308 lacked the pure kinetic energy needed to do much more than penetrate the depth of a pencil eraser. We were in trouble, this I was sure of.

The beast reared its head back to bellow another roar as a second wave of runners came from the surrounding buildings to join the party.

As its fists, torso, and even head impacted the building yet again, I pitched the shotgun over the edge and fired. The gun bucked and damn near jumped out of my hands as it fired. The shot hit the beast in the crown of its head, stumbling it back.

As I fired round number two, and missed, the hulking freak put its shoulder into the next blow, caving in a huge section of wall and making the building feel as if it jumped entirely by several feet.

I loaded yet another round amid yells and shouts from my team interspersed with bursts of fire. The acrid smoke of cordite burning filled our area, and my nose and eyes as well.

Third time is the charm, right? The third slug caught the creature in the eye, nearly dead center, and sent a small fountain of blood, tissue, and ocular fluids skyward as it penetrated into its head. The resulting pressure caused the remaining eye to bulge grotesquely as the creature fell forward, faceplanting the wall, and then slid down to the ground.

We had no time to celebrate as I watched cracks spread across the roof right under our feet.

The building began a new kind of rumble. An aftershock of the assault it had just endured, it would seem.

"It's falling in!" I alerted the others. "Guys, get back! GET THE FUCK BACK!"

We scrambled back just in time for the roof to fall into the office below us, giving a clean line of sight to the final half of the second group of infected, about ten of them. They began pouring into the building, so we began firing into the remaining stairwell behind us as they funneled in.

Bodies piled up in the open doorway and down the flight of steps as we all bled our magazines dry. The stench of Big Mac mixed with that of the other monsters and began overwhelming us as dark rust brown infected fluids pooled on the rooftop and ran down the stairs into the office below like a water runoff alongside a street in anytown, India.

Within seconds we were alone again. I couldn't hear a damn thing from the ringing created by so much heavy gunfire, but I couldn't see anything else approaching us. We climbed down, helping each other onto the rubble since the stairwell was blocked by corpses. A final shot from Rich as he took out an infected that was only trapped by its friends, barring its entry to the rooftop.

"Okay, over to the equipment," I said breathlessly. "We'll rest there. It stinks here."

The others murmured agreement. I think. I honestly couldn't tell to this day if they were quieted from fatigue, or my own battle with post-fight tinnitus.

TWENTY-FIVE

We rested for perhaps a half hour and confirmed the keys present in all the vehicles save for one dump truck. After a little searching, we found that, too, in the pocket of a pair of torn and bloody jeans laying nearby with a scattering of bleached white bones.

Returning to the equipment with a set of keys for each, we took a moment and busted out the lights on each vehicle. No sense in adding more markers to the presence of such lumbering mechanical beasts, we were certainly visible enough as is.

The only illumination that was left was done so at the behest of James. The work lights, site illumination, just in case our personal duties carried on beyond available sunlight.

As luck would have it, there were enough radios to give one per vehicle. We checked them, made sure the batteries had some juice, and that they were each on the same channel.

It was decided that the excavator was going to be the slowest vehicle, but it also left the driver very exposed, so we put one dump truck in front, then the heavy tracked vehicle, followed by the backhoe, and myself in the dump truck in the rear, with Tony riding shotgun.

Pulling out onto the main road from the work zone, we began our arduous parade back home, making a fraction of the pace we had when inserting to what would prove to be a quick, but very tense fight.

Passing so slowly through the town, and in the daylight, I was able to see how much further the decay had spread since the previous journey here on day one of our vacation away from home.

So many shops had been broken into and left in complete disarray. They weren't even completely ransacked, several shops still showed things we were more in need of than those with a short-term mindset, including clothing, personal care products, feminine products, and I'll be damned, toilet paper!

I called a stop to our short convoy.

Once the vehicles had ceased their forward momentum, I got out of my truck, leaving Tony to keep an eye on it, and I took Dave along with me.

I approached the front of the small convenience store, and, reaching through the broken front door, I unlocked it, and swung it open as Dave led the way, pistol forward and ready as we swept the darkened interior.

There wasn't much left, the food and drinks had essentially been cleared out, save for a few small items here and there. We moved toward the toilet paper and care products, and grabbing a couple of nearby shopping baskets, we started to load up.

The sound of a single footstep drew our attention toward the back of the shop. Then another.

Quietly placing our new-found luxuries on the tile floor, we each moved to the shelves lining the nearest aisle, and, keeping a low profile, moved forward with as much stealth as could be mustered. We each stuck to our own side of the aisle, freezing in unison at every whisper of another presence. We were close now.

A short, chuffed breath near the closing end of the aisle told us as much. It froze the blood in my veins, and my heart felt that pressure as it began working double time. In the open was one thing with these freaks, but in this small shop, every narrow aisle and blind corner felt like death would be waiting.

I could tell Dave felt the tension just as I had, his knuckles turning stark white on the Beretta he carried, I could sense as much as feel every breath of his coming in short puffs of stale shop air.

Just as I was about to motion him a few paces forward, the first shriek came. Its tone blasting through my body, my entire being, as we both opened fire at the speeding shape hurtling towards us.

The Smith & Wesson recoiling in my hands, its leaden breath slamming into the speeding shape, twisting it, nearly spinning it into a nightmare form of blood spatter and bone fragment as it lurched and fell.

As if this signaled a party, several more shrieks came from another corner of the store. I dropped my magazine free of my pistol and slid another one home, releasing the slide just as Dave did the same quick dance.

"I hear more!" I called to Dave.

"Yeah no shit! But how many?" he retorted, clipping the rest of what he intended to say as the shop filled with the tremendous sounds of rifle fire followed by the tinkling of glass as the entire storefront exploded inward. The hail of bullets blindly fired into the area could be felt as much as witnessed as they flew by like angry hornets, making a mess of whatever they impacted.

"HIT THE DECK!" I screamed at Dave as I pulled him to the floor, "HIT THE FUCKING FLOOR MAN!"

We both dropped, full prone, side by side, and began sending our own weight in metal projectiles into the corner that made the most noise. Without being able to actually see what we were hitting among the explosion of debris all around us, we fired anyway, both pausing only to reload our weapons.

On my final mag change, I noticed the rest of the noise, save for the next level ear-ringing I now had, had vanished. It was nearly silent in the store, though through the foggy downpour of exploded flour bags I could still see very little.

As if from a nightmare, a single hand clawed out, desperate for purchase, mere inches from my face, reaching through the powdered fog as if trying to grasp me and drag me into a whole new level of existence. Not today. I flinched back, and opened fire, the muzzle blast from the small 9mm clearing just enough floating enriched white flour for me to watch the head attached to my attacker snap back, fall forward, and stay still after thudding dully on the tile. A puddle of rust marking it on the floor as holy men were once marked in Renaissance paintings.

Then the voices of our comrades became evident. Shouting into the store, asking for proof of life, apparently.

"We're good!" I called back. "We're safe, it's clear!"

"What the FUCK, man," Dave exclaimed as he pulled himself up to stand next to me.

"Yeah, we're going to have to work on some safer practices, I think," I said, bending down and fingering a bullet hole in what was left of a bag of flour just over where my head was.

I turned to the front of the store and started barking orders, not even trying to hide the anger in my voice.

"Next asshole that fires with friendlies downrange and no clear lineup on a threat gets shot in the fucking kneecap," I told the group of friends gathering around the front of the shop.

"We were-" Tony started.

"Fuck that," I snapped back. "You of all people should know better. No target, no fire."

"Yeah," Tony resigned. "Understood, man. Sorry."

"Okay!" I began, "Let's get a count of dead freaks, and anyone not counting, is carrying everything useable to the lead dump truck. This is now a scavenging mission."

"I sure hope it was worth it," Clara spoke, as she tried to move past me.

"It's two-ply. Fuckin' two-ply. Of course it's worth it," I challenged, shoving a pack of toilet paper into her chest to carry outside before turning to the countertop.

There, Dave and I began loading loose rounds into our empty magazines, checking and clearing the pistols, and getting ready for whatever was next.

The report came back, eight infected dead in that shop.

TWENTY-SIX

Everything of use loaded into the lead dump truck, we were ready to set out again. Our dreadfully slow and noisy walking pace set, we went.

Dave now took Tony's position in my truck, allowing the infantryman to be in the point vehicle and keep a constant visual on our avenue of approach. The odor of a joint burning slowly in Dave's hand filled the truck's cab.

I continued searching storefronts, not seeing anything worth a repeat episode of what we'd been through. Leaning low in my seat of the tail dump truck, I chanced a glimpse in the mirror at where we'd just came from. What I saw didn't completely register at first. I took a second, longer look.

"Team." I spoke through the two-way radio and received a mixed reply from three different handsets.

"Full-stop, guys," I instructed, and nearly had to stand my truck on its nose to stop it as the backhoe jammed to a standstill.

"What's up, man?" Tony's crackling voice questioned.

"We got company," I reported. "Six o-clock."

"Infected?" Tony crackled again.

"Nah," I started, catching the chrome reflections in my mirror as our new company came closer. "Nah, man, not unless they can ride four motorcycles and drive a red car."

"What's the plan here?" Clara called in.

"Sit low, stay calm, but have a gun ready," I explained. "We'll see if they're friendly, if not, I'll call it out."

As I finished this and listened to the calls in the affirmative to come back, I grabbed the shotgun off of the floor next to me and began loading the tube with buckshot. Dave nodded, checked, and locked in his AK47 from the passenger seat, and laid it across his lap with the muzzle pointed at the door.

A few beats later, the first motorcycle passed us, then another, the other two stopping by my truck, one per side, as the car pulled past and parked in front of our lead truck. Not good, if they just wanted to be friendly, they wouldn't box us in.

The guys on the motorcycles stayed stoic, one smiling and nodding to me.

A middle-aged man exited the car, his burnt umber skin shining with sweat in the sun. He walked up to the door of the truck that Tony occupied with Clara. After a moment of conversation with them, he pointed toward my truck, as if seeking confirmation, and turned his scuffed and worn Air Jordan's to walk in my direction.

A few breaths later, he was by my door. Smiling jovially, and showing a few gaps where teeth once were, he climbed the step and hooked his elbow over my windowsill to steady himself.

"Mornin'" he greeted, I remained steady. My shotgun casually lain across my lap, and my thumb nonchalant in its position against the trigger.

"Not much for talkin', huh?" the man goaded. "Well, you will. Because we need to have a talk."

"You're off to a good start," I replied, ice in my voice, something about him set my nerves on edge. "So why don't you continue, so we can get on with our day."

"You see," he continued, not missing a beat, "we scavenge here. And you've taken from here. We've had our eye on these machines for quite a while."

"Yeah, so have I," I replied, the same level tone. "Guess you should have been here yesterday, you could have had them."

"Son," the man replied, "I'm reasonable. I'd like to cut you a deal for half. Of everything you've got. You see, my boss has a compound, and our people could re-"

It was then I cut him off with the back of my fist across what was left of his teeth. My goal was to take him off the truck completely, he merely staggered on his perch and came right back with the muzzle of a pistol pressed firmly against the side of my head. Well...fuck. It wasn't supposed to work like this. Not at all.

"Okay. Okay," I cautioned the man, "I'm sorry about that. I'm nervous, I've never done this before."

Grinning, he spat blood onto the street surface.

"That's fine, it's easy," he climbed back into his sales pitch, "as I was saying, our people could really use the supplies. Looks like two-thirds now, you know, split lip tax."

"I'm going to reach slowly for my radio," I warned, feeling the pistol press tighter into my skin.

"Only if it's to tell your friends to comply," the man warned.

I nodded and reached for the radio.

"Everybody." I spoke into the mic, and waited for all cars to check in, "This man happens to be one hell of a salesman, and he wants two-thirds of everything we've got."

"No," Tony's voice crackled in. "Fuck that."

Tony was met with agreement from our peers. Good. I hope they caught my intention with my next words.

"Now guys," I calmed, "he's coming from a good angle. But, instead of two-thirds, let's give him all. We aren't far from home."

I could see the man's smile widen in my peripheral vision. I keyed the mic to stay open.

"Now," I spoke, as in one motion, I ducked my head forward and depressed the shotgun's trigger with my thumb and prayed. The gun dug into my thighs as it went off. The sound of the shot inside the cabin of the truck was beyond deafening. The shot was true, ripping through the door of the truck and catching him square in the midsection. The force of the blast did what my backhand couldn't and sent him sprawling onto the pavement clutching and clawing at his gut.

A moment after, Dave opened up with his AK, and every other vehicle began spitting ammunition through doors and windows and...receiving fire. By the time the wave of panic for my friends washed over me, it was over. Gun smoke rolled across our area and people began scrambling out of vehicles. That's when I heard it. It was Clara's voice.

"Tony's hit!" she yelled. "He's fuckin' hit!"

"So am I," Dave called from behind me, as I turned in horror to see my friend of many years passing the front of my truck, clutching his chest.

"Shit hurts more than I thought it would," he said as he leaned against the front of the truck.

"Ah fuck man. Fuck, fuck, fuck, Dave, fuck!" I chanted, then yelled to the others, "Can you move Tony?"

"He's coming," replied Rich. "He's okay. Shoulder got grazed he says."

On cue, Tony came from the line of vehicles, a thin line of blood dripping from his shoulder. Then he saw Dave and started running.

We got Dave's hand away from his chest and saw three neat little wounds right across the mass of his narrow chest. Each wound wept with blood. Getting him laid down on the pavement, I pulled my knife and cut the front of his shirt open.

"Give me some water," I called out, and immediately received a bottle.

I punched a hole in the top of the lid with my knife so I could squeeze the bottle and create enough pressure to clean the wounds out. Then, while Clara knelt next to him, and Tony stood over top, I began irrigating his wounds, washing blood and dirt away as gently as I could.

When the water hit his chest, Dave let out a gasp of air. Poor fucker.

With the wounds cleaned, I could look at what we were working with.

"What the fuck?" I inquired.

"What is it?" Tony asked, panic in his voice.

"Get me a med kit," I instructed Tony, who dug into his backpack and handed his to me.

I searched the kit and found exactly what I was looking for.

"Okay Dave," I said soothingly. "Do you want regular, or Lion King?"

Everybody, even Dave, shared a near identical inquisitive expression.

"You weren't shot, dickhead!" I chastised Dave. "Probably shrapnel, it hit you but didn't even penetrate. You're missing skin, it will sting for a bit, but you're probably okay."

"Oh!" Dave said, shocked, then laid his head back on the pavement, looking like the fool he probably felt he was. Tony erupted in peals of laughter, and Clara got up and walked away shaking her head and squeezing the bridge of her nose.

"Why do I deal with you guys?" Clara asked, turning back around, her expression halfway between exasperation and humor.

"We're family," Tony replied, before bursting with laughter again and helping our friend to his feet.

"Hey!" Rich called, "We've got one missing and one alive!"

"Keep that fucker breathing," I instructed Rich as I marched over, then barked to James and Clara, "Go find the other guy. Alive, if you can. Dude mentioned they have a base. I want to know our neighbors."

Just then we heard the rattling of a trash can next to an adjacent building.

"He went that-o-way," I said, pointing, as the pair took off after him.

Turning to Rich, I asked, "Where's he hit?"

"Twice in the leg, looks like," Rich replied, then added, "I'll clean and wrap the wounds."

"Tie his hands and gag him first," I ordered, just as Clara and James rounded the corner of the near building with a white guy in his early twenties between them. Must have been a short hunt.

They pushed the guy down to his knees in front of me.

"Look, dude," I said in explanation, "I don't want to be a dick. All we wanted was this equipment, now all I want from you is info on your, uh, your settlement."

"Nah," he replied cockily. "Fuck you, homie."

"Okay," I started, then, giving my best Gary Cooper impression, "We have ways of making you talk."

Rich finished up with his guy, and we were just about ready to get underway again.

"Tie them both up, legs, hands, and gags," I instructed. "Then put them in the back of my truck. Just push that car of theirs out of the way with your truck, leave the bikes where they are. I'm hungry and tired, I want to go home."

Everybody complied, and in no time the sounds of our engines filled the air, and we began our slow parade back home once the car was nudged aside by the massive dump truck.

"You know," Dave began, "I really liked that shirt."

"Shut up, Dave," I replied.

TWENTY-SEVEN

The rolling chain link gate moved out of the way as our vehicles approached the compound. Compound, I like that. I think I'll keep it.

My truck being the last, I pulled up to where a smiling Henry stood and leaned out my window.

"You done good, my brother!" Henry called cheerfully. "Real good. Praise God!"

"Thanks man," I replied, then, "Hey, listen, Dave's going to walk with you to get your storage keys for the south building. Then you're going to meet in the parking lot with the equipment and start assigning jobs. We begin gathering wall materials and digging the dry moat tomorrow morning."

"Okay," he replied, ponderous. "Okay yes sir, that sounds like a plan my friend."

Dave climbed out of my truck, still shirtless, and joined Henry as the older man slid the gate back and locked it, then headed toward the motor pool. The other construction vehicles made their way to the far side of the parking lot. I didn't want the whole community to witness us offloading prisoners. I didn't know how well it would sit with them.

I pulled my truck to the front doors of the south building, and then put the back of it to the double sets of doors and waited. I was halfway through a cigarette when Dave came walking up the motor pool ramp, across the way to my position, tossing a large set of keys from hand to hand.

As I disembarked from my vehicle and headed to the front doors, Dave followed, wordless. We were here to do work that needed to be done, but clearly neither of us enjoyed.

Into the front doors, to the west flight of stairs, and down. There were storage lockers here, tenants could lease them for a little extra, each one about six by eight feet in size. They had solid doors, and could lock. This would do fine for containment.

We found a pair of lockers, unlocked them, and left the doors hanging open. We then retrieved the two men and placed one in each…cell, I guess. They're cells now. Looks like we have a prison. Now, how do we get information out of the prisoners?

I started with the basic questions. Grandma stuff first. Have you eaten? Do you have enough to live on at home? You're not still dating that girl, are you? Okay, maybe not as far as the last question, but the most I could get out of either of these wannabe gangsters was that they were both hungry.

Playing the nice guy, I had Dave grab some MRE's from our scavenge bags, and we set them both up with full bellies. Still, no breaking. They didn't even so much as breathe what side of town they were located.

I was about to start asking a bit more firmly, if you will, when Tony appeared.

"Nobody saw you heading here?" I asked him.

"Nah man, nobody," Tony replied.

"Good," I answered. "I don't know how many of our people would be on board with keeping prisoners."

"Makes sense," Tony concurred. "Anything from them?"

"Nah bro," I replied. "Not a peep, and we should have been smarter and blindfolded them. One of them recognized our buildings, so we can't just sneak them back out and send them home."

"Damn," Tony grunted. "Well, we need someone to watch them. A guard, I guess."

"Someone who doesn't mind being alone, and can keep this secret," I speculated. "Has anyone seen Chris?"

Both Tony and Dave exchanged puzzled looks, then admitted they hadn't. Neither had noticed him in a couple of days. I hadn't either. Where the hell could the guy be?

"Okay, we'll figure that out later," I relented. "Looks like you two are on rotating guard duty tonight. Give them each a bottle of water, don't talk to them unless they are willing to spill it all."

They agreed, and I left. I joined the group in the parking lot just as Henry was going over the final revision of the plans to bolster our defenses.

Work and security in shifts, with two teams. One team starts tearing down houses for materials and space, the other, smaller team, runs and guards the equipment as efforts are made to build a lengthy dry moat two blocks out from our original wall, buying us farming and living space, with enough land between walls to create a no man's land for anything trying to intrude. The moat was to be about eight feet wide, and just as deep.

Eventually, all the houses would be torn down, save for a sporadic few new constructions that could stand a while with little to no maintenance. The basements left behind would eventually be filled in with soil as we got bored and dug the moat deeper and wider, the land made then to farm to supply ourselves for a longer period of time.

These were solid plans, and everybody seemed positive in their shared outlook. Safety and security. Sustainability. I wasn't sure if I was the only one aware of the long-term implications, but this had a depressing undertone. The talk of things built to last and planning so far ahead. We were resigned. We were giving up hope of this ending. We were colonists in a new, hostile, dead world. This was our lives now.

I broke the mood anyway, but in a different manner.

"Hate to break up the positivity everyone," I broke in, "but has anyone seen Chris in the last few days?"

Nobody had.

"Okay," I stated. "From now on, everybody checks in with Jennifer at dinner time. Spread out, I want the compound searched for him. I'll start in the basement of the south building. Everyone else check everywhere. In pairs. Let's go, people!"

We searched through the afternoon, and a team went out to give a check outside the wall for a block in each direction. They found a flashlight, and a strange looking glass smoking pipe a half block away, but reported no blood. Well, at least he didn't appear to have been eaten. Now, where did he go?

I advised the team that was to go out scavenging in the morning to keep an eye open for him, and to do their job in the direction that his clues led. Maybe we'd get lucky. Maybe not. There was so much going on, we could try, but, where the hell was I supposed to have the time and resources to search a dead town, attached to a dead city, for one guy?

***

Dinner was the typically joyous affair, this time complete with Henry and James keeping busy assigning positions for work teams for the next day, and Rich with his own plans. He was talking in my ear about how he needs this and that, how his future armory could be waterproofed and secured. I told him my new favorite go-to response.

"Make a list, give it to Bri."

After finishing the food and what conversation that felt pertinent, I retired downstairs. Jennifer and Gwen were nowhere to be found, probably still conversing on the rooftop. That was okay, I undressed and flung myself on the bed. Jennifer was still recovering, in a sense, from the loss of Melissa. If she could have some time with friends, I was thankful. It was time to distract herself, and time to give myself to get lost in other thoughts.

I didn't. I was asleep before I could reach that damned itch in that weird spot on my back.

TWENTY-EIGHT

I rolled out of bed in the morning, Jennifer still breathing lightly, fast asleep. Walking past Gwen's room, I noticed she was still out cold, too. Good. At least I didn't have to explain my plans for the day to anybody.

Making my way out of the entrance to the building I paused, taking in the warm early morning, the sun not quite having broken the horizon yet, though its heat was still apparent.

I looked around to make sure nobody was watching and noticed Henry on the southern rooftop keeping guard. I decided he wasn't looking my way so I took a moment to relieve myself on the nearest bush and began walking to the entrance of the southern building.

Once inside, a left turn, one flight of steps down, and I found myself looking at Tony. He was sitting slouched in a lawn chair in the middle of the hallway, fast asleep.

I folded my arms, and loudly cleared my throat. He stirred a bit, then casually opened his eyes and promptly closed them again as he fell into a deep yawn, followed by a stretch.

"Wake up, you fuck," I grumbled, trying to project some jest into my tone.

"Oh!" Tony replied lazily. "What's up, dude? I figured they weren't going anywhere."

"You're lucky you were military," I replied. "Otherwise I'd question your ability to wake up from a snooze if they made noise escaping."

"It's an acquired talent," Tony said, grinning. "So what are we going to do?"

I whispered some quiet instructions to him, and he left.

Looking around at the hallway I occupied, I took it all in. The occupied section of the corridor was lit by candlelight, the light ending just past the area needed to view. Eyeing the two securely locked doors, our first prison cells, I recalled all the power generation equipment we'd gathered on the rooftops and retrieved the radio from my side.

"James, you up?" I spoke into the handset.

After a moment, "Yeah, barely, boss, what's up?" James' voice crackled through the device.

"Where we at with getting power hooked up?" I questioned, then, "Over."

"Uhhhh Rob says he has everything just about ready in the security room," he said, recalling details. "I've been busy with y'all but I can get the rest of the power ran in a few hours probably. Over."

"Get you some coffee," I instructed, "and get on it then. I'd like to be able to heat up a Hot Pocket by lunch time. Over."

"Sir," James began, "we don't have any of those. Over."

"Yeah," I replied with a chuckle, "but the thought is nice. If Henry asks, tell him you two will help him with the dry moat after your job is done."

A new voice broke the line as soon as my last words left my mouth.

"Loud and clear my friend." It was Henry, "We'll get the streets emptied in a short while, I'll begin digging and building after that. Oh, and, uh, copy on James and Rob. Over."

"Good shit, brother," I replied. "I'll be busy with my own project, I'll find you later on. Over."

We finished our conversation and James began hailing Rob, who replied, eventually. They sorted out a meeting in the security center and broke radio contact. Henry quickly picked up the line and started calling people to put out the breakfast call to the local freaks. I'm sure Dave and Tony were sore they were missing that, but we had our own business to attend to.

A few more beats and here they came, each one carrying their own end of a large folding card table with an assortment of things piled on top, including a couple of heavy wooden folding chairs from the floor above, some rope, and other items I'd asked for.

Arguing amongst each other like a couple of siblings, they finally set the table up lengthwise in the hallway and began organizing its contents.

"Okay," I began instructing, "I want each of them in their cell, shirtless, and tied very firmly to a chair. I've got some questions to ask these fine young gentlemen."

Both of my friends agreed, complied, and in a few more minutes both of our captives were tied, scared, and complaining.

I stepped into the first room. The younger white guy tied to the chair did not look too pleased. His shirt off, patches of tattoos covered his body, including 'Always Faithful' stretched in an arc across his narrow belly.

"Mornin'!" I said cheerily. "I've got questions, of course, if you work with us, I set you free, maybe even drive you home. Give me shit, and I'll have to find another place much, much further away to deliver you to. I don't really want to kill off the living though, so, please, work with me here."

He glared at me like I had kicked his mother. Okay. Not much progress so far.

I retrieved a pack of cigarettes from my pocket, a lighter, took one for myself and lit it, and shook another loose to offer to the young man tied to the chair. He shook his head and grinned.

"Nah asshole, I don't smoke that shit," he replied, sly venom in his voice. "That's why you bitches gonna lose. We stay fit."

"That's nice in theory," I began, exhaling a cloud of smoke into his face, "but you're the one half naked and tied to a chair in my basement, fuck head. Would you like to reconsider your cockiness?"

His grin disappeared, replaced by a scowl in an instant. Good.

"Not gonna be so sure of yourself when Big Tyler find out about this spot," the man spat.

"That's your leader?" I asked. No reply. "Okay then, what's your name?"

Nothing.

"Where is your home in this new world?" I tried, still nothing. He just sat tied to the chair looking straight down between his feet.

This continued on for nearly thirty minutes. He wouldn't answer anything at all.

"You can beat me, starve me, whatever you want, bitch," he finally offered. "Ain't selling out the family. You ain't gettin' shit out me, home boy."

"Oh, I think I will. I've got a backup plan," I said, smiling wide, and whispered something quickly to Dave, who disappeared for a moment and came back in with a small armload of items.

Since the guy wouldn't break eye contact with the floor at his feet, that's where I placed my tools. In this space, I laid a metal serving spoon and a quart of heavy weight motor oil. With my hands free, I retrieved the lighter from my pocket and used it to light the MAP gas bottle torch I still held. This was also placed at his feet, flame pointed toward him, just far enough away for some of the heat to reach the man.

He started visibly changing his firm position, a thin bead of sweat breaking out on his brow, but he remained silent and tried to project as much resilience as possible.

"I want to be a good host," I explained, straining to retain the cheer in my voice, despite my own admonitions at what was to come.

I picked up the motor oil and cracked the top of the container open.

"In respect to my graciousness," I continued, not letting any of my own tension break the calm of my tone, "all I ask, is that you provide us with some info. Maybe we could even open up trade, and positive relations with your...Big Tyler. That's really what he goes by?"

The man remained firm.

I proceeded to pick up the serving spoon, and, in clear view of his eyes, measured out a brimming spoonful of motor oil.

"This is probably the last chance to offer me what I'm asking for," I cautioned. He spat at me, a sticky, dehydrated stream of spittle landing on the front of my shirt.

"Okay." I strained to remain calm, outwardly, at least, "You must just be tense. I'll help you relax."

I removed my now saliva-tainted shirt.

"Tony, gag him with this," I instructed calmly.

Tony, looking a bit uneasy, took the shirt from me and approached the man. He resisted, clenching his jaw and not allowing the cotton tee any passage.

"I'd like this to be as easy as possible on our guest," I offered, "so, if the shirt won't fit, remove some teeth. It should work then."

Well imagine that. Suddenly his jaw relaxed and he allowed himself to be gagged.

I picked up the still-lit torch and motioned toward the captive with it.

"I've never done a massage like this before," I explained, touching the flame of the torch to the bottom of the spoonful of oil, "but, from what I understand, the oil should be heated to relieve tension and help calm you."

The man's eyes widened a noticeable amount.

"You sure you don't want to help us? I may write a book about this someday, I want to make sure I've got the information just right!" I explained.

His eyes narrowed, he stared straight ahead, and he puffed his chest slightly. Okay. I'd have given up the ghost at this prospect, apparently this guy is, as his tattoo would indicate, Always Faithful.

"No problem!" I said, my stomach turning behind my Pleasantville grin. "Let me know if this is too warm for you or just right."

The oil in the spoon began bubbling and letting off a pungent blue-white smoke.

I stepped to the man, removed the heat from the spoon, and began to drizzle the oil over his back and shoulders. The skin began to turn and crackle everywhere the heated honey-like fluid contacted it. The screams emanating from his throat resonated through the whole corridor despite their muffle.

The stench of hot oil and burning flesh filled the room, stifling the already thick air, and permeating every bit of my being.

As if queued, the rifle fire from outside began, signaling the start of the neighborhood watch, as Tony began calling our morning clean-up of the area. The shots were light, sporadic in their staccato, apparently less partygoers each morning, as this sounded lighter than the last.

After moments that seemed to be hours, the spoon was empty. The prisoner slouched in his seat, against his bindings, panting and sobbing heavily. Tears mixed with long streams of snot dripped in runners down his face and over the shirt still occupying his mouth. The oil-soaked flesh looked as ugly as any horror movie makeup I'd ever seen.

My stomach threatened to give up everything it didn't contain inside of it, but I steeled myself and began anew.

Filling the spoon back up with oil, and reapplying the heat source to it, I asked again, struggling to remain casual.

"Now, are you relaxed? Would you like to help me out a bit here? Oil isn't made anymore, and it's kind of a commodity now."

The response was, in truth, not what I'd expected. He arched and pressed against his bindings, letting out a muffled bellow as every tendon, muscle, and vein popped to the surface and the chair creaked heavily before he relaxed and locked eyes with me, glaring as rage broke the surface in his expression.

"Okay, your choice," I called to him. "Usually we only offer a twenty-minute experience, but we'll give you the full hour session, since clearly you're still tense."

The spoonful of oil brought back to a heat so warm you could see the heat roiling on its surface and I approached again. I began allowing a long thin drizzle to fall into his close-cropped hair, then, impatient, I dumped the whole large spoonful at once over his head. The oil and skin fizzled and even popped as it came into contact with sweat, exploding pockets of the bodily fluid with audible snaps and sizzles. The substance rolled down his head, hissing more as it came into contact with his ears, and his neck, hungrily transforming the flesh it contacted. His muffled screams reached such a pitch as to be inaudible as he pulled and strained before finally going limp.

In my distance I could hear Tony retching in the corner as Dave began calling my name.

"Scott! Fuck, man!" Dave bellowed. "Enough, god dammit, too much! He's done!"

Pulling myself back to the world I quickly pressed my fingers into the cooling oil on the side of his neck. A pulse.

"He's still alive," I whispered to my buddies. "We can use this. Tony, say he's dead."

"Okay, he's dead," Tony whispered, his voice soft but very matter of fact.

"No, dude, say it so the other guy hears," I urged as realization dawned on Tony's face.

"Dude!" Tony called loudly, "What the fuck did you do? We needed answers and you killed him! Shit!"

"Well," I began, equally loud and clear, "I guess it's a good thing we brought a spare."

As a trio, we exited the room, turned, and entered the storage locker next door. Here, a slightly larger, slightly heavier built black man of about the same age sat in the same bound position as the other man. Again, tattoos present here and there. Except, this one didn't appear to be as ready to fight as the other.

"I'm going to cut to the chase here because I don't want to waste any more time," I counselled. "Your buddy next door just died from shock, from the pain, and didn't even give a name. Your choice. Think fast."

I immediately poured out a spoonful of oil and began heating it up.

"No need," the man said calmly. "I've got no family to protect there. The other guy was Big Tyler's nephew, Johnny, and you just brought a war down on yourself killing him. You need to answer for that. He will end you."

"Yeah?" I paused, both perplexed and relieved at this one's compliance, "Okay, where?"

"The old high school in the North of the city," he informed, then added, "By the fire department."

"Okay good," I replied, dousing the torch and setting my things aside. "How many are there? How well supplied and armed? What's their disposition?"

"All I can and will say," he continued, "is that Big Tyler intends to take over the city. He's enslaving anyone weaker and recruiting those loyal."

"How many people, how many weapons?" I asked again.

"I won't give that much up. I'm sorry," he admitted, looking resigned, "you can torture and kill me, too, I just can't."

"That's okay," I said easily. "We have a location, we can scout it easily enough."

"That's fair," the man replied. "Name's Tyrone, by the way. I didn't get yours."

"Sir," I replied firmly. "You can call me Sir. Hey, Tony?"

"Yes sir," Tony reported.

"See, Tyrone? Sir works for me," I smiled, then, to Tony, "Go get some shit to clean and patch the other guy up and get him woken up. We'll find a plan for them, they can't go straight home."

Confusion crossed Tyrone's face as Tony disappeared into the hallway.

"Yeah, sorry for the deception," I informed Tyrone, "Johnny isn't dead, but he is badly burned, and the pain did cause him to lose consciousness."

"You'd have been better off killing him," Tyrone cautioned, "Tyler is a dangerous man."

"Oh well. So am I," I warned. "Dave, get this man together, and get him some water and a little food. Wherever we go, he's got a journey tomorrow. He'll need to be ready."

"Got it," Dave replied.

TWENTY-NINE

Out in the morning sun was a beautiful sight to my eyes. Henry was out directing and supervising a full set of both construction, and armed escort. Most of our available people were here as backhoe and excavator worked in tandem digging out a trench two full blocks away from our existing fence. One team was assigned to each vehicle, as well as another for the people working on foot.

While the machines dug, another team stripped fencing and any other large flat materials they could grab from the surrounding neighborhood, including the plywood lining the inner walls of an adjacent garage. I could count only a half dozen people not present, presumably Carolyn with the kids, Rob and James working in the north building, Dave and Tony, and, still no Chris.

Henry turned and waved to me and promptly turned back and started directing the next section of wall into place. They'd been at it for probably an hour tops and already had a twenty-foot section of earth moved, eight foot wide and just as deep. The wall that was going up on the inside perimeter of this was being backed by the dirt being dug out, and the front being braced by 2X4's, I assumed just until supports could be dug and fastened and the dirt behind settled.

It was truly a beehive of activity. I think, out of all we'd been through, this level of teamwork made me most proud of our little community. Even Katie and Parker were fast at work and doing so with only a little grumbling.

Deciding not to bother the progress, I started walking back to the apartment buildings, confident that Henry could keep everything running smoothly.

About halfway there, I noticed the front of a boat trailer sticking out from next to a garage. An idea hit me all at once, and I walked over to investigate the find further.

I approached it and grabbed the fasteners to the cover and stripped it from the machine. What sat before me was a boat. Clearly. About 25 ft in length, maybe? Had two engines, seating, and what looked to be an interior cabin with a small bed, storage, and more seating.

The wheels in my head started turning faster. I grabbed the two-way radio from my hip and spoke into it.

"Hey, Tony?" I said into the microphone, "Y'all done up there? Over."

"Yeah man," he replied, "Dave's just finishing up."

"Over?" I questioned, half serious, half joking.

"Over," he replied lightly.

"Good shit," I said in turn. "Grab Dave and a truck with a trailer hitch. I've got a boat I need you to pick up, get it set up by the river and park it."

I rattled off an address when he was ready and ended the conversation, thinking I was done, when another one started up.

"A boat? That's frickin' cool man, we going fishing?" It was James, "Oh, uhh, over."

"Nah, man," I spoke back. "I'm going on a trip up the river. What's up? Over."

"Hey if you got a second, come up to security. Over," James replied.

"Yeah. On my way. Over," I replied, replacing the radio on my hip and starting in the direction of the towers.

I walked into the security office on the ninth floor, still a bit out of breath from all those steps but not as much as usual. I'd cut back on smoking, next is to quit all together, right? Probably easier to do since tobacco wasn't so easily accessible anymore as each trip to the gas station could kill you.

Looking around the space, it had been set up more cleanly and smoothly than before. The masses of wires and cables had been tucked and hidden. Everything appeared to be hooked up. James appeared in the doorway of a nearby walk-in closet.

"Hey boss!" he said cheerily, grinning.

"I can only assume this is good news?" I asked, caution breaking my tone.

He retrieved the radio from his belt and spoke into it.

"Hey Rob, stand by, over."

Rob's voice came back through the radio, affirming what he had been told.

"Okay boss man," James continued, "Rob's watching the equipment topside, I've got to keep an eye on the power closet for any issues. Whenever you're ready, flip that switch over there."

He motioned to a forearm-sized red lever on the back wall before returning to his closet hideaway.

"Uh, okay," I replied to the empty room.

I moved to the switch and paused. What was going on here? Some kind of trick? Or...?

"Hey James!" I yelled over to him, "Just flip the switch?"

"Yeah!" he replied, "Go for it! Just don't look right at it as you activate it, in case there's an issue or surge!"

"Okay," I said with a shrug, grabbed the switch, turned my head, and pulled it down.

A loud click followed by several smaller ones resounded throughout the room. The lights overhead flickered, and then died, then flickered back to life to stay. All of the screens and computers on the partition flickered on, flooding the area with a whitish-blue light, although they all had error prompts on screen.

Then, a sound I had all but forgotten flooded my ears. Its sweet low song permeated every bit of my being. It tugged at me. It pulled me and drove me. Within moments, I was standing in front of the source. A wall-mount air conditioner. My God.

"James?" I called loudly, "James, I think I love you, man!"

James appeared, grinning like a child.

"A/C in here only, to keep the equipment cool. I need to monitor the power draw," he explained. "We should have basic power throughout both buildings though. A couple refrigerators, maybe, but nothing drastic."

"How?" I asked, realizing the power draw needed just to light both buildings, and Henry's garage. Plus, whatever else came up in the future.

"Well, I'm going to monitor all that," James explained. "We should have enough. Of course, more will always be better, and we'll look for ways to do that. The good news is that it took a hell of a lot of juice to run everything they had. Grow lights, hydroponic systems, climate control, ventilation…"

He trailed off, shrugging one shoulder. Just then, Rob made his entrance.

"Now to get all the programming talking to all the cameras and the DVR the right way," he said, taking a seat in front of the bank of monitors.

"How many cameras do we have?" I asked. "I thought the complex only had about ten, didn't it?"

"It did," Rob answered, "but one of the last scouting runs brought in some real nice outdoor units and plenty of wiring from local stores and the bank. We have twenty-three now. One was damaged when Parker dropped it off its perch, or we'd have every box on each screen filled."

"Of course," I said, resigned that Parker would never be quite great. "Well, you guys got everything handled here? When you're done see if Henry needs anything."

Both replied in the affirmative and I departed, putting out a call on the open channels to everybody in our community.

"Listen up, everybody with a radio, relay this message," I started. "We have power thanks to James and Rob. Don't use it. We need to figure things out for now. Power only basic lighting, and, if your apartment doesn't have window tint or blackout curtains, then lights off completely at dusk. Not so much as a reading light, or night light for that matter. Do not bust down the airwaves replying, we'll talk more at dinner about this."

As I broke the threshold downstairs and into sunlight, Dave and Tony passed blindly by in a pickup truck. I could hear the nearby construction project. Kids playing on the other side of the common area. My skin could still remember the recent blasting of cold air. Most of us were still here. Things were looking to be going quite well, all things considered.

Rich came by on foot with Willy. They barely noticed as they passed by.

"Hey!" I called to them, they both stopped and turned, "Where you two going?"

"Willy says we should be able to break the pool drain to open it without power!" Rich said cheerily.

"Should be able to drain it," Willy offered, "and keep the basin mostly dry still when it rains."

"Henry don't need help?" I questioned.

"Nah," Rich replied. "They're running smooth, that's why we're going up here."

"Okay." I shrugged, and they shrugged, then we parted.

I crossed the common area to the opposite side, where the kids were playing. Carolyn had gotten her hands on a box of sidewalk chalk, and the result was a smear of color that would actually be considered art in some modern colleges.

Naturally, Gwen saw me and ran straight for me, yelling "Daddy!" over and over. She met me with her trademark knee-level hug, so I picked her up and squeezed her.

I felt a little guilty, mornings and evenings were spent with her, but the time was always short as there was never a time without a series of fires to put out. I needed to get this place situated so I could give her the time she should have with her father. That was something I'd never get back with Melissa. Yet, here I was, planning at least a few days journey for the next day.

Gwen and I played for a while. By play, I mean she'd make a series of haphazard lines in the three colors of chalk she was afforded, occasionally finding a random piece of nothing on the ground to come over and shove in dear old dad's face. I accepted every piece I was given, and without hassle. After all, the toddler always knows best.

Eventually, Tony and Dave pulled up in the truck, boat in tow.

"It's the fuckin' Catalina Wine Mixer bro!" Tony cheered.

"Boats and hoes!" Dave shouted in turn.

"Christ," I replied. "You two need more than help. That movie sucked!"

"We got the boat, dude!" Tony replied, without breaking stride in conversation.

"What's this?" I asked, eyeballing the mass of rubber bungee straps around the trailer coupling.

"Wrong size hitch," Dave explained, then, "Dipshit here gave me the wrong info."

"Hey, I didn't know!" Tony retorted, to which Dave reached out, grabbed Tony's nipple through the shirt, and twisted, eliciting a shout and arm punch from Tony.

"Okay, alright love birds," I chided. "Go get this pig in the water and moored to the shore. It needs five days of supplies for a half dozen people. Should do it, I think."

"You got it!" Tony replied cheerily, then the two drove off toward the riverfront side of the compound.

I entertained Gwen a bit longer, or maybe much longer, until the work crews started back our way in small vehicles, leaving the equipment where they finished, ready for the next day.

I questioned Henry as he approached about the wisdom of leaving them there, but he assured me they couldn't be started easily. He did, however, express concerns over fuel, as they already siphoned most of what the dump trucks had to keep the equipment running. I agreed that we'd address that issue shortly over dinner.

THIRTY

Before long, the entire populace, save for some sentries left to keep watch, were on the rooftop of the north building. The fare was fancy as ever. Tonight, what Dave referred to as a jail break, noodles, spam, and a few types of cobbled together sauces to choose from.

Food came in with every supply run, and it came in armloads and boxes, but enough of one type to make a meal for everyone the same was running thin in a hurry. It didn't seem like it would be much longer until we were on individual meals, or seemingly worse, everyone with their own can of food or sharing an MRE with a companion. We'd need to send a long-term team out soon, with the goal of bolstering our food stores as much as possible. The heat of the year was peaked, and soon it would only get cooler, then, finally, the Ohio winter would come to settle. That time of year, with our bitter cold and mountains of ice and snow, you had to eat double just to stay warm and healthy.

Everyone had seemed to form their own little groups for dinner time. Friends and family sharing tables. The table I claimed for myself was near the entrance end of the rooftop, the west end of the north building. It had become common for me to hold less formal meetings here, outside of our makeshift council meets with the heads of each department. It was time for another, Tony and I had the table to ourselves as Jennifer and Gwen had made their own friends to spend time with.

"James, Henry, Rich, Dave!" I called out. Several heads turned my way, and I motioned the four over to the table. "Leave your food, grab a seat, guys. This won't take long."

They all approached, sat, and pleasantries were made before beginning the night's meeting.

"I'm going to be as quick, and to the point as I can be," I explained. "Henry?"

"Yeah?" Henry inquired.

"Your work crew just got cut to a smaller size for the next several days," I said, as I watched a cloud of confusion move over his face, and I explained, "Tony, you're going to be in charge, as my second in command, for the next few days. You saw that coming?"

"Well, yeah, with the boat and all that," Tony opined.

"Rich and Dave are going to come with me," I explained, "we've got a boat, and we're going up river and back. Probably gone two to three days."

"Why up the river?" Rich questioned.

"I'll explain in private in a minute," I answered, then, "Henry, this means you'll be short on that end, and James has a job to do for me for a few days or so as well, he'll take as many as a half dozen with him. Your work capacity will be diminished, but I expect you to do the best you can. You're project foreman."

"Well, I guess, but we won't make as much progress," Henry explained.

"That's fine, I expect that. All I ask is you do the best you can. Now go get to your meal before it gets cold, brother." Henry and I shook hands, and he departed. As he passed Jennifer, I noticed her watching the meeting.

"James," I stated.

"Yeah man what's up?" James inquired.

"You've driven heavy vehicles, any good with a semi?" I asked, eying his expression.

"If it's auto. I'm shit with manual. Those non-synchronized things..." he trailed off, shaking his head.

"That's fine," I said, then retrieved a notepad and pen from my pocket and began writing. "You're going to take four people. I'm taking Rich and Dave. Tony needs to be in command here, so whoever is left that you have confidence in their discipline and marksmanship. Take a week of supplies, but I don't want you gone longer than four days."

"Uh, okay, yes sir," James said, unsure and a bit concerned. "What are we doing?"

"We need you to scout something, and we need fuel, food, and whatever else you can find," I instructed, then, sliding a page from my pad across to him, "Old Northern High School. Keep your distance, and, at all costs, do not engage. Run if you're spotted. Do not fight. These guys aren't good nor are they neighborly people."

"Fuck," James muttered softly. "How do you know about them?"

"A friend told me," I offered. "What I need is detailed on that page. Numbers. Bad guys? Do they have good guys? Hostages? How well supplied are they? Are they comfortable? Disciplined? Draw a rough map of their grounds. Their defenses. Vehicles, locations of who and what. Take pics. Bust the flash bulbs in your cameras so there's no 'oh fuck, they saw a flash'. Scout them for 48 hours, then you move on, no matter what, to your next objectives. Understood?"

"Understood," James stated as the others exchanged glances. "Yes, sir."

"Very good," I commended. "Now, part two. We need fuel, so you need to find a tanker. We need diesel as priority, but, if you can't find it, gasoline will do, but we need diesel the most, okay?"

"Yeah, sure, how do I tell them apart though without opening the tank?" he questioned.

"Easy," I replied, writing more on a new page. "Here. The front, back, and both sides of any tanker will be labeled with diamond shaped placards. They'll be considered bulk, so they'll have what's known as a U.N. number in that diamond. Gasoline is 1203. Diesel is 1993. And if you're not sure, you know what gasoline looks and smells like. Diesel will have a blueish-green tint and smell kind of oily."

"Oh, okay," James replied. "Makes sense."

"Trucks can pull a lot of weight," I continued. "Even if it's full of fuel, load it with whatever you can fit or strap to the outside. Stock us up. You've got 48 additional hours to do this. Most newer semis in company fleets are automatics anyway, you should be okay there. Just watch out for off-tracking."

"What the fuck is off-tracking?" Dave interjected.

"Trailer will always turn in sharper than the tractor, dude," I told Dave. "That's why semis always pull forward, then turn in, to clear turns, otherwise you could end up wrecking, or getting the trailer stuck."

Dave simply nodded and leaned back, clearly satisfied with having learnt something new.

"There's a second part to your scavenging," I continued. "The military seemed to have the outskirts of downtown blocked and guarded. It's a long shot, but continue south once you've left the school, see if they left anything at all useful on the bridges and venues over and through the gorge and valleys near downtown. And, finally, while you're scouting, keep an eye on any parts stores, fuel stations, and private garages you see. We need every drop of any fuel stabilizers and additives you can find."

"Okay, yes sir," James responded, now miles deep in thought. "Yeah, sounds good to me."

"If there's no further questions," I ordered, "go finish dinner, figure out who you're taking with you, and get a week of shit for y'all gathered up. You leave here no sooner, no later, than 10:00 hours. Get it together tonight and your crew can sleep in tomorrow. Dismissed."

James got up, shook my hand, and left promptly.

"Tony," I said, turning to my close friend, "Don't fuck up. Do what I do. Help where needed, drink a little, make sure everything gets done and the place doesn't burn down. I should only be gone three days."

"I got it dude," Tony assured. "It will be fine."

"Good," I replied. "Stay out of my good liquor."

"Wait," Tony interjected, smiling. "Where's the good liquor?"

"Not telling," I replied, grinning as I watched his expression drop. "Rich and Dave now."

Both leaned forward in anticipation.

"Dave and Tony have the boat loaded for our trip. All we need is to release the moorings and leave." I informed Rich, "I have a hypothetical for you."

"Alright!" Rich said, an eager expression shading his face, "Shoot!"

"Let's say," I postulated, "there's bad guys, bad guys with info that could be pertinent to the safety of our entire compound, and all our friends and family within. Would you be above kidnap and torture to extract that information?"

"I mean," Rich said, pondering the question, "there's kids here. I'd kill for the info."

"Good," I stated, lowering my voice and moving in closer to be heard. "We've got two of the gang bangers from Old Northern, we're dropping them off alive far up the river, and scouting things along the way. One's hurt, both are very bad guys, but I don't want to murder them, so we're giving them a chance."

"Makes sense to me boss," Rich assured. "I'll get a kit ready and see you in the morning?"

"Yes, you will," I concurred. "Be up early. We load the guys up at 03:00, before anyone else is awake to see. This stays between us at the table. See you at a quarter till."

Rich departed and James passed by on his way to the stairwell, nodding, and had Willy Grey, Clara, and Frank in tow. Looks like he had his crew. Jennifer then approached with Gwen, having left her spot at the table with Shannon and Ashley.

"Hey!" I said. "Wanna sit and finish eating here?"

She didn't, instead, she questioned, "I heard you guys talking about a boat trip tomorrow?"

"Yeah, we're going to go up river and do some scouting," I lied, "see if anyone else has a camp on the water like us."

"But only three of you?" she persisted. "I don't really like it. There's room for more people on the boat, and it's not safe out there."

"Less people, lower profile," another lie, "and we should be safer in the water. Those fuckers don't go anywhere near it."

"I could come," she began, "if it's safer."

"Not that safe though," I admonished. "I'd rather only one of Gwen's parents risked at a time."

She sat and we continued conversing, catching up a while longer until Tony left for bed, and Jennifer and Gwen departed soon after. I took that as my cue to clear my table and go down to sleep as well.

THIRTY-ONE

My little wind-up alarm clock went off promptly at 0200 hours. As usual, it took me little to wake up fully, and I was up and dressed in little time. I washed my face in the water basin wedged into the bathroom sink, brushed my teeth and left after kissing both Jennifer and Gwen as they lay sleeping.

Promptly at 0245 we met near the boat and Tony and Dave and I led Rich to the spot the prisoners were kept.

Both men were as they'd been left, Tony the last one having been on guard duty for them. They had both been fed and given water. Tyrone and "Mr. Always Faithful" were both tied, gagged and bags placed over their heads, and two of us at a time carried each of the men to the boat and placed them below decks, as far forward as possible and well hidden behind a pile of blankets and gear.

We worked nearly without a word, but the noise clearly drew Fred's attention, as he made his way across the south building rooftop to look down at us and wave.

I returned the wave, and made my way onboard the boat, starting the engines to an idle as Rich and Dave cast away our moorings to the shore. It was all such quiet work, but even the low tone of the engine seemed to echo through the area like a child shouting in a cave.

I kept the engine as low as I could, and we made maybe only a couple knots speed over the water at most, between the low power of an engine near idle, and the river pushing headlong against us. We did our best to maintain silence throughout the predawn hours, the constant rumble of the engine only occasionally broken by muted conversation.

From time to time, we could make out the silhouette of an animal, or a man-shaped figure either on the banks, or further back into the neighborhood. Aside from these sightings, and us, there was not much more to be seen, just the long black tape ribbon of river stretched out through the area, lazily reflecting a near full moon as it passed through the ghost town of a once-thriving population.

We agreed to untie our guests to allow them some food, water, and a restroom break once the sun was up. Didn't want to let them out blindly if there was a chance of being watched by anyone we couldn't see.

The morning had passed lazily, surprisingly calm, as we wound our way slow and steady up the waterway. Dave and Rich had settled themselves into watch positions at the bow and stern of the boat, I kept steady on the wheel to guide us and provide a 360-degree watch. Still, barely a word had passed.

***

Sometime just after dawn Rich spoke up from his position forward.

"Hey!" he said in a harsh whisper. "Guys I've got a small group of them!"

"Hold fire," I ordered in return. "Let's see what happens."

There was indeed about ten figures spread out haphazard on the banks of the river. They seemed to have found their way within the confines of the chain link surrounding the business, apparently not been given a reason to find their way out. Held back on this side only by a short concrete ledge.

As we got closer in the boat, they began to take notice. Most were of the slower variety, and they would take notice, follow with their eyes and feet, but they would not drop into the water.

This was more apparent with the few quicker infected that were present. A couple paced, right there against the edge of their water barrier, as if they were hyenas on the fence at a wildlife preserve. Grunts and chuffs coming from both, interspersed with low vocalizations, reminiscent of a drunk mumbling on the phone in the next room while you're drunk yourself, trying to sleep on the couch. Distant and muddy, nothing but a string of vowels you'll never quite grasp.

A third member of the faster party was a bit further off, closer to the building in the center of their zoo pen. Once he took notice of us, he let his head fall back and shrieked to the heavens, then charged. All three of us audibly tensed up on our weapons.

"Hold fire unless he hits the water!" I called in a low voice, "I don't want the world to know we're here."

The form flew through the streaks of breaking sunlight, highlighted by sunbeams here and there, the shirt to his service uniform flapping out behind him. His chest was streaked with blood and the skin of the freak glowed under the contrasted lighting, broken up by patchy tattoo work.

Then, he just stopped. Okay, he didn't *just* stop. It was a nearly comical display, if you stripped away the dark undertones of this world, that is. The monster broke into full stride about twenty yards from the water. But, once he got closer to it, he began a cartoon-like backpedal. As the freak dug its heels in, one of the shoes split and gave way. Having spent months on a likely rotten foot, it just gave up under the task at hand. This put the freak firmly on his ass, where he slid another yard or so and stopped just short enough to let its now bare foot hit the water.

This set off a short string of those near-barks, grunts, and finally, once the freak found its feet again, a few coughs broke the mostly silent night. He quickly joined his buddies, pacing and vocalizing while shaking his now wet foot about like a dog that found a puddle.

"I'll be damned," Dave muttered.

"Yeah, freaks don't like water then I guess," Rich observed.

"Makes sense why we don't see many of them right around the compound," I opined.

"Compound?" Rich questioned, "I like that name. But, what do you mean?"

"Only two, maybe two and a half sides they can approach us from," I explained, "the bend of the river. It's kind of securing us from them in the west and most of the north of our area."

This set off quiet talking about us having a good spot. Ideas were kicked around regarding making our dry moat into an actual moat. It was quickly decided that as good an idea as that was, it would be impractical to do. And we still had no idea if it was water in general, or a depth thing, or even residual mental conditioning from their previous life. You just simply don't swim in the Cuyahoga River. The damned thing caught fire in the sixties, and I don't personally know anyone who's trusted that water since.

The low chatter eventually wore away as we made our dreadful slow way up the lazily flowing river. We returned to silence as the warmth of a new day began to grow.

The drawn-out quiet brought me to my thoughts. The loss of Melissa. Jennifer and Gwen having to live the rest of their lives like this. No more chance of normalcy. No worries about grades, new school clothes, family holiday dinners.

I wondered where my mother and father were, or if they were even okay.

The sun had just started to break fully free of the horizon as the first tear fell unbidden from my cheek. No way was I letting the guys, let alone anyone else see this. I wiped my face and announced I was going to go below to let Tyrone have a chance at relieving himself and getting a little in his stomach.

Removing my trusted Smith and Wesson from its holster, I went below. I had to walk at a crouch to begin with, and, now, the cabin was even more cramped. Piled high with supplies, and with a large hollow at the front for our two guests, there was no room to get comfortable on board.

Tyrone was closest to me. Good. I found I was having a hard time looking at Johnny. So loyal that he was willing to be tortured and disfigured while retaining all obstinance even long after. We needed something good to shake this crew up enough to give us the advantage.

I nudged Tyrone with my foot and he stirred.

"Wake up, dude," I spoke. "You got to piss? Hungry? Thirsty?"

"Yeah man," he started, then paused, "You been crying? Your eyes are red."

"Nah," I stated. "Just stoned."

"Not quite the goody two-shoes after all," he observed, chuckling, "but we already knew that, after what y'all did to him."

"Tell me his name I'll let you up," I suggested.

"Nope." He objected, "What's it matter anyway?"

"True. Very true. We'll hopefully never see each other again anyway," I concluded.

I let Tyrone out of his bindings. I started warming up a can of Ravioli over a small camp stove for him while he took care of his business and took a seat adjacent to me with a bottle of water. Dave never left his side, the muzzle of Dave's AK47 never straying from the man more than a few degrees. Enough coverage with the rifle to remind the man who's in control here.

Once Tyrone had eaten and been taken care of, he was returned, bound again, to the space reserved for the two of them.

The other man got the same treatment, though Rich was the one who wordlessly watched over his every move while a can of green beans and corn was heated up.

After he was brought back below deck, we each had our own small meal, in turns, and then returned to our posts.

The rest of the morning passed with little to no excitement.

THIRTY-TWO

About midway through the day, we had our first sighting of anything truly interesting since the discovery of the freaks' water phobia. Rich was the first to notice once again.

"Hey, guys?" he asked, then, "I see smoke."

He pointed to a few smallish columns of smoke rising in the near horizon, barely visible against the blue sky.

"What about it?" Dave asked. "We've been seeing smoke here and there all morning."

"This is different," Rich replied. "Look."

"He's right," I concurred. "This is just thin grey smoke, and all I smell from it is wood."

"You thinking people?" Dave asked.

"Yeah man, I am," I agreed. "Keep your weapons ready, but don't fire unless we get shot at first."

We all remained at the ready as we neared the area of the smoke's origin. As we came around the bend of the river, there was a guard post positioned right in the outer elbow of the next bend, a couple hundred yards down from our current position.

As we approached, the top of a man's head became visible in the turret. It soon disappeared behind a cannon-like barrel of a Ma Deuce. That's a fifty-caliber machine gun, if you didn't know. It was nestled behind the armored protection of what appeared to be a turret salvaged from a military vehicle.

"We're not surrounded," I began, "but we are definitely fuckin' outgunned. Be real friendly now, guys. Lower your guns and don't piss off the man with the machine gun. Please."

Dave and Rich both lowered their guns, as did I.

I stood up fully from the driver's seat and began a slow, friendly wave.

"Rich," I said under my breath, "Go below deck, gag both of them, and make sure their ties are secured." Then, almost as an afterthought, "And bring up that bottle of whiskey and hold it up like you're showing it off."

"Okay," Rich complied, "sure thing."

Rich disappeared and I continued my wave as we slowly approached the guardian of this river section. Then the man in the turret also rose and waved back. From this distance I could make out long, dark hair, a shirtless body covered in tattoos depicting demons, skulls, and various metal bands. Everything below the guy's neck appeared to be covered.

Just then, Rich appeared back above deck, holding a bottle of Jack Daniels up on high as if he were showing off a trophy. To this, the man in the turret laughed, pointed at the bottle, and gave the sign of the horns.

"So far so good," I told my friends. "He look friendly enough to you two?"

"That depends," Rich spoke up. "Friendly by our old standards, or friendly to normal standards?"

"Yeah, no shit," I chuckled. "Let's go with the former, and hope for the latter, eh?"

"Just be careful," Dave warned.

The boat neared the little docking area by where the guy was situated.

"What's up dude?" I asked. "You cool?"

"I'm alright!" the man called back. "Nice fuckin' shirt, bro!"

He pointed right to me, to which I looked down and realized I was wearing my Slayer shirt today.

"Oh, thanks." I laughed. Keep it friendly.

The boat neared the dock, and we threw our ropes out to another man we hadn't noticed until just then. He carried the same look, all black clothes, despite the summer heat. His hair was closely cropped, but he too was covered with a variety of ink.

The man pulled our mooring ropes and wrapped them around the cleats on the dock to tie us in firmly. He stood up, and went to speak inaudibly to the first man, who motioned and said something in reply, to which the second guy departed up the flight of steps and out of sight.

"He's going to go get the boss man," the first man explained. "That's normal, man. He meets everyone who stops in."

"That's cool man," I ensured. "I'm Scott, this is Dave, and Rich."

He shook each of our hands in return and introduced himself.

"I'm Jason," he greeted. "Sorry for the gun in your face, can't be too careful."

He pounded the inside of the turret he still occupied with aplomb.

"Nah," I began, "I understand, dude. What kind of guy is your boss man?"

"Oh, he's cool," Jason stated confidently. "He's a real reasonable dude truthfully."

"Nice," I stated. "Hell of a setup you have here. This come from the military?"

I was trying to pry and I think he knew it.

"Yeah, we got some Marines here," he replied with pride, "real cool dudes. They had some guys called Motor T that saved this off a wrecked truck so we could set it up down here."

"How many Marines you got here?" I asked, trying to be innocent, "How many people in general?"

"Oh, I don't know," he replied wryly. "Never took the time to count everybody."

As we chatted, a few men came down the stairway. A couple weren't dressed as military, but the way they carried themselves, they had to have been.

The man in the middle of the group was thicker, not fat but definitely heavier built than the others. He had a rounded, friendly face. An almost permanently jovial expression set, slightly rosy cheeks and he was already smiling upon making eye contact. He wore long black shorts, and a T-shirt displaying the local nu-metal band, Mushroomhead.

"What's up guys?" he exclaimed, almost too friendly in the way he carried himself.

"Not much," I said, smiling my best 'pleased to meet you' grin.

"You all good?" he asked, his friendly tone and expression never changing, "Oh! Shit! Did you guys check them?"

"For what?" Jason asked. 'Clearly they're armed, but they aren't shooting, so I assume they're cool for now."

"Yeah, good point dude," the boss man replied. "You guys good? Like, you're doing alright? You from around here?"

"Yes, we are," I informed him. "Uh, on both of those questions. I'm Scott, by the way, you?"

"Mike. Mike Hashman," he stated assuredly, shaking my outstretched hand, "but you can call me by either."

"Good to meet you, Mike," I said in return. "Shall we?"

He nodded and led us up the stairs, a few other guys, included the presumed military, in tow. I left Rich and Dave behind to watch over our supplies, and make sure our guests stayed undiscovered.

"What brings you guys out this way?" Mike inquired.

"We were scouting up the river a little way, curiosity, really," I lied.

"Cool, cool," Mike replied. "Most of us that started here were on a bus going to a concert in Cleveland. The party buses? Shit was so fun!"

"Nice," I replied. "How many people you got here?"

"Around sixty-five," Mike stated, as we crested the top of the steps. "We started with like forty, some Marines showed up, other people coming down the river from Cleveland decided to stay."

I didn't get the chance to reply before we reached the top. What lay before me was a relatively small gated community, a few more than a dozen houses, all similar, gathered around a large cul-de-sac of sorts. All houses were around three-quarters of the central area, with the riverside left open. We stood in a large patch of land facing the scene from the river side.

Between us and the homes, was a small road that circled the central area, and connected in the center on the other side to provide a way in and out. The loop of the road made up another field of sorts, in which I could see people tending to various types of vegetables, melons, and various other things. A handful of cattle, sheep, pigs, and chickens actually freely roamed the grounds amid the people.

Surprisingly, everybody looked mostly healthy. Whereas people in our compound weren't exactly thin, even Katie and Bri had lost weight since the beginning, and the rest of us had toned up probably more than ever in our lives.

Nearer us, closer to the path to the water, a few women washed clothes in basins and hung them on lines and over plastic chairs to dry.

Small fires burned here and there, both open, and contained to metal barrels. Most had various types of meat, fish, or vegetables being dried and smoked around them. There was even a large water still that had been set up, made out of an old tanker and various plumbing.

When you took it all in together, the scene would have fit in any picture from the old settler's days, save for the invasive anachronism of modern vehicles, housing, and clothing.

Altogether, it was fairly pleasant. They'd had themselves a thriving community here. The one thing to give it away was a definite small-scale military presence. I could spot a few HUMMV's, and a small handful of clear military types. And furthermore, every single citizen in sight was outfitted with a modern battle rifle and sidearm of their own.

"Quite a setup you've got here, Mike," I said, earnest astonishment not hidden.

"Yeah, we're doing alright," he said proudly.

"How'd you end up here, if you don't mind my asking?" I inquired.

"Man, so we were on that party bus, right? There were two buses," he explained. "Major traffic everywhere, and the driver got out of ours to see if he could talk to someone and find out what happened. That's when they attacked."

He detailed a flooding of the infected much like the one I'd experienced, and a short journey that paralleled my own in many ways. With the driver dead, Mike had taken the helm, and through a series of risk, chance, and blind luck, he got both buses full of people to safety in this small gated community.

Being 'everybody's buddy', many followed Mike closely, and the rest went where the numbers were, for the most part. He'd told the story of a few who tried to flee in the beginning, and how quickly and brutally they met their end.

One had tried to run for a shop filled with people hiding. He got tackled before he even reached the door, running along the front, and was speared through the glass storefront, ending the tale for himself, as well as the thirty some odd people taking refuge.

Mike showed me around the majority of his compound, barring the homes. He showed where a deep incline was being dug out of the earth, a full team working on it, being assisted and instructed by a couple of the military types. Mike described it as their bunker project, to hold more goods, and provide a safer fallback point should the walls of their community fail.

"Might happen sooner than you think," I warned. "Have you seen the big fuckers yet?"

"No, I haven't," Mike replied, concerned and not without a bit of suspicion.

I described the giant we'd taken down, and the details of how much it took, as well as the amount of damage it did to the building we were on. I told him of our dry moat, he agreed that he was going to be finding something then to bolster their defenses. He said he'd get with his engineers to plan that project.

I won't lie, the guy surprised me. He was so young, maybe early twenties. So lively, so friendly, but he carried himself in a way that told you he had things under control. A young metal head exterior backed by a fifty-year-old businessman on the inside. He departed for a few moments to use the restroom and grab us all some water bottles.

"Don't let him fool you," one of the military types accompanying us spoke up for the first time. "Mike's a hell of a good guy, acts almost clownish at times, but he'll handle the things nobody else wants to."

"What do you mean?" I questioned.

"He's exiled people for theft, dishonesty, stuff like that," the man continued, "even had someone executed for rape. Pulled the trigger himself, then went and had dinner. Guy's good, wholesome as fuck, but don't cross him."

"Thanks for the warning," I replied, and before I could dig further, Mike returned, handing out plastic bottles of clean, crisp water.

"We purify our own here," Mike said, holding up his water bottle, "they set up a system that filters it, distills it, filters again, then it gets cleaned up one last time."

We made more small talk about the way things were run here. Mike maintained direct control on most things, but when it was a larger matter, category three to five issues, as it was told to me, they would vote as a community. Every vote was private, and every vote counted. Fair as can be, he said.

It was then that I'd suggested setting up trade between our communities. I gave our approximate location. General commodities, help with whatever projects, defense as a team, even river patrols between the colonies.

He, of course, said he'd be down, but it would have to be put through a vote. We spoke on the subject a while longer, until I decided it was time to depart for now, promising we'd be back the next day on our way down through to home. I wonder what category he'd classified this as. I didn't ask.

I brought a handful of fresh apples to Rich and Dave, and we all stopped and had a bit to eat before setting off again.

After we'd set off again, waves and good tidings exchanged on both ends, I felt confident we were parting on good terms.

Once it all had been detailed and explained to Rich and Dave, they agreed it had a lot of promise if all went well, and that we should definitely bring it up as soon as we got back to our home.

We travelled the rest of the afternoon and into the evening, until we were sure we were far enough. At least, as far as we dared to go. The city limits of Cleveland, Ohio, loomed ahead of us, and none of us wanted to dare venture any further. Not a place as populated as that, though clearly the military had been here as they had in Akron. Pillars of black smoke still showed, rubble still smoldering even this long after everything had been bombarded. At least, we'd assumed that's what it was from.

Cleveland wasn't the best city to visit even when things were normal, let alone in the end of times. No thank you.

We allowed our guests topside, one at a time, same as twice before. They did their necessary, ate, drank, Tyrone bargained for more time topside, but, eventually they were both stowed back away.

Anchor was dropped right where we sat, and there we camped for the night. We all sat in near silence. No lights, no engines, nothing but the sound of the water lapping against the side of our vessel, and occasionally a low whisper between us.

Okay, actually, Dave or Rich, and once, both, had to wake me up at various points due to my snoring. Aside from that, we were just shadows inhabiting this small section of the water, just for the time being.

THIRTY-THREE

Dawn broke slowly. It illuminated shadows into shapes, shards of glass as mirrors, then finally brightened the whole landscape.

On my command, everyone was awake, and both prisoners were roused from sleep and brought up topside.

"Can you both swim?" I asked, to which they eyed me suspiciously.

"Of course, we can," the unnamed man scowled.

"Good," I said, direct and without the positivity the word implied, "this is what happens from here. I'm turning this boat around and getting ready to raise anchor. These? These are yours."

I held out a small backpack for each of them. Neither man looked pleased. Tyrone was downright confused.

"I thought you intended to execute us and dump us," he said. "You're letting us go?"

"I can't kill you as you've done nothing but pose a threat," I explained. "You didn't kill or harm any of us, but I couldn't let you just walk straight back home from our place. You're in Cleveland now. Catch a ballgame or something."

"What's these?" no-name asked.

"You ever going to tell me your name?" I asked, to which he turned his head and spat, "Okay. Well, Tyrone, Asshole, you each have three bottles of water, three cans of food, one of you has basic fire-starting tools, the other has a basic med kit. Oh, and you have these."

I retrieved and offered two revolvers, one .32 ACP, the other a .22 LR. Both basic, simple, black, and cheap, but better than nothing at all. Each man took the proffered weapon and inspected them.

"We get bullets, or we gotta find those?" Tyrone asked.

I held up two packs, each about the size of a fist. Both packs resembled lumps wrapped in duct tape, and they'd been spray painted florescent orange.

"Rounds for each. A full cylinder, and three full reloads for each gun," I explained, then, "The second you two hit the water, I gun the engine, Rich throws them ashore. Best of luck, guys. Get in the water."

Tyrone dropped into the river and waited for his partner, holding the side of the boat as he bobbed along. The other guy, no-name, hesitated.

"You fucking asshole, you can't just leave us here!" he exclaimed.

I wasn't in the mood to bargain. I motioned to Dave and Rich, the two approached him, and as no-name swung his fist, Dave ducked and the two shoved him straight off the boat and into the water, sputtering and flailing for a moment until he got his bearings and started swimming. He muttered and cursed as he went. Tyrone nodded and began moving to the shore as well.

As promised, I gunned the throttle, and Rich launched both neon colored packages to the shore, where they hit, rolled, and came to a rest in each their own tiny little dust cloud.

Back southbound we went.

***

The day remained warm and sunny as we made our way back down the river. We picked up a bit more speed, having reconnoitered the area we were now passing through. Conversation still remained muted at best, as we all felt the distance from home that we now held. What was once a thirty-minute car ride now had taken all day with a one night stay afterward. It was exhausting, to say the least.

The boat still wasn't exactly soaring through the water. Just a few knots faster seemed to be the ticket. It brought us into the realm of moving target, but felt safe enough, as we hadn't had a chance to fully scan the river and remove any debris capable of causing hull breeches.

An hour or so into the trip and something caught my eye. I was scanning debris along the bank on the starboard side when I caught a stir of movement. What had, on first glance appeared as a rock and some debris, stood up. I mean, it literally stood up, took the shape of a man, and crept away at a hunch.

Rich and Dave clearly saw the man as well.

"Sniper," Rich said, matter of fact yet quiet.

"Yeah," I confirmed. "Holy fuck I thought he was just junk."

"Fuck that," Dave proclaimed as he disappeared below deck.

"Yeah, best of luck," Rich confirmed as he followed Dave. "Best of luck boss man."

"You fuckers!" I exclaimed. "Fuck, man. At least give me something to hide behind."

I was expecting a pile of ballistic vests, or at the very least, some of the pressure treated boards we'd stacked our supplies on.

Instead, Rich's freckled arm appeared just long enough to toss a large piece of cardboard at my feet.

"You're getting your rations cut, you fuck!" I said, chuckling, as I lowered myself until I could just barely see the river ahead, crouching behind my protective...cardboard.

For the next hour, I kept watch, while the other two sat below decks. They were stuffing their faces, as the smell of freshly heated and opened MRE's wafted up out of the cabin, and I could hear the rustling of plastic.

Finally, we rounded a sharp bend in the river, and were met with the now familiar MCTAGS turret containing the familiar head of long, dark hair that I knew as Jason.

I cut the power down on the throttle, and slowly stood up to wave. For a moment, the turret swung my way, then as Jason recognized us, he too stood up to give a big wave.

We pulled up and moored as we had before. This time, the smell of freshly cooking meat wafted down from the settlement above.

"Jason." I nodded to the man in the turret.

"What's up, dude!" he replied cheerily.

"Y'all having a cookout?" I asked, smelling the air and eyeballing the smoke rising above us. My stomach grumbled on its own volition.

"Oh! Shit, yeah, man! Go on up!" he replied. "You'll find the boss man around the food!"

The three of us thanked Jason and made our way up the stairs to the ground level. We had no hidden prisoners, and not much but day bags with us, so keeping someone with the boat didn't seem as prudent this time around. Especially with Jason and his armored turret of death.

We reached the top of the flight, and before us, maybe a dozen yards, was a large smoker. It was the kind you see the barbeque guys pulling down the highway. It was open and Hashman and another guy worked as a team pulling chunks of meat off of a smoked pig. I couldn't believe my eyes! It was like I'd just walked into a dreamland.

"Hashman!" I called.

"What's up, buddy!" he turned and replied with his usual upbeat tone. "You guys have a good trip? See anything cool? You hungry? Check it out man, we got plenty!"

"I see that!" I replied, still astonished. "Is this typical?"

"Kinda, man, yeah!" he said thoughtfully. "Every third Sunday."

"Sorry?" I replied, confused.

"Every third Sunday we have a big barbeque," he explained. "Nobody goes without, it boosts morale, and we dry whatever meat is leftover so it lasts us a while."

"No shit?" I replied, my mind finally grasping that yes, this was indeed a freshly smoked pig in front of me.

"Yeah dude!" he replied with enthusiasm. "Jerry's the shit with this stuff! Have you heard of pemmican? We make a lot of that with the leftovers. I guess you can't with pig, but we still dry it and store it."

"How are you storing it?" I asked.

Jerry, a robust biker looking type with a shaved head, full beard, and tattoos was the one to reply.

"We dug up a root cellar," he explained. "Dry that pig out, use lots of salt and pepper. It keeps purty good."

"Really?" I replied, "Nice!"

I whispered quickly to Rich, who disappeared back toward the docks. Dave was already at home conversing with another group and passing around what looked like a joint the size of a finger. A few short beats later and Rich returned, our two bottles of whiskey in hand.

I retrieved the bottles from Rich and handed them to Hashman. He took them graciously and invited us to eat.

I was starved. Dave, of course, had the appetite of a stoner and didn't hold back, either. Rich on the other hand was still full from their stowaway lunch in the cabin. He still managed to take a small portion of each item and do his best to stuff it in.

Aside from the hog in the smoker, which was being doled out in great piles, there were many other items. Several large cooking pots stood on grates positioned over a rectangular cooking pit. Within the pots were creamed corn, canned green beans, and a favorite of mine, Bush's baked beans. I was clearly in heaven. I had to be, right?

"Well go ahead brother!" Hashman encouraged from just behind me, pounding me on the shoulder. "Looks good, right? They do so good with this!"

"Damn, man," I said, beginning to scoop food onto my tray, then, laughing, "I'm thinking about those beans."

We shared a laugh over this, then a meal together. Most of his crew seemed much like him and Jason. In general, they were good, warm, friendly people, despite their looks giving off standoffish vibes. A few weren't as sociable as others, but that was fine, we had a similar mix in our community. As a matter of fact, I don't think I'd ever seen Chris Simmons say more than a couple of words at a time to anybody at all. Even Rich.

There was clearly a pecking order in play here though. Without a word, Hashman, Jason, and a few other guys took seats and invited us over to the sturdiest, most prominent table. Others grouped together in their own circles at other tables, and children sat happily with their mothers and caretakers in the grass. I wondered if the totem pole was this clearly established in our own camp. As I thought about it, I began to believe it was.

We ate until we were so stuffed with food we became lazy. A nice slow buzz from the shared whiskey bottles crept in. Rich and Dave were having a great time. It really made me start to consider some better morale boosting for our own people. I'd honestly never considered it, what with all the projects and other goings-on at home.

After the meal was finished, we invited Hashman to come down to our own place and marked it on the map for him. We talked again of trade and support between the settlements. He said he would love to check it out, and even offered us a couple of animals with promise we'd open up relations by gathering supplies that they might need in anticipation of his visit in return.

We parted on a good note. We loaded up a male and female goat that he had chosen for us himself, both very healthy animals. Saying goodbye, we released our moorings and set off.

The rest of the day passed with startling calmness. Almost lazy in its cadence of just birds, bug noise, and water lapping at the boat as the motor purred out its one long story.

We began to see familiarity, and with it, a gauge of distance.

Once we were close enough, I retrieved the flare gun to announce our arrival, and set the glowing reddish orb high into the sky about an eighth of a mile from our compound. It arced high, reaching its apex, and began to slowly fall back toward Earth.

Approaching our mooring site slowly, I swung the boat wide in the water, and positioned it to park with its bow northward, facing upriver.

Tony, Jennifer, and several others greeted us as we began unloading.

"Are those goats?" Jennifer asked, amazed. "Where the hell did you get goats from?"

"No, they're chickens. Clearly," I replied, which earned me a slap across the back of my head. "Seriously though, we all have some catching up to do. I've got some big news."

"Oh, you have no idea," Jennifer replied, trailing off in a way to appear vague.

THIRTY-FOUR

I instructed Tony and Jennifer to get all the department heads they could, save for Carolyn to watch the kids. Rich and Dave were told to go straight up to the Command Center on the ninth floor, and everybody else to join them soon. This meeting couldn't wait for a post-dinner affair. We officially had neighbors! Hey, you can't blame me for getting excited about this, it was a big development!

I made my way promptly to the construction project, opting to jump in a nearby Smart Car instead of hoofing it.

I pulled up near where the equipment was working. Henry was doing a fine job leading and directing project operations. Everyone had fallen into a solid swing of things and all seemed to have their own positions and duties. It was truly moving along like a well-oiled machine.

The large excavator was running full bore and surprisingly, Parker was at the controls. It seemed as though the dry moat, as we'd decided to call it, had been deepened and widened. It was now a good ten feet in each dimension.

Another crew was busy tearing down walls and roofs from the nearest houses. These were being repurposed. The side of the dry moat nearest the compound was being lined with a bare stud skeleton just a foot or so away from the moat. At regular intervals, post holes had been dug for supports, and then the remainder of the space in each hole was backfilled with concrete being mixed in a wheelbarrow with river water. This supported skeleton was quickly sandwiched between pieces of scavenged plywood, and then braced with more studs and lengths of rebar against the far bank of the moat.

I was informed by Henry that these braces would only be temporary, just used to keep the wall's shape until everything had settled. As the excavator dug, it piled its dirt and debris to the inside, and, once another section of wall was completed and braced, the backhoe got busy pushing sloped mounds of dirt behind it to bolster it, and provide a natural guard walk the length of the platform. Finally, at regular intervals, flat platforms jutted out to the inside, providing seating, and a spot to line up sandbags and pressure board to create regular guard posts.

It was, to say the least, impressive. And they had nearly a third of the project finished already. If only we could have gotten road crews to move this well back when.

"You could hit it with a tank, or even run one of your semis into it and the wall won't move," Henry finished explaining proudly.

"Nice," I started, "but I sure as fuck hope it doesn't come to that."

We shared a laugh about that thought and I asked, "Any problems with the freaks?"

"Nah brother," Henry stated. "Few small groups here and there. Our morning dinner bell has been working well. We had a few inside the perimeter, must have stayed hidden in houses. We opened a garage and three of them came running from inside."

"Nobody got hurt from that?" I inquired.

"No sir," he assuaged, "we took care of them bad mamma-jammas"

"Not as bad as I'd expected them to be then," I admitted. "That's good news. Hey, listen, there's been a big development, I need you to ride with me to the north building, we're having a meeting with all heads as soon as I get up there."

Henry obliged, and we got into the tiny car and made our way back to the north building, parking right out front and making our way up the stairs again.

"One of these days, Henry," I said, half joking, "you and James are gonna get the elevators running again."

"That sure would be nice," he replied, laughing, yet as out of breath as I was.

We both walked into command, and each found a seat. Naturally, mine was at the head of the table there.

Tony, Jennifer, Henry, Rich, Bri, Shannon, Ashley, and Dave were all present.

Most were at the table, in actual seats, while Dave and Rich lounged sidebar on a couple of black leather couches that had been brought in and pushed against one wall.

"Dave, Rich," I instructed, "keep your seats, but you're going to have to sit up. It's meeting time."

Rich sat up, Dave gave me the finger and continued lying where he was. That's fine. It's Dave. That's my buddy, regardless what level of defiant dickhead he's capable of being.

"Alright," I started, "We have neighbors. About ten miles upriver. Good people, leader's name is Hashman. Mike Hashman. We've invited him to come by, via boat, tomorrow morning. Don't shoot the fuckin' guy, he's invited."

I let everyone in the room that was unaware digest this. It didn't go down as big as I was expecting.

"Well," Jennifer began, after exchanging looks with Tony, "at least those neighbors are friendly."

"Huh?" was all I could say in reply.

"We had another group show up at the front gate yesterday evening," she explained. "Tony handled them, but we don't think it'll be the last we see of these ones."

"Tony?" I questioned, looking in his direction.

"Yeah, a small group knocked on the main gate yesterday," he repeated, adding, "Said they were looking for a couple of their guys."

Tony eyed me carefully, and the two on the couch both perked up.

"A couple of their guys?" I asked, putting on an innocent face for the benefit of the majority here.

"Said they found and collected their dead at a spot a ways west of here," Tony continued. "There was apparently a fight. They said they followed oil here."

"I'm sorry," I began, "followed oil? Were they with the government?"

"No," Tony said, chuckling. "No, they said whoever hit their guys must have taken damage, there was a puddle of oil there, and a steady trail of drips leading right to our gate and into the compound. I checked after they left, they were right."

"Yeah, Henry said one of our dump trucks had a gouge in the oil pan that cracked it a bit," I recalled, "but, we were attacked, we didn't hit them. And we damn sure haven't had any new people here."

"We have, but that's next to talk about," Tony said. "They demanded we owned up to it, and wanted payment. Said he'd forget all about it for half of our supplies, and two truckloads of good scavenged things every couple of weeks for six months as restitution. If we don't pay, they claimed they would attack, or find another means to get back at us."

"They're fucking raiders!" I exclaimed. "They tried running a fuckin' racket on us then, too. Fuck those guys. What did you tell them?"

"I mean, I was there. Me and Dave both got shot," he paused, so we could all share low laughter at Dave's expense. "I had half a granola bar I was eating. I threw it at their leader's feet and told him to consider it a down payment."

"Nice!" I replied, laughing. "Did he even give a name?"

"Big Tyler," Tony stated dryly, narrowing his eyes at me.

"Never heard of him," I stated, keeping my façade. "Anything else?"

"Yeah. Guy basically said we'd be sorry," Tony elaborated. "Fred was up in the building, in a blind, he placed a rifle shot right at the guys feet when he started moving closer. Dude's gonna come in real handy, we should run him on more scouting missions."

"Yeah, he's been so busy and keeps to himself, I forgot he was even here," I replied sheepishly.

"Yeah," Tony said. "Anyway, they said they will be back in 24 hours. That's this evening. If they don't have at least one truck filled with supplies waiting outside the front gate, they said we'd pay anyway."

"Okay," I began instructing. "Everyone who can hit the side of a semi with a firearm needs to be on guard. Pull in the work crews, everybody incapable, including children, come up to this building's rooftop. Let's get people rounded up and ready an hour before they're supposed to be here. Soon as this meeting is over."

"There's more," Shannon broke in.

"Yeah, but this is good news," Bri interjected. "We have new people!"

"New people?" I asked. "I didn't see anybody…"

"No, you wouldn't have yet," Shannon replied. "They all went through intake, and I've got them on the medical floor in pairs, waiting a 48-hour quarantine, just in case."

"Good work!" I congratulated. "Anybody useful?"

"Um, well," Shannon started. "One guy, some kind of prepper and country boy. And an older woman who can drive trucks. The rest aren't as much use, three children under twelve, one sixteen-year-old girl, four adults who had no transferable skills, but they're healthy enough. I figured they could join work crews where needed?"

"The girl, too," I confirmed. "I think it's fair to ask that if you can hold a legitimate job before the world went to shit, you can work here, too. I got my first job at fifteen, let's use that as the age to start working here."

"Sounds fair," Shannon agreed. "They should all be coming out of quarantine tomorrow morning, they showed up the afternoon of the day you left."

"Good," I stated. "I look forward to meeting them."

"Hey, since we're all here," Jennifer offered, "Why don't we use each of us here, plus James and Rob, as like the heads of a committee?"

"Not a bad idea," I concurred. "That would streamline the process of anyone who needs anything and allow us to make large decisions faster. Carolyn holding up alright with the kids?"

"Yeah," Bri said, bringing up her notebook. "Every scouting run has been good about bringing things she could use, and that they need. They even had cookies for snacks today."

"Awesome," I said. "Anyone else, before we call this meeting over?"

"We need supplies," Bri started. "Well, we always need them, but right now, including the new people here, we'll last until mid-January. We need bigger scavenging runs, and our medical department has requested to, and I quote, 'Grab every last band-aid and aspirin', so there's that, too."

"Cute," I said flatly, eyeing Shannon and Ashley as they grinned broadly, quite pleased with themselves. "Okay, well, any form of public transportation should have a small med kit, and fire extinguishers at the very least. Always empty every medicine cabinet, every time we scavenge, fire and police should have stuff in their vehicles and buildings. Relay that all to James when he gets back tomorrow."

"On it, boss!" Bri said, as she wrote everything down in her book. "Anything else?"

"Any home with a decent aquarium, especially if there's more than one," I kept on, to a now confused looking group. "Several of the antibiotics used in aquarium care are the same, or can be used in place of what we use for people."

"He's right," Dave agreed. "Also any boats or watercraft. Our boat had a nice first aid setup and two fire extinguishers."

"And to answer Bri's long term supply question," I closed, "we have more people, we're just gonna have to scout more and bigger. Take two trucks, fill them every trip out. We'll come up with more suitable plans for the winter. Henry can also devise some kind of rudimentary heating for the buildings, too, I'm sure. Once spring is here, we should have enough land, and enough houses torn down to start farming. Raid every garden shed for seeds."

Bri finished writing everything down and smiled.

"If there's no further questions, I'll let everyone get back to what they were doing," I offered, and everyone began leaving. "I'll be napping, I'm sure Dave and Rich will, too. Good job everyone."

THIRTY-FIVE

It was decided that an early dinner was in order, so, after my short nap, I joined everyone in the usual spot, on the rooftop of the north building. We ate with little conversation. Those of us that were to be watching for these assholes ate less, consumed enough to keep us steady, but not lazy.

After the meal was finished, shooters left the rooftop, Carolyn and the kids remained.

Even Frank, despite his recent injuries, was there. His bad arm held in a sling, that side also sporting a crutch he'd had tied into place around his shoulder. In the other hand, he brandished a Colt Python. He even stood idly by with Willy, joking about how he had a few speed-loaders tucked into his sling.

***

We chose Willy to go place our offering outside the gate. He wasn't willing at first, but Dave made sure to talk some sense into the guy.

He ambled meekly to the front gate, and there, he pushed one single granola bar through. Its shiny wrapper catching the low evening light as it fell through the chain link gate and met the dirt with a soft thud.

Having done his job, Willy walked back to join Tony and me in the doorway to the north building. From here, we could easily see the front gate and a large stretch of the wall, but still afforded ourselves some distance and cover.

A few moments after Willy departed, we got a report on the radio from Henry.

"South tower roof here, over," he said quietly through the radio lain next to us.

"Go ahead South, over," I replied, then listened for the response.

"Got one vehicle that left after Willy did his thing," Henry detailed. "Left quietly and headed south, what next? Over."

"Now," I began, "Now we wait. Keep an eye out. Over."

***

About an hour had passed. The sun had gone down over the horizon, and the light had nearly completely faded from the sky, showing a blanket of brilliant stars that otherwise would never have been seen in this part of town prior to the end.

I could tell everybody was getting restless. Hell, I was getting restless. We'd been standing there watching nothing the whole time.

Just as I was about to call an end to it, the radio on my hip crackled to life. It was Henry.

"We've got two vehicles coming from the south that I can see. Over," he informed.

"Heading this way?" I asked in turn. "What kind? Over."

"Can't tell brother," Henry replied. "Too dark to tell anything. Over."

A few beats later, the noise of engines reached our position.

"One of them has stopped," Henry reported, "About half a block away. Over."

"Okay, keep an eye on it," I replied, almost forgetting, "Over."

As I'd ended my words, the first vehicle pulled within view of the front gate, visible from my position.

"I've got one dark colored Chevy pickup," I described into my radio. "See two in the cab. Hold up, other vehicle is approaching. Over."

As I'd ended my radio call, the nose of a white truck creeped into view. I tightened my grip on the rifle and buried it into the sweet spot in my shoulder. In my periphery, I could sense Tony, and even Willy, doing the same.

In an instant, the area flooded with a pulsing amber light. The rest of the second vehicle came into view. It was a tow truck. What the hell was going on here?

"Everyone keep ready," I ordered into the radio, "only fire on my mark. Over."

Three different voices came back to me, all in the affirmative as the tow truck swung around and backed up to the gate. I could make out some kind of large object hanging from the back, I know what it looked like, but it couldn't be...

"Is that what I think it is?" I said to Tony, who remained stoic and poised with his rifle, not saying a word.

The amber light continued pulsing, coming from the light bar on the vehicle. Before I could distinguish more of the shape on the back of the vehicle, the horn began blaring. Letting out one long, obnoxious, screaming note from its horn, as the driver of the vehicle bailed from his seat, ran, and jumped into the bed of the pickup truck, which then sped off in a roar of engine noise and cloud of tire smoke. This was not good.

"We need to get that horn shut off!" I shouted into the radio, breaking cover and running toward the gate, just a moment before everyone else left their positions to do the same.

"They're going to draw every infected fuck in this part of the city with that shit!" Tony yelled as he ran, right on my heels.

Before I could reach the gate, nor anybody else, for that matter, all Hell broke loose.

The scene became something of a frantic horror house shooting gallery.

The wail of the horn, the flash of the amber light bar, the shrieks of infected. Then the sharp crack of gunfire.

Rich met the wall at the same time as the rest of us and began handing out a dozen road flares in pairs to those of us who made it there first. We each started lighting them, and then, everyone following Rich's lead, began throwing the flares far out, over the wall in long arcs.

The angry red glare of each stick of light floated through the tar black of the night, landing in no particular order, only to light up the spot where each landed with a hellish glow.

The nightmare forms of freaks of every human shape and form nearly immediately began appearing, flitting along the edges of the light, appearing long enough to draw a bead with a gun, and then gone. A few sprinted straight through the flare light. They stayed lit long enough to draw the gunfire. Each demonic form sprinted, lit up in a red otherworldly glow which made them appear to be straight from Hades itself, only to catch small arms fire. Every one that fell twisted and jerked to find its spot on the ground, disappearing in an illuminated cloud of blood and bodily tissue, and was immediately replaced by yet another. They were drawing our fire. I was sure of it.

The remaining forms, the ones that skirted the glow of the flares, soon reached the full brilliance of the amber tow lights. As they were illuminated, they dropped low, and actually began heading right for the tall grass around the wall, the truck itself, and any other obstacle that could even temporarily block them from sight. They were trying to distract us, sure, but they were also trying to seek cover. These fuckers were *learning*.

The first freak hit the chain link of the front gate, almost just arms-length from my position. She came out of damn near nowhere, I was close enough to read the word 'Hope' on her Tiffany necklace. All hope was lost for that one as Dave loosed a half-dozen shots from his AK-47, shredding her from the voice box up. As the freak hit the ground with a jerk and a final spasm, two more hit the gate.

Dave ripped the first to pieces with another volley, and as he changed magazines, I let my rifle fall loose on its sling and pulled my shotgun off my back. After disengaging the safety, I let one round of twelve-gauge buckshot fly, hitting the beast squarely in the face, and wiping its memories for good.

"WE NEED TO SHUT THAT SHIT OFF, NOW!!!" I shouted over the cacophony. *"TONY, DAVE, ROB, RICH, HENRY, ON ME! WILLY GET THE FUCKING GATE!!!"*

Willy did as he was told, and the others moved right to me as rounds from everyone else whizzed and snapped past us, seeking whatever moving body they could in the dark.

Another freak hit the fence, and was quickly disabled, though not killed. Whoever shot him hit him right in the center of the upper chest. It must have passed through and destroyed its spine, as what was once a man dropped to the pavement before reaching up and attempting his journey up the chain link anew, until Tony drew his sidearm and planted a single forty-five round into its cranium.

We tightened up into kind of a rough phalanx, and the couple of us with lights on our weapons clicked them on. Willy eased the gate open enough for us to pass through, then slammed it shut behind us.

We began getting rushed on step one. The first freak making a beeline right for me as I first caught it in the light on my shotgun, then with a load of lead pellets to the face. The others began firing. Not as panicked and sporadic as those left inside the walls, but more controlled. More experienced, these were my guys. My core survivors, and it was not our first close encounter.

"Keep tight!" I ordered, straining my voice. "Keep firing, we got ten more feet!"

We approached the truck with as much speed and grace as we could muster. One round from inside the wire whizzed past me in the lead, then a second actually tugged at my shirt sleeve.

"HEY!" I shouted behind me, "WATCH YOUR FUCKING FIRE!"

I could hear no response over the noise of the horn.

We got to the truck, and, looking at the form hanging from the tow boom, I could tell it was a man. Then I started to recognize things. The tattoos. The striped shirt. The head had lolled forward, the face was pointed straight down, but I could recognize the guy immediately.

"It's Chris!" I declared, amazed, and a bit in shock. "Fuck! Tony kill this dinner bell! Rich, Dave, get him off of there! Everyone cover them!"

I couldn't tell if anyone agreed verbally. It was just that fucking loud there, but Tony reached the driver's door, exploding the glass with a couple of pistol rounds, and reached in. He removed a long dark-bladed hunting knife from the steering wheel, silencing the horn for good, then started flipping switches on the dash until all of the vehicle's lights shut down, drowning us in darkness only penetrated by our weapon lights, and a few handheld floods from the compound as everyone frantically tried to pick off scurrying shapes.

The guys got Chris down, and draped his limp form over their shoulders as we made our way back to safety. My shotgun had run dry, I tucked it under my left arm for the light and drew my Smith and Wesson 9mm: spot with the shotgun light, shoot with the little guy. Everyone else had apparently hit the same snag, and the crack and boom of rifles and shotguns quickly subsided into the pops and bangs of various pistol fire.

"WILLY!" I shouted, "GATE!"

Just as we reached it, the gate slid open and we piled through, half of us tripping on the other half.

Just then, an infected hit the gate right where Willy was holding it, causing him to yelp and jump back.

Before he could recover, or anyone else could react, another freak lunged straight through the opening. It hit Henry, who was trying to gather his feet after a tumble, and flew another six feet forward, coming down on top of him with a loud thud. Before the creature could gather itself, Henry whirled around on the ground, found Earth with his back, and placed his large revolver under the creature's chin, simultaneously pulling the trigger.

The gun barked a muffled report. The .357 round thundered out of the barrel, immediately ripping apart flesh and pulverizing the monstrosity's skull like an overripe melon.

Henry wriggled his way out from under the thing as Dave got the gate slammed and latched shut.

The gunfire continued as Tony and I reached Henry, and we locked eyes with him, horror playing over our faces at the same time it reached his. He was covered from the chest up with infected gore. His frightened expression was soaked with blood interspersed with bits of bone and flesh.

"It's in my mouth," he said softly. "Oh Lord, it's in my mouth. It's in my eyes. I'm going to be one of them."

Resignation washed over Henry's face as suddenly his own revolver met the side of his head. He lined the barrel to his temple before either Tony or myself could react, and he pulled the trigger.

Click

Tears began falling from Henry's big brown eyes as he pulled the trigger again. And again. And three more times, while Tony and I stood there paralyzed. Every chamber clicked empty.

"Get me some water," I said to Tony, who immediately reached into his pack and produced a large bottled water.

I poured it over Henry's face, trying my best to rinse away the threat. He shook and kept repeating over and over that he was infected.

"We don't know that, dude, you're going to be okay," I said, pleading with the universe as much as I was reassuring my friend, "It's okay, everyone I've seen changed instantly. You're good, man. SHANNON!!! Where the fuck is Shannon and Ashley?"

My shouting brought both girls over, and as per my orders, they began tending to a sobbing Henry before leading him away to quarantine.

"Shit," I muttered, turning on my feet, "Chris! Where's Chris?"

I found a small group gathered around a large, limp form on the ground.

I approached, and, finally, in the light of so many flashlights mixed with the fire of a nearby woodfire barrel, I could just make out the battered face of Chris.

"Rich?" I questioned as I approached the scene.

The last few rounds of gunfire faded away as Rich looked up.

A single tear line from each eye cut the dirt, grime, and blood on his face. His usually piercing eyes appeared dimmed, and all he could manage was a shake of his head. Negative.

Stooping down to find the carotid artery for a pulse revealed a long deep gash across his throat. Not abandoning hope yet, I gathered myself and felt for his pulse in his wrist. After a moment, I dropped the hand I held back to fall limply to the ground. Nothing.

Chris Simmons was no longer a part of our world.

Attached by a string to his other wrist was a Ziploc bag.

"What's this?" I asked, motioning to the plastic dangling on a string.

"Let's find out," Tony replied, his voice bare and emotionless.

He slipped his knife under the string, and with a flick, separated it from Chris, then tossed the bag to me.

I immediately opened it, finding a piece of paper inside, which I then withdrew and unfolded it.

On the piece of paper was a printed picture of a cozy looking townhouse-style apartment front. Across the top, it read *Timberland Properties LLC*.

Then, at the bottom of the page, it read:

Have you forgotten? Just a friendly reminder from those of us at Timberland Properties LLC, you are __ days behind on your rent. Please process late payments directly through the management offices. Have a beautiful day!

"What the fuck?" I asked, before turning the page over and finding a handwritten note.

Tony leaned over my shoulder to get a better view himself.

Tried being diplomatic. Now we do it MY way.

You have 48 hours to bring the amount of supplies I asked for with generous interest to

Old Northern High School

Or we come back. We come in force. We take everything, and everyone left alive.

You are property now.

B.T.

"B.T.?" I asked.

"I'll give you one guess," Tony growled.

"Fucking Big Tyler," I stated. "Check Chris' pockets and shit. See if there's anything else."

Jennifer joined us and looked over Chris' body as well. Lifting his shirt, and the legs of his Dickies pants, revealed a mass of bruising everywhere. His face, pallid and drained of blood, was swollen and lacerated almost to the point of being unrecognizable.

"The rope marks where they tied him…" Jennifer began.

"Fucking crucified him," I corrected.

"Right. Crucified," she said, almost sheepishly at the confrontation in my voice. "They're bruised. I think he was alive when they did that. His whole body is a mass of contusions and blunt force trauma. I feel broken ribs. I think one knee has been shattered, and an elbow. Jesus."

Clearly, she'd been learning a lot of medicine in her free time with Shannon and Ashley. In any other situation, I'd be impressed with my wife. Right now, as a new friend and a major player in our survival lay dead before me, I just wanted answers.

"What's all this mean?" I asked, perhaps more sharply than I'd intended.

"He's missing all his finger and toenails, too," she continued. "Deep lacerations to his throat, under his armpits, and the femoral triangles near his groin. I think…"

"Think what?" I urged.

"I think he was tortured. A lot. While he hung there," she stated with a tremor, and then they bled him like a pig for slaughter when they were done."

I clenched my shotgun so tightly the polymer stock creaked.

Rich finally lost his shit completely. He stood straight up and stormed over to the gate, clenching the links in his hands and shaking them violently as he began yelling.

"Big Tyler!!!" he bellowed, "You fucking fuck!!! I swear to God, you fucking fuck!!! I'll kill you myself! You fuck! FUCK!!!"

He continued yelling as Dave grabbed him under the arm and led him away toward the north building, yelling profanities the entire way, his throat growing more hoarse nearly with every syllable.

"Jennifer," I instructed, standing up, my eyes burning from trying to hold back tears, "Get some people to help you. Get him somewhat cleaned up and buried. We'll schedule a memorial service for him once we can. Then get everyone rounded up on the north rooftop. Even the ten new arrivals.

"But," she began, "Shannon's quarantine isn't up for twelve more hours."

"Fuck her quarantine," I stated firmly, walking away, then, over my shoulder, "I'm going to need warm bodies with guns in their hands. If they were infected, they'd have turned already. Everyone on the roof in 30. Let's fucking go, people!"

THIRTY-SIX

Some people stayed behind to bury our large friend. Tony followed, and we stopped on the Medical Floor to speak with the ladies.

"Henry?" I said upon entering the makeshift doctor's office, making eye contact with first Shannon, then Ashley.

"He's good so far," Shannon offered. "He's moved to individual quarantine. Forty-eight hours. We'll check his vitals and overall condition every six hours. Nothing to do but wait and make sure he's comfortable. Everything seemed normal once we got him cleaned up."

"That's great so far." I agreed. "So, he's doing well, but how's he doing?"

"Emotionally," Ashley chimed in, her voice low and solemn, "he's a wreck. He has signs of mild shock. He's not spoken a word since he quit muttering about being infected. He just kind of clammed up and withdrew while we ran tests and got him settled in. He'll need time, but the mental trauma could stick with him long-term."

"Thanks, ladies," I stated. "Which room is he in?"

"Last one on the right," they said in unison.

I departed without a word, Tony silently in tow.

Upon reaching his room, I stretched a hand out and knocked on the door.

"Henry," I called, "It's Scott. I'm sorry buddy. I think you'll be fine. Try to rest, we have a meeting, I'll be down after with a gift for you. I…I love ya, buddy. It's going to be okay."

"Damn, man," Tony muttered quietly, "You said you love him. You really are worried."

"Let's go have a drink," I replied softly, then, to Henry, "Okay, I've got to go. I'll be back, man."

We made our way back down the hallway, passing our medical staff as they knocked, then unlocked and opened the first closed room by the main office. I assumed they were getting new members gathered up to meet with us.

We reached the end of the hallway, went through the open stairwell door, and wordlessly began making our ascent.

***

Taking seats on the rooftop, I cracked open a bottle of scotch I'd retrieved from my apartment on the way.

I took a long pull straight from the bottle. The burn was a welcome sensation as the liquid settled firmly in the pit of my stomach. Breathing out and tasting the peat to the drink, I passed the open bottle to Tony, who took his own long sip.

We maintained muted conversation about the events that had just transpired, and those to come. A course for the meeting was laid out as first Dave, then Rich joined us.

Rich's eyes had been rimmed red from crying, and as he passed to a seat at our table, he plainly snatched the bottle from my hand and took a large gulp himself before handing it back.

Dave looked simply tired, the layer of grime that had collected on his skin and clothes was streaked through with sweat. He informed us he had helped bury Chris, and he was thanked for it.

Before long, the rooftop was flooded with people. Men, women, and children all mingled together. This included the new survivors, who held tight to their own little grouping in an obvious attempt to maintain familiar company in an unfamiliar face.

I'm sure we looked more than simply rough to them. Every one of the adults, even Carolyn, wore the visage of recent tears, or anger. Most of us had a mix of blood spatter and grime still clinging to us, as a telltale of how close quarters some of the fighting had gotten.

"Everyone is here, except Henry," Jennifer informed me.

"Okay then, let's begin," I stated firmly.

I stood up in my place at what was essentially the head of the entire rooftop. A few took notice, but most were still in the process of muttering to each other about what just happened. Some more ambitious individuals were in the process of cleaning their weapons and reloading magazines. Tony had definitely been spending his free time wisely, as he'd taken it upon himself to educate small groups of our community on their weapons and their function.

"Everybody listen up!" I barked, and was satisfied when all conversation ceased and every head, even those of the children turned my way.

"My daddy!" Gwen exclaimed from her mother's arms, and a soft chuckle from the people gathered wavered and then died as Jennifer shushed the little bundle of energy.

"We have some new faces with us tonight," I pointed out. "I'd love to meet with you newcomers as a group, but for the moment, we have more pressing matters to attend to."

A few nearby the new people reached out in handshakes and greetings, and a murmur rose and fell before attention was once again brought my direction by Tony clearing his throat loudly.

"The man responsible for this...issue...tonight, goes by the name of Big Tyler," I informed the group.

"He's not actually that big though," Dave interjected.

"Yeah, he's pretty average, I'd say," Tony added.

"Shut up, you two," I ordered, trying not to grin at my idiot friends. "He literally signed his work with this note."

I held up the note, then passed it to Jennifer to pass around so everyone could read it. I then continued my speech, if you could call it that.

"His men attacked us when we retrieved the construction equipment," I stated firmly, matter-of-fact. "He is the one who met Tony at the main gate. He threatened us. He accused us. He tried to extort us into giving up our hard-earned, hard-won supplies. Many of you know Chris Simmons went missing some time ago. Clearly, it was this man who held our own friend, our partner. A member of this community."

A murmur rose across the rooftop at the realization. The gravity of this situation began to level the mood like a road grader.

"He not only held one of our members since long before we made contact," I continued in explanation, "but once his petty demands were turned down, he tortured, then murdered that man. *Our* man. Then he brought a spectacle here that he was sure would flood us with infected. He has kidnapped and killed a member of our own safe home. He then put every one of us, new and old, even the children, in danger."

Voices began to rise across the group gathered here. Cries ranged all over the spectrum. Fear, anger, retribution, some pure venom, especially from my table.

"So," I began anew, pleased with the feedback and the rally of our people, "We need soldiers. I'm personally declaring war. You will be in danger. You will be shot at. We will attack their compound. James is returning midday tomorrow with a full recon spread of their location. I expected them to be an issue, but this... This is above and beyond. Those willing to join us in arms, raise your hand and remain. Those not willing, go to bed. No hard feelings against you, I'm asking a lot here."

Hands slowly began to spread, raised up in the air, across the rooftop.

Katie began to stand and tried to grab Willy by the arm to lead him away as well. Jennifer, mid turn, grabbed her arm, yanking the overweight woman back to her seat forcefully.

"Sit, and raise your hand," Jennifer spat at her. "He's not going to take your fat ass anyway, but you better volunteer."

Katie, then Willy, both complied.

Only the new arrivals remained. Still in their own group and mostly looking quite unsure of themselves as to what to do. Then, surprisingly, one of them stepped forward. A heavier-built man nearly my age, with a scruffy dark beard and a black ballcap displaying the American flag pulled low over his eyes. He wore a large chrome revolver on an open hip holster. If I was the least bit sure that this was the aforementioned country boy, the bottle in his hand half full of tobacco spit erased all doubt.

"Cody," the man stated, his voice much smoother and more casual than I'd expected. "Cody Freeze."

"Freeze?" I asked. "Is that your real name, or your rap name?"

"I definitely don't rap," he replied flatly.

"Well," I began in earnest, "Welcome, and, thanks, Cody."

As if he spoke for the rest, the other adults in their group raised their hands as well.

"Full community of volunteers," I observed, astonished. "Okay. We'll see what intel and supplies James brings us. He was to watch their camp for 48 hours, then scout the military supplies. We'll see what he gives us in the morning and go from there. I'll keep you all in the loop. Everyone is dismissed. Have a good night."

We spent the next thirty minutes or so saying our goodnights as people departed the rooftop. We also addressed and did our best to soothe concerns.

Cody began to walk past, and I called over to him.

"What's that you got on your hip?" I asked.

"Smith and Wesson 500," he stated and grinned broadly.

"Biggest handgun in the world, isn't it?" I inquired, to which he grinned even bigger, tipped his ballcap, and went to find an empty room to call his own. I liked the guy a little already.

The roof had cleared, even my own friends, leaving Jennifer and Gwen.

"Why don't you two go get some rest," I offered. "I'm going to grab some glasses and a bottle of CC and head down to see Henry, probably going to spend the night down there."

We said our goodnights and loves, and they left as well.

I stopped by the supply floor and grabbed a brand new fifth of Canadian Club blended whiskey and headed down to Henry.

***

I reached medical and found only Shannon still on duty after the meeting. With a few words, she retrieved a pile of blankets and a pillow from one of many closets and handed them to me before going back to the triage journal she'd been reading.

I reached the end of the hallway and spread my bedding out. I was not going to leave Henry's side this night, even if there was a steel door between us. I'd known the guy for years, and never had a word of bad to say about him.

"You there?" I asked as I slid the homemade meal slot on his door open. "Brought some of your good ol' CC, dude. Here."

I poured a healthy glass of the liquor and set it on the ledge.

"Thank you, brother," he replied, almost inaudibly, and took the glass. I poured a second, for myself, and settled in.

We spent what felt like an eternity sharing the whiskey like that. I finally got him talking, though not nearly as animated as he used to be. We talked of all of our past stories between us. We spoke of people we both knew, things we'd both been through, anything and everything. I still to this day could not tell you if we were merely chatting as old friends or catching up to possibly say goodbye forever.

Whatever the case, before the night drifted too far, the bottle was empty. Our words were slurred and heavy. In my candlelight, I could make out the visage of my friend. First, he merely sat near the door. Then he slumped, deeper and deeper, until finally, I heard snoring. I took this as my cue and lay my head on my pillow in my makeshift bed.

Before I could recall taking another breath, I was fast asleep.

THIRTY-SEVEN

I woke to a gentle shaking sensation. It was Shannon, and she had me by the shoulder.

"Hey," she said softly. "Didn't want to startle you. I just need you to roll over that way, so we can get into Henry's room."

"What?" I asked, shaking my head and rubbing sleep from my eyes. "Is he okay? What's happening?"

"Nothing's wrong," she reassured. "I've just got to get in to check his vitals."

I noticed Dave standing next to her, his AK-47 at the ready, cradled in one arm, a key in the other hand. He was covered with strange lumps that I couldn't quite make out at first.

"Mornin', sweetheart!" he said cheerily.

"Are those...pillows? Strapped all over you?" I asked, slightly amused, and sitting up I continued, "You look ridiculous. You here to cuddle?"

"Best we could do at short notice," Dave informed me solemnly. "In case he's more hungry than usual."

Shannon touched Dave's arm, and he put the key to the door. He turned the lock over and shoved the door. Hard. Shit, I didn't warn them that Henry might still be slumped up against it.

"Hey hey HEY! Ow!" I heard Henry's voice bellow. "What the fuck are y'all doing here?"

"You hungry?" Dave asked casually. "Wanna take a bite off my ass, big boy?"

"I'ma take a bite of something, damn you!" Henry shouted. "No I'm not hungry. I'm old. I'm hungover. And you doin' way too much, brother Dave. Too much, Lord Lord."

I gathered myself and started to depart as they began questioning Henry. He was reassuring them his headache was from last night's liquor. He's fine, he said. Shannon began checking his vitals. Dave asked where they were planning to put the thermometer, which sparked more yelling and vulgarity from Henry.

I decided to skip heading upstairs. If Jennifer and Gwen were asleep, I intended to leave them there as long as possible. I'm sure they needed it.

Instead, I made my way out the front of the building and into the morning. It was overcast, and threatened rain, but the heat of the waning summertime still held. The air was somewhat thick with humidity.

The carnage from the night before was still evident. I began rounding people up who milled about nearby and directing them. With Henry down, it looked like the work project would be up to me to direct.

"Get these infected in a truck and take them to the dump site," I instructed and watched as people began wrapping their faces with rags. The dead didn't even stink much yet. Why the need for cowboy bandanas? I inquired as much and was met with a basic response.

"These don't stink much," Willy offered, "but the ones on the highway where we dump them? They're getting bad. You can smell them from here when the wind blows right."

"We'll get a burn going then," I concluded. "One of these days when the wind will take the smoke away from us. For now, do the best y'all can."

He complied, as did everyone else, and in short order, they had the dead in the back of one of our new dump trucks. It was interesting to watch the work. The backhoe, being the more mobile of our two equipment pieces, was brought out. The bucket was then stuffed with as many dead infected as they could, then elevated to be dumped carelessly into the back of the truck.

It wasn't so much a recognition of the loss of humanity in the infected, nor was it a telling of the hardening of our people. It was just work. Something else to do or clean up, and they treated it as such.

Before long, the truck was departing for the overpass, and Jennifer had approached me. Sleep still clouded her face, but she had a fresh cup of coffee in hand. Thick, black, and bitter just the way I preferred. But, this time, it had a little extra to it.

"It's hot," I observed, turning to her. "Hot coffee? We have hot coffee?"

"We plugged a pot into the command center," she smiled, handing me a thermos full of the beverage. "Just, don't tell James."

"Thanks." I smiled in return and kissed her on the forehead. Then, I turned to the rest of the people in the area.

"Get everyone gathered up, I want full work crews on deck in fifteen!" I barked. "Henry's down, but we got shit to do, people! Rich!!!"

"Yeah man," he appeared behind me, startling me. "What's up?"

"Fucker," I murmured, gaining his grin in response to my startle. "Grab two people. I want your armory idea at fifty percent by tonight or we're scrapping it."

"Oh, trust me, we got this!" Rich replied, still grinning, then departing to begin work.

"Come on Dave," I called over just as he appeared from the front of the building. "Let's go, cuddles!"

Dave met me on the way to a Smart Car, and we loaded up and departed for a few blocks away to the worksite, Katie opening the gate for us to pass.

"You know Henry usually runs a morning dinner bell, right?" Dave reminded me.

"Don't think there's any left, man," I replied, as I eyeballed the puddles of congealed blood we passed. "Least not this morning. How is the old man anyway?"

"Shannon says he's not infected," he replied, shrugging. "I don't fuckin' know, dude. He seems okay. She wants to keep an eye on him though."

"I think he'll be alright," I confirmed. "Why don't you think it got him?"

"Hard to say," Dave replied. "Not really my area of expertise, anyway."

We pulled up to the work zone and I got out of the Smart Car and immediately into the excavator. It couldn't be that hard, right? Everyone else had been operating it. I should be able to as well.

I couldn't. At least, not at first. I got the machine started, and with the first pull of the lever, the machine swung about, just missing Dave, and burying its bucket into the side of the car I'd just departed.

I shut the machine off and left the cab.

"Well then," I spoke to nobody. I tried wiping my hands off nonchalantly and acting casual. Dave had streams of tears from laughter as he doubled over.

Just then, Rob appeared with the backhoe, pulling it to a stop and shutting the machine off.

"What the hell happened here?" he said, eying the scene, then Dave, and finally me.

"I fucking hate Smart Cars," I grunted, then, "Okay, you're on the excavator, let's get moving."

Chuckling to himself, Rob climbed aboard and flawlessly removed the bucket from the small vehicle and positioned the machine to dig.

Before much longer, we had a full operation going despite Henry's absence. Everyone filled their own roles just as they'd been doing for so long under his lead.

We were steadily pulling up sections of earth and building sections of wall and barrier. Everything was going well when I heard the grinding of metal, and the crack of something as it gave way.

"Whoa guys, hold up!" I called, eyeing the long section of piping that protruded from the newly dug section of ground.

"Just a gas line, boss," Rob called down from his machine.

"Just gas line?" I asked, a bit cross in my tone.

"Nothing left to it," he explained. "Utilities long been shut off, no danger in an empty line."

I grudgingly, though carefully, watched as he used the machine to pick the busted section of gas pipe out and got back to his work. Okay then, I guess he's right.

Work kept trudging along when I noticed movement to our southwest. It was one of our trucks I had recognized first, a red pickup, as it came around one corner and made its way toward our gate. Following this was a sight to behold.

Even at this distance, I could make out a white Peterbilt pulling a long tanker trailer. To the outside of each were strapped many, many things I could not discern at this distance. It swung wide around the turn and kicked its burners on, belching black smoke and rolling faster toward our main gate. Following it, a dark blue Smart Car, one of ours, that made its way in the truck's wake.

I started walking toward our own little car before recalling the earlier incident. Dave and I instead loaded up in a nearby Ford Ranger and, after instructing the others to keep working, we headed to meet James and his crew.

***

We arrived at the gate just in time to follow the last vehicle in.

Pleasantries were exchanged, James and the three that went with him were filthy, tired, and looked like they'd been rolling around in pig slop, but they were all intact and unharmed. Thank God.

"Got your diesel!" James exclaimed proudly, "And a whole lot more goodies. More than we expected to find, in all honesty."

James cut me off from replying as he swung open the passenger door of the truck and reached up into the cab, withdrawing a large black gun. It was an M240E1, a belt-fed machine gun used by the military. It even still had the ammunition belt locked into place, though the top cover was crushed.

"Doesn't fire, but I thought we could maybe figure it out and get it working with time," James offered.

"I'll get right on that!" Rich, coming up to take possession of the weapon, his eyes glowing with excitement. "Shouldn't be too hard, right?"

"Maybe have Tony give you a hand with it," I opined. "We could definitely find a place for it if it'll work."

Tony appeared, as if sensing his name being mentioned, and he and Rich disappeared with the gun before I could add anything else to the conversation.

"Tons of ammo for it, too," James continued. "Actually, we found lots of various ammo and things the military had left behind. Lot of it got blown clean off the bridge, we had to get crafty to retrieve it from the tree branches below and stuff. Lot of fun, that was."

"What's this?" I inquired, motioning to a series of tubes sticking out from under the tarp covering the bed of the pickup truck.

"Mortars," James said, smiling broadly. "They only had illumination rounds, but again, it was there, I figured we could use them."

"Lucky Rich and Tony didn't see those first," I chuckled. "What else we got?"

"Tanker's full," James continued. "It's diesel. We cleared out a couple of auto parts store, every drop of any kind of fluid they had. Batteries, big and small. Military left a lot of radio gear that didn't get pillaged, and we salvaged every piece of combat gear or supply we could find."

"Any vehicles left behind?" I inquired.

"Nah, anything that would have been salvageable was destroyed from inside," he admitted. "Clara said it's SOP for the military to not leave vehicles behind intact. Don't want them in the wrong hands type of thing, I guess."

"You've done very well, James," I congratulated. "I'm impressed, and we're all proud of you four."

"Thanks," James replied, then his expression darkened deeply. "The, uh, the guys at the school. Real bad dudes, man. I want to get rid of them. We all do."

"Oh, brother, you have no idea," I assured. "They brought Chris back to us. And a whole swarm of infected. First things first though, let's get Bri down here with her notepad."

I motioned to the freshly dug dirt nearby, topped with a rudimentary wooden cross with Chris' name painted on it. James muttered a curse and began helping to unload the trucks and line things up for cataloguing.

I raised Bri on the radio and she came down and began happily attending to her duty of documenting and directing all the supplies. There even turned out to be several boxes of toys and school supplies on the roof of the smart car, held down by scavenged ratchet straps from the parts stores.

I walked over to Rich's pool. They'd had it completely drained, and, I was informed, the drain valve was wedged open to keep it from building up water.

Rich had already constructed three of four walls, standard-issue studs and plywood packed with anything he could find to insulate it. He also had what appeared to be a slightly raised floor, also joisted and laid in with heavy plywood. He told me it bought a little elevation from the pool floor, there'd always be some standing water, and this kept things dry.

"Going to move my things out here, too," he told me. "That way, there's always somebody to keep an eye on things."

"What about your wife?" I asked. "She moving in, too?"

"Carolyn?" he asked. "Nah, she doesn't want to sleep near anything that goes boom. Scares her. It'll be okay."

"You're doing good, man," I said, reassuringly.

"Thanks," he accepted. "Going to section it off before the roof is put on. Building a chain link wall and a counter at the front, with a door, I want to make it function as a regular armory window."

"Nice. Nice," I stated.

We continued talking about his plans for a moment, and when James was ready, we left Rich to his own devices and made our way up to the command floor. I radioed for Tony, Dave, Jennifer, and a few others to come join us so we could go over James' recon, and begin a plan.

***

"We've got it all," James began, "but our files aren't tidy. Let's see what's on this one."

He placed a memory card from one camera in the reader, made a few clicks of the mouse, and in an instant, one of the security monitor screens minimized and we were greeted with a full color video of downtown Akron, as seen from the main bridge from the north leading over the valley.

"Oh, shit, yeah," James exclaimed, "you need to see this. The way the infected are acting. It's, it's just weird, man."

We all became silent and watched intently.

The scene was clearly from a shaky digital camera, but it showed what we needed to see very clearly. Downtown appeared as completely wrecked as any warzone images I'd ever seen.

From the firebombing early on in the end of things, the buildings were all scorched as far up as several floors. Windows were blown in, and even on floors above the primary burn line there were black streaks reaching up like fingers from many windows.

Vehicles left in the roadway were little more than burnt-out hulks of what they'd used to be. Smaller piles of debris, and what I'd assumed to be long dead

200

infected, littered the streets and sidewalks. Street lamps were blown out and bent at odd angles, and the road surface itself had even appeared to crack and been bubbled in weird ways.

In the following moments, a scene unwound that made me feel like I was watching a Hollywood film instead of real-life footage from a scout team.

One freak came blazing full speed around the corner of one building. It started that strange bark, and a number more spilled out from the hidden corner, almost like legged marbles being shoved aside by a broom.

Then the first giant flew into view. Yeah, I said flew.

A behemoth much like the one at the construction site was picked up off of the ground and entered the scene horizontally. It hit the pavement, leaving small bits of its mottled skin behind as it found its feet in a hurry.

A second behemoth entered the scene, taking a swing at the first and landing a glancing blow before the first tyrant lunged, spearing the second against the remains of a parked car.

Smaller, well, normal-sized infected scurried about. Clearly, they were interested in the action, but did their best to not get involved. They made an effort to avoid the struggle going on, and most of them managed.

One got tangled up around the second beast's feet, nearly tripping it. The beast seized this opportunity for a weapon, grabbing the smaller infected and throwing her like a spear at the first monster. She hit him head first, stumbling him, before he regained his balance and lunged again.

It was like watching a pair of mutated gorillas battle it out during mating season. The scene continued for perhaps another fifteen seconds before one got the upper hand.

The first giant grabbed what appeared to be a burnt-out Vespa scooter from amid two crashed cars. He turned, and swung it like a giant hammer, catching the second right in the side of the head, staggering it until it fell flat on its back.

Taking this as his chance, the first lumbered forward, smashing again with the scooter, bringing it down overhead and smashing the other creature across the center of the face. Again and again it raised the little motorbike, and brought it down, each impact heard audibly despite the distance of the person filming it.

Finally, convinced that it was dead, the first monster stood straight, pulled its arms back, head arched to the sky, and let out a bellow that turned my stomach even through the digitized sound system. This sent all the other smaller infected scattering. They actually cowered around building corners and behind cars.

"These fuckers are all, even the little ones…" Tony trailed off.

"Getting smarter?" I asked. "Yeah, we've been seeing that, haven't we?"

"I don't know what they were fighting over," Jennifer added, "but they definitely seem to have some kind of structure forming. Like, social stuff."

"That they do," James confirmed. "We've seen lots of examples of it, too. Working like pack animals, too. Eight of them had us cornered in the local parts store. If we didn't have guns, we'd have lost to them."

"Okay, I want all this relayed to the medical team," I instructed. "Earmark it for them to use to learn more about what we're up against. Anyone who's a hunter, or good with animals, too."

"Got it," James said, withdrawing the memory card and inserting another.

"Ah, okay, here we are," he said, "Old Northern High School."

He began scanning through the pictures and video clips the team had gathered. As each frame passed, he said what he'd learned about whatever was on screen.

Most of the information regarding the infected was old hand already. What was of note was the locations and conditions of things that could help us greatly in the foreseeable future. James even took the initiative to locate several private garages with wood and coal burning stoves for heating, making mention of their usage for our own purposes.

Next, he reached the files containing their scouting imagery from Old Northern. Flicking through image after image of the complex owned and run by the micro-tyrant, there was plenty to see. One shot, however, captured Tony's attention.

"That guy," he said. "Right there. Stop scrolling."

"Yeah," James confirmed, "he seems to be running the show. He doesn't do any actual work, but orders people around and in the evenings, he takes one of the women, or one of the girls, into the school building with him."

"That's Big Tyler," Tony confirmed. "Yeah, he's asshole number one around here. Fuck that guy."

We quickly caught James up to speed on what had been happening while they were gone. The news of the Hashman compound brought light to his eyes, but the news about Chris and what Big Tyler's guys had done quickly darkened them again. He was visibly angry, shaking and squeezing the camera in his hand until the case began to creak.

"They have a tent city in the southern parking lot," James explained. "Civilians, captives, slaves, whatever you want to call them, they keep them there. I counted 39. A few men and a few women, the rest younger. High school aged, mixed group. We figure they were holed up at the school when everything went to shit. They look bad, man. Real bad."

"We'll get them," I promised, watching a single tear fall from James' cheek. "Keep going. At your own pace."

He wiped his eyes and continued.

"There's a rotating guard," he continued. "One main gate, the rest is all original chain link with the other gates barred and closed off. We counted maybe forty-five of this Big Tyler's guys all together, unless some live completely inside and never see the light of day."

"We'll count for sixty of them, then," I concluded. "Better to overestimate them. We've got thirty-ish adults ourselves. Fuck."

"They do leave in groups of ten to twelve," James advised. "They go out at various points during both the day and night, nothing seems to be on a schedule. They're well-armed, well-fed, but they're loosely organized, and they do bicker quite a bit amongst themselves."

"We need to find a way to thin them out when they leave," I surmised. "They follow a usual path out of there?"

"Uh yeah," James confirmed. "The main east and west stretch that the school sits on."

"We need traps, or ambushes. Tonight, and in the morning. We're down to about 36 hours to do this," I opined. "If they stay true to their threats."

"What about them big infected?" Rich's voice broke in. "We could lure one right to them somehow."

"What about the innocent people there?" I questioned, then, seeing the figure next to Rich, "Ah, Mike! You made it! Everyone listen up, this guy is an ally. Meet Mike Hashman."

Everybody took turns introducing themselves to Hashman, and we quickly got him up to speed on what we were talking about. He knew about our plans to attack, I guess he and Rich had been standing there for a few minutes before breaking their silence.

"Let me call my boys," Hashman offered. "If they're down, we could get maybe 25 more people in a few hours down here?"

"Sounds good to me, Mike, and thank you." I offered, "Guys, Mr. Hashman here has a handful of Marines, and a bunch of metalheads. They can definitely help."

Conversation rose and fell as soon as I silenced it to bring attention back to our planning.

"Rich, take Mike and show him around," I instructed. "I'll be with you guys shortly."

"Will do," Rich complied. "Hey, Mike. You guys have lots of crops, do you fertilize them?"

Mike nodded wearily.

"Good." Rich grinned, clapping Hashman on the shoulder. "We're going to have to talk about the joys of fertilizer and diesel fuel, too, hope you've got some to spare."

The pair left. Poor Mike, already in Rich's insane hands while we began planning our avenue of attack. I pinched the bridge of my nose and got back into the conversation.

Before long, a plan had been constructed. Everyone left to begin to prepare, leaving me with my two closest friends.

"Think we can pull this off?" I asked Tony.

"I sure as fuck hope so," Tony replied.

"We don't have a choice," Dave added. "These dudes are worse than we thought. They need to go."

"Agreed," I stated, as I leaned back in my chair and lit a cigar. "We can't let this kind of evil grow in our own back yard."

THIRTY-EIGHT

As promised, within a few hours a pair of boats eerily similar to ours were spotted heading toward our compound down the river. I got the call on the radio from Dave, who was by the river having a smoke on our own boat. I made my way to the shore, Hashman joining me and a dozen others.

After Hashman confirmed they were his, those with us visibly relaxed, allowing their weapons to rest on slings and in holsters and instead, standing by to grab ropes and find anchor points to bring the boats in.

Both vessels were loaded with an even mix of Marines, metalheads and others. Everyone was kitted out, as it were, and took on the look of any small-town militia from before the collapse of civilization.

"Where's Tim?" Hashman asked as Jason began helping unload supplies and people from his boat.

"Sick. Again," Jason replied, exasperated. "Says it's his stomach."

"He's so full of shit," Hashman shot back. "That's the fifth time this month. He's just shirking duties."

"Definitely not full of shit," Jason replied, chuckling. "Actually, he's so not full of shit he's not even allowed to use the latrines. Ramirez dug him out a shit trench by the fence line. Dude has to have IBS or something."

"Tim somebody important?" I asked, eyeing the pair.

"Explosives guy," Jason replied. "But, I think he's afraid to be outside the gates."

"Every time his rotation comes up," Hashman explained, "he ends up fuckin' sick. Guy's smart, but he's useless. No matter, you guys have a dude that seems as good as Tim."

"We do?" I questioned.

"Me," Rich spoke up.

"You speak boom?" I asked him. "Why didn't you say anything?"

"Never needed it," Rich replied flatly, then, motioning to the second boat, "Is that for me?"

"Yeah," Hashman replied. "Fifty bags. It's the right shit, isn't it?"

Rich approached the boat, climbed aboard, and began inspecting the pile of bags that covered the entire bow of the boat, making it sit funny in the water.

"That's the shit, good stuff," Rich announced and began directing people to carry the bags to the swimming pool armory.

Rich grabbed a pair of the 50-pound bags of fertilizer and departed as well.

"Alright," I stated, "Let's get ready to brief everyone. We have a fuck ton to orchestrate, and the clock's ticking."

"Let's do it, dude!" Hashman agreed, clapping me on the shoulder jovially.

I pulled the radio from my hip and spoke into it, instructing everyone with a handset to get everyone else together, we'd meet outside the south building as there were too many present to reasonably fit in the command center, and I wasn't making everyone walk up the flights of stairs. I wanted us fresh, we moved tonight.

***

"Everybody take a seat, relax, chill out, but listen up!" I barked out to the group of about sixty people gathered around.

Tony and Dave had found a white board and pack of dry erase markers. The board, propped against the front doors of the building, held a crudely drawn map. The map laid out the school, the surrounding property, and a rough sketch of the surrounding neighborhood up to two blocks away from it with various symbols drawn upon it.

"Here we are," I advised. "We take up places on the south, west, and east of the school and break into four teams."

I pointed to various points on the board as whispers and low conversation started, presumably people trying to buddy up with each other.

"Tony and I lead one team," I continued, "Rich and Dave have their own place, and they'll handle their duty alone."

"Yeah!" Dave called from the back, "We're gonna fuck some shit up!"

"Yes, Dave," I replied, trying not to laugh. "Clara and Frank will lead the team to the east. Hashman and Jason will lead the western team. Tony and I will be south, as it's our job to get as many innocent people through the fence and to safety as we can before Rich and Dave show up."

"When do we start it?" questioned a man whom I didn't know, one of Hashman's metalheads.

"They're good and drunk, probably high, after dark," James supplied. "Except for a team they usually send out to do some night time scavenging."

"Correct," I offered. "Ideally, Rich will show up when they've got their gates open to allow their scouts to leave. Either way, once we have word he's coming, Jason's team will set off a distraction just north of the compound before moving to position, we want them all looking away from where we will be extracting people."

"With a little luck," Jennifer opined, "them being intoxicated will make them easier to distract."

"That's the plan," I agreed. "Everyone only need worry about their roles. West team will get the call from me, after Rich contacts me. Once their distraction is working, we get people out of there. Then, we wait."

"For?" Jason asked.

"For our crazy redhead," I replied, grinning broadly. "He's going to do his part, and get the fuck out of Dodge, then we wait again. I suggest you all find solid cover, cover your ears, and open your mouths once he does his part. You'll know beyond a shadow of a doubt once the waiting is over. Then, we all move in, staying in cover, and clean up the rest of these assholes until they either surrender, or whoever is left is dead."

Tony stepped forward and started letting people draw straws, the tip of each one was colored a different color, one color for each team needed.

"Red with me," I instructed. "Blue with Hashman, white with Clara. Let's move, people! Triple check your shit, be ready for a fight. Each team, follow your leads. Hashman has given us some radios and earpieces that are bound as a set."

"Everyone on my team let's go!" Clara ordered. "We're going to help Rich load up this truck, then we're out! Check your gear, don't fuck around, don't test me!"

"One last thing!" I shouted. "There's infected out there. Only kill them if you have to, do it quietly. Give us away, get our civilians killed, disobey your lead, or otherwise fuck this up, and I will shoot you myself. This is real, people!"

***

Everybody had brought their straws to their respective group leads. Every group lead was busy assisting with gear checks and getting everyone prepped as the sun crept a bit lower in the sky, nearing the horizon.

I met with Rich and several others near the back of his dump truck. It was the typical, lighter, worksite type of dump, painted bright city worker yellow.

The crew had just finished loading up several 55-gallon drums. A half-dozen were left standing and strapped into place, two more in the very back were lain on their sides. Those two had been strapped into place, ensuring the others didn't move. One of Hashman's men was busy screwing wooden boards into place to secure everything further, while Rich had just finished securing a few car batteries with the rest of the load and running wiring through the whole mess. Every barrel had already been connected, and a series of wires ran to what looked like a mechanical timer from a clothes dryer.

As I approached the back of the vehicle, Dave stood with his AK-47 cradled in one arm, a joint slowly burning in his free hand. He approached me as I approached them.

"Sorry sir," Dave directed, putting the hand with his joint in it up to me, "this area is currently off limits to all non-authorized personnel."

"Fuck off Dave," I replied, laughing. "Should you be smoking that here?"

"He's right, man," Rich called down. "Put that shit out."

"Fine, fine," Dave relented, moving out of the way and off to smoke elsewhere.

"Jesus, Rich," I exclaimed upon taking everything in. "Timothy McVeigh much?"

"Should do the job nicely," Rich replied, grinning as he fastened a couple more wires together. "I just hope it's enough."

"It better be," the unnamed Marine retorted. "You got half our fuckin' fertilizer in these barrels."

"He's got a ton of our diesel in there, too., I added. "No worries, we'll repay you guys greatly for all the help."

"I'm not worried, we're not worried," Hashman supplied as he also approached. He took one look at Rich's setup, then the cigarette in his fingers, uttered a singular "Oh, shit," and disappeared again.

"Got an estimate on when this will be finished?" I asked, turning back to Rich.

"Now, pretty much," he stated, jumping down from the back of the truck, "Let's go, Dave!"

"Hey," I said, putting a hand on my friend's shoulder, "You guys be fucking careful, dude. Don't get in over your head. Be smart."

"You know we got this," Rich replied grinning as he climbed into the truck.

Dave followed by climbing into the back of the truck with the barrels, and pounding twice with his fist on the roof of the vehicle. He then turned and eyed me, a somber expression crossing his face and clouding his eyes.

"Man," he began, gaining my full attention, "if it all goes bad, if we don't make it, I just wanted to let you know one thing."

"Yeah?" I replied, curious. "What's that?"

His only response was to extend his tattooed arm, hand facing me, with one inked finger protruding right from the middle.

"That's great, Dave," I laughed. "Hey, I know where your stash of Arizona tea is. You die, it's mine, bitch!"

He thumbed the safety off his AK and glared at me.

"You don't fuck with my tea, dude. Don't fucking touch it."

I didn't have much of a chance to reply as the truck sputtered to life, eliminating the chance for further conversation, then it rolled to the gate, and departed.

Clara approached as they left.

"That our cue, boss?" she inquired as she walked up.

"Yeah, you good? Got a good team?" I asked in return.

"Mixed bag," she started. "We got Fred, too, but we have both Katie and Parker."

"Yeah," I grinned, "I got Tony, Wayne, and James, but also Willy."

"Could be worse, wanna trade?" she asked, grinning in return.

"Fuck no," I shot back, "we drew straws, fair is fair!"

"Yeah, okay," she relented, then turning to the mass of people, "Load up, guys! Let's move, we're losing daylight!"

She was right, the sun had touched the horizon, and the temperature was already beginning to drop. Wouldn't be many more weeks and the cold weather would be upon us. I didn't even have a spare moment to start contemplating what this meant for us when my earpiece began speaking. The first time hearing a voice through it, and having forgotten I'd put it in, it nearly made me jump out of my skin.

"West and east teams are Oscar Mike,"sSaid the voice, one of Hashman's men.

"Solid copy, let's get south team gathered and moving now," I replied.

I got loaded up in the bed of a full-size Chevy pickup with a half-dozen others, including Tony. Just before we hunkered down and got ready for the ride, Jennifer came up to wish us well and planted a kiss on my cheek.

"Make sure Gwen's daddy comes home to her," she fairly pleaded. I could read the worry on her face, and I replied in kind.

"Don't think that's possible," I explained. "I think our mailman is long dead, woman."

She chuckled and reached out to slap me upside the head for my joking, which I dodged and then waved as the truck pulled away. She returned the wave and Gwen did as well, from her perch in her mother's arm.

***

We departed through the front gate and began moving southbound in a small convoy. We had moved into the shadows of our own wall, and then crossed the main avenue, taking side streets that I hadn't seen since we first got to the apartments in what felt like another time ago.

As we rolled on through damaged and abandoned neighborhoods, I took it all in again, as if it were the first time. The carnage looked much the same as it always had. Some houses had been left wide open, our own scavengers symbols spray painted across walls and garage doors. The basic FEMA scripture, marking them as safe, but empty of any goods.

The scenes of carnage and devastation had faded in their own ways. Once fresh, maggot-ridden piles of decay from people who had fallen victim to the ravenous infected had turned to bare bone, puddles of blood long washed away with the sporadic rains that came at night in the Ohio summer. Houses and vehicles that had burnt no longer smoldered.

The only familiarity was the sight of the infected freaks. They seemed to sense that what they were seeing was no longer an easy meal, as they paid attention, and took notice, but mostly just viewed us in passing. A couple here and there in front lawns, some visible between buildings or in open garages, ghostly figures letting us know that we were never truly alone in this world, and never truly safe.

A few very freshly dead infected passed us as we swerved around them in the streets. They had been taken out either by our lead vehicle, or one of the other groups that had left shortly prior to our departure.

One of the Marines with us nudged my shoulder.

"Mike wanted us to give you and a couple of your buddies a gift," he stated, "should help with this mission."

I watched as another Marine kicked the crate he was sitting on into the middle of us. It came to a stop in the middle of the pickup truck's bed, and the first Marine withdrew a large survival knife and pried the top of it off, tossing it over the edge to clatter to the street.

As he did this, and the box top came to a rest on the roadway, three infected came running from a two-floor home to one side. They barked and grunted to each other but didn't screech or scream. Presumably, they didn't want to share their prize with anyone else. They skidded to a halt, inspected the offering, and one-by-one they turned away from it and left the scene to search for something they could actually eat.

I leaned forward in anticipation and viewed a handful of very short carbines arranged side-by-side in the crate. The guy pulled one from where it rested and handed it to me. It looked very much like an M4, but much shorter, and lighter, with a suppressor attached. The guns were dressed in a beautiful combination of black and desert tan.

"Name's Rogers, by the way," he stated.

"Hell of a name for a rifle," I shot back, slightly confused.

"Rogers is my name," he corrected, not a drop of humor in his tone.

"I know," I informed, "I was being facetious."

"We all handle the pre-battle jitters in our own way," Rogers stated, then continued, "Anyway, this is an Mk18 Mod 1. That's a basic Surefire SOCOM suppressor, it will be very quiet for you. It's chambered in 300 Blackout. Basic setup, collapsible, vertical foregrip, EOTECH holographic sight. If you can work an AR15, you can work this, it's no different."

He handed them around to Tony, James, and Wayne. Each man accepting and inspecting his new rifle. Tony eyed his almost adoringly, as if he'd been handed his life's dream on a street corner.

Rogers grabbed mine from me, chambered a round, and took aim at an infected who had wandered into the street in our wake. Once the freak drifted to about 75 yards behind us, Rogers squeezed the trigger.

Typically, a suppressed weapon will not be whisper quiet. In real life, as opposed to movies and video games, you're looking at a screen door slamming for volume. So, I wasn't expecting the results we were shown.

One smooth trigger pull, the rifle jumped, emitted a sound no louder than a soft sneeze, and the freak's head exploded like a firecracker went off inside of a watermelon. You could fire one of these in your living room and not alert anybody upstairs. I don't even think it would wake the guy on the couch. I was in love. I was astounded, but I did my level best to remain business like and not show those emotions.

Rogers safed the weapon and returned it back to my eager hands. I accepted it graciously and spent the rest of the ride speaking with him about the weapon platform. I kept watch on the others out of the corner of my eye, laughing internally at the wonder on Tony's face. I hoped Hashman wasn't expecting to get this back. I didn't want to see Tony cry if he had to hand his in.

Before too much longer, as we neared the neighborhood that the school was located in, the hushed calls began coming across my earpiece. I took note of Rogers and Tony both looking distracted as they too listened to the voices that only we could hear.

"West team in position, prepping distractions," reported Jason.

A few blocks travel later, and another report came in.

"East team is settled in and waiting, boss," Clara stated.

"Solid copies on all, south team moving in shortly." I confirmed.

We all stayed hushed and low as the truck took a right to head west and skirt fairly far away from the main school area. We directed ourselves to the south again, crossed the main throughway, and disappeared back into the neighborhood just southwest of the school.

The sun had gone down, leaving only a trace of its essence in the western sky as we wound our way through the neighborhood to our destination. I pressed on my earpiece and spoke into it.

"Rich, what's your status?"

"We found what we're looking for, you ready?" he replied after a moment's pause, his usually boisterous scratchy voice nearly inaudible on my end.

"Stay put, we're moving in now. I'll advise shortly," I instructed.

Rich complied, and our conversation ceased as the vehicles slowed to a stop behind a small strip mall facing the main street directly across from the school. We all quietly and quickly dismounted the vehicles and made our way to the back doors of the businesses. Thankfully, our adversaries had most likely looted them already, as both back and front doors all stood wide open.

I let Tony, Wayne, and Jason dispatch the few nearby infected outside of the buildings as we moved, their weapons' barely audible report still seeming startlingly loud. The rest of our group filed into the businesses on each side of us, and we went straight in through the middle one, a long-abandoned and looted dental office.

Without a word, we made our way through a small break room. Keeping low, we passed a trio of work rooms, their chairs and overhead lights now long defunct. The whole place seemed incredibly eerie as we made our way up front.

"Contact," Tony stated coldly, followed by three spaced out hushed rifle reports as three infected met their quick demise.

His third round exited the head of the obese woman it had entered. As she fell, leaving a dark spray of brain matter and skull fragments, the round continued on. It punched a neat hole through the shop front glass, travelled straight across the street, and embedded itself in the back of a chair next to a tent.

The woman sitting in the chair jumped, startled, and spun around in her seat to look behind her.

We all froze, watching with great apprehension, as she scanned the area behind her, then the ground around her, said something to the man next to her, and continued sewing whatever the garment was that she'd held.

Collectively we all breathed a sigh of relief. I punched Tony in the arm, and he apologized before continuing to the large pane of glass to peer through the hole he made. The other 8 of us took up positions low along the wall under it. Rogers and myself posted near the front door, looking across the street at the scene before us.

The area with the tent city was nearly pitch black. No lighting, and only a single burning barrel was afforded to the people that these guys held captive. After a few moments of watching, we concluded that there was only a pair of bad guys left to watch over their herd of civilians.

Nearer the north end of the school, we could hear a mix of rap music, and rock music being played from portable speakers and stereos. Several small fires and burning barrels were scattered about, and we could make out a number of figures moving about them. Some would put a cigarette or other to their lips. Some others could be seen taking swigs from bottles. It was definitely a party of sorts.

As we watched, it became apparent that a third man was with the prisoners, as the tent flap nearest the fire barrel opened and a middle-aged guy in jeans and a leather biker vest exited. He zipped his fly and nodded to another man on guard duty. I could just make out the form huddled near the back corner of the tent. Her knees drawn to her chin, arms locked protectively around them. My blood boiled at the sight of it. We've got to get these people out of there.

Rogers viewed the scene almost casually, making mental notes of the position of everything. Clearly, he was not a stranger to the ways people can get, having spent time overseas with our armed forces.

I pressed my earpiece and began to speak.

"All teams check in."

I got okays and positions from everybody with an earpiece almost instantly. All, except for one.

"Rich," I called into my earpiece, "Rich, where you at?"

The tone of Rich's voice, and the panic, sent a shiver up my spine.

"We're going to be early!" he nearly shouted, the sound of Dave's AK47 cracking in the background. "We got spotted."

"Fuck," I replied. "Okay, how long?"

"Uhhh," he began. "Maybe 8 minutes, maybe less?"

"Copy," I replied, nothing we could do now but go, "West team let's move, set those distractions off NOW!"

"Got it, moving now dude!" Hashman replied.

I turned to the guys with me, and also spoke into my earpiece so the teams in the adjoining businesses could hear.

"South team," I ordered, "shut and block your back doors. As these people get to you, usher them in and get them behind as much wall and protection as you can."

The teams on both sides of me replied in the affirmative just as a pair of illumination rounds from our scavenged mortars took to the sky. They glowed brightly against the dark background above and threw everything below them into startling contrast with our night time surroundings. As the shells slowly fell, they cast an alien pulsing glow across all of us.

In the new man-made daylight, we could clearly see a growing number of figures departing from their small groups to look up at the spectacle. As if to punctuate the point of the distraction, a series of firecrackers and bottle rockets began to take on life and flight, creating a racket right at the northwest corner of the school's tall chain link fence line.

Some of the enemy that still had their wits about them began to drop low and find cover, but, thankfully for us, even the three closest to us kept their attention focused near the north end of the school.

Myself and four more of the south team reached the southern fence at a dead sprint. We all took aim and dropped the three sentries with several body shots each. The civilians began to take notice of our presence.

"We're good guys, hang tight," I said in a voice that I hoped was calming, and barely audible to just my chosen audience. Some of them seemed placated, others began to panic. Wayne and Jason pitched in, trying to calm those closest to us as Rogers and Tony began cutting the fence apart.

One man worked with bolt cutters, the other with heavy wire cutters. Soon, they had the fence split large enough for a man to easily fit through. Each side was peeled back as a flap and secured in place with a padlock for each side, to hold the gap wide open.

As we spilled through, Wayne, Rogers, and Tony took up watch as Jason and I crept in low and began herding people to the gap.

We instructed each of them to gather up more people and get everyone corralled and heading to the businesses across the street. We each reassured them that there were more of our guys there and that we were here to help and rescue them.

Some hesitated, some outright refused and had to be coerced both by us, and their companions.

"How can we be sure you're good?" asked one emaciated teenage boy. His clothes hung loosely off of him, and they were so soiled that the smell nearly rolled off him in waves.

"If you're not sure," I explained, "I'm not going to force you. If you think the life you live here is better than what we can offer…"

I finished with a shrug as he pushed his thick dark hair out of his eyes and viewed me suspiciously.

"What's your name, kid?" Rogers questioned as he approached.

"Colby. Why?" the teenager replied, almost exasperated.

"Colby, we need to get moving," Rogers urged. "Help us, or find a tent and-"

Rogers never finished his sentence as a gunshot sounded from the school, then several more.

Most of us ducked low, but before Colby could be pulled to safety, a round entered his neck on a path that was nearly jaw to shoulder. He dropped faster than his own blood did. Arterial spray painting an abstract on Rogers' web gear and my face alike. Colby's dark eyes went wide as he fell, his hands reaching up to his neck, clawing at his wound as a drinking fountain arc of blood left the ragged hole.

"Contact! Fuck!" Rogers shouted as more gunshots sounded. "School! Second floor!"

The three not occupied with saving the teen's life began firing in a controlled, hushed, staccato of suppressed rifle fire as more unsuppressed shots sounded from the businesses we held as a safe zone.

More members of our south team met the civilians at the fence and brought them through as Rogers kept pressure on the wound. The poor kid was already pale, his movements and desperate attempts to figure out what happened to himself began to wane. The pool of blood spread out around his pale thin body as more of the life-giving liquid left. Despite his best efforts, Rogers could not stem the flow of liquid escaping the teen. His life was leaving fast, the effort futile, and there were many more people to save. A moment later, Rogers abandoned his attempts and began trying to console the kid as he faded away.

A very short while later, he left him completely and began helping me check and clear the last couple of tents as Tony and the other two moved away from us, trying to draw fire while also trying to lay down suppressing fire. More guns joined in on both sides, but as directed, the east and west teams remained quiet.

The buzz of a round whizzing past my head forced me to drop as I exited the last tent, pulling a teenage girl in little more than rags by the hand and shoving her in the direction of the hole in the fence that everyone else was funneling through.

That same round found its mark in the shoulder of a man in an old ratty button up shirt and khakis. It spun him, and he hit the dirt before getting back up and stumbling the rest of the way, only to be helped through the fence by Rob, and then directed to the dental office.

Several more rounds landed too close to us for comfort as I called the east and west teams into action as well. A couple of more civilians and two metalheads took superficial wounds from the gunfire. As I turned away from emptying a magazine and ducked behind the fire barrel to reload, I witnessed one of our Marines take a round directly through the face and collapse in a heap amid calls of 'Sanchez!' and strings of obscenities.

I began to get reports of more wounded and two more dead from Hashman's west team, and was just about to put in the call to ream Rich out for not being here yet as a pair of headlights to the west flicked on. I could make out the shape of the dump truck approaching at a bit more than a running pace. He was only maybe a half dozen blocks away.

"We need to move, NOW, people, clear the area!" I shouted over the cacophony of gunfire and yelling, "Fall back! *FALL THE FUCK BACK!*"

The rest of our team and few remaining civilians began fleeing even more panicked through the one-man gap in the fence. People flooded across the street as members of our team covered their departure from the gunfire behind us and a handful of odd infected that came to investigate all the noise.

Rich was now only three blocks away from us and I could see a dozen runners in pursuit of his truck, as well as the lumbering figure of one of the behemoths. The truck would slow, and Dave would rake the ground with his AK. The behemoth reached the truck on one occasion and smashed flat into the back of it, nearly lifting the rear wheels off the ground before Rich mashed the throttle and the vehicle lurched forward again.

Rob left his spot with the rest of the people from the school, leaving just me and Willy. I made my way through the gap and Willy and I paused momentarily to watch as the truck approached.

As Rich hit the intersection that put him two blocks away from us, a second massive infected freak barreled down the side street, meeting the side of the dump bed with a massive crash of steel, raising one side of the truck and nearly throwing Dave out of the back before Rich gained control.

"We got two now!" Rich called over the radio.

"Yeah, yeah I see, keep to the plan, one more block and punch it!" I yelled, ducking my head as another handful of rounds whizzed overhead in both directions. "Gate's still closed, hit it fuckin' hard!"

"Roger!" Rich called back.

He cleared the next block and the truck picked up speed as I darted across the street, with Willy just a handful of yards behind me. I burst through the front door of the dentist's office just as Rich crashed through the main gate to the school compound. The truck shuddered as it smashed through the chain link and continued on, taking out one unsuspecting gang banger. It hit the man dead on and he got caught by the front bumper, soundlessly leaving a streak on the pavement as the truck entered the compound, now with well over 20 infected, and a pair of behemoths still giving chase.

I reached my hand out to Willy just as he neared the door, and his eyes widened with surprise as three or four rifle rounds stitched their way across his back and exited out of his chest, leaving ragged holes in his shirt. He careened toward the door and hit me like an accidental linebacker as he collapsed face down.

"Willy!" I cried as I rolled from my back and moved to meet him.

Tony also rushed to my side as we rolled Willy onto his back. The damage had been done as his torso was already blotched with angry patches of blood. The bleeding started quickly, as where he'd landed, there were bright red patches lined across the floor in the path he slid.

He coughed up a spray of more blood, and it began to trickle from the corner of his mouth as a tremendous crash could be heard over the gunfire. I craned my neck to witness a cloud of dust and debris at the side of the school. The swarm of infected began spreading out, and the behemoths zeroed in on the closest people to them left out in the open.

I turned my attention back to Willy as he coughed and gasped in only to cough again, more blood mixing with the air around us in a fine mist. Tony was busy coaxing him, telling him to take it easy as he ripped his shirt free and began dumping water on the wounds to evaluate him.

Willy locked eyes with me and uttered a single question.

"Did..." more coughing, another gasp, "I do good?"

"Yeah, man," I replied, feeling the hot sting of a tear as it formed in my eye. "You did your best, dude. We're all proud of you."

Before I had finished, Willy had already gone still. Tony felt his neck for a pulse, and turned to me, his blue eyes meeting mine as he shook his head in the negative.

The moment was cut short by another burst of nearby gunfire and a new string of yelling and expletives out on the street. I turned my attention to see Dave picking Rich clean up off the ground and putting him into a fireman's carry over his shoulder. My blood went cold until I could hear Rich telling Dave off and yelling at him to put him down, but the stream of blood running from Rich's leg was already apparent as they made their way into the dentist's office.

Their entry was followed by another salvo of gunfire that ripped through the doorway behind them and found homes in the walls and reception desk near us.

Turning to view the outside again, I witnessed infected falling as the full attention of the gang bangers was brought to bear on the new intruders. The gunfire stopped coming our way and instead chased those who used to be human.

Smaller infected fell to the copper and lead as readily as they always had.

One of the behemoths picked a man clean off the ground with one hand and bit into his chest, arcing blood and tissue like someone had tossed a bucket of it into the air. The man's screams cut off instantly. Another guy began dumping everything he had into the massive beast, only to have the body of his own recently dead comrade thrown at him.

I could view the second giant making its way through the rest of the compound, chasing anything that moved, completely frenzied as it ignored the gunfire sent its way.

"Hey guys?" Rich called as we were engrossed in the scene outside, "Remember that bomb I made and just drove into there?"

"Uh shit, yeah," I replied, peeling my attention away. "Oh shit, that's right. Everybody down, find heavy cover!"

I pressed my earpiece and began speaking loud and clear into it as we scrambled around.

"All teams, all teams," I ordered. "Cease fire and find cover! Get to cover right now! Over!"

Dave and I dragged Rich by his armpits as he held pressure on the nasty looking bullet wound in his lower leg. Tony and Rogers began instructing everybody else to seek cover as far back in the building as they could. This left the break room full, and the furthest dental room mostly full as everyone dug in and crouched. As instructed, everyone got low, hands protecting their ears, eyes closed, and mouths open.

"How long did you set the timer for?" I asked Dave as we put Rich down in the dentist chair itself and got low.

"I don't know," he replied flatly.

"Fuck do you mean you don't know?" I shot back, knives in my tone.

"I mean I don't know!" he snapped back. "Dingus here used a dryer timer, no minute marks."

"I didn't think that through," Rich grimaced as he continued putting pressure on his own wound.

"Well, what did you set it to?" Tony broke in.

"Wrinkle free," Dave replied, shrugging.

Tony fell over laughing. Rich just stared blankly at him, so did pretty much everyone else in the room.

"Let me get this straight," I clarified, wincing at the bellow of a behemoth as another burst of gunfire sounded, "you set a thirty-five-hundred-pound bomb, to wrinkle-free? Dave? Fucking wrinkle free?"

"Yeah. I thought it was a nice touch," Dave replied, a bit indignant.

"Jesus fu-" I began, but never finished.

I'll be honest with you. To this day, I'll swear the world collapsed, then expanded again.

Time itself may have shifted, I'm not quite sure.

What I know to be fact, is that the entire front of the dentist's office blew inward. What followed was a crack that sounded like all the thunder in the world hitting at once. Even mouth open and ears covered, the ringing I experienced nearly drowned everything else out in an instant.

The shockwave could be felt immediately after. It swept clean through the area we occupied, followed by an oven blast of heat.

Debris large and small pelted the entire area. I witnessed what appeared to be the metal fuel cap from a truck zip through the wall next to me and embed itself in the far wall. Other various items crashed into the building we occupied as smaller bits fell across the entire area. It rained down on our shelter like a hail storm.

We began to regain our senses just in time to be overtaken by a rolling dust cloud.

I could still hear essentially nothing. I nodded and directed Tony away as he made it to me in his rounds of checking on everybody. As best I could tell, everyone felt the explosion much the same as I had, but there were no major injuries.

As my sense of hearing came back to me bit by bit, I found my feet.

"All teams, check in," I spoke into my earpiece.

Hashman's team reported much the same as we had. Some wounded, a handful of dead from the fighting, but nothing more than hearing loss and minor scrapes, cuts and contusions from the bombing.

Clara, to the east, and the far side of the school, reported a few wounded from the fighting, but almost no effects from the explosion aside from collective tinnitus.

"Okay good," I replied into my earpiece, then, as much to the other teams as everyone else, "Okay, let's waste no time. We rendezvous in one minute at the main gate. Weapons hot, everyone not wounded and with a flashlight meet up. Sweep and clear."

We gathered ourselves and made our way out of the ruined dental office and to the front gate.

Having figured the time for stealth was over, I slung my new rifle to my back and brought forth my shotgun. Clicking on the light in front of the fore end, I led the way out of the building and across the street, cutting a bit over and making my way along the fence line with a dozen guys behind me.

The beams from our lights danced all over, keeping watch inside the fence line for anyone left, as well as outside the fence line for anyone infected. The entire path of the lights could be seen through the heavy haze that the dust cloud had left in the air.

In a few more beats, these beams were met with many others, converging from two directions besides our own, as we met with the other two teams at the front gate.

"Check it out!" I called to everyone gathered, about 35 in total, give or take. "Two teams, every other person through this gate is on me. Those not with me, are with Tony. Tony's team will work up this side and cut across the North. My team cuts across the south and up the east side. We'll meet at the northeast corner and sweep the school."

"We killin' everyone, boss?" Hashman asked, a bit too eager to pull the trigger some more.

"We aren't these assholes, dude," I replied flatly. "If they're being hostile, kill them. If they aren't, leave them face down with one or two to watch them, we'll round up any survivors and figure out what to do after."

Everyone voiced their agreeance and understanding, and we began to sweep the grounds.

My team found and rounded up four that were no longer in the mood to fight and we killed none. We met at the northeast corner and joined Tony's team to split up once again inside the school. Six more in total were found alive in the school. They were in such bad shape that they needed to be carried out. One man missing half his leg from a hallway collapse. A chunk of the floor above had fallen flat and caught him from the knee down.

We wrapped the leg and applied a makeshift tourniquet and brought him outdoors with us. The dust had nearly faded and let the entirety of the scene around us be known. I was in full-on disbelief at the devastation our very own Rich Lester had cooked up.

Where there once was a full, intact, brick and mortar school building, there was a disaster scene. I'd joked with Rich about taking inspiration from Timothy McVeigh, and the Oklahoma City bombing, but what we were seeing was actually a pretty good representation of that scene.

It was like a God-sized ice cream scoop was taken out of the side of the building. This missing space was matched by a crater in the ground as deep as a man was tall.

Debris was spread out as far as our lights could let us see. So were the bodies. Ironically, the largest piece left of the truck that we could find was the tailgate, which appeared to have ripped clean through one of the behemoth infected and scattered its inner workings like candy from a child's piñata. That was somehow worse than the human bodies that were left behind. The large monstrosity, once made into a freak lasagna, put off a horrible rancid fish odor that overpowered everything else around. It was all any of us could do to keep from gagging because of it.

The other behemoth was nowhere to be found, having been so close to the epicenter of the blast, there likely wasn't anything left.

We rounded up the handful of people that survived. Twelve men, four women in total. Placed them all near the main gate on their knees.

"Hey Scott," Tony called to me. "This one looks familiar!"

"Well I'll be damned," I stated, as I joined him, "Big Tyler, is it?"

The man just stared at me, his brown eyes wide, mouth slightly agape showing a few gold front teeth.

"I asked you a question," I restated, staring into his eyes.

"Don't think he can hear you," Tony said, and he moved Tyler's head to the side with the barrel of his rifle. He was right. The explosion did its job in a different way. Both of Big Tyler's ears had thick streams of blood and fluids running from them. At a glance, I could see several more members present had the same condition.

"That's a shame. Poor bastard won't be able to hear his own trial," Dave interjected with a toneless laugh.

"Those of you that can hear, raise your hands," I called out. Nine hands went up.

"Those of you who witnessed Big Tyler take part in the torture and slaughter of a good man, before crucifying him to the back of a tow truck," I continued, no emotion in my voice as I eyed the small group, "keep your hands up."

Three hands stayed up.

"Very good," I began again. "Bear with me, it's almost over."

I eyeballed Big Tyler as he started to look around, quite nervous, at what was left of his old crew. He may not have been able to hear us, but I had the feeling he was beginning to comprehend.

I moved forward to a position directly in front of him. I planted my feet and made sure there was a round of buckshot in my shotgun. Closing the breech on the weapon, I began to speak loudly, clearly, and with the tone of a professional.

"Big Tyler, you have been found guilty of murder by a panel of your peers. As we are not in the prison business, you will be summarily executed without further trial or process. I'll give you a moment to get right with God or what have you."

Upon realization of what was happening, one of our captives began to wail.

"He's gonna kill us all anyway!" cried a woman no more than 20 years old. Blonde hair tipped in the faded remains of blue dye that had long since grown out.

"No, I'm not," I replied in a firm, business-like manner. "Just him, because he killed our friend."

"You're not going to let any of us go, you piece of shit!" she continued. "Don't you fuckin' lie to us! We're as good as dead!"

"Maybe," I replied, "but I will let you go, and I won't be the reason you die. Wayne, you're closest, shut her up."

Wayne nodded and approached the woman, who began to fight and try to flail until Wayne backhanded her one time. It knocked her loopy and calmed her long enough for her to be gagged with a kerchief from Wayne's pocket.

"Anyway," I said to nobody in specific. I proceeded to raise my shotgun, and without further process, leveled it at Big Tyler's chest. The trigger broke through as clean as ever, and the lightweight shotgun came to life in my hands.

It sent eight double-ought buckshot pellets forth, right into the center of Big Tyler's chest. The rounds ripped through his chest cavity, exiting, and taking blood, tissue, and even bits of spine with them in a dramatic display. Big Tyler hit the pavement like a sack of potatoes. Wisps of smoke leaving the wound as he twitched once, twice, and then lay completely still after the third.

"The rest of you, get the fuck out of here," I instructed dryly. "Head east, west, south, wherever you want, but I want you out of my city forever. Don't even look back, but you're free to go. We don't do prisoners."

Some of them got up and took a few nervous steps before breaking into a dead run. Others stayed, looking confused, and watching their peers leave. I assumed they were making sure nobody was getting shot in the back before making their own escapes.

Wayne took the cloth from the girl's mouth and she spoke again.

"Are you at least going to give us a weapon?" she asked, this time, nearly pleading.

Looking down near my feet, my eyes fell upon what I needed. I kicked the piece of rubble from the school toward her.

"Take this brick," I offered, to which she scoffed, and was led away by two friends before she could run the risk of becoming aggravating again.

***

We got our crew, the rescued people from the school, our wounded, and our dead out of the area and back to the complex.

THIRTY-NINE

There was much hustle and bustle as the dead were interred. We had no way to preserve them, and it was decided it would be more dignified to do it now instead of waiting. I waited in place for the burials for each of them as the closest to each person mourned. Out of eight dead, the only one of ours to be lost was Willy, and even that felt like too much, though his sacrifice allowed us to free nearly forty innocent people. A half-dozen adults, the rest were children from the school. I say children, but teens would be more fairly worded. To each their own.

Whatever you wish to call them, these people truly were rescued. Underfed, overworked, abused and mistreated. Big Tyler's gang had run them like slaves. They lived in all weather in a series of worn-down camping tents with concrete under them. The girls, and even some of the boys, had been used by Tyler's men for whatever purpose they saw fit. They were basically fed table scraps. Never new clothes, or personal care. They were forced to live in fear and squalor. I was very pleased we were able to give them a new lease on life.

As they would heal and recover, the extra hands would be a blessing around our compound. They weren't even forced into quarantine, despite Shannon's protests. They'd lived as prisoners and slaves, and as it was, they were clearly not infected at any rate. The best thing they had going for them previously was safety from the outside world.

Shannon, Ashley, and Jennifer triaged the wounded and provided the best care they could. Henry filled in and gladly helped bandage and care for any of the teens that had minor injuries.

As our group had nearly doubled in size now, the already established members settled into sleeping in shifts, while those awake spent the night helping in whatever way they could.

Bri busied herself assigning people to rooms, quickly filling the rest of the space in our building and moving others into the south building.

Carolyn made herself at home socializing with the two school teachers that came in with the new adults.

All in all, things were a busy mess, but they were going smoothly.

Hashman and his crew began loading their boats, and we parted ways with agreements to help each other and establish the river as trade route between the settlements. Yeah, we had a lot of fertilizer to find and send up river, and other supplies for the help and a heap of condolences for the seven people killed from their camp. And, yes, we kept the rifles.

FORTY

The following day proceeded much the same. Hustle and bustle mixed with rest and recovery.

Dave, Tony, Jennifer and I had a meal in the command center as we watched the movement nine floors below us. It looked like Henry had already started making his rounds and was explaining to people how work crews would run. He roped James in as his own second-in-command to help with the new, much larger crews. This meant they could also get many more projects done in one shot.

It was a beautiful thing we'd done, and we had much better to come just over the horizon. I was nearly about to comment on this when there was a flash and a large *woosh* from Rich's armory that caught our attention. This was immediately followed by a thick cloud of white-grey smoke that poured out of his half-built armory and began rolling over the compound, following the wind, but too thick to be truly dispersed.

"Rich what the hell is going on down there?" I called into my radio, then, "Over."

"Sorry man," he replied. "Just experimenting with a little bird shit and sugar."

"With what?" I asked. "Never mind that, you're supposed to be on light duty until that leg heals! Over."

"This is light duty though!" he replied. "It'll be okay. Over."

Sighing, I replaced the radio on my hip and we all relaxed and shared a laugh about it.

"Thank God we gave that boy a place of his own to play," Dave laughed.

"Yeah," I replied, "don't know though, how mad could we ever be at him after yesterday?"

"This is true," Tony supplied, followed by a boisterous belch that could be felt as much as heard.

***

The rest of the day was largely uneventful.

People were sorted and, for the most part, rested. Everyone was given new clothes and began to settle into their living quarters. Bri ended up flooded with a landslide of new requests and was doing her best to process it all. I explained to her that it would be days until scouts were sent out, we were on break while the dust settled, but she insisted. The only time she took a break was when Dave came by to take her for a private lunch by the river. The pair had grown quite well as a new couple.

We all met on the roof of the north building, now nearly bingo on seating with the new additions. I just finished making a big welcome speech. I laid out our basic rules and explained that Tony would begin familiarizing people with firearms in groups. James, Clara, and Wayne would spend our next couple days off running informal classes on the basics of scouting and gathering, and Henry would begin assigning work crew duties to everyone aged fifteen and older, no exceptions.

We detailed each department, how our council system worked, and every department head introduced themselves to the new group.

It was Tony's turn. In the fading sunlight, he stood up and began to introduce himself.

He got no further than his name, and that he was my second in command, however, when the most peculiar thing happened.

As he raised his glass, there was a tug on his T-shirt. Just a tug. He looked down as a tear became visible just inside of his right nipple.

At this moment, a far-off crack sounded, like the snapping of a large tree branch.

As we all sat in silent, stunned wonder at what had just happened, a trickle of blood began to tint the blue of his shirt, just under where this strange hole, or tear appeared. The trickle became a flow.

"I-I think," Tony stammered, looking at his chest, then locking his bright, vibrant blue eyes on mine, "Ah shit, man."

He fell forward. He landed face first on the rooftop as his drink glass met the ground with him, shattering and sending shards of crystalline glass tumbling across the rough surface.

I was the first one to him. I was in pure shock, not processing what was happening.

"TONY!" I cried as I reached him. "God, no. Fuck, man, no, no, NO!"

Others gathered round and we could see a corresponding hole in the back of his shirt, also bleeding.

I rolled him onto his back to see the ugly dark patch of blood spreading from the wound on his chest, and it dawned on me. My life long best friend had been shot. The tree branch was a rifle report, coming after the impact because of distance.

I pulled him in close to me. The commotion on the rooftop drowning itself out in my own shock. The sounds fading, seeming so far away as I cradled my buddy tight against me. I could barely even hear Dave screaming for Shannon, Ashley, Jennifer, fucking *anybody* from medical, get here *now* for the love of God.

I cradled his head against my chest as he was pulled away from me by the girls. Shannon immediately removed his shirt and began doing what she could while barking orders to the others.

I still can't recall it all. I can't remember if I cried. Can't remember if I just sat there, numbed by fear and shock. It was all so far away from where I actually was.

My buddy for so, so many years, lay there with a sucking chest wound. Lay there by me, while others worked to do the best they could for him. How? Why? Who? We were just having dinner.

I tried to grasp thought after thought as it floated by my periphery. Nothing made sense. To make matters more convoluted to me, it all got further away as it faded to nothing.

I don't recall fainting, but they say I did.

EPILOGUE

The burn of tears forming reached my eyes once again as I relaxed against my restraints. My head lowered, and I allowed a few drops of the saline liquid to fall from my eyes as I remembered the sight of my good buddy laying there on the rooftop, bleeding from a neat puncture that went from his back, and through his chest.

Upon seeing my emotional pain, and not for the first time that day, the temperature of the room went from cold and investigatory, to something just a bit warmer. Cold? Maybe, just maybe, cool, but nothing more.

Grayson motioned to Munoz, who pressed a button on his device and ceased the recording.

"Scott," he began, "I think we can call it quits for the day."

"You think?" I asked, sarcasm brimming in my voice. "My ass went numb from this chair hours ago. My throat is dry, but I've got to piss so bad I'm afraid to drink any more water. And we're just getting into the meat of the story, if you recall. My buddy-"

"That's enough, Scott. We'll call it finished for the day," Grayson reiterated. "No point in trying to rush this, I understand, it's hard. We'll pick it up again tomorrow."

"I want out of these bindings," I began, "and I want to visit with my friends and family."

"Unfortunately, Scott," Grayson replied, "we can't do that. This is still an investigation, and the order to keep you confined and separated comes straight from the President."

"The President?" I retorted, slightly amazed. "He's here? Is it still..."

"Oh, no!" Grayson chuckled, "No, thankfully he's no longer around. Best thing to come of all of this."

"Eh, fifty-fifty," I answered. "Can you show me them again, at least? Please?"

Grayson flicked through the screen on his tablet and handed it to me again. I must have been the last one still in my interview for the day. Everyone else was seated in what appeared to be individual cells. Some eating a meal from a tray, others reading. Henry was the only one being active, quickly and furiously belting out a series of sit-ups. The young kids, including Gwen, were in a larger room. Bunk beds lining the walls, and a giant rubber mat in the middle of the room that was scattered with toys. They looked well cared for, but no child appeared very happy.

I sighed as I settled on flicking between the screens showing Gwen, and Jennifer.

Grayson earmarked the stack of paperwork he'd done as I rambled on about our story. Then, he shuffled everything into order, tapping the edges on the table to straighten them, and then sliding the whole works into his folder.

Munoz busied himself by returning the equipment he'd been using to the case it belonged to, then stacking our used cups neatly by the water pitcher.

As they finished their chores, Grayson retrieved the tablet from my reluctant grasp, and placed it on top of his folder.

"What's your name, anyway?" I asked him.

"I told you, Scott," he informed me. "It's Grayson. Agent Grayson."

"Your first name, Grayson," I clarified.

"Agent," he replied, smiling warmly as I rolled my eyes.

"Dick," I replied coldly.

After a soft laugh at my indignation, Grayson motioned one private forward. Munoz brought the other one to him, and he left with the case carrying the recording equipment, as well as Grayson's tablet, returning a few moments later.

The privates then joined me, one on each side, and began undoing the bindings that kept me in that Godawful chair for an entire day. As they worked, Grayson spoke again, inflecting his most calm and personal tone I'd heard thus far, certainly to placate or reassure me.

"Scott, I just wanted to reiterate. This is a hearing," he intoned, "not a trial. It's more like an interview. We want anything that can help us with research regarding the infected, but it's also informational about you, and your comrades. We just want to get to the bottom of what happened back in Ohio and make informed decisions from there."

"Whoa dude hold up," I started, freezing myself, "back in Ohio? Where the fuck are we?"

"I'm not at liberty to say," he replied, his grave expression returning.

"What *can* you tell me, then?" I asked, my indignation also making a return.

"Meat loaf. Instant potatoes. Corn," he said, nearly monotone.

"Excuse me?" I replied.

"It's what's being sent to your room once you get there," he said. "That's about all I can tell you for now."

I glared at him as the two uniformed men released my body and brought me to my feet. He turned and departed through the door, which he left open for us to exit as well.

I followed the private in front of me, and was tailed by the other, as well as Munoz.

We exited the 1980's classic interrogation room and entered a state-of-the-art...hallway.

Colorless tile made up both the floor and the ceiling. The walls done in such a typical white and green two-tone, split down the middle, that it was almost laughable at how expected it was.

What wasn't expected was the mix of people. Everything from nurses and orderlies, to guards, to people dressed in civilian and street clothes were present.

We took a right, the opposite of Grayson's direction, and began walking down the hallway. We passed room after room, none of their purposes apparent save for the glowing electronic labels positioned just above varying levels of security. I assumed the remainder of the rooms we passed to the right were like the one I'd left. I didn't really pay much attention. My focus was on the young, uniformed man walking just ahead of me, as well as trying to track Munoz and the other behind me.

A minute or two later, and after several turns through hallways of varying degrees of sterility, I felt my chance coming.

Munoz quietly excused the guard to my front and took his place. One more turn, and six more doorways lining only one side of the hallway, and we stopped.

Munoz approached the door we'd reached and leaned in to allow his retina to be read.

With his full attention diverted, I drove my bare foot into the back of his knee with everything I had. He collapsed as his knee gave, and his face met the scanner.

Then, using the moment, I ran backwards into the private, the back of my skull connecting with his nose, and my weight and momentum catching him off guard and allowing me to drive him into the wall, knocking the wind from both our lungs.

Before I could even recover, I felt a cold steel presence just off center on my forehead and heard a click. Looking up, I gazed straight into the angry brown eyes of Munoz as he held his Beretta to my head, his other arm propping himself against the wall.

"One wrong move, puto!" he challenged. "Breathe wrong. I fucking dare you."

I said nothing, but slowly brought both my hands up as I tried not to piss myself.

The Private joined in, a thin stream of blood trickling from each of his nostrils. He cradled his rifle in one arm, the barrel pressed into my side, as he lifted me by my armpit with the other.

The door Munoz unlocked clicked open, and I realized it was not the grand escape I'd hoped for. It was my cell.

"You almost got out of your shackles and got to be comfortable, dickhead," the Private growled as he shoved me into the room, slamming the door behind me.

I resigned myself to my situation and sat down on the thin padding of the single cot-like bed.

The room was just like my old days, when I'd have the occasional visit to county jail. A bed, table, and chair, all steel, all bolted firmly to the wall. The toilet and sink were formed from one piece of stainless steel, and also bolted firmly to the wall. The room was about double the size of a standard jail cell, but that was it. The main difference here was the solitary security camera over my door in the corner of the room, wrapped safe and sound in a thick metal protective box.

I relieved myself in the toilet, and sat back down on my bed, just in time for the meal slot to open in my door, and a tray pushed onto the ledge.

It was exactly as Grayson said it would be, with a fruit punch in a cardboard carton for the drink. The meatloaf was flavorless, as were the runny mashed potatoes and rubbery corn. If I didn't know any better, I'd think certain TV dinner companies had been contracted for this mess.

Nonetheless, I picked at my food until I'd gotten through the ordeal and attempted to lay down and get some sleep under the single thin blanket I was provided. No dice. Not with the hospital glare of the fluorescent lighting burning brightly overhead.

I got up, and searched for a switch, my shackles jangling the whole way. No switch. I clapped. Yeah, okay, nothing there, either.

Finally, I went over to the camera and tried waving and calling to them, to be met with a response in the negative regarding the lights. Lights stay on, and I am to be monitored like everybody else.

Okay, that's fine. I guess. Looks like I'm not masturbating any time soon.

I returned to the poor excuse for a bed, faced the wall as I laid down, and covered myself again. In the process of staring at said wall, and reliving everything I'd gone through, my door clicked, then opened.

Munoz stood there, on a single crutch. This brought a grin to my face, though, to my surprise, he returned the grin. He then stepped aside and nodded to someone else.

My blood ran cold.

Into my room walked a man I had recently become well acquainted with.

Colonel John Parker.

He was still in full uniform, and he strolled into my room with all the confidence any man could possess. Taking his jacket off, he turned to the camera box, smiled and waved grandly, then placed the jacket over it.

"Don't bother getting up, Mr. Pfeiffer," he told me as he placed his hand on his sidearm, "I won't be long."

"What. The. Fuck. Do. You. Want?" I replied, venom dripping from every word I spat.

"Your cooperation." He smiled, ignoring my disposition. "If not for our sake, then for that of Jennifer and little Gwen."

"Touch them, and the entire world wouldn't be able to keep me from you," I retorted, tensing every muscle, despite my impotence in my bindings.

"I'm making the threats here," he replied, every word calibrated. "Your case is against the United States military. You're a group of yay-hoo civilians. You'll accept full fault for your actions against the military, and we may go easy enough on you and yours."

"What's your end game, Colonel?" I asked, trying to peer through the curtain of rage I could feel coming.

"We're going to rebuild, and I'm key to this." He continued his explanation, "Now, I know you can be reasonable. For the U.S. to be able to be rebuilt into the great and wonderful Union, we can't possibly have you slandering the name and actions of one of the new Founding Fathers, now, can we? Work with me, and I may be able to get you a sweet deal on a farm somewhere that nobody can bother you, and you can't bother me. Alaska? Maybe somewhere through Mexico? It'll surely be better than the alternative."

The guy was a snake, and somehow, the way he pronounced Mexico got him even further under my skin. May-hee-co. Fuck this prick.

"You need to find the exit, Parker," I snarled, "before you find yourself as wrapped in my shackles as I am."

"I'll give you some time to mull it over, pardner," he sneered. "Oh! Here, this is for you."

He tossed a square piece of paper on the ground, grabbed his jacket, and departed the room. The door slammed, and the lock worked itself into place in his wake. I got up and retrieved the paper he'd left.

It was a color Polaroid of him. Sitting, smiling, one hand waving, the other firmly wrapped around my very blonde, very innocent looking daughter.

I'm going to end his life.

I sat on the side edge of the bed in silence. I'd begun sweating and shaking like a junkie needing a fix. There was, at that moment, nothing I could do save for fantasizing how many different ways I could hurt him when I got the chance. They'd have to shoot me to get me away from that man.

Eventually, I returned to my original position, laying on my right side, facing the wall. I lay like that for so long I finally found sleep by complete accident, never letting go of that picture. Never letting go of my thoughts, my anger, and my pain and frustration.

THE END

AUTHOR'S NOTE

I write this segment with a tear in my eye. A tear borne from realization of a dream. I never in my wildest imagination thought I would write this. So much time and effort has gone into it. Time and effort that I never thought I had in me.

I did not do it alone. Many, many people have had a hand in this creation coming to life, and at the point this note is written, there will be many more to come.

I want to thank you all. From the bottom of my heart, I will be forever grateful.

I could write another book in itself just listing names and reasons, but, if you even suspect your name to be on that list, just know that it is.

Most of all, I want to thank my readers. Whether there are ten of you, or a million. You're amazing and instrumental in helping me realize the dream, and I hope the journey has been a positive enough experience for you to hang around for the next installment. Part Two is coming, have no worries, this ball is rolling!

www.ingramcontent.com/pod-product-compliance
Lightning Source LLC
Chambersburg PA
CBHW022215170626
46807CB00005B/2373